KNOW YOUR BEHOLDER

ALSO BY ADAM RAPP

NOVEL

The Year of Endless Sorrows

PLAYS

*The Hallway Trilogy • Red Light Winter •
Stone Cold Dead Serious • Nocturne • The Metal Children •
Kindness • Blackbird • Finer Noble Gases • Animals and Plants •
Essential Self-Defense • Gompers • American Sligo •
Ghosts in the Cottonwoods • Trueblinka • Bingo with the Indians*

NOVELS FOR YOUNG ADULTS

*The Children and the Wolves • Punkzilla •
Under the Wolf, Under the Dog • 33 Snowfish • Little Chicago •
The Copper Elephant • The Buffalo Tree • Missing the Piano*

GRAPHIC NOVEL

Ball Peen Hammer

KNOW
YOUR
BEHOLDER

A Novel

ADAM RAPP

Little, Brown and Company
New York   Boston   London

The characters and events in this book are fictitious. Any similarity to real persons, living or dead, is coincidental and not intended by the author.

Little, Brown and Company
Hachette Book Group
1290 Avenue of the Americas, New York, NY 10104
littlebrown.com

First Edition: March 2015

Little, Brown and Company is a division of Hachette Book Group, Inc. The Little, Brown name and logo are trademarks of Hachette Book Group, Inc.

The publisher is not responsible for websites (or their content) that are not owned by the publisher.

The Hachette Speakers Bureau provides a wide range of authors for speaking events. To find out more, go to hachettespeakersbureau.com or call (866) 376-6591.

ISBN 978-0-316-36891-9
LCCN 2014955121

10 9 8 7 6 5 4 3 2 1

RRD-C

Printed in the United States of America

For Paul, Rob, Chernus, and Ray

CONTENTS

PART ONE

SMALL-TOWN SNOW

I haven't left my house in almost a month.

It's either Tuesday or Wednesday—most likely Wednesday—and three days ago a foot of snow fell on Pollard, Illinois, and its surrounding farmlands: storybook snow as soft as sifted cake mix. Although an old municipal plow has scraped down the street exactly twice—the driver's head enshrouded in wool—clearly it's been an effort in futility as the snow continues to fall at a dizzying rate.

I'm in the attic. I've been spending the last few hours counting the number of people laboring down the middle of my street on cross-country skis. Laboring, not gliding, as one might expect from a sport that uses a pair of long, preternatural runners. There have been seven skiers so far. Velocity-challenged and hunched over, the cross-country skier fights the snow, driving his poles into the frozen crust, desperate for purchase. The snow doesn't welcome his pursuit the way it coaxes the downhill skier with its powdery, virginal shimmer. It bewilders rather than bewitches.

The cross-country skier exists as if trapped in a purgatorial silent movie.

It's strange how full-body winterwear makes gender difficult to identify. Each goggled cross-country skier seems androgynous, machine-like, somehow pneumatic. It appears that the sport is a solitary pursuit, as I have yet to witness duos or trios. Perhaps there is something about the threat of being snowbound in a small town that inspires the lone adventurer? Where are they going, one by one? Are they skiing away from lives of ill repute? Or to a lover? Or simply to the library to return overdue books because the car won't start?

Whatever the case, those lone skiers, as they probably already know, are not going to find much in Pollard aside from Our Lady of Snows shrine, an embarrassing, miniaturized counterfeit of the shrine at Lourdes, France (ours looks more like an interstate rest stop for science-fiction enthusiasts than a place of pilgrimage dedicated to Christ's mother), and an enormous bookbindery on the outskirts of town.

What snow does to a small town like Pollard is vastly different from what it does to a mountainside. Whereas it beautifies the mountainside, beckoning photography and sporting life and teams of people in expensive, pastel-colored, waterproof Gortex to gather on outdoor lodge decks and drink mulled wine and hot toddies, it shuts the small town down, rendering it municipally constipated.

Mountain snow has the power to be painted. Small-town snow just gets dirty.

Architecturally speaking, the houses on my street are sort of interesting in that they are mostly mid-nineteenth-century, three- to four-story Victorians in various states of structural and aesthetic decline. The less compelling houses are a pair of low, flat Tudors and something four lots down that looks unfortunately log-cabinish. From my vantage point (the attic), the neighborhood has been suddenly blessed with an innocent gingerbread-house quality, featuring meringue-like gables, sugar-glazed finials, and frosted yards. Things look downright Alpine. But Pollard is no mountainside. Soon it will be dirty.

It's warm and dry here in my attic room and the portable humidifier beside my writing desk issues a calming, attendant hiss and the occasional gurgle. It smells cedarn up here today. I'm dressed in two pairs of slightly yellowing, old-school, waffle-patterned long johns (long johns on long johns, if you will), a moth-bitten, Brillo-pad-gray cardigan sweater, a pilling wool winter hat the color of kelp that mostly hides my asinine hair, merino Ingenius camping socks, and a light-blue terry-cloth bathrobe that has become a low-grade monastic cloak. It is definitely the outfit of the nonattendant. The uniform of a Life in Default.

I am also now sporting a beard, and have developed a very real anxiety about it smelling gamy, like wet squirrel or coon. Beard pong can be an acute social/hygienic problem and when I encounter my tenants at the front porch mailboxes or in the basement laundry room I make an effort to keep at least an arm's length between us. Though I twiddle and stroke the beard compulsively, I don't know what it looks like, as I've been doing my best to avoid mirrors and reflective surfaces of any kind out of fear of what I'm liable to see staring back at me. I'm starting to imagine the beleaguered Civil War soldier. Or the banished indie record store warlock. Or a derelict from the northwest United States. Like one of those Olympia, Washington, societal dropouts who eats only frosted Pop-Tarts, living out a nineties grunge fantasy. The beard is mangy and random, with riptides and lots of wiry rogue strands.

The word wayward comes to mind.

But I'm a musician, so doesn't that make my current state

okay? Musicians have beards. And many musicians live outside of time. There's Time and then there's Musician's Time.

This morning the molten plates of my personal history took a tectonic shift when I realized it's been nine days since I've removed the bathrobe. Yes, attired in ancient terry cloth, I've slept, eaten, landlorded, gone to the bathroom, washed dishes, and guitar-noodled for some unfathomable number of hours.

One of the strange symptoms of even the mildest form of agoraphobia is that it gets progressively difficult to distinguish between personal and household odors. Beyond my beard, which I really can't smell, as I've no doubt grown immune, the rest of my person stinks of the attic's aged cedar, fiberglass insulation, and the faint aroma of dead mice. Mold memory. A skosh of Lysol-covered bird death. At least I'm still brushing and flossing. My mother used to say that when you give up on your teeth you might as well lie down in a ditch and wait for the dirt. I guess I'm still keeping that proverbial ditch at bay.

I inherited this house from my father, Lyman Falbo, after he retired from the accounting firm Falbo Financial Management, which he founded in the early seventies with his college roommate, Big Stu. Three years ago, upon selling his share of the company and handing over the reins to Big Stu (now Skinny Stu after turning vegan), Lyman took his second wife, Sissy Bisno (now Sissy Falbo), to live out their days in a cream-colored, heavily stuccoed ranch house in a cul-de-sac retirement community in Jupiter, Florida.

Sissy, a waggly-breasted, six-foot Lutheran widow, boasts burled hands, the shoulders of a veteran lumberjack, and a face somehow reminiscent of a young Garrison Keillor. I'm convinced that if I were to challenge her in any number of one-on-one combat exercises, she would put me on my ass six ways to Sunday. Her bidirectional, east-west breasts jiggle around so much underneath her many lilac-colored church sweaters that you have to wonder about not only their shape, volume, and bra strategy, but also their quantity. Does she possess three breasts? Five? Some large, some small, some upside-down or sideways? She's forty-nine but looks sixty-five, and I would swear one arm is longer than the other. I keep looking for the thing that attracted my above-average-handsome, sixty-two-year-old, semi-wealthy, charming-in-a-golden-retriever-sort-of-way father, but I'm at a loss.

Lyman claims she's a great swimmer, uncorks a deadly tennis serve, and possesses a beautiful singing voice. Her former husband, the late Southern Illinois meat-packaging mogul Chuck "the Bull" Bisno, died under the knife, during bypass surgery following a massive heart attack, and Sissy and Lyman "found each other" (the agreed terminology of their first encounter) at the weekly Wednesday night Grief Support Meeting held in the basement of First Lutheran Church. They fell in anodyne love shortly thereafter.

Why Lyman, a stalwart Roman Catholic his whole life, suddenly decided to sample the First Lutheran programming is anyone's guess. My dead Roman Catholic mother, Cornelia, would be horrified.

Cornelia Wyrwas and Lyman Falbo fell in love in Chicago. Having just graduated from Kansas State University, Lyman was on an entry-level-job interview at an accounting firm in the Loop. Cornelia, seventeen at the time, was changing linens at her parents' small bed-and-breakfast on Milwaukee Avenue, where Lyman was staying. I don't know the moment they found each other, be it on the stairwell, in the dining room, or at the threshold of some potpourri-scented linen closet, but I imagine them making love on the B&B's creaky antique furniture, Lyman covering Cornelia's mouth, my virgin mother biting his fingers and bleeding onto fresh sheets (which she would later have to abscond with and drop in some far-off Dumpster she would walk to in hand-me-down shoes), the two of them spooning awkwardly afterward, my father inhaling the scent of her blackberry hair, the light from a bedside harlequin lamp spilling softly across their young, postcoital faces, my mother whispering Polish into the musk of his boyish neck.

Lyman's new wife likes to make casseroles and Lyman likes to wear suits even when he's not within twenty miles of an office building. They like this about each other and they both like that they like this about each other.

Since meeting Sissy, Lyman has been taking a large daily dose of Lipitor. He also rides a stationary bike until he starts to wheeze asthmatically, and eats a low-cholesterol, high-fiber diet.

Despite her seemingly plentiful mammae, Sissy and Chuck Bisno never had children, so marriage was a relatively clean move for Lyman. In the twilight of his life, he pretty much gets to have his new lady all to himself.

Based on an early visit to their Florida home, this is what I observed: Sometimes they play gin for a buck a point. Sometimes they'll watch PGA golf and she'll sit on his orthopedically replaced knee and he'll position his hand between her gargantuan shoulder blades and call her his "girl" as if he's talking to a beloved German shepherd. She doesn't mind his taking his post-dinner carminative pills in front of her, and doesn't mind even further when, while encamped on the living room sofa (Sissy crocheting scarves for Midwestern relatives, Lyman watching his prized DVD boxed set of <u>B. J. and the Bear</u>), he releases farts that sound like a drunk attempting a blues scale on a waterlogged clarinet. Lyman will even pat his tummy and send her a thumbs-up down the sofa.

It took more than a year after they left for Florida to rid the house of the scent of filterless Pall Malls and hemorrhoid ointment. The Preparation H was my mother's, bless her heart, and even though she died of a brutal, soul-crushing stomach cancer two years prior to my father's leaving-slash-retirement, I believe Lyman still hoards tubes of the ointment, whose strange medicinal odor of mink oil and boiled turnips serves as a sentimental reminder of his true love and substitute mother. The Pall Malls were Lyman's and I'm convinced that despite his grisly alkaloid teeth, receding, stout-colored gums, and two-packs-a-day habit, he will live to be a hundred and twelve.

The house is a Queen Anne Victorian with a wraparound porch; deep, overhanging eaves; decorative milled panels; pointed dormers; lots of well-glazed, double-paned, stormproof windows; authentic nineteenth-century wainscoting; ample parking space; three ancient climbing trees; and a handsomely paneled, industrial-carpeted, mold-free basement that has never flooded. Despite recent insulation upgrades, it still gets cold in the winter but stays somewhat cool through the humid part of the summer. In other words, heating it is a hellacious money-sucking bitch, but it's tolerable in August.

During my time on earth, the house has survived three tornadoes, a first-floor electrical fire, an authentic wild boar, and a wave of resilient, late-seventies termites that took six months of an archaic baiting process to get rid of.

In the house's original state, there were three upstairs bedrooms and one on the first floor, just off the living room. Now the first floor functions as a single-family unit. A year ago I converted the second floor into a pair of one-bedroom apartments, adding a dividing wall of Sheetrock, a bathroom, and two kitchenettes, whose need for a shared wall and shared plumbing and electricity eliminated my boyhood bedroom. Three months before that, half the basement was outfitted with a false gypsum ceiling, the industrial carpet, pairs of bathrooms and kitchenettes, and eight panels of Sheetrock, to prepare for the two one-bedroom units down there as well—humble, dormitory-like, but very livable—I'd even say cozy. Although I've been running oscillating fans for weeks, however, the basement still smells like joint compound and bleach.

My first basement tenant is scheduled to move in the day after tomorrow. His name is Bob Blubaugh, which sounds like some unfortunate character in a bad American independent film. I don't know much about him beyond that, like me, he is in his midthirties and, unlike me, he was an alternate on the 2002 American Olympic luge team at Salt Lake City. Over the phone his voice was soft and clear, verging on soprano, and I imagined it emanating from someone with an inflamed, permanently chapped face.

Also living in the house are my ex-wife's brother, Bradley, who stays on the second floor; the Bunches, a former circus couple who rent the ground-floor family apartment; and Harriet Gumm, an art student who occupies the other second-floor unit.

The remaining basement unit will be filled soon. Just this morning I received three responses to my Craigslist posting, which makes eight total. Of those eight, I will winnow it down to five and I predict three of them will actually show up for a look-see. It's winter break at Willis Clay and outside of a man with the unfortunate name of Victor Mold, each person who responded to my ad claims to be a student, which means they will likely be financed by their parents, which is as close to a sure thing as it gets when it comes to renting out a basement apartment with a false gypsum ceiling during the worst economic crisis in recent history. Tomorrow I'll do some reaching out via e-mail.

In the attic, to which I repaired almost two years ago, after my ex-wife's departure, I have a twin bed (the one from my childhood) with a good mattress. The small bed affords me a surprising amount of floor space. I have a wall of paperbacks, mostly twentieth-century American fiction, arranged alphabetically by author; a dozen binders containing my complete baseball card collection; two wave-shaped CD towers; a few crates of beloved vinyl; and a midlevel stereo system featuring a Crosley Tech turntable finished in fine mahogany, a mini-CD jukebox, and a pair of state-of-the-art Polk Audio R300 tower speakers. I have an unremarkable stuffed chair (burnt-orangish and corduroy) and a vintage freestanding gooseneck Zoalite reading lamp that Lyman didn't bother taking with him to Florida. It's the lamp my mother used to read under in the living room, and I honestly believe that having it near him would make him feel like an infidel.

Other possessions worth mentioning: My authentic '69 Les Paul Epiphone electric guitar and a small Marshall kick amp, on top of which rests a wireless telephone and analog answering machine from the late eighties that requires authentic mini-cassettes and makes people sound trapped and desperate, as if they're transmitting vocal arrangements from outer space.

I haven't changed the strings on the Les Paul in over a year and I recently sketched it in the margins of the very manuscript that I am using to chronicle all of this. (Whatever this winds up being—a novel, a confession, a grand, self-indulgent, one-sided palaver—is anyone's guess.) Sketching things that historically resonate with me is perhaps my one sentimental guilty pleasure. I sketch my ex-wife a lot. I am not a very good artist. My faces have a tendency to look unfortunately lagomorphic. As a child I was fascinated by Watership Down, and harelips seem to plague my drawings of human faces.

No one has seen the margins of whatever this is, so between my guitar and the various curves and planar pleasures of my ex-wife's anatomy, I'm confident that the drawings' various implications will remain an author's secret.

I also have my own bathroom up here, properly tiled, with what I'd wager to be the quietest toilet in the Midwest (I splurged at Home Depot), a working sink, and a showerhead with enhanced water pressure. My kitchen is elfin, with a half-fridge, a portable double-burner stovetop, and a lone Formica counter space crowded with enough English muffins, Skippy peanut butter, instant oatmeal, wild flora honey, and Maker's Mark to get me through the winter. From the top of the minifridge rises a pyramid of canned goods: beef Burgundy, stewed tomatoes, chicken giblets, pears, sardines, Green Giant corn, myriad Campbell's soups, etc. I eat my meals at a portable "Nantucket" kitchen island. Yes, I have become a man who spends a good portion of his time bellying up to a mostly useless three-foot-high rectangular mass.

Centered on the attic floor is a bearskin rug that Glose, the troubled drummer in my band, left crudely folded and boxed in our rehearsal space. I had the surprisingly high-quality bearskin professionally flattened and steam-cleaned, and I will occasionally lie on it and think of my ex-wife, Sheila Anne:

Her strawberry blond hair and small perfect breasts.

The beautifully arranged astral dusting of peach-colored moles descending below her right ear.

The slender subtle natural arc of her back.

Sheila Anne left me for another man.

A man so intergalactically fit he could be cast as some physiologically advanced alien on the SyFy network. A man whose teeth are so white and straight it almost hurts to think about them (Sheila Anne insists that they're natural). A man five years my junior whose chiseled, perfect jawline is deftly offset by one of those undeniably aquiline Mediterranean noses. A corporate alpha male who dresses like an adult and shaves every morning. A man with a wolfish, charming smile who can no doubt execute twenty military-regulation pull-ups while carrying on a lighthearted conversation about the pleasures afforded by his new, ergonomically contoured office chair.

Sheila Anne and Dennis Church live in New York City, in what I imagine to be some cobalt-blue-themed, sleekly furnished apartment located on the twenty-third floor of a gleaming high-rise overlooking the Hudson River. They eloped on a beach in Mexico with only a priest, an authentic mariachi band, and a local photographer as their witnesses. Sheila Anne accidentally posted public-access wedding photos to her Facebook page, and I was dumb enough to let curiosity get the better of me. Though my band did have a fan page, I refused (and still refuse) to become a member of Facebook. But after I learned of their elopement from Bradley (Sheila Anne's younger brother), I couldn't help putting myself through the misery and wound up clicking on her unrestricted page.

After she heard from another bandmate, Morris (via Facebook message), of my being crushed by the photos (I was bedridden for close to four days), Sheila Anne changed her Facebook settings and sent me an e-mail of apology:

> Francis,
> I'm so sorry you saw those photos. I hope you're okay.
> > With love,
> > Sheila Anne

Yes, her farewell salutation was distinguished by a lowercase l. She obviously exclusively reserves the capitalized version of the word for her new husband.

In the photos, Sheila Anne looks nauseatingly beautiful in her sunflower-yellow summer dress, with Mexican poppies arranged in her hair and a bouquet of the same flowers in her hand. Her ankles are ringed with braided sea grass and anemones, the tops of her bare feet flecked with damp, Yucatán sand.

Dennis is wearing seersucker shorts; a matching jacket, the sleeves rolled to the elbows; a white dress shirt with a yellow bow tie; and a straw porkpie whose hatband smartly matches his neckwear, not to mention his bride-to-be's dress and floral accents. He too is barefoot and his tan, ultrafit legs look somehow appropriated from a world-class tennis pro.

He's one of those guys who can wear pastels and not in any way compromise his masculinity. I suspect you could walk up to him at a cocktail party and say, "Why, Dennis Church, what color is that four-hundred-dollar, seemingly-normal-but-designed-to-the-tits casual shirt?" To which he might reply, "It's actually blood-orange-infused salmon," then sip from a glass of chilled rosé in sort of a faggy way and manage to somehow <u>in-crease</u> his masculinity quotient.

The uncredited photographer captured their nuptial kiss while a corona of Mexican sun was forming a divine, perfectly timed halo around their soft joined faces, the porkpie off now (perhaps flung down the beach dramatically), the ocean calm and cerulean and twinkling behind them, an impossibly white Caribbean seagull passing overhead, high in the cloudless blue sky, wings wide and still as if in benediction.

Sheila Anne and I were married in the back room of a steak-house in Branson, Missouri (B. T. Bones Steakhouse), during what would wind up being the band's final tour. That morning I had passed a kidney stone and managed to sprain my ankle at the precise moment it disgorged itself from my urethra. I was high on Morris's Percocet, and in the few Polaroids chronicling the sad but perfect little evening of ribs, smoked sausage, and pulled pork (the Three Amigos Combo), assorted sides, and a red velvet cake that the B. T. Bones manager allowed us to bring into the restaurant, bless his mom-'n'-pop heart, I look like I'm about sixty-three years old. I'm wearing a Carolina-blue cotton-blend suit that I'd purchased from the local Sears and a pair of canvas Chuck Taylor low-tops, also Carolina blue, with white laces and white athletic socks.

My collared shirt, also white and also from Sears, is too small, and my tie is of the paisley variety, phantasmagoric in that insane way paisley can be, and knotted with a misshapen Windsor that was executed by Glose while in deep, furrow-browed concentration. Despite my garroted neck, my facial muscles are somehow either so relaxed or so pain-fatigued that I appear to have jowls. Sheila Anne is wearing a candy-striped fifties thrift-store dress she bought in Branson and baby-blue rain boots (not quite Carolina blue, but close enough) and her hair is in French braids and she's laughing sweetly at my terrible state.

We're so in love that just thinking about it makes my viscera feel like it's turning to landscaping mulch.

Bassist and childhood best friend, Kent, deejayed with his cheap portable boom box, pulling CDs out of an ancient duct-taped binder, while Morris and Glose basically got shitfaced on consecutive tumblers of the B. T. Bones signature drink—the Slippery Tin Roof—which, if I remember correctly, included "ice cream" vodka, chocolate syrup, and coffee liqueur, among other ingredients you might find stockpiled at a four-year-old's birthday party.

The said Polaroid is currently affixed to the bottom of my minifridge with a plastic carrot magnet, which means I have to lie prone and drive my chin into the backs of my hands to really look at it.

I've been doing exactly that a lot lately.

I have never been to New York City but I visit often via the Internet. Someone called Ivan Ivanovich authors a blog chronicling the streets of Manhattan, with little abstract captions below photographs of storefronts, bridges, an East Village farmers' market, Central Park, ethnically diverse children frolicking in urban playgrounds, the Hudson River at dawn, pigeons posing along the edges of tenement rooftops, etc.

When the band was touring we got as far east as Pittsburgh, but the Big Apple has eluded me the same way large game bass elude certain kinds of cursed fishermen.

Oh, the band.

The band the band the band the band the Motherfucking Band...

The band is—or <u>was</u>—called the Third Policeman (a flagrant plagiaristic homage to Flann O'Brien's underappreciated masterpiece), and we made a pretty good go of it here in the Midwest, mostly headlining college bars and occasionally opening at larger venues for some younger, sexier indie/new school postpunk outfit from Portland or Akron or Walla Walla; some slack-haired, waif-thin copycat quartet brimming with wit, donning perfectly distressed clothes (matched only by their carefully ragamuffinized hair) accented by trust fund–financed tattoos and exhibiting a lazy live-performance habit, unwarranted industry irony, and stupidly large amps.

The Third Policeman, on the other hand, was a well-aged, anti-industry psychedelic semi-jam band with a penchant for outro pop harmonies and the occasional speedy punk vibe. We had smallish amps and old duct-tape-corrected quarter-inch cables that had survived the spaghetti-blob insanity of years of bad postshow breakdowns and crammed-to-the-tits gig bags.

I mostly fronted, wrote a good share of the lyrics, and played rhythm guitar. Backed by a small label out of Madison called Slowneck Records, we recorded an EP and an LP. After the LP (Argon Lights) was released we spent most of our time touring highbrow indie music towns (Cleveland, Louisville, Chicago, Austin, Pittsburgh) and making the occasional college-radio appearance.

At our best we were as tight as anyone, and when our drummer, Glose, wasn't fucking us (and himself) over during his huffing stage (as in airplane glue out of small brown paper bags), we looked like a band that could break through the ranks and make a real go of it on the national level. Before Glose wound up in an emergency room in Lawrence, Kansas, for accidental self-induced septicemia (blood poisoning) that he'd contracted from a dirty fork he'd been using to pop a blood blister on his foot, Slowneck Records had planned a monthlong European tour that included Berlin, Amsterdam, Copenhagen, and Paris, which would have surely taken us to the next level, or simply improved the quality of our lives by a modest percentage.

Glose has since sworn off forks, though I have no doubt that his lifestyle still affords him ample opportunity for some other form of accidental self-poisoning. Once he ate a TV Guide just to see what would happen. Nothing happened, so he decided to follow that up by ingesting the first three books of the New Testament. The shame about Glose is that when he has his head on straight, watching him drum is like witnessing someone operating a flying machine.

Besides Glose's erratic episodes, which included shoplifting, public nudity, urinating on small-town barbershop windows, and several fistfights (for some reason he liked to head-butt other bands' bassists, rugby-style), our biggest weakness was our lack of focus. Or maybe it was fear of success, or some combination of the two. We were creepily Chekhovian. Our Moscow was New York and LA, and we talked about testing those larger markets with emphatic music in our voices. But whether our handicaps were financial (no one made more than $300 a week), romantic (what became fondly known as the Third Policeman's "Yoko Factor"—my bad, fellas), spiritual (depression, lack of artistic faith, fear, etc.), or transportation-related (no one ever seemed to have a large enough car to fit two guitar amps, a bass amp, a drum kit with hardware, and a bunch of gear, or good enough credit to rent one), we couldn't manage to get our shit together. Everyday distraction is a syndrome that can cripple any band, especially one with four members. At least one of them has to be the organized one who keeps things rolling with the booking agent and label rep, not to mention manages the responsibilities of maintaining the website, silk-screening the T-shirts, preserving a good vibe with the tour manager, etc.

Of the four of us, Morris, our lead guitarist, pedal collagist, and minimaster of the Arto-Lindsay-No-Wave-inspired punk incantation (in one of the Third Policeman's signature bits, his voice would break through an aurora of guitar shimmer like a mad dog barking down rabies), was that guy. He knew it but didn't like it. I could have been that guy, but I was too in love with Sheila Anne and my priorities were shifting away from the band and toward the false ether of married life. For seven thousand reasons, Glose most certainly wasn't that guy, and Kent, despite his genuine Third Policeman enthusiasm, had a hard enough time simply balancing his checkbook.

Sitting here, at this very moment, it's somehow Morris I miss most. Morris "the Cat" Sparks, who ran a 10.8 100 meters in high school and was the first white male to win the state of Ohio in that event in almost thirty years. Morris turned down Division I track scholarships to three Big Ten schools to attend the nonathletic, cannabis-saturated Reed College in Portland, Oregon, for the sole purpose of studying with the poet Gary Snyder. Morris, the left-handed "white Hendrix." The enigmatic master of the upside-down imitation Danelectro with which he could make more exciting noises than a guitar jock with a five-thousand-dollar axe and nine-hundred-part loop station.

Morris came to Pollard by way of the Wicker Park area of Chicago. He wanted to live cheaply while writing prose poems about power stations and dirty Midwestern children and the encroaching dominance of what he called the "Great Digital Eye." He was a graduate of the U. of Chicago (he transferred from Reed after his sophomore year), and I happened upon him playing an open mic at Pollard's lone independent coffee shop, Hello Hi Coffee on Plano Street. He had long dirty-blond hair and a reddish beard, and was busing his solid-state imitation Danelectro through a delay pedal and triggering some other low-end sound bed with his left foot while performing selections of his poetry. It might sound like utter pretentious nonsense, but it was one of the purest forms of human expression I've ever heard and witnessed. His face did honest things, as did his voice. It was as honest as milk from a cow squirting into an aluminum pail. He performed barefoot, and his slender, surprisingly clean, feminine feet, which he didn't even bother tapping time with, seemed honest too. When I later asked him why he chose to perform barefoot, he said it was important for him to feel the vibrations come up through his heels. The thing about Morris is that he meant it when he said and did stuff like that—stuff that, coming from anyone else, would likely seem affected or snake-oily or just plain random.

He rented an apartment above the coffee shop and survived by working as a barista at Hello Hi Coffee and giving guitar lessons. For nearly a year I courted him to form a band with me, and when he eventually caved, I thought I'd acquired a great secret that would solve perhaps .3 percent of humankind's foibles.

After Slowneck Records was absorbed by a soulless industry monolith, they dumped us; at least that's how I've managed to arrange that narrative. The truth is, we sort of dumped ourselves. Imploded is a good word. Before Slowneck made the move to the big leagues, they actually tried to rally us to stay together and keep grinding it out. But unfortunately things were already too far gone.

After the band split up Morris stuck around Pollard and we jammed in my basement for a few months, trying to work up new material, but there was something missing that the four of us had had together—something intangible and tense and roundly inspired—something that made jamming feel necessary, even religious at times.

Morris eventually left without a good-bye, which would continue a recurring theme for the Third Policeman.

He currently teaches language arts at a junior high school in Durham, North Carolina. I imagine him barefoot in the classroom, still long-haired, clad in chinos, a plaid button-down and navy knit tie, reading Edgar Allan Poe to eighth graders by candlelight while scoring it with one of his guitar collages. The kids probably love him.

All four members of the Third Policeman had always held day jobs. Glose was a technician's assistant at Pollard's lone stand-up MRI clinic. Morris eventually became the lead barista at Hello Hi Coffee. Kent, a certified librarian, worked at the Pollard District Library re-shelving books and on the sly sold vintage rock 'n' roll T-shirts to the kids who would frequent the library's surprisingly sophisticated, Kent Orzolek–curated Young Adult section.

I wrote a column for the local alternative weekly, the <u>Pollard Pigeon</u>, mostly charting my experiences, opinions, and attitudes about the regional and national music scene. I would occasionally embed a record review in my generous thousand-word allotment, which was no problemo for my editor, an old hippie who called himself Chuckie Skyhawk. I'd been a writing major in college (Grinnell College, Grinnell, Iowa), so my byline gave me the false sense that I was actually applying an otherwise wasted higher education.

My column was called "Notes from a Rock 'n' Roll Windsock," and I had a good readership and a modest but lively online dialogue that would follow each entry. I thought about continuing the work as a blogger after the <u>Pigeon</u>, like so many other small-town weeklies, folded, but I couldn't get beyond the pride-spurning, reductive fact that I would no longer be getting paid for my important, expectant work. Despite the <u>Pigeon</u>'s meager circulation (2,500), the byline was surprisingly good for my ego.

For reasons I don't completely understand, my Sheila Anne did not take Dennis Church's unfortunate last name, so it is a consolation to me that she did take mine, the unlikely Italian cognomen Falbo, which translates as "fair-haired" or "blond of beard." Unlike Lyman's prior to midlife, my hair is not fair, though my beard is sort of reddish. I believe I inherited most of my external physical attributes from my mother's side. She was a hundred percent Polish, dark-haired and pale-skinned, with icy blue eyes. I got the dark hair and pale skin from her, and the tired, grayish eyes from God knows where, as Lyman's hound-dog-sad eyes are one of his best, most lovable features.

Perhaps my eyes are simply Pollardian?

Sheila Anne and I were Mr. and Mrs. Francis Falbo for exactly three years, eleven months, and twenty-two days. I arrive at my number based on the Thursday evening she walked out of the house, not the postmarked date featured on the top left corner of the divorce papers, which arrived by way of certified mail not even two months after her leaving. In official terms, our divorce was based on "irreconcilable differences," for which Illinois law requires a two-year separation before the divorce can be completed, but the separation can be reduced to six months if the proper waiver and stipulation are filed correctly. And, yes, I somehow agreed to all of this, always the gentleman, always the fool.

The summer following our elopement, in an effort to satisfy both sets of parents, we held a Commitment Ceremony in the backyard, where we recited carefully composed vows to each other under Cornelia's copper beech. While I know Cornelia and Lyman would've preferred a Catholic church, they were more than happy to host. Sheila Anne and I were staunch agnostics, so we didn't want to go anywhere near a place of worship.

Cornelia's cancer treatments hadn't become too debilitating just yet, so she was in great spirits, making her signature paczki (Polish donuts) and welcoming everyone with smiling eyes, offering shots of Nalewka Babuni, an ultrasweet Polish liqueur.

Sheila Anne's parents and several members of her extended family drove down from Minnesota. They were a tall, hearty lot, some of whom looked Nordic, others more ruddy and Irish. They wore a lot of Ralph Lauren and liked to drink Budweiser out of the can and talk loudly about their baseball Twins and football Vikings.

This was the first time I met Sheila Anne's parents face-to-face. Her mother, Erin, a beautiful former model <u>and</u> tennis pro, immediately hugged and kissed me on the cheek, welcoming me warmly to their family. Robert Farnham, on the other hand, a tall, broad-shouldered corporate attorney with unimpeachable silver hair, was more than a little circumspect. He was handsome in the same way sailboats can be, and when he shook my hand it felt as if I were being administered a gentle life-or-death warning.

Glose oversaw the proceedings wearing what appeared to be a white pleated muumuu that was supposed to be some sort of official-looking garment.

Our vows were embroidered with words like <u>eternity</u> and <u>collaboration</u> and <u>life-partnership</u>. And <u>humor</u> and <u>fun</u> and <u>devotion</u>. <u>Authenticity</u> was one particular word that seemed to hang in the air that night like a magic spinning platter.

Morris performed a genuinely moving ballad on his nylon-string guitar, and Glose played accompaniment, using only a brush and his fingers on his snare drum. After this, drinks were served and Morris and Sheila Anne's brother, Bradley, sixteen at the time, took turns deejaying and both sets of parents lit tiki torches and citronella candles to keep the mosquitoes at bay and everyone danced under the copper beech. It all went down without a hitch in that no one tore an ACL or passed out in the front yard.

I spent most of the evening avoiding Robert Farnham's stern, emasculating gaze, keeping within arm's reach of Sheila Anne, who acted as a buffer between her dad and me after our tense handshake.

Kent, who was not in attendance for reasons I'll get to, was sorely missed, of course. I e-mailed him the few digital photos that Lyman took with his iPhone, but I never heard back.

To bring things to the present, Sheila Anne now uses her maiden name—Farnham—and mine has been deleted from her identity like a smudge Windexed from a bathroom mirror. She has recently been hired onto the elite sales force of Astra-Zeneca, a leading pharmaceutical company that specializes in medications designed to combat, among other embarrassing afflictions, cholesterol, hypertension, and prostate cancer. It's no coincidence that Dennis Church also reps for AstraZeneca.

I imagine my ex-wife walking around New York City in mannish suits and heels fit for a venture capitalist, talking to accounts on her Bluetooth headset, clicking across serious avenue pavement, the <u>Wall Street Journal</u> tucked under her arm, a to-go cup of barista-made cappuccino in her hand, some impossibly crafted foam art like President Obama's face or a rare rhomboidal leaf keeping its shape through sips one, two, and three, Sheila Anne defying pedestrian traffic signals, hailing a cab on a whim, multitasking her tight little ass off, carrying an expensive but sleek leather attaché full of high-end sales materials and brightly colored pharmacological samplers that would probably do a world of good for Yours Truly.

*   *   *

Although she makes frequent visits to Milwaukee, Chicago, and nearby St. Louis, I haven't seen my ex-wife in almost two years (688 days to be exact).

Sheila Anne and I first met after a gig in Louisville, where she was getting her master's in health science at Bellarmine University. The Third Policeman had just played one of that particular tour's best sets at the Rudyard Kipling, a small but indie-respected mom-'n'-pop venue that Slowneck had booked us at as part of one of our many meager six-city treks. While we were breaking our equipment down (we never got to the level that garners guitar techs or roadies), Sheila Anne introduced herself. Those eyes of hers were set against pale, lightly freckled skin and marmalade hair, and although she hid her figure under tomboy-ish corduroys complete with fob chain running back pocket to belt loop, and an oversized plaid button-down shirt that at one time might have been her uncle's, there was no doubt that she possessed a killer, extremely feminine body. But in the grand scheme of indie-rock regional chilliness, which was infecting my entire life at that time, it was her engaging warmth that was almost shocking.

Later at the bar, after we'd loaded everything into our institutional-looking rental van, and following small talk during which I couldn't really focus because I was so immediately smitten, she offered to take some photos of the band at our next gig in Cincinnati the following night. I hadn't even noticed the digital camera around her neck. It was her spring break and she had some time off, and although she wasn't a professional she'd studied photography as an undergraduate (College of Saint Benedict, MN) and had recently developed a passion for shooting the interiors of Louisville bars: those dank, old-school joints that still serve cheap bourbon and don't give a shit about cleanliness, coolness, or closing time. Classic analog juke-boxes. Fading beer light signs. Bartenders donning flea-market wigs. Half-burnt-out Christmas tree lights twinkling sadly.

Sheila Anne was only twenty-five at the time, with long braided hair and those eyes that never seem to tire, age, or lie. I invited her to have a few more drinks with the band over at Freddie's, another local dive bar that kept later hours—and one that she'd recently photographed—but she declined the offer, saying that her boyfriend wouldn't approve and that she always got herself into trouble when she went to Freddie's because the Maker's was so cheap. The fact that she drank Maker's was an immediate turn-on, but the mention of her boyfriend made it a bitter one. Profound disappointment spread through my limbs like nerve damage. I wound up going to Freddie's with Glose anyway and drinking several consecutive shots of said holy bour-bon, chased by cans of aluminum-tasting Miller High Life, whereupon I passed out in a vinyl booth riddled with duct tape, knife lacerations, and cigarette burns.

Nevertheless, Sheila Anne showed up in Cincinnati and shot much of what became the first images on the Third Policeman's now semi-frozen website (it hasn't been updated in well over a year). That night she decided to stay out late with us. We drank at a bar near the ballpark, and I couldn't keep my eyes off her. While she was in the bathroom, Morris kept insisting that she was into me, which I didn't believe, despite the fact that, as our resident chick shaman, Morris could suss out these kinds of things the way pigs can find truffles.

Upon returning from the bathroom she took my hand under the table. Morris and Kent were at the jukebox, and Glose was skulking around, beating the busboys to leftover baskets of chicken wings. I was overwhelmed with the sensation that my stomach had disappeared and I was turning to powder. I think I fell in love with her at the precise moment she took my hand. And though it was brief and likely unremarkable, it is a feeling I will never forget and one I'm afraid I will never experience again. Elysian Fields and all that.

She stayed with me in my hotel room that night, but we didn't sleep together. We mostly shared a bottle of Louisville-purchased Maker's Mark, passing it back and forth, with no assistance from the Quality Inn's faulty ice machine. She really liked our music, especially the lyrics, and thought the way I played the guitar was "quietly sexy." The highest compliment an attractive, intelligent woman can pay to a rhythm guitarist is to tell him that he is "quietly sexy." It's like telling a young center fielder that he "runs like a deer." I felt a surge of confidence, as well as a surging boner.

She wouldn't talk about her boyfriend, though she did mention that things weren't going in the right direction. (They were both master's candidates in the same health science program. His name was Laird.) But instead of taking the men-as-stepping-stones theme as an early sign, I egomaniacally interpreted the declining Laird chapter as an invitation and opened my lonely heart the same way seventh graders thrust their chins heavenward and free their tender souls after a hoped-for love note is discovered in a homeroom locker.

Sheila Anne followed us to Cleveland and Chicago, shooting our shows and helping us manage the merch table. Morris was cool and slept in Glose and Kent's room, and Sheila Anne and I made love for the first time in Chicago, at the Days Inn off Clark Street—appropriately a legendary rock 'n' roll hotel— with a Lake Michigan wind rattling the window like intermittent applause.

Miraculously, those brief seven minutes—perhaps the most perfect seven minutes of my life—produced simultaneous orgasms, yielding zoological noises from us so hilarious that upon completion we were immediately seized with hysterical laughter. Someone on the other side of our door might have thought we were watching Monty Python. There's nothing better than coming and laughing at the same time. It had been a first for both of us.

The following morning, while I paced along the carpeted hallway outside our room, Sheila Anne called Laird and, through a long, teary phone conversation, ended their relationship. Over the course of the next few days I asked her repeatedly if she needed time to recover/decompress/heal from her breakup. Nobody worth his salt wants to be a rebound lay. But she insisted that we dive right in, headfirst, eyes wide open, and continued from these clichés to her platitudes about how we only lived once and life was too short and we had just a few tragic years to flop around and be foolish and dare the gods of love.

Again, I should've taken note.

A few days later we got married in Branson, Missouri. Branson was the next leg of the tour. It's situated in the Ozark Mountains. The Third Policeman got booked to play a Journey tribute set at the God & Country Theatre. This was the kind of gig that would essentially pay for the entire tour. Somehow, Morris can hit all of Steve Perry's impossible high notes, a challenge for any man who still possesses testicles.

High on Vicodin after the gig, I took a knee in front of a packed house of die-hard Journey freaks, professed my love to Sheila Anne, offered her a braided cocktail straw arrangement as an engagement ring, and asked for her hand in marriage. She accepted, laughing, no doubt equally high on Vicodin, and pulled my head into her midriff. She then kissed me so passionately and fully that I could have died right there.

The following day, a Monday, after I had passed the aforementioned kidney stone and sprained my ankle (were these not omens?), we obtained a marriage license from the local recorder's office, a document later signed by Morris and Kent in the back of B. T. Bones Steakhouse after a municipal judge named Lester Moncrief, a half-blind, wheelchair-bound albino whose business card we'd found resting on a little shelf beside the marriage-license window, solemnized our marriage.

While my marriage to Sheila Anne was in full bloom, Kent was heading in the opposite direction as he and his girlfriend, Caitlin, a professional quilter (meaning she hand-made and sold quilts on consignment) as well as our minitour merch manager and occasional head barbecue chef, were about to go through a painful breakup.

Caitlin Carr of Indianapolis joined the tour in Pittsburgh, five days after the Branson show. Little did we know that she was less than twenty-four hours from leaving Third Policeman bassist and my best friend since sixth grade, Kent Orzolek. She wound up publicly accusing her boyfriend of some three years of being a homosexual. This little imputative nightmare took place in a dive bar on Pittsburgh's South Side, while we were playing electronic darts on a Friday night in the middle of hockey season among scores of shitfaced, pissed-off Penguins fans, who had just witnessed a hard-fought loss to the New York Rangers.

Caitlin's accusation seemed preposterous, but was in fact, as we were about to discover, wildly and unpredictably true.

Poor Kent.

It turned out that he'd been in love with Glose for several months and that the reason he'd been putting on weight was that he knew Glose preferred fat girls. Kent had grown particularly heavy, pushing 250 pounds (at a generous five foot ten).

He came out to Glose roughly at midnight, the night before our Pittsburgh show, in Glose's Holiday Inn motel room, as Caitlin, Sheila Anne, Morris, and I were getting stoned and streaming a <u>Three's Company</u> marathon on my laptop in another room. I think Kent got inspired by my sudden, impulsive marriage to Sheila Anne.

According to Glose, this is what happened:

Wearing a tight sleeveless T-shirt featuring a Shazam thunderbolt, perhaps to highlight his plump pecs and bulbous tummy, Kent Orzolek professed romantic love to his longtime rhythm section partner. Glose, in response, vomited his Dairy Queen double cheeseburger, root beer, and vanilla shake onto the fire-retardant carpeting. Then he (Glose) freed his uncircumcised penis from his underwear-less pants and proceeded to urinate on the plot of regurgitated matter, at which point (according to Glose) Kent actually went to his knees. This, I assume, was probably out of desperation or relief or horror, or some combination thereof, as those extraordinarily heightened moments in our lives have a tendency to naturally lower our center of gravity, thus the need for phrases like "She took my legs out" and "He made my knees go wobbly." Glose, however, obviously misinterpreted Kent's genuflection as an inspired offer of fellatio, and according to Kent, Glose struck him square in the face with the cheap digital clock radio he'd aggressively snatched from the bedside stand. Glose claimed he thought Kent was coming by simply to huff a little glue and watch reality TV, something they'd been doing ad nauseam the entire minitour. (As an aside, Kent swears to the God of Rhythm and Blues that Glose has three testicles.)

The following morning, while Kent was out gophering coffee (it was his turn), Glose went straight to Caitlin and told her everything, which Kent, of course, despite his inflamed and bruised face, vehemently denied, calling Glose a liar, an iconoclast, and, of all things, a hairy, emotional Nazi.

That evening's gig at the legendary Gooski's, in Polish Hill, was, for good reason (and to put it lightly), a sloppy, unfocused mess, and we lost the room halfway through our set. The rhythm section was a horror show. Glose refused to look at Kent, whose eyes were bulging with tears. To make matters worse, because of his recent weight gain, Kent was short of breath and double-chinned and sitting on his amp the way old people sit on buses, and he was making a lot of faces that the middle-aged antihero stroke-victim character tends to make in American films just prior to having to go to a knee at the wedding reception for his estranged daughter who hates him but will likely grant him for-giveness.

We muscled through the set and broke our gear down in front of a disappointed crowd and sold a whopping four CDs and maybe three T-shirts, and only half-a-dozen people signed the e-mail list and we loaded into the van and headed back to the motel with our collective tail between our legs.

Later that night, Caitlin's Inquisition reached its peak at the aforementioned dive bar on Pittsburgh's South Side. Through several rounds of Iron City Lights, Kent couldn't convince his girlfriend of three years that Glose's story didn't hold water. It was his word versus Glose's and Caitlin believed Glose, whose version was sadly and inexorably the truth.

It turned out that Kent and Caitlin had been having sexual problems for months. She told me the only way Kent could achieve an erection was if she turned the lights off and lightly blew into his rectum while he brayed incoherently on all fours. And if that didn't work, she would have to gently jab at his puckering anus with the tip of her thimbled index finger.

The breakup was inevitable. Caitlin wound up boarding a Greyhound bus, leaving Kent and the band for good.

Along with my marriage, Kent and Caitlin's breakup was one

in a confluence of unfortunate events that would lead to the demise of the Third Policeman. Glose, who'd exposed himself as a passionate homophobe, a terrible friend, and dare I say a hairy, emotional Nazi, basically stopped speaking to Kent altogether, which broke Kent's heart, smashed it like a felled swallow under the wheel of a two-ton truck. After Pittsburgh we canceled gigs in Morgantown, West Virginia, and Bloomington, Indiana, and returned to Pollard.

The van ride home was eerily quiet, to say the least. I drove most of the way while Sheila Anne sat beside me in the passenger's seat. Behind her, Kent basically stared out the window catatonically, while in the far back, amid a lot of equipment, Glose disappeared under a Hawaiian shirt he'd mysteriously acquired in Branson. Morris, as even-keeled as ever, manned the seat between Glose and Kent, reading a paperback and writing in his notebook.

Despite the tension between Glose and Kent, Sheila Anne and I couldn't have been happier. In a few days I would be putting her on a bus back to Louisville so she could complete her master's work at Bellarmine. We held hands and doted on each other the entire ride back. We were newlyweds, after all, and our whole life was ahead of us.

Back in Pollard, within days, Kent quit his job at the library. Without farewell, no doubt shamed and embarrassed, he packed his things into his '79 Ford Fairmont and drove north to his parents' poorly insulated winter cabin in Michigan's Upper Peninsula, where he currently resides doing God knows what. He does not answer my e-mails or his cell phone. I'm told it snows six months out of the year in the Upper Peninsula, and I worry about my best friend since sixth grade being gay and alone and cardiovascularly challenged in the hinterlands. Perhaps the saddest part of it all is that he did not take his bass with him. It's still zipped in its Reunion Blues pleather gig bag, standing upright, leaning against one side of my wall of paperbacks.

Without any of us realizing it, Gooski's in Pittsburgh's Polish Hill would prove to be the Third Policeman's final show.

So now I am a landlord in the house I grew up in. Lord of the Land. Francis Falbo, Landlord, take my card, won't you?

My mother died on the first floor, in her converted hospice room, roughly where Bethany, the three-year-old daughter of my longest nonfamily leaseholders, the Bunches, used to sleep. I don't make a habit of discussing my mother's death with tenants. No one wants a ghost around, especially the ghost of a woman who spent a lot of time swallowing screams precipitated by intestinal pain.

I'd like to think that after a failed marriage and a semi-promising rock 'n' roll career, which has evaporated into the Mist of Destiny (or Irony), I have found comfort in coming to accept the clear simplicity of my life. The practical duties of landlording are satisfying and chock-full of miniprojects that are actually solvable (unlike my personal life).

Such as: Replacing water heaters. And keeping raccoons out of the trash and bats out of the attic. And clearing gutters and battling ants and devising strategies for eradicating mid-July wasp nests from under the rear eaves. And installing bathtub drains or snaking a sewage pipe when the plumber isn't available. And the acquired skill of speaking to sunburnt, potbellied, Kodiak-chewing contractors about installing drywall or routing conduit or reglazing windows while they spit tobacco juice into a 7-Eleven Big Gulp cup.

Is this approaching grace? I wonder. Or is the aggregate narrative of my life a series of small, ill-shaped rationalizations that mask an enormous failure? I probably won't know until I reach old age, if I'm that lucky, as cancer runs on my mother's side of the family like salmon in the River Tweed.

Is becoming the landlord in the house you grew up in sort of like running a funeral home? Or is it awesome and humble and rife with the coolness of familial legacy?

Two weeks ago, just after New Year's, Todd and Mary Bunch's three-year-old daughter, the aforementioned Bethany, disappeared. They were purportedly at the local Target, perusing the Outdoor/Camping aisle, when toddler Bethany wandered off, as toddlers throughout history have been wont to do. Was she kidnapped? Conveniently left?

The local media has made a pretty big stink about "Little Bethany," although both the Pollard Pioneer (our daily ultra-conservative newspaper) and the WKCG evening news seem to be in cahoots, hell-bent on treating Bethany Bunch's disappearance more like an alien abduction than something actually disturbing and real.

Meanwhile we are halfway through the month, and while I try not to dwell on it, Todd and Mary Bunch still owe me rent for January. It's not easy wrangling money from tenants when they're down on their luck, let me tell you.

The Bunches are former trapeze artists in the Ringling Bros. Circus, from which they retired after their daughter was born. They were apparently married during a performance, shouting their I DOs midflight in front of a paying audience in Cedar Falls, Iowa. Todd, a short, quiet, wide-shouldered redhead with "invisible" adult braces, is now a rookie at the local fire department, and Mary, a petite, doll-eyed, slightly haunted-looking milkmaid of a girl, spends almost as much time moored to the house as I do.

This morning a detective came by. We spoke to each other on the front porch. His last name is Mansard and he is tall the same way high school history professors can be tall and he is severely bowlegged and sports a flesh-colored hearing aid. He possesses the face of an insomniac, distinguished by a nicotine-stained brown-gray mustache, and his line of questioning had mostly to do with the Bunches' domestic habits, specifically odd behavior, and whether or not there has been any sign of spousal or child abuse, to which I could only answer—and honestly so—that I didn't know, that I'd never noticed anything out of the ordinary like bruises or limps or silent cries for help. I explained that the house was nearly two hundred years old (it's 134 years old, actually), with thick walls, fireproof-carpeted floors, and a layer of acoustic vinyl I had installed underneath the carpeting on each story.

Mansard seemed suspicious of me, as if I was somehow protecting the Bunches. "You really haven't seen anything?" he asked.

"No," I said, my wool hat snagging briefly in the synthetic holiday conifer wreath I've yet to remove from the front door. "They come and go, keep to themselves."

He asked me what I charge them for rent, and how large their unit is.

Was this guy actually an undercover rep from some government agency created to investigate amoral landlord behavior? I told him they had the entire first floor, gesturing toward the window behind me, whose heavy brown drapes suddenly made it look funereal. "It's roughly nine hundred square feet." Perhaps he was asking about their living conditions because a cramped unit might be motivation for creating more space, thus eliminating a three-year-old?

"Is it nice in there?" he asked.

"Nice enough," I replied. "Simple."

He asked me if I spent a lot of time with the Bunches. I told him that I didn't make it a habit to socialize with my tenants. He wanted to know if they went to church, to which I answered I had no idea. Then he actually asked me if I went to church, and I told him I attended the Church of Neil Young and Crazy Horse.

"It takes place in my headphones," I added.

"You're Lyman Falbo's kid," he said.

I told him that indeed I was.

"He did my taxes once. Got me a pretty decent return. How's your dad doing these days?"

I told him he was down in Florida with his new wife.

"He was a helluva bowler," Mansard said. "Didn't he bowl a perfect game?"

"Nineteen seventy-nine," I said. "He had the score sheet framed."

Mansard stroked his calico mustache. He took his time. He acted like someone trying to portray a detective on a TV show. Like there was a camera set up at the other end of the porch and he was filming an audition. At home he probably wears a plaid flannel bathrobe and smokes a pipe. No wife. Maybe a two-decade-old cat sinking into a matching plaid armchair, fat and slow, runny-eyed, blind.

A tree branch down the street cracked. It sounded like someone's femur breaking at close proximity.

Mansard eventually said, "You know, it took them four days to file a missing person's report."

I didn't reply.

"That's ninety-six hours after little Bethany disappeared," he continued, touching his archaic hearing aid. "Usually, the parents'll file within four or five hours."

I asked him why he was telling me this and he replied that as their landlord I should know the kind of people I'm renting to. "They do hold a proper lease, I presume?"

I said nothing, but nodded.

The snow, which had ceased for almost an hour, started again. It looked somehow theatrical, from the Ice Capades or some other holiday extravaganza, as if it had been cued and someone hiding across the street in the Grooms' ancient sycamore was turning a dial.

Hazard Groom, the retired Pollard Memorial football coaching legend, was shoveling his driveway in what appeared to be a Formula One fire-retardant racing suit. He also was wearing hiking boots and a hat that made it appear as if an owl had landed on his head. He stared up at the heavens, indignant in the face of the incessant snow.

"It's about twenty-four degrees out here," Mansard said. "Aren't you going to invite me in?"

I explained that there was no common area.

He asked if we could just go to my unit and I said something about cramped quarters, so he suggested going to get a cup of coffee.

I told him I was expecting the plumber.

Then he mentioned the cold again, saying, "I'd really love to get the heck out of this weather." He blew into cupped hands and stomped his feet.

I asked him if he'd tried ringing the Bunches' doorbell.

"I did," Mansard replied. "If someone's in there, they're sure as hell not answering." His face was starting to contort from the windchill.

My unclean, riptiding, transmogrifying beard was protecting me brilliantly, and I was quickly tiring of the storkish bastard and his calico 'stache.

"Couldn't you <u>force</u> them to come in for questioning?" I said.

"Oh, sure I could do that," Mansard answered obliquely. "Not sure that's necessary just yet."

Was this guy lazy or did he have some weird veteran detective strategy?

Through gritted teeth he added, "I understand the husband's a firefighter?"

I told him that as far as I knew this was true.

"Former circus couple going straight."

"Straight?" I said.

"The straight life. No more big top. No more freaks. Clowns. Contortionists. Midgets with cardboard swords. The smell of big-game dung and hay. All that fantasy. Suddenly deciding to hunker down and do the neighborly life in a place like Pollard. Going for the quiet America. It's bound to do a number on your head."

"I suppose it could," I said, and wiggled my toes, which were safely warm inside my merino Ingenius socks, which were covered by a pair of Scandinavian ergonomically advanced wool slippers that Sheila Anne had gotten me for our first Christmas.

"What do you do," Mansard then asked, "besides chase down the monthly?"

I told him I used to be in a band.

"Like a rock 'n' roll band?"

"Um, yeah," I said. "We played rock 'n' roll."

"What instrument?"

I told him I mostly played guitar and sang. "Some hand-clapping, too," I added.

Then he asked if he would have heard of the band, and I said probably not.

"What were you guys called?"

"The Third Policeman."

"No kidding?"

"You've heard of us?"

"No," he replied. "I mostly listen to Mickey Newbury, Waylon Jennings, that sorta stuff. Kristofferson." Then he asked if we were interested in police work.

"Only the police work of the soul," I replied.

"There's no other kind," he said.

We were practically flirting, and it felt just plain weird.

He cocked his head to the left a bit, as if suddenly beholding something. The gesture was distinctly beaglelike. "Do you always wear the robe?" he queried. "I only ask because there appear to be about thirteen different species of mustard stains at play."

I told him I eat a lot of sandwiches.

"And the hat?" he asked.

I told him it was part of my landlord ensemble. "I have an evening robe too," I lied.

"Comfortable living," he offered, somewhat gently, though I could sense the hidden barb in the cotton ball. For the first time I noticed that his mustache hairs looked like they were growing into his nostrils and that his nostril hairs looked like they were braiding into his mustache. Mansard gave me his card, touched his hearing aid again, and said, "If you speak to your dad please give him my best."

Then he descended the porch steps, his head still tilted slightly to the left.

Across the street, Hazard Groom was taking a break, leaning on his snow shovel. Plumes of lung smoke escaped his mouth, and his silver racing suit reflected squibs of light.

Mansard started whistling as he fished for his keys, or maybe it was his hearing aid feeding back. He walked with a hitch. Something to look forward to: arthritis in the winter. I briefly imagined him bowling with my father back in the seventies. Sideburns and turtlenecks and polyester pants. Disco playing over the PA.

Mansard's car—a metallic-gray Lincoln—squawked as he engaged the remote to unlock his door.

Although, as I've said, I haven't seen Sheila Anne in nearly two years, my ex-brother-in-law, Bradley, who was staying with us for a few months before she left, still lives in the street-facing second-floor apartment (Unit 2). For unexplained reasons, Bradley, twenty-two now, had dropped out of the University of Wisconsin–Whitewater and arrived on our doorstep after the first semester of his sophomore year. He'd been wrestling a pretty ferocious weed habit, which, since the acquisition of his sister's thirty-seven-inch high-definition Sony plasma flat-screen television, has been recently upgraded to Lifestyle status. The flat-screen was de-installed from Sheila Anne's and my former living room and reinstalled onto his freshly Sheetrocked bedroom wall once he moved into his own unit, roughly a year and a half ago.

He simply knocked on my door and stated it plainly: "She said I could have the plasma." As if I were giving him the very stuff of my blood, or my ex-wife's.

I didn't fight him for the TV. It had to be de-anchored from the wall with a special tool that only the guy from Best Buy has, so it cost me a hundred and fifty dollars to have him come to the house, de-mount it from my wall (now the Bunches' wall), then remount it to the virgin Sheetrock in Bradley's unit.

Bradley is one of those handsome, athletic-looking men who, aside from Hacky Sack, Wiffle ball, and occasional stints of skateboarding, has never played a sport in his life. Women seem to descend on him the way crab apples fall out of trees in the late fall, yet he seems only vaguely interested at best. In my opinion it's not his sexual orientation that accounts for his indifference to women—he seems pretty obviously straight—but rather it's a kind of general disconnect from the world. This detachment in its most elemental state is plantlike. And like most plants, marijuana included, it is only sunlight and water that he needs, a condition that might be called human photosynthesis. Recently, like me, Bradley has grown a full beard and exists largely in his underwear, though he wears simple V-neck T-shirts and boxer briefs, not long, waffle-patterned double-layered thermals.

We obviously have more in common than I'd like to admit.

When he does leave the house he dons a long black trench coat and a navy-blue knit skullcap, as if he's heading off to work at the docks, though aside from the Blackhawk River, which is a stagnant, sulfuric glorified tributary with a cement prom-enade featuring an outfit that offers summer paddleboating, a Baskin-Robbins with faulty refrigeration, and a dozen or so va-cant, suspicious-looking storefronts, Pollard's only other body of water is a crappie-stocked man-made lake glutted with Jet Skis and pontoon boats.

Despite the fact that my ex still pays his rent, Bradley and

I seldom speak, and when we do, the conversation is executed with the fewest possible syllables.

"Hey," I'll say, after he opens his door, upon which I was knocking for several minutes.

"Hey," he'll reply in his sleepy baritone.

"What's up?" I'll ask to ease into things.

"Nothin' muh." The words are almost breathed out, a somber little anti-song, the three syllables getting equal exhalation and drone.

For some reason I feel it necessary to hang on to the thin vestige of familial tissue—however dehydrated by marijuana, baseboard heating, or general male sadness—that connects Bradley and me.

He'll say, "She sennit, righ?" <u>Sennit</u> meaning "sent it." <u>It</u> meaning "the rent."

"She sent it," I'll confirm for him.

"Coo," he'll say, after a genuinely blank moment, the word sapping one of his few remaining available breaths for the day, his face as vacant as a Tupperware lid. Not "cool"; "coo," and sincerely uttered, not hipstery, and with absolutely no intent of sounding urban or in any way ebonical. I'm convinced he drops the <u>l</u> out of classic stoner elocutionary fatigue.

"I just wanted to see how you were doing," I'll offer, feeling my blood pressure, which is already low, dropping to match his.

"Coo," he'll say again.

"You're good?"

"Yeah, I'm coo..."

Then we'll stand there and stare at each other, the smell of reefer creeping into the hallway, almost manlike in its sharpness, with his sister's state-of-the-art TV murmuring in the background and <u>Halo</u>'s pause-mode riff looping maddeningly.

Bradley and Sheila Anne have mouths shaped the same, the upper lip fuller than the lower, perfectly imperfect, and they have the same color eyes, somehow sea-foam green. It pains me to look at him.

"Heard from your sister?" I'll finally ask, trying with all my weakened will not to pose this question, but ultimately failing, like some pathetic crystal meth addict breaking down in front of a stranger at the Greyhound station.

"Other day she tole me to check my e-mail," he said recently.

"She called you?"

"Lef a message."

"But you don't have a computer."

"True dat."

"Do you even have an e-mail address?"

"Think so."

"You can borrow my laptop anytime," I offered.

And he nodded, evidently having exhausted himself of any more verbal energy. And I nodded too. And when the nods decayed to cranial stasis, we just sort of stood there like cows in a field of mud.

"You have Cheetos in your beard," I said, or something to that effect.

And then he mustered one final nod, almost infinitesimal in its movement, and shut the door not quite in my face, and I turned and headed back up to the attic.

Since he became a leaseholder I've seen exactly thirty-two women knock on Bradley's door, which is just at the landing of the eight stairs that lead up to my attic unit, so it makes it easy to spy. And yes, I count them (I actually keep a tally on a piece of paper that is thumbtacked to a small corkboard over my desk). Both the front and back doors are well secured; you have to be buzzed in to get into the house, which means that most of these girls are waiting around for someone to leave the premises so they can sneak in, likely because Bradley is too lazy to cross the necessary square footage of his apartment to reach his intercom. And because I am by all definitions housebound and beyond Bradley and me there are only four other people living here (well, three now, considering the fact that little Bethany is missing), I imagine this waiting could get exorbitant. I estimate most of the women to be in their twenties. They are all above-average-looking to beautiful, slim, if not blatantly fit, and slightly agitated. The majority of them leave dramatic notes taped to his door.

Notes like:

Bradley, you really hurt my fucking arm . . .

Or:

Thanks for all the lying!

I have no idea where he meets these women or how he goes about accumulating them. I thought for a while that it might be some sort of personal dating enterprise developed through one of our more mainstream social media platforms — Facebook or Twitter or what have you — but in addition to not owning a computer, Bradley lives without the services of a smartphone. His telephone is of the analog rotary-dial variety. In fact, I'm almost positive that it was a phone I grew up with. So he assembles a stable of women without click, drag, text, post, tweet, or any other missive from the digital world. Which makes his babe magnetism all the more remarkable. Aside from the plasma TV, he is the Luddite Lothario of Pollard, Illinois.

Bradley owns a silver Toyota Celica with one brown door and a replacement tire. It's a car he parks in the back of the house, but rarely drives. I've seen him mostly getting stoned in the driver's seat, pulling from a seven-inch, sunburst-orange fiberglass bong, the stereo system playing Bon Iver or Bill Callahan or Sufjan Stevens or some other soul-blighted "In" or recently "Out" Midwestern indie crooner.

Next to Bradley, in Unit 3, which faces the backyard, whose majestic copper beech is perhaps the property's greatest natural asset, is Harriet Gumm, a twenty-year-old art student attending Willis Clay whose current project involves nude studies of local middle-aged African-American men. Like Bradley and his stable of women, I have no idea how she finds her subjects or where they come from. Despite its rural profile, Pollard is ethnically diverse, with a surprisingly large African-American population, upwards of something like 27 percent. Lyman, my quietly racist father, always claimed the majority of them were Southern blacks who didn't have the resources or the will to make it all the way north to Chicago. My mother would shake her head disdainfully, only half-joking that she married a racist.

"You married a realist," Lyman would contest, dead serious. "A realist!"

Harriet Gumm boasts dyed black bangs over mischievous Coca-Cola-brown, heavily lined eyes, and she is one of those sun-phobic loners whose ears are perpetually plugged with iPhone buds. She wears mostly navy-blue or black clothes, often covered by a charcoal-gray wool pinafore, a silk headscarf, knee-high white socks, and black leather, brass-buckled children's shoes. She seems somehow out of time, as if she could have been a troubled silent-film star, or some haunted character from an Edward Gorey fable. In a more pedestrian context, at a glance she could be mistaken for a parochial junior high school student. But then she'll turn and cast her large brown eyes at you with such intensity it's as if a four-hundred-year-old witch is glimpsing the damp, thin paper napkin that is your soul.

Our exchanges have been limited to brief hellos in the basement laundry room—her voice surprisingly quiet and girlish—and minimal discourse about the rent, which she always pays in cash (invariably twenty-five twenty-dollar bills), which she wraps in scented white, patterned Kleenex and stuffs into a white business envelope with "Mr. Falbo" printed on the front. The strange thing about her penmanship is that it's an uncanny replica of my manual Corona typewriter font. So much so that I took an eraser to it only to discover that it was composed in fine-point charcoal pencil.

When she moved in she brought with her a duffel bag, a waxed canvas backpack, and a wooden easel. Once, when I had to fix her window, which wouldn't close, I noticed that she had turned all of her artwork around, so that it looked like she was hanging blank pieces of sketch paper on her walls.

Her music of choice is a multitude of African-American female classic soul singers, ranging from Etta James to Tina Turner. Her skin is so alabaster white it's almost blue, and as far as I can tell, she doesn't appropriate cultural "blackness" in any way. If anything, she presents herself as a prog-rock/goth chick, and I would expect her playlist to contain more Ministry or PJ Harvey than Sister Sledge.

There is something porcelain and doll-like about her. She is slim-hipped, not quite long-legged, not quite full-lipped, and, like Dennis Church, possesses a long yet unapologetic nose. But her icy pallor dominates. For some reason I can't quite imagine her with pubic hair. I see a small series of pyramid-shaped gemstones instead. She is attractive in the same way that certain kinds of high-end candy dishes can be.

The man whom she is currently drawing, Keith, is an over-weight, slow-moving, light-skinned perpetual smiler whose extreme positive nature could be misconstrued as Christian. He's always beaming, or at least on the verge of it, and the grooves in his deep-guttered corduroys produce such loud swishing noises that I can hear him approaching the back porch all the way from my attic room. Keith stands a hulking six-four, with oddly thin, vermiform arms. He apparently doesn't own a car, as I've witnessed him only afoot.

As I sit here in my yellowing, decade-old thermals, while the ghostly snow (it has officially been declared a blizzard) passes through the spill of weak moonlight outside my attic window, I am seized by the certainty that I am still obsessed with a woman who no longer wants me, and has not wanted me for a good long time. This certainty I picture with a large Marfan hand, one that might be wearing a thin, black, homicidal-looking leather glove, and it hurts. It makes it ache in my Adam's apple, this certainty. It makes me want to drink consecutive bourbons and play Minnesota-based, midnineties slowcore music, which doles out fewer beats per minute than Chopin's brutally sad nocturnes.

Other than the wretchedness of cancer, which I came to know vicariously through my mother's suffering, there is perhaps no greater misery than the loss of the Love of Your Life. I know it's hyperbolic and sentimental and whiny, but those are the truest words I can type.

The Love of My Life. The One Great Love. Miracle Love.

As if I were some sad-eyed, slope-shouldered, prehistoric mountain creature roaming the antediluvian earth at night, and was befriended by a lonely, nocturnal, equally prehistoric bird, say, a kind of burly, mechanical-looking but kindhearted loon of the night who saves the prehistoric mountain creature from the terror of Epic Loneliness.

In other words, Love So Special It Might as Well Be a Children's Fable kind of love.

I could certainly use the services of one of Bradley's visitors. I'd like to believe that, like my former brother-in-law, I have willingly devolved into my own monastic plantlike state, solitary, self-sustaining, animated only by moisture and an attic window's worth of sun, but I can't deny that I long for the simple creature comfort of companionship, specifically female companionship. It's not sex that I'm talking about, although that certainly accounts for something; it's the warmth of another. The reliability and purity of a woman's shape moving through a shared room. The cast and cant of her shadow on a wall. The warm apples-and-smoke scent of her hair hanging faintly in the air. The perfect spiderweb smallness of bras and panties clinging to a hamper's wicker skin. The minty effluvium of her toothpaste breath on cold winter mornings.

In the simplest of terms, according to Sheila Anne, she left me because I lost my ambition. Because I settled—that was the word she kept throwing around.

Settle: to decide on something; to solve; to make or become resident; to colonize place; to stop floating; to pay what is owed; to move downward; to subside; to stop moving; to make or become clear; to end a legal dispute; to make or become calm; to put details in order; to make somebody comfortable; to put something in place; to establish or become established; to compact something firmly; to assign property; to impregnate or be impregnated.

I'm fairly certain that, with regard to me, the definition Sheila Anne was referring to was "to stop moving."

And why did I stop moving? Because I grew to be satisfied

with our life in Pollard and the cresting of the Third Policeman and the cluttered familiarity of the basement recording studio. Perhaps the most troubling reason I stopped moving is because of love itself. Because I let love become my priority, which, I realize in retrospect, results in too much doting, a compulsive need to touch and cling, and the dissolution of any mystery that might exist between intimate companions. It is mystery, after all, that keeps a marriage interesting. Things secreted in drawers. Unknown telephone numbers on the long-distance bill. Unusual URL addresses on the web browser.

I think I took marriage to be a kind of pre-midlife apotheosis, but instead of it inspiring me to continue to grow as Francis Falbo the Man and Francis Falbo the Rock Musician (thereby increasing my mystery quotient!), it pushed me into a strange mode of self-satisfied semiretirement. I loved getting domestic and cuddly. I practically swooned at the dependable regularity of shopping for groceries and the weekly Laundry Day and tri-weekly scheduled Magic Hour Sex and morning coffee/newspaper reading and making "team" decisions about dinner and evening entertainment and whether or not we should get a Puggle (we never did).

Sheila Anne commuted to work ninety minutes away, where she managed the Human Resources Department at Decatur Memorial Hospital. Route 41 is not the most exciting drive in the state, and the boring commute, combined with my boring car and her boring, mostly devout Christian staff, made her tenure at Decatur Memorial pretty uneventful, if not existentially challenging. Then she would come home to a cookbook dinner, prepared by her domestically satisfied, bemused-by-a-midlife-type-lifestyle-but-actually-only-thirty-two-year-old husband, and a few glasses of twelve-dollar Merlot, and maybe a semi-interesting studio film foisting itself off as an independent dramedy about a small-town varsity wrestling coach or lawn-furniture salesperson or some such middlebrow, down-on-his-luck-despite-being-world-class-handsome hero, and then we would bed down to sleep and wake up early and she would man the espresso machine and scan the newspaper while wolfing down the granola and the antioxidant blueberries and then once again the ninety minutes in the fuel-efficient Volkswagen Jetta to clip time at a hospital where it rarely got better than talking to disgruntled nurses about when they could expect to be fully vested 401(k)-wise.

The beige Midwestern hamster wheel spins and spins.

I suspect Sheila Anne met Dennis Church at some hospital function where pharmaceutical sales reps were rubbing shoulders with pharmacists, pain management buyers, psychiatrists, and other hospital higher-ups. I imagine the scenario unfolding at a Ponderosa, Glen Campbell on the radio, Sheila Anne and Dennis Church falling in love-at-first-sight across tubs of hi-cal/low-cal dressings at the buffet-style salad bar.

"Hey," he says.

"Hey," she replies.

"I'm Dennis. Two <u>N</u>s."

"I'm Sheila Anne."

"You're with the hospital. According to your lanyard you run the Human Resources Department. I'm with a top-three pharmaceutical conglomerate. That's Glen Campbell on the radio. 'Rhinestone Cowboy.' Great tune. You know it was actually written by an Australian? Great American country-and-western pop song written by an Australian. Dingo ate my baby. Go figure."

"How long are you in town for?" Sheila Anne asks, warmed by his Top 40 trivia charm.

"Only tonight. Why do you ask?"

"Because I find you incredibly attractive, particularly your masculine, aquiline nose, and I don't want to go home and face my mediocre husband whose recent increase in body-fat percentage is only seconded by his declining mystery quotient. Plus, our sex has become like the mechanical, shame-tinted, physiological sawing you read about in Christian reproductive books written for children, where the husband and wife look like pancake people and don't have genitals per se, but sort of smooth, glabrous, Teflon-like surfaces."

"Awesome. You have beautiful, sea-foam-green fuck-me eyes."

"And you have an interesting, incredibly strange but undeniably sexy fuck-me nose."

"And without going too hyperbolically off the rails here, I have to say, glabrous—what a cock-smoking word choice."

"Learned that word from my husband. Good with words. Bad in bed."

"Dingo ate my baby."

"Put that heaping plate of low-cal lentils down, cowboy, I'll follow you out."

But it really probably went like this:

"I'm Dennis."

"I'm Sheila Anne."

"You looked marooned at the salad bar."

"Oh, I'm just being vague and noncommittal. There are too many options."

"The variety of croutons alone."

"It's all just so complicated. And is that supposed to be blue cheese or ranch?"

"I'd bet my baked potato that it's ranch…I gather from your lanyard that you're with the hospital. I'm from AstraZeneca."

"Is that a new addition to our solar system?"

"It's a pharmaceutical company. It would appear that I've lost my lanyard."

"Maybe it's down at the other end of the salad bar, deeply recessed in that tub of cottage cheese and pineapple bits."

"I'm one of the reps. This is part of my new territory. Illinois, Indiana, Iowa. Do you live in Decatur?"

"I live in Pollard. Southwest down Route Forty-one. Two-lane highway, lots of nice arable fields to take in. Corn. Cows. Silos. What about you?"

"I live in New York."

"City?"

"The Big Apple, yep."

"Never been."

"Instead of corn, cows, and silos, we have skyscrapers, pit bulls, and the smell of salmonella in August. I'm actually originally from Colorado. Little town called Yuma, about two hours northeast of Denver."

"What lured you east?"

"The job."

"They bring you all the way out to New York City so you can work in the Midwest?"

"They fly me out here once a month. Put me up in decent hotels, rent me quality sedans."

They smile. He reveals his white, nonbleached, staggeringly irresistible teeth.

Sheila Anne's larger upper lip dimples up adorably.

"Mind if I join you?" he asks (finally).

"Not at all," she answers.

And then they finish filling their plates with low-cal, colorful salad bar selections and sit together at an imitation oak, poorly padded, ass-cheek-hardening booth and talk about things like the Wellness Profession and the pros and cons of socialized medicine and why maybe the French and the Swedes have figured it out and the insane hours doctors put in for the good of mankind and how fluorescent hospital lighting makes one look and eventually feel bloodless as a macadamia nut, which can be generally counterintuitive to healing, and how the cafeteria fare at Decatur Memorial has actually improved quite a bit since they brought in the new eco-friendly food services company.

And over his medium-rare porterhouse steak, in between graceful but without a doubt masculine mastication, Dennis Church, in his lightweight, well-tailored spring/summer business suit, tells the sea-foam-green-eyed beauty across from him about the loneliness of traveling and how low-down and just plain weird it is to have your only companions be your company-bought MacBook Pro and your tricked-out company-financed smartphone, and how sometimes he wishes he lived a simpler life, in a small town with like a Little League diamond and a swimming hole and a barbershop with one of those swirling red-white-and-blue barber poles and ceramic Nativity scenes erected on the lawns of churches during the holiday season and a really high-quality miniature golf course with a windmill that's so big it almost looks real and a shopping mall with an authentic food court and a grade-A Fourth of July fireworks display at the local speedway and a lima-bean-colored water tower with the town's name featured in black majuscule letters.

And in between his words, Sheila Anne imagines her life in New York. The faster metabolism it would educe and the taxicabs and the inconceivable volume of humanity teeming on actual boulevard-sized streets and wide cement sidewalks and sluicing bike messengers and the unspoken rules of engagement on subway cars and the new urban way of walking and

the learned skill of avoiding insane encephalitic homeless people with swollen carbuncular faces and leaky eyes and Pilates
at dawn and bartenders who can knock your socks off reciting
Shakespearean soliloquies while shaking the daylights out of a
martini and high-speed elevators and crammed espresso bars
and the yeasty sweet smell of Broadway theater lobbies.

And every other sentence or so Sheila Anne starts to imagine
this New York life with <u>him</u>, this incredibly magnetic Dennis
Church, who has undone the top button of his oxford now and
loosened his tie so his impressive, well-shaven Adam's apple can be
free to dance a bit. And although at this point it is an absurd, pre-
mature notion because she is very much married and supposedly
in love with and spiritually and legally committed to a man she
lost her mind over some four years earlier, she lets her imagination
run like a wild horse galloping along the cliffs of the Costa Brava,
and all she can see is Dennis's presumably fit, low-fat, highly con-
ditioned body poised over hers, the two of them composed
missionary-style in some cheap roadside motel room off Route
41, with great classic soul music like Larry Graham's "One in a
Million You" playing at a volume so perfect that they can inhale
the music with the pores of their conjoined bodies and yet also
hear each other's animal pleasure—the wordless mewls and
whimpers—releasing into and infusing with Larry Graham's velveteen baritone and by the end of their meal, which she can't
even remember eating, let alone choosing, Sheila Anne Falbo has
decided to give herself permission to fall under the spell of this
extremely thoughtful, surprisingly charming, endlessly interesting
gentleman with the aquiline nose who is sitting across from her.

*   *   *

Earlier I keyed into the Bunches' unit. The grief over their missing daughter tinges the air like a spoiled egg. Their apartment is surprisingly neat, with furniture that is as beige as it is simple. I assume their plain living is due more to ignorance than some minimalistic aesthetic choice. They were itinerant circus travelers after all, most likely living out of secondhand Winnebagos and camper-trailers, enduring and adapting to gypsylike caravanning. Perhaps they have yet to experience the challenges of domestic stability and therefore know nothing of the concept of classic American household clutter.

I was surprised by the lack of toys. Aside from a stuffed corduroy cat that was more of a throw pillow than a child's companion, there was little if any evidence of toddler life. Regarding Bethany, I thought I might find a series of circus-themed photos of her arranged around the living room walls, the sequined trapeze-artist parents thrusting her joyously into the air as celestial big-top lights glint overhead...a clown riding a miniature tricycle over a sawdust floor, little Bethany perched on the handlebars...an elephant standing in the center of a ring of paper lanterns with Bethany cradled safely in its trunk. But save for what appeared to be a wool Navajo blanket hanging above the sofa, their walls were blank.

In their entertainment console, an archaic TiVo's red light was engaged. I imagined them recording <u>The Oprah Winfrey Show</u>, an episode dedicated to the epidemic of Missing Children in the Heartland. The Bunches would view it encamped on their itchy calico sofa, their legs extended on their unremarkable coffee table, as they ate microwaved Stouffer's.

Mary Bunch keyed in while I was clutching their remote control. I have no idea why I was suddenly holding it, and I was forced to hide it in the pocket of my bathrobe.

"What are you doing?" she asked. Her voice was high and faint and trapped in her nose.

I told her that I'd heard a strange noise in her apartment as I was walking up the stairs. She asked me what kind of noise, and I said, "A sort of scrabbling. There were coons in the attic last night," I lied.

"Coons?" she said.

"Yep," I replied. "Scrabbling raccoons."

She said she was under the impression that raccoons were in hibernation mode.

And I told her that, yes, the majority of raccoons were indeed engaged in deep hibernation mode, but that sometimes it was necessary for a few of them—a brave select few—to venture out for the purpose of foraging for food. I could hear my voice sliding into its higher bullshit register.

"During a blizzard?" she asked, dubious.

"Especially during a blizzard. The stakes are higher. Hunger becomes paramount. They have to refuel."

"<u>Whose</u> apartment did you hear them in?"

I told her in rare cases such as this—in "coon cases"—that I always do a quick check of the other units. "A cursory inspection," I offered, and explained that I had keyed into Harriet Gumm's and Bradley Farnham's apartments too.

She hadn't blinked yet, and the space between us was acquiring a strange density, like the air before a thunderstorm. Her light-blue ozone eyes appeared to be somehow glued open. I had never noticed it before, but Mary Bunch has freckles. The kind where the pigment appears to have dissolved and settled over the paler layer of skin, more infusion than dusting.

"They're pretty resourceful creatures," I added. I breathed through my nose. A trail of cold sweat was running from be-

58

tween my shoulder blades to the small of my back. Time was slowing down. I said, "By the way, how's your heat been?"

"Our heat is fine," she replied.

A dollop of embarrassment began slogging through my intestines. "Sorry if I crossed a line," I finally offered, swallowing the dry mouth. Swallowing twice actually.

She was wearing a ski vest over a weather-resistant anorak, accompanied by a gnomic, conical red winter hat and mismatching collegiate jogging pants. The ski vest, puffy and hazard orange, looked bulletproof and gave the impression that she was either a municipal worker or a deer hunter.

"Can I help you with those?" I asked, pointing to her bag of groceries.

"I can manage," she said.

There was another awkward moment, during which she sniffled back a snot globule and finally blinked. It was as if the blink somehow reset her. She exited into the kitchen with her groceries.

The warmth of their unit was making my pulse drop and my feet felt incredibly thick. Sweat was now also forming at my temples and soon my beard would start glistening repulsively. Something beyond the embarrassment of having been caught nosing around in one of my tenant's apartments, something beyond the clammy humors of shame, was overwhelming me. Something sad and heavy and haunted.

I could suddenly smell freshly cut apples. And Mary Bunch was putting groceries in the fridge. I imagined it filled with doubles and triples of things. Jars of mayonnaise and bottles of ketchup. Four-packs of butter. Eight quarts of whole milk, most of which would never get drunk. A dozen misshapen grapefruit. Overbuying to compensate for their missing child. Little dimple-cheeked Bethany with her baby teeth and her impossibly large blue eyes, her wheat-colored hair.

Once she knocked on my door. She was wearing only a saggy cloth diaper and holding a dinner fork.

"Hi, Bethany," I said.

The flaxen hair, duck-curling at the base of her neck. Her tiny pink hands. "Fork," she said, thrusting the utensil high in the air. The word was a perfect note, almost pure oxygen. I wasn't sure if the fork belonged to the Bunches, if it was mine, or if it was one that had been randomly left in the stairwell.

"Thank you," I said, taking it from her.

She then plugged her mouth with her thumb and headed back down the stairs, all on her own. I remember being vaguely troubled that it was the beginning of December and the Bunches were letting their daughter wander around the house unsupervised, wearing only a saggy diaper.

When Mary reentered the living room she'd removed the ski vest and anorak and was now wearing a Phish concert T-shirt, too large, probably her husband's, with a long-sleeved black T-shirt underneath.

"You think we did something," she said. "To her." Her voice was still congested, and I had the strange impulse to go to a knee, to actually genuflect; perhaps out of some expression of abject, confusing shame for trespassing in my own house, or worse yet, for being a completely neutral human who exists mostly in wool camping socks.

Still standing, I said, "Did something to who?"

"Our daughter."

"No," I said. "I don't."

Mary Bunch was surprisingly attractive in her <u>Billy Breathes</u> T-shirt, and our proximity, likely tweaked by my recent extended lack of female companionship, felt weirdly romantic. Was there a sudden charge between us? A little ionic landlord/tenant valence? Whatever it was had taken me by surprise.

I quickly fantasized that she was trapped in a bad marriage, that her lack of blinking was in fact a dry-eyed cry for help, that behind her retinas a home movie was playing that featured Mary being emotionally terrorized by her husband, Todd, with his invisible braces and inescapable circus strongman holds, and that I was the only one who could save her. I would invite her up to the attic and we would simply spoon in my boyhood bed. And then I would wash her hair in a basin of water, frontier-style.

But what about little Bethany? Was she actually alive, being held captive by her parents, gagged and duct-taped, locked in a closet somewhere?

Mary Bunch's nostrils were gluey with snot. I got the sense that it was more than just a cold, that she was somehow spiritually congested, that her soul was heavy with some unnameable guilty paste. She wiped her nose with the back of her wrist. I realized that, like me, she didn't appear to have showered recently. Her face had a film. The hair sneaking out from behind her ears was matted and dirty. I wanted to smell it. I imagined the sharp odor of her unclean scalp embedded deep in the fibers of her gnomic ski hat.

Finally Mary said, "I saw you speaking to that man yesterday." I asked her what man she was referring to and she said, "The tall creepy-looking guy with the mustache."

"So you were here," I said. I told her how he'd claimed to have rung their doorbell several times.

"Who was he?" she asked.

"A detective," I replied.

She said something about how "these people"—I supposed

she meant cops—were "relentless." She asked what he wanted, and I told her how he'd simply asked a few standard questions. "About Bethany?" she asked.

Hearing her say her daughter's name was strangely shocking in that it revealed nothing more than if she'd uttered "clock" or "can opener."

She said, "What exactly did he ask?"

"If I'd seen anything out of the ordinary."

She started bobbing her head. Tiny little nods. It was almost parkinsonian, this bobbing.

I was confused, back on my heels, defensive, yet I still had this impulse to pull her close and feel her breasts press into me. Something about our mutual desperation. Or maybe it was just my hormonal loneliness, my proximity to an unwashed woman pheromonally spiking my testosterone. Despite our many respective thermal layers, I was convinced that an old-fashioned breast-to-chest hug would do us both a world of good.

After her head came to rest, she said that they hadn't filed a missing person's report because they didn't even know what that was.

"Of course," I said.

She said that when they signed the lease they told me how they were "different." "We're still getting used to this kind of life," she added.

I told her I totally understood.

"Why did he give you his card?" she asked, and the space between her words had shrunk, her breath had quickened.

I said I was pretty sure it was standard procedure and that he had given it to me unsolicited.

Then she asked if she could see the card, and I told her it was up in the attic.

"What's his name?" she asked.

I told her "Mansard" and she asked what kind of detective he was. "Just a regular detective," I said.

Her eyes seemed to go soft-focus, and she mouthed his name a few times. Then the head bobbing started again. "Are you gonna call him?" she said.

"Should I?" I asked.

Her blue eyes seemed to surge. She regarded me with an attitude I can only describe as ultracontained vitriol, her mouth a small knot of bitterness. "We didn't know about the Office of Missing Persons," she said.

"There's no need to explain anything to me, Mrs. Bunch."

"Mary," she said.

"I mean Mary."

"I'm not a librarian."

"Of course," I capitulated yet again.

"She disappeared while we were shopping," she said. "Someone took her right out of the fucking Target."

Their refrigerator hummed in the kitchen. Hides of snow calved on the roof. Someone in the neighborhood was trying to start a chain saw. Plows scraped by on distant streets. These were epic sounds.

Then, to change the subject, perhaps cheaply, almost in the voice of another man, someone I've never heard speak before, I said, "I don't mean to have to be a landlord right now, Mary, but you're almost three weeks late with the rent."

"We'll have it to you in a few days," she replied tersely.

Her large, unblinking eyes, their pupils enormous again. This is what grief does to your eyes, I thought. It turns them into doll's eyes. Grief or sociopathic numbness.

"Todd's waiting on a check," she added.

"Don't worry about the late fee," I offered.

For which she didn't thank me. Mary Bunch was about as thankless as an interstate tollbooth attendant.

"By the way," she said, "are you planning on shoveling the front steps? Todd almost slipped and fell this morning. It's starting to get dangerous and we can't afford him losing any days."

"I have someone coming by," I lied.

She asked me why I couldn't do it.

"Bad back," I lied again. "But don't worry, they'll be shoveled and salted first thing tomorrow."

Then, without looking at my hands, she said, "Why are you holding that?"

I hadn't even realized it, but I'd removed their TiVo remote from the pocket of my bathrobe. I was squeezing it so hard my knuckles were pearling. I loosened my grip, handed it to her.

She gently snatched it and wedged it into her armpit. "I think you should go," she said, her arms folded in front of her, her chin still jutting.

I found myself wondering how many times she'd fallen into the net while doing trapeze. Twelve? Two hundred? And would it have been a product of bad timing or a missed cue? Her body hurtling through the air as if thrown from the window of a high-speed train.

The remote fell from her armpit to the floor, and the cover for the batteries popped off and one AA battery rolled across the space between us and kissed my slippered left foot. We froze in recognition of a kind of mushroom-cloud moment. Neither of us would look down.

I realized I was squeezing my butt cheeks together with all my might, which I surmised was related to my acute dehydration. It somehow felt like the AA battery was now lodged in my rectum.

"I'm sorry," I said, hoarse now. "Next time I'll make sure someone's home."

She uncrossed her arms and then crossed them again.

Then I bent down, which allowed me to release my butt cheeks, engaged my unfit, atrophying hamstrings, and grabbed the remote, its small plastic battery cover, and the battery. On one knee I negotiated the battery into its correct plus-minus position, clicked the case closed, and rose to hand Mary Bunch the remote, which she accepted with cupped, rigid hands, as if being forced to inherit a piece of unwanted heirloom crystal.

Up close she had soft, perfect skin, and despite her mucoidal nostrils, her breath smelled like maple syrup and pancakes.

Later in my room I took a Viagra. Earlier I'd procured a vial of the little blue rhomboidal pellets from my pot dealer, Haggis, who, in addition to the popular erectile dysfunction pill, is now selling Vicodin, Xanax, and chocolate bars infused with psychedelic mushrooms. It seems that when it comes to matters of small-town drug dealing, expansion is more than possible, even during a recession.

Despite the blizzard, Haggis wore frayed corduroy cutoffs and hiking boots with no socks. I could smell his feet. Oddly buttery, deeply fungal. Like multiplex popcorn and the between-the-toes cheese of masculine decomposition.

Haggis lives out of his car—a venom-yellow midnineties Nissan hatchback that boasts a suspicious-looking Nevada license plate and many dings and dents. He'd recently fashioned ghetto-style valance curtains from what appears to be the felt hide of a pool table, which he uses to conceal his front and back windshields and all windows. He's one of those post-post-post-college-aged eccentrics who spring for custom curtains but won't fix the dents on their car.

Haggis came up to the attic, and after completing the Viagra transaction, we drank instant Folgers and listened to side A of Fleetwood Mac's <u>Rumours</u>.

Inspired by his shorts, I offered him my corduroy reading chair. I manned my twin bed, which sort of sags in the middle.

Our hands were interlaced around kooky gift-store mugs. Mine had a snoozing Garfield the cat on it, the phrase "Anybody can exercise... but this kind of lethargy takes real discipline" splitting at the ellipse, ringing either side of the rim. Haggis's mug featured the words BEST WIFE IN THE LAND OF LINCOLN in large red letters, which were superimposed over the silhouette of our great sixteenth president's profile, the profile framed by a cookie-cutter outline of our twenty-first state. A joke gift from Sheila Anne. Given that I am the one who was technically cuckolded, <u>wife</u> now carries with it an ugly, stomach-turning connotation, yet I keep the mug around the same way people who suffer through excruciating toothaches keep extracted wisdom teeth in jam jars.

We both drank and re-interlaced our hands around our mugs. I think Haggis really appreciated the company.

"So you chose the attic," he said. "Cozy."

I told him that I felt better having everything going on below me.

"Like a lordship."

"I never thought of it that way," I said.

"You're lording over your subjects, Fran. You're like a fucking monarch."

I imagined actually commanding this kind of status over my tenants. I'd have to start showering and wear jackboots or something. Jackboots and a greatcoat. I could shape my beard into a kingly Shakespearean spade and speak in declarative iambs:

Come live / with me / and pay / me rent.

"I dig the stairwell paneling," Haggis said.

I told him that I'd been thinking about adding a workout room in the basement. "Treadmill, StairMaster, rowing machine, some dumbbells."

"Fitness," Haggis replied sadly, as far away from the concept of the word as a shipwrecked man from a fax machine.

I wondered if Haggis was one of those men who doesn't die a human death, but dissolves like a piece of wood in a barn.

"Diggin' the beard, dude," he offered after a silence. "You're startin' to look downright apostolic."

Despite his nearly forty years, Haggis hasn't gone gray and still possesses a boyish, clean-shaven face. His jet-black hair, like my apostolic beard, is wayward and at certain angles looks like a smashed crow clinging to his head. He has the strange habit of absentmindedly stroking his left nipple, over the shirt, in a curiously circular fashion, as if perpetually haunted by a life-altering grammar school tittie twister. His teeth are dim, so dim they're almost blue. They belie his youthful face and non-gray, unwashed hair.

Stevie Nicks's syrupy voice began "Dreams," the second song on side A but easily the record's true beginning. I've always thought the first track, "Second Hand News," sung by Lindsey Buckingham, to be an asinine, herky-jerky chest-wiggler better suited for the end credits to one of the Muppet movies. It's totally beneath the rest of the album.

"So, Viagra," Haggis said. "Gettin' back in the game?"

"Trying to."

"Seein' someone?"

I told him I was pretty much just watching Internet porn

and whacking off, which was a lazy half-truth. I've actually been thinking about my ex-wife and whacking off.

"I could use a laptop," Haggis lamented. "When it comes to lovin' Old Lefty, I have to rely on my faulty memory."

"You're left-handed?"

"No, but I like changin' it up. Makes me feel like I'm gettin' away with somethin'."

It gave me hope that a lost man living in his car could still be blessed with wit and ingenuity.

After Haggis finished his cup of coffee we said nothing for a while and listened to the rest of side A. "Never Going Back Again" into "Don't Stop" into "Go Your Own Way" into "Songbird." I have always loved Stevie Nicks's voice the most, but lately Christine McVie has been winning me over. Her voice is less bewitching and not as haunted with the troubles of the world, but clearer, stronger. You're not as fooled by it.

When side A was over, the wind whistled through the cracks of my attic's finial window, which made everything suddenly forlorn and remote, like Haggis and I were the only two people left in some shack in the Arctic. In a semi-arthritic three-part move, Haggis wrested himself from my corduroy chair and buttoned his capacious loden coat. His calves peeked out from underneath, pale and bald as freezer-aisle chicken breasts.

"Hey," I said, "you know anyone looking for extra work?" I figured one of his clients would be desperate to make a quick buck.

"Not really," he replied. "Why?"

I told him I needed someone to come by every few days and shovel the sidewalk and porch steps. "Salt them down afterward. Just a few times a week. Someone sort of dependable."

"I could do that," Haggis offered, his voice suddenly hopeful, childlike even. "Shoveling's my thing."

I was surprised. He was obviously making good money dealing drugs—enough to finance homemade valance curtains at least—and I presumed he had very little if any overhead since he was living in his dinged-up car.

"I'd pay you twenty bucks a go," I offered.

"Oh, keep your money, bro. God knows my flat ass could use the exercise."

"I'd do it," I said, "but I tweaked my back the other day."

"Say no more," he said.

I asked him if he could get it done by tomorrow, explaining how one of my tenants had been complaining.

"I'll do it tonight," he said. "I just have to run a few more errands. I'll be back later."

I told him he was the best.

After he left, I placed his mug in the sink and turned <u>Rumours</u> over to side B.

The whistling again. The blizzard passing diagonally across the attic window. That snowplow was back, scraping by on the street below.

When "You Make Loving Fun" started, I lay on the floor, pressed my ear to the central air duct, and listened, hoping to somehow bypass the second floor and hear into the Bunches' apartment. I imagined Todd and Mary Bunch not talking, but passing notes to each other across their kitchen table, their daughter's small half-rotted body interred in some frozen field on the outskirts of Pollard, her ice-blue cyanotic face arrested in an attitude of calm certainty, as if she glimpsed something beautiful just before Mommy and Daddy forced her to drink from her sippy cup of strychnine-laced cranberry juice.

After the Viagra finally kicked in, I powered down the turntable, manned my desk, opened this manuscript to page 29, where I had sketched a fairly decent likeness of my wife's naked body, her eyes staring back at me, irises larger than her real ones, the pupils dreamy and crepuscular, her rabbitlike mouth filled with yearning. Her breasts small yet full, nipples erect. Her perfect hips, shaded with faint cross-hatching.

I masturbated with the intensity of a thief pillaging a dark room. Crazy images bloomed in my mind: Sheila Anne on all fours; Sheila Anne morphing into Mary Bunch with stelliform eyes, fellating me on my bearskin while clutching her TiVo remote. Even Kent's ex, Caitlin, made an appearance, her feminist thatch absurdly large and dark, simian-like. She rode me while I clutched her bush. But it was Sheila Anne who returned and brought me to the promised land, in a classic missionary formation. Though I aimed for the nest of paper towels I had fashioned in my lap, I accidentally orgasmed copiously onto the reverb and volume knobs of my Marshall kick amp.

Later I was awakened by strange, guttural huffing noises coming from the front of the house. From my attic window I could see Haggis, down on his hands and knees, using the back of a hammer to chip away at one of the four ice-encased steps leading to the porch. He had already cleared the walkway from the street, and there was a big bag of melting salt on the lowest step, against which leaned a snow shovel.

Haggis's grunts were impressive, and he seemed to be making great progress, clawing away with his hammer as his breath smoked up through the now thinning snowfall. Behind him, as the dawn just started to silver the Grooms' rooftop, a lone cross-country skier clad in goggles and head-to-toe sky-blue Thinsulate passed down the middle of the poorly plowed street.

PART TWO

THE SNOWMAN
MYSTERY

Bob Blubaugh moved in four days ago.

Bob Blubaugh Bob Blubaugh Bob Blubaugh...

Stating his name over and over sounds like a septic tank going bad.

His possessions include a steamer trunk, an aluminum-surfaced kitchen table, two matching dinette chairs, a small wooden desk, five milk crates filled with books, and a full-size mattress and box spring.

On Friday morning, just as the blizzard finally died, he unloaded his few things from a green Family Truckster station wagon boasting a wood-brown stripe and Minnesota plates. Filigrees of snow made his passengers' windows look ornate and otherworldly. The backyard was effulgently white under the bright morning sun, the copper beech majestic and silver.

At the back porch we shook hands and I halfheartedly offered to help him haul his stuff down to the basement, but he politely declined. I was still wearing my ensemble of double thermals, bathrobe, slippers, and pilling knit hat. I had gummy eyes, and my nose felt like a swollen, hemorrhoidal ass haphazardly arranged on my face. My head was starting to itch, as were my cheeks, and I had genuine concern about psoriatic scales radiating through my beard. Despite having to lug myself out of bed at the sound of his car pulling into the back lot, I was grateful for his early arrival.

From the porch I watched him carry both mattress and box spring on his back in one go, Egyptian-style, slightly bent at the waist, with an athletic grace that I've rarely seen. I held the door open and he thanked me every time he passed, seemingly not at all winded. He was clean-shaven and his breath had a wintergreen kick to it.

When he was done moving his stuff in, I gave him a quick tour of the house's ground-level communal spaces: the mailboxes, the wraparound porch with its white wicker patio furniture and standing ashtrays, and the backyard, where behind the copper beech someone had erected a child-sized snowman, complete with a carrot nose and two pieces of charcoal for eyes, but no mouth. Draped around its neck was a pink scarf. The snowman threw me. I hadn't noticed it when Blubaugh was unloading his things.

To Blubaugh I explained that in the spring, just after the thaw, I would arrange the three-piece wicker furniture set under the copper beech, which was also a smoker-friendly area and available to all tenants. Setting up the white wicker ensemble each spring was one of my mother's simple pleasures, and I'll admit that I've made it my own little Falbo tradition, a kind of sentimental elegy to Cornelia. The copper beech was her favorite tree after all, and in the summer months she would often read under its branches well past dusk, sometimes using a flashlight, unconcerned with the insane number of bug bites she would acquire. From my bedroom I could sometimes hear my mother laughing. She liked Kurt Vonnegut, J. D. Salinger, Anne Tyler, and John Irving. She especially liked the precocious children in Salinger's stories. It was the only time I would ever hear my mother laugh, while she read late at night under her tree.

I pointed out the alleyway Dumpsters and gave him the low-down on the weekly Thursday garbage pickup, the importance of separating the recyclables, etc.

Then I gave him a quick tour of the basement. I showed him the coin-operated washer-dryer and next to that the storage room, which houses an ancient manual lawn mower, a few boxes of fifty-watt lightbulbs, and retired Falbo family bicycles, including Lyman's bad-ass-looking Schwinn Fastback (which he never used) and my seatless Huffy BMX with yellow mag wheels, which I once manned with the asinine intention of jumping over Kent's secondhand Yugo until the makeshift particleboard ramp collapsed midlaunch and I wound up bouncing off the driver's side door like a confused porpoise sailing into an ocean liner. I sustained a mild concussion and a deep thigh bruise that put me on crutches for nearly a week. Behind the remains of my BMX junker and mounted on the wall is my mother's ancient burgundy Raleigh three-speed, complete with whitewall tires and Wizard of Oz handlebar basket.

I'm not sure why the bike is mounted. I sometimes think Lyman was confused about the purpose of her gravestone. After her death he mounted not only her bike but also her prized enamel colander, a red straw sun hat, and the clarinet she played as a girl. These items were randomly displayed around the house: the colander on the wall over the downstairs toilet; the sun hat over the old RCA console TV in the living room; the clarinet in the kitchen, in the small wall space over the microwave. At first I was touched by Lyman's meticulousness. He measured the walls to find their perfect center point. He used a level and special curved braces for the clarinet and made sure the sun hat was hung in a way that wouldn't damage the brim. Hanging the bike took him half a Sunday. I realized he was starting to lose it when I found him standing over her wedding dress, which he'd smoothed out on their bed and was attempting to clean with a toothbrush.

When I began the renovation I put the colander, straw hat, and clarinet in a box, which I shipped to Lyman down in Florida. I had the wedding dress repaired and dry-cleaned and sent it to Cornelia's mother, my grandma Ania, who is still alive, living in a nursing home in Chicago. For unknown reasons, Grandma Ania and Lyman have stopped speaking. I suspect the moratorium has something to do with his remarrying, although he is financing her residency at the home.

After the storage space, I showed Blubaugh the boiler room, which is probably as totally unnecessary as it is uninteresting, the space being a dank fungal cement bunker that reeks of mold and dust and corroded iron. I always show it on the tour out of some need to illustrate the authentic bowels of the house. I mentioned that I'd been considering turning the storage room into a mini fitness center. I thought Blubaugh, being a former Olympic athlete, might perk up, but it didn't seem to excite him at all. In fact, I think he yawned and flared his nostrils. Then I pointed out the dropped ceiling, which one could easily argue to be counterintuitive, lowering an already low ceiling. But it actually needed to happen to hide the old beams and termite damage.

"Brand-new ceiling," I said. "The whiteness actually opens things up." I stretched and pushed up a gypsum tile to feature the hollow space. "Good for hiding illegal substances," I added, jokingly.

Blubaugh offered a half-smile that was probably actually a quarter-smile, maybe even an eighth.

"And there you have it," I said. "The grand tour."

Blubaugh finally broke his silence and said, "The fundaments."

We shook hands in a gentlemanly fashion (again) and I left him alone.

Up in the attic, I looked up the word <u>fundaments</u>, which is a noun whose first definition is cited as "the buttocks," the second definition, "the anus," and the third, "a base or basic principle, underlying part; foundation." The final part of its tertiary definition was a relief, to say the least. I wrote the word down in a notebook I keep for lyrics, weird words, and other errata.

I also drew a small, blank-eyed, mouthless snowman wearing a child's scarf. I did some nerding out on the Internet and found that another word for <u>mouthless</u> (which actually isn't a word) is <u>astomatous</u>. I wrote that down as well, just to the left of the snowman.

<u>Astomatous</u>.

A few hours later I knocked on Blubaugh's door with two copies of the lease and a bottle of Côtes du Rhône, which I always offer a new tenant. I keep cases of red and white wine at the foot of my bed. As a general rule I offer the men red and the women white. It's one of the few pieces of Neanderthal advice I've taken from Lyman, who is by no stretch of the imagination an Epicurean, but simply believes that one's gender and one's wine should have a corresponding natural order.

Blubaugh appeared to be entirely moved in. There was something spartan going on. At a quick glance I noted the lack of an entertainment system, which would bode well for the overall sanity of the other tenants, the Bunches in particular, whose bedroom sits directly above Blubaugh's living room. Some weeks before, over the phone, I had explained to Blubaugh that while I had done my best to soundproof each story with acoustic vinyl, the Sheetrock, though of decent quality, is by no means the intricate, labor-intensive, mid-twentieth-century lath-and-plaster system that traps and eats sound waves, and tenants were expected to keep loud music, television, and other potentially noisy activities to a minimum. As far as I could tell, at least with regard to unit noise, there would be no problem with Bob Blubaugh. If anything, his apartment emitted an absence of sound. Aside from the faint hum of the refrigerator, there was almost a palpable, vibrating silence.

"Welcome," I said, offering the bottle of wine and the two copies of the lease.

He thanked me and took the Côtes du Rhône, placing it in the center of his kitchen table. He seemed intensely preoccupied with the table's true center point, adjusting the bottle until he was satisfied. Then he sat and started going through the lease.

"I have white too," I offered. "A Clairette."

"I'm fine with either," he replied.

Lyman firmly believes that men who drink white wine are homosexuals, whether they know it or not. "A Chardonnay man is not a real man," he would say. So according to my father's theory, I was renting to a sexually neutral being, which no doubt would drive Lyman batshit crazy.

At a glance, there is something almost shockingly, well, normal about Bob Blubaugh of St. Paul, Minnesota, former first alternate on the American luge team that competed in the 2002 Winter Olympic Games at Salt Lake City. In terms of physical stature, he is maybe five-ten, of normal build, neither chiseled nor flabby, handsome nor homely, with hazelish eyes, Clydesdale-brown, slightly thinning hair, which he parts to the side Robert Redford–style, and an impressive cleft in his chin that might be deep enough to hide a lemon seed or two. He wears aluminum-framed, amber-tinted glasses, and on the day of his arrival, he donned a light-blue button-down oxford, navy Levi's corduroys, a thick, ropy, gray wool cardigan over the oxford, and penny loafers.

In short, Bob Blubaugh looks more like a reference librarian who might also collect vintage eyewear than a former Olympic athlete. And he might be as ageless as a cardboard cylinder of Quaker Oats.

In the living room, his steamer trunk was opened vertically, revealing a five-drawer wardrobe and a miniature closet, the two sections separated by three ancient hinges. It gave Blubaugh the air of someone from a distant land, a traveler of oceans, a secret hoarder of rare spices.

Next to the steamer trunk was his desk, which had a soft leather top, embossed with what appeared to be the outline of deciduous deer antlers. Stacked on the floor, in small thigh-high towers, was his modest library, book spines facing out. There was nothing on the walls, not a single framed photo, a poster, a clock, or a wall calendar. If he possessed a computer, it wasn't anywhere to be seen.

This was apparently a man without history or family, birthed in a luge chute, ejaculated from a frosty tunnel fully formed. He will live for two thousand years, following blizzards around, snow and ice being his only true ancestry. Windchill his lone friend.

His small dinette set was centered in the kitchen. He sat in one of the two chairs. I stood a few feet away, fighting the urge to twiddle and claw at my itchy beard.

While he signed both copies of the lease, I said, "How was the drive down?"

"Not too bad," he replied.

His voice has a distinct lack of music in it. It subtly modulates in one slightly alto-ish register. Adult men with high voices always surprise you, though. They're either incredibly well-endowed or know karate.

"You just missed the blizzard," I said.

He nodded like he was gesturing hello to the postman.

"Nothing you haven't seen before I'm sure," I offered stupidly. The last thing a fellow Midwesterner wants to commiserate about is the harsh winters in the Midwest. It's like dentists making small talk about teeth.

He handed me the two copies of the lease. His penmanship was the cleanest I've ever seen. On the underlined space beside "vocation" he'd printed "person" with a lowercase p.

"You're a professional person?" I said.

He smiled and adjusted the bottle of Côtes du Rhône yet again.

"You get paid for that?" I asked, joking.

He smiled like taxidermy. Meaning his mouth in that position appeared to be somehow stitched and glued.

He then produced a royal-blue, vinyl-skinned checkbook, which must have been living in the pocket of his cardigan. He filled out a check, signed it, and handed it to me, though I can't be certain that I actually caught all of these movements. In some strange way it almost felt like the check had written itself. Or maybe it was prewritten and Blubaugh simply tore it from the book.

I studied it briefly and said, "Bob, this is over six months' rent."

"Which includes the security deposit," he replied.

Again his penmanship. Each letter rendered masterfully.

I told him that I had no problem with tenants paying me on a month-to-month basis.

"This is better for me," Bob replied. "Simpler."

I folded the check in half and placed it in the pocket of my robe.

He remained seated at the table and I was starting to realize that my new tenant moved with such restrained, kinesthetic efficiency that it was sometimes hard to catch him moving at all. There was something Eastern going on. Dare I say ninjafied. He existed with such rarefied functional stillness that there was the odd sensation that I was talking to a life-size painting of Bob Blubaugh, not Bob Blubaugh the actual man.

"Not to get too personal on day one," I said, "but do you mind me asking what brings you to Pollard?"

"I was just looking for a quiet place."

"To do what exactly?"

"To live."

I asked him if he knew anyone in the area.

"No," he replied.

I noticed that the checkbook was gone, and although I had turned away only briefly to look at the actual check, I had no idea where. However, there was still a ballpoint pen on the kitchen table, this much I know for sure.

"Here," I said, handing him a small Post-it note, "the Wi-Fi code."

He accepted it and blinked. Or maybe he didn't blink. Maybe he didn't even accept the Post-it. A few breaths later, I did notice the Post-it note affixed to the anodized surface of his kitchen table, near the base of the bottle of Côtes du Rhône.

We were quiet. Above us Mary Bunch was running a vacuum cleaner.

"The Bunches," I said, pointing toward the ceiling. "I'll be sure to introduce you."

Bob Blubaugh said nothing. He simply sat there, motionless, his face blank, almost blissfully neutral. Eyeballs framed by his tinted glasses. It was all so fucking subtle. Maybe he was undergoing some strange process of meditation? He knows how to make time slow down, I thought.

"If you ever need anything," I offered, "don't hesitate to knock on my door. I'm up in the attic. Accessible from the aft staircase. Welcome to the building."

Still nothing from Blubaugh.

I turned to go but stopped. "By the way," I said, "will you be getting a landline? I only ask because I have a pretty good connection with a guy at the phone company. With a day's notice he can get it installed in no time."

"No, thanks," he said.

"You're exclusively mobile? I only ask because I'm looking at your lease and I'm noticing that you didn't fill in a cell phone number."

"Because I got rid of it."

"Oh."

"Yeah."

"So but what if I have to get in touch?"

"I'll make sure you can."

We looked at each other for a full five seconds. I think I actually counted them out in my head.

"Oh, and no pets," I added for some reason. "Meaning mammals. I'm cool with fish, or something that can be kept in a terrarium, but no mammals. Guinea pigs, dogs, ferrets, cats, gerbils, hamsters, that kind of thing."

A bustlike response. Complete stillness. An expression I would describe as Beethovenish.

I left with my copy of the lease, feeling sort of gently freaked out. When I got back to the attic, I filed his lease in a cardboard legal box under my desk and took a shower for the first time in two weeks.

Before I got under the water, I finally looked in the mirror, focusing exclusively on my beard, which had begun to look like it was made of granite. I tried to avoid my eyes. Somehow I knew they would be ringed with shameful, baggy, bourbon-colored circles. Of course I failed. When you start to become your own science experiment, you can't help looking. They weren't as bad as I thought. I looked mostly sad. Sad in the same way that weather can be sad. I was the human equivalent of a cold, rainy day. I was a brown puddle in the middle of a dead-end street, with maybe a Popsicle stick or two floating in my dank, dog-slobbered water. If Sheila Anne were to see me I would be embarrassed. The thought sent such an intense pang of shame through my stomach and kidneys that I had to sit on the toilet for a moment.

I realized that I hadn't left the house since around Christmas. This was my second one without Sheila Anne. I thought it would be easier than our first one apart, but it was harder. On Christmas Eve I wound up drinking a bottle of Maker's Mark and crying myself to sleep and staying in bed the entire next day and maybe even the day after that. It was a bad forty-eight hours. I'm pretty sure that was the beginning of not being able to leave my house. You figure there'd be some horrible inciting incident, but there wasn't.

The hot shower felt like needles on my skin. To rid the oil slick that had congealed on my head I had to shampoo my hair three times. I really dug into my scalp and sideburns, which actually burned a little, giving newfound literalism to the word. I shampooed my beard too, an act that gave me so much relief I whimpered.

So I have a bad tooth.

My lower first molar on the right side zings when I drink anything cold or inhale the winter air. Almost a year ago, I was supposed to have a root canal, but I kept putting it off, and I now get repeated calls from Dr. Hubie, the Falbo family dentist. Yes, the calls are from Dr. Hubie himself, not his secretary, the ageless, honey-voiced Julie Pepper. I don't have the heart to tell him that I'm having serious problems leaving the house, but I need to get this tooth fixed before it rots through my jaw.

Post microwave lunch of Dinty Moore beef stew, I was flossing in front of my bathroom mirror, trying to wrest material from my bad molar, when I heard something being slid underneath my door. No envelope, just a blank piece of heavy-bond sketch paper, one fold, elegantly creased.

It read:

> Mr. Falbo,
> My toilet's running again. Would you mind taking a look?
> Sincerely,
> Harriet Gumm, Unit 3

Harriet Gumm often almost smiles when she speaks to you, as if she's constantly harboring a secret. It makes her a little sexy in a mischievous sort of way.

Her apartment is set up as a portrait studio. There is a simple mahogany stool in the center of the living room, surrounded by a handful of wooden easels, each easel loaded with large, variously grained sketch pads. There is no furniture here, nothing cozy or domestic, nothing feminine, a simple iPhone dock resting on the floor, no magazines or books—only the stool and the easels and the iPhone dock and an apple box filled with countless stubs of charcoal and pieces of colored chalk. Under the centered stool, a large piece of muslin, gathered around the legs. I couldn't imagine this girl owning clothes or shoes or makeup, but she obviously did. She practically wears costumes! Her bathroom contained only a cake of generic, peppermint-smelling soap, a bottle of No More Tears shampoo, and a simple white towel hanging from the chrome rack that I installed on the inside of the door. It could be the bathroom of a construction worker.

Affixed to the living room walls with blue masking tape were drawings of all the black men she'd been studying, mostly in charcoals. I recognized the African-Americans who'd been coming to the house over the course of the past several months: Cozelle; Markeif; Jershawn; and her present subject, Big Keith.

Each man had a seven-part narrative progression.

Panel One:

Nude slave being purchased shipside by a plantation owner, ankles and neck ringed in medieval-looking iron shackles.

Panel Two:

Semi-clad, barefoot slave engaged in some form of plantation work involving cotton picking, soil tilling, or field clearing.

Panel Three:

Freed slave fighting in Civil War setting, dressed in makeshift Union Army soldier's garb, aiming a musket at unseen Confederate enemies.

Panel Four:

Educated freed slave sitting in a high-gloss university lecture hall, bespectacled, in collared shirt and tie, slacks, and fine leather shoes.

Panel Five:

BCS college football player striking a Heisman pose in the end zone, white Amazonian cheerleaders going apeshit with oversized pom-poms.

Panel Six:

Wealthy professional football player manning the wheel of the infamous O. J. Simpson white Ford Bronco, a trio of bikini-clad, blond Caucasian women fawning over him from the backseat, one of them fondling him under his uniform pants.

Panel Seven:

Modern-day, twenty-first-century African-American, nude again, confident in expression, staring straight at the viewer, holding a smartphone, a Bluetooth device in his ear, penis dangling midthigh, a noose around his neck, an ancient Southern oak tree in the background, conflating the literal and ultrasymbolic "lynching" theme, bringing the whole thing full circle, back to the Inescapable South.

Each subject has a slight variation to his story. For instance, the thin, sinewy Cozelle, instead of scoring a touchdown, is playing NCAA basketball, knees bent at the free throw line, mid-rhythm-dribble, wearing a North Carolina Tar Heels uniform and classic Air Jordan high-tops.

In his slave work setting, the dark-skinned, abdominally endowed, large-eyed Markeif is picking cotton, bare-backed, with grotesquely raised flogging scars, whereas the light-skinned, GQ-handsome Jershawn is dressed as a white-gloved butler, fully wigged and facially powdered, serving silver platters of food to the plantation owner and his family in their decadent dining room, ghostly portraits of patrician, Hircine-faced forebears looming on the walls above.

The only panel that is exactly the same throughout is the rendering of the white Ford Bronco; the one thing changing being the actual subject, but each receiving a handjob.

"What are you calling these?" I asked.

"The Seven Stations of O. J. Simpson's America."

"Wow," I said. "Intense title."

"It's my senior thesis project."

"You've really nailed Keith's face." She had obviously nailed his enormous penis, too; vermiform like his arms.

"Thank you," Harriet said shyly, wearing the faintest hint of a smile.

"They all pose nude for you?"

"That's what they agree to."

"Do they sign a contract?"

"We simply have a conversation over coffee. If it feels right, we agree to meet for one sixty-minute session, for which I pay them twenty bucks. If that goes well, we continue the process, hopefully eventually arriving at the white Ford Bronco."

I asked her if she ever felt unsafe.

"No," she replied.

I asked if her subjects ever get excited.

"You mean erect?" she said.

"Yeah, that."

"One of them had that happen the first few sittings, but the problem resolved itself."

I tried to imagine what this could possibly mean. I envisioned Harriet handing Markeif a tube of Astroglide and a paper towel and leaving the room.

She asked me if I've ever posed nude.

I told her that I hadn't, that I couldn't even imagine it.

"It's surprisingly liberating," she said.

"You've done it?"

"In my life drawing class we all do. Even Professor Chubb models."

"Wow," I said, taking in the detail work. "Jershawn..."

"What about him?"

I told her it was hard not to notice his "endowment."

To which she replied: "The African-American male is perhaps the most unfairly sexualized archetype in modern culture."

I told her that according to her drawings, it didn't seem to be unfair at all. "The word <u>ample</u> comes to mind," I said. "The word <u>fortunate</u>. The word <u>blessed</u>."

"Those are not exaggerations. The renderings are physiologically accurate."

Cozelle had the most normal penis, meaning normal-looking by comparison. And even his was impressive.

"What's unfair about a large penis?" I said.

"I would argue," Harriet said, "that the owners of these penises are not seen as full human beings. The African-American male is blatantly heralded for his athleticism and genital endowment. It's as unfair as Marilyn Monroe being worshipped for her body."

I told her that I worshipped her face too.

Harriet shot me a circumspect look.

"And her underrated singing voice," I added.

She told me I should pose for her. "In all seriousness," she added.

"Why?" I asked, totally thrown.

"Why not?" she replied.

I took a half-step back, still holding the cardboard and plastic packaging for the toilet's new refill flap. "How old are you?" I said.

"I'll be twenty-one in March."

I asked her if what she was doing was even legal.

"Of course it's legal. My subjects come to me by their own volition. They're grown men. They're not mentally challenged in any way. It's not like some form of reverse statutory rape."

"Do you even like me?" I said.

"Sure," she said. "Why?"

I told her that I wouldn't want her to render me if she didn't at least like me a little. "You might be predisposed to highlight all my flaws."

"I like you," she replied. "You dress like you live in an institution, and I think you have a secret life."

"You think I have a secret life?"

She sort of squinted and pursed her lips.

Arranged on the cutout over her kitchenette was a set of three charcoal drawings unlike the others. The subject was a small blond girl wearing fuzzy, footy pajamas, wandering through a dark forest. In the drawing her figure is illuminated by a long blade of light too narrow and focused to be from the moon. Its source is unseen, but the feeling its omniscient perspective evokes is one of surveillance, be it government-, Hollywood-, or UFO-motivated. The only colorized elements are the long beam of light cutting through the forest, the lit-up trunks of trees featuring oily snakes, an owl, some nocturnal rodents of prey, and the little girl's blond hair and Pooh Bear pajamas. The subject appears to be either oblivious or gently bemused that she is being followed through the tall, dark, and hairy forest.

"Who is that?" I said, completely absorbed by the three-paneled narrative.

"A girl."

"Anyone in particular?"

"No. Why?"

"It's just that everything else on your walls is based on actual people."

"Maybe she's me," Harriet offered mischievously.

"But you don't have blond hair."

She said she dyed it.

I asked her if she was a natural blond.

"I feel like you're asking me if the curtains match the drapes. Do you like it?"

"Your hair?"

"The triptych."

"Yes," I heard myself say.

She asked me what it was precisely that I liked about it.

"The little girl," I said.

"What about her?"

I told Harriet that it really felt like she was somewhere. "Lost but definitely somewhere," I added.

"Else?" she said.

"Yes," I said, "somewhere else."

"Well, she's definitely somewhere."

I'm not sure we were talking about the same thing. Of course I was thinking of Bethany Bunch, but who knows where Harriet Gumm was coming from.

"She's in a never-ending forest with slithering nocturnal creatures," she said.

I asked her why the forest was never-ending.

"Because that's what I wanted it to be," she replied.

"And the light?"

"What about the light?"

"What's its source?"

"Who knows?" Harriet said. "Maybe you are."

That's where she lost me. Harriet Gumm liked being provocative for the sake of being provocative.

"You should seriously pose for me," she said.

Again I asked her why.

"Because I think you'd make a good subject. I'd pay you twenty bucks a sitting."

"Nude?"

"Yes."

I looked at the surface of the stool and imagined all the large black men who'd sat upon it, their anuses and perinea, their bulbous testicles dangling. Did she disinfect the top of the stool after each sitting? Was there like some special disposable doily that was utilized?

"Okay," I heard myself say.

We were quiet for a moment. Harriet wouldn't take her eyes off me. It was like she could see me naked. My atrophying muscle tissue and fish-belly skin. My average, flaccid, circumcised penis. The strange mole in my belly button that Kent used to say was Nestlé Toll House's lost chocolate chip.

Her buzzer sounded. She crossed to the front door, let in whoever it was.

"A subject?" I said.

"Keith. Final session."

"Time for the noose?"

She didn't answer.

Before I let myself out, I said, "Should I shave?"

"No," she said. "Keep the beard."

And then I glanced at the triptych again and asked if she'd made a snowman in the past few days.

To which she answered: "I've never made a snowman in my life."

I didn't want to run into Keith, so I exited toward the second-floor aft staircase. From the stairwell window overlooking the backyard, I spied Mary Bunch on her way to the alleyway Dumpsters with a bloated black Hefty bag. With great effort, she lugged it through two feet of snow. I had an impulse to scream out to her. From behind the double-paned window she likely wouldn't have heard me, but I still had to cover my mouth to stop myself.

What the hell was in that Hefty bag? I couldn't contend with the dark possibilities, so I went down to the basement and started pacing the laundry room. There was a load tumbling in the dryer. Was it a load of the Bunches'? Were they washing bloodstains out of their clothes? I couldn't quite get myself to open the dryer door and check.

After I heard Keith's heavy feet pad across the second-floor hallway and disappear into Harriet Gumm's apartment, I headed to the front porch to check the mail. Bradley was coming up the steps, wearing the black trench and skullcap, carrying a bag from Ace Hardware.

"Bradley," I said. "What's up?"

"Hey," he said, the y barely resonating.

His beard had really cool cowlicks in it. Sort of silvery-blond

whirlpools that seemed to have their own little fairy-tale universe. I imagined Lilliputians emerging, stealing crumbs, and
diving back down into the depths. He could probably store
things in his beard. Like almonds or match heads or even a
mailbox key. He was almost fifteen years younger than me and
his beard was teaching my beard a serious lesson.

For someone so low-pulse he seemed a bit agitated. It could
have been the simple fact that he'd been walking and was out of
breath. If he'd hoofed it all the way to the Ace Hardware and
back, it meant that he'd covered some four miles.

"Everything okay?" I asked.

He didn't respond, so I said, "Long walk?"

"Longish," he replied, hardly hitting the g.

He wore old mustard-yellow Chuck Taylors, which were
soaked from the snow, and no socks. All of the buttons but one
were missing from his black double-breasted trench. He kept it
closed with a brown extension cord. Underneath the trench he
wore a white thermal not dissimilar to the one I was wearing.

I pointed to his footwear and told him that he was going to
get trench foot walking around in all the snow.

He didn't respond.

He was starting to look homeless, a little malnourished. I could
sense that we were about to start another awful, thick silence, one
that contained the sad realization that I was the loser whom his
sister had left and that I was even more of a loser because I tried
to access her vicariously through her younger brother who didn't
even like me. For a second it felt as if our beards were communi-
cating animalistically, independent of their owners, like two dogs
sniffing each other's asses on the street. Bradley's beard smelled
like weed and nacho cheese Doritos and some other faint but ripe
moschatel odor I can only describe as deeply wrong.

"What's in the bag?" I asked, worried about power tools, drywall anchors, carpentry nails, etc.

"Supplies," he answered obliquely.

"Home improvements?"

"Yep," he said.

I asked what needed improving, and he said nothing major. I said, "Anything you need help with?"

He shook his head.

What could he possibly be up to? I wanted to look in the bag. Was he making something? A new kind of bong? A nursery for growing weed? A pipe bomb?

Just then Mary Bunch walked onto the front porch and stomped snow off her boots. She was again in her many layers, the hazard-orange vest and conical winter hat. Her nose was running and she held two grocery bags from Econofoods. She said hello to Bradley, but her eyes bounced off me like I had a huge raised facial birthmark with fuzz. Then she keyed into her apartment and shut the door, turning the deadbolt on the other side.

I pointed to Bradley's Ace Hardware bag and said, "No holes in the walls, now. That Sheetrock was expensive."

He replied, "Okay, Dad."

Somehow I liked Bradley calling me dad. An absurd notion, I'll admit, but it made us feel related again, which meant that in some ludicrous reality burbling in the sad part of my mind, I was still in his sister's life. I said, "You're free to go, son."

It came out way more paternally than I'd intended. I didn't even recognize my own voice. I sounded like a high school principal who wears chinos or something. Bradley pushed past me and up the stairs.

*   *   *

It nearly gave me a heart attack to stray from the back porch and forge out into the alleyway, but I had to see what Mary Bunch had left in that Dumpster.

For the first time in a month I actually ventured from the house, trudging thirty or so feet through twenty-two inches of snow. At first I took baby steps, carefully lifting out of the depths of snow. It was slow going. My teeth chattered uncontrollably in that weird way that has nothing to do with the cold. My heart triple-timed in my chest, as if I'd been injected with some stimulant intended for racehorses. My mouth went dry and my tongue seemed to shrink. I thought my throat would close. I might as well have been teetering on an ancient mountain precipice.

I had stupidly worn my wool slippers and my bathrobe. A sudden gust sent a snow shower from the branches of the copper beech into my face and eyes, and a blackbird flapped wildly, as if on cue, and disappeared over the garage. It was as if someone had planted the bird. My blood pressure spiked. My heart beat in my mouth. I could feel my dick shrinking.

The tar-paper shelter over the Dumpsters gave me the false sense that I was at least partly enclosed, so that made it a little easier. Hands on thighs, like an oxygen-starved, postrace miler, I breathed through my nose and tried to calm down. I honestly thought I might have to go to a knee. I'd left my cell phone in the attic, so aside from shouting out to the snowbound neighborhood, there was no way to call for help.

What a terrible way to die this would be. A heart attack at thirty-six. Out back by the Dumpsters. In thermals and wool slippers. In not even two feet of snow. Literally scared to death for no good reason.

After I regained what was left of my composure, which wasn't much, I worked quickly. Inside Mary Bunch's Hefty bag, scattered among household refuse, were children's clothes: a pair of navy sneakers with rainbow stickers on the sides; white T-shirts; old bibs with food stains; a few pairs of cotton pants; a denim jumpsuit with an elastic waistband; socks so small they seemed more suited for a doll; a baby bonnet; cotton turtlenecks; and a set of pink poly-blend mittens, joined with a clip.

Panic seized me again. The only thing that mattered was getting back inside.

That night I dreamed there was a basement under the basement. A subbasement, if you will, whose floor was soil, black as pitch. A distant crying lured me down there. Crying from a child, muffled and desperate. I had to enter the washing machine and shimmy down a flagpole, fireman-style. The pole was slick with a kind of warm, gelatinous substance and during my descent I had the distinct dream-mind thought that it would be impossible to climb back up, as the flagpole was without ruts or anything to grab hold of.

My mother was standing in the center of the soil floor, in her hospice gown. She was thin from her cancer, the bones in her face sharp and prominent, her collarbone enormous, a wisp of hair matted over her soft, pale skull. Bethany Bunch was pulled into her, held close, and my mother was covering the little girl's eyes with her hands. Bethany wore only a diaper, though she seemed old enough for clothes. Her hair was a dirty-blond galaxy, almost pulsing with life. The room was very warm and humid. They were both covered with a film of sweat, both filthy from the soil. It was as if they had walked hundreds of miles and had nothing left, too tired even to sit.

Then I was suddenly barefoot and could feel between my toes the damp, cold earth, where worms wriggled.

"She's blind, Francis," my mother told me. Her voice was tired. It sounded like it was coming from somewhere else. From somewhere and everywhere. Below and above me. "The little girl is blind."

I had the strange sense that there were other subbasements below this one, going on for infinity, with other lost children. A threnody of children's voices sang from some recessed place. Ugly, unresolved, incomplete harmonies, wailing and feral.

The copper beech was suddenly in the little room. My mother and Bethany Bunch were gone. I had the horrible, certain feeling that the tree had swallowed them.

I woke up with such tenacious cottonmouth I had to check to make sure there wasn't actual cotton in my mouth.

After instant coffee and some unamplified guitar noodling (unamplified guitar noodling always seems to help rid a bad-dream hangover), I called Mansard and told him about the Hefty bag.

He said, "Children's clothes, huh?"

I mentioned the snowman and the pink scarf, the matching mittens.

Mansard said, "The mittens were in the garbage?"

"Yes."

"And the scarf was on the snowman?"

"The scarf was on the snowman."

"And you're certain that it matched the mittens."

"The mittens were pink and the scarf was pink."

He said he would come by and take a look.

Later today, Baylor Phebe, a man in his early sixties, is coming by to have a look at the available basement unit, opposite Bob Blubaugh. According to his e-mail, Mr. Phebe is a retired junior high school teacher from down in Little Egypt—Cairo, Illinois, to be exact. He's attending continuing ed classes at Willis Clay and is interested in a two-year lease. Mr. Phebe's been staying in a local motel, paying a steep monthly rate, and is ready to make a larger real estate commitment. He has an authentic Southern accent, as do most people who hail from the lower third of the state, and the deep melody of his voice alone inspired me to move his request to the top of the small pile of three candidates, the other two being an undergraduate junior-college transfer student and a guy from Arkansas named Reggie Reggie. Both had poor references and nothing to speak of in terms of guaranteed income, and the landlord part of me is loath to offer a lease to someone who calls himself Reggie Reggie. Sirhan Sirhan comes to mind, or some homeless drag queen with third-degree burns. I think having a senior presence like Baylor Phebe around could be good for the overall ecology of the house.

"You're going back to school, huh?" I asked him over the phone.

"Spring semester," he said. "Just a few classes."

"Are you married?" I asked.

"I was," he said. "My wife passed away three years ago."

"I'm sorry," I said. "It's a formality. I have to ask."

"Oh, no offense taken," he said.

I asked him if he had kids.

"I have a daughter, lives up in Milwaukee."

"Pets?"

"No pets," he said. "No wife, no kids, no pets, no attachments whatsoever. It would just be me and my fishing poles."

*   *   *

I called Dr. Hubie and spoke to his secretary, Julie Pepper. I told her about the pain in my tooth. I think I actually pretended to cry a little.

"Dr. Hubie doesn't do house calls," she said. "Most dentists don't."

I told her about my back. I was starting to really carve out some good fiction regarding the injury. A slipped disc. A "hot" disc fragmented onto one of my sciatic nodes. Shooting pains radiating down my left leg. A terrible snowballing ache. I learned about all of this on the Internet.

"I really can't get down the stairs," I told her. "Can you at least ask him to call me?"

"I'll put you on the list," she said.

Around noon, Todd Bunch knocked on my door. I was rotating thermals, sending the under layer to the laundry basket, replacing it with the outer layer, and adding a new set on top. I also had changed into a new pair of wool socks, probed my ears with Q-tips, applied Mennen Speed Stick, musk-scented, and trimmed a few nose hairs that were on the verge of autogenously braiding themselves into my mustache, à la Detective Shelley Mansard.

Tying the terry-cloth sash around my bathrobe, I said, "Mr. Bunch."

He was sporting a crew cut, which, in sharp contrast to his former floppy head of spaghetti-sauce-red hair, made him look like a young Marine in training. Either that or a counselor at a Christian youth camp. Was the crew cut an attempt to change his image? To avoid being publicly recognized as the evil father of little Bethany, the prevailing media opinion of him?

Photos were starting to be shown on the evening news. The famous black-and-white Target surveillance still of Todd and

Mary Bunch standing in the stuffed-animals section, almost the same exact looks of abject shock on their faces. Holding a stuffed panda bear, as if Bethany had dropped it in that very aisle and they were summoning her spirit.

Todd Bunch was wearing his navy-blue Pollard Fire Department uniform shirt, with official patches on the shoulders. He had a few days' growth of a sandpapery beard, fine as mica dust. He seemed tense, ultracontained. I was struck by how small his head was, as if the cavity containing his brain was smaller than most. His hands were fists at his sides. There was a little white bloodless halo around his wedding band.

He said he just wanted to personally thank me for taking care of the front steps. He spoke slowly, deliberately, almost as if delivering a memorized recitation. "The walkway too," he added. He was having a hard time making eye contact.

I told him it wasn't a problem, that it was my duty as his landlord.

He opened and closed his mouth in a guppylike fashion, then proceeded to unclench his left fist and drive a knuckle into the meat between his eyes, as though warding off a migraine.

I asked him if he was okay.

He exhaled through his nose, a whistling noise. His eyes, open now, fluttered nystagmically, the pupils contracting to little black pinpricks. I thought he might keel over, but he remained standing. Knees slightly bent, extremely still, shallow of breath, he opened his mouth again, closed it yet again, and then launched in, saying, "Mary and I would really appreciate it if you didn't go through our garbage."

It suddenly felt like there was a piece of gravel caught in my throat. I swallowed hard. I think I said, "I" and "uh." I retched and swallowed again.

"Mary saw you out back by the Dumpsters." His lower lip was trembling now. When it came to classic man-to-man confrontation, it was clear that we were equals in the discomfort zone.

I coughed again and then cleared my throat. I explained that I'll occasionally do a garbage check to make sure tenants are recycling properly, that I get fined if the city finds recyclables in the regular trash and vice versa.

He looked down at his feet and said, "Our garbage is not your concern."

This was obviously the next thing on the list to say. He wasn't interested in engaging in a dialogue; he was checking off bullet points.

My arms folded now, I said, "But it's my duty to execute the occasional Dumpster check."

"We recycle," he replied quickly, a little too loudly.

Then his lips got really small and taut. His clenched teeth, which were showing now, seemed to radiate a white-hotness behind his dull braces.

In my most soothing FM-radio voice I said, "That very well may be true, Mr. Bunch, but I still have to do the compulsory checks. I do it to Bradley Farnham's and Harriet Gumm's garbage too. As a safeguard."

Then he closed his eyes and breathed through his nose intensely, as if there weren't enough air in the small space between us. That faint whistling noise again. The tiny head, seemingly shrinking further. The rubbery dome of his skull, visibly pink underneath his crew cut. He turned to the side as if consulting invisible counsel. I realized for the first time that in profile Todd Bunch has almost no nose. This combined with his thick, furrowed brow made him look like the enormous mahimahi trophy that Lyman had had mounted in his office, above the tufted leather sofa in the waiting area. The similarity was almost breathtaking.

Through his rose-tinted orthodontia, Todd Bunch said, "We threw her clothes out because it's too hard having them around—" He stopped and made a sound like he was choking, then exhaled powerfully and continued. He explained that he had suggested giving Bethany's things to the Goodwill, but that Mary couldn't bear the thought of other children wearing their daughter's clothes.

In that moment I felt this man's heart breaking. I could almost hear it. Like the smallest pinion snapping in a clock's delicate machinery.

"Can I ask you a question?" I said.

"Not about Bethany," he replied. His voice was suddenly small and boyish.

I told him that my question didn't involve his daughter.

"What, then?"

I asked him if he'd made the snowman.

"What snowman?"

"The snowman in the backyard," I explained. "Someone made a little snowman."

"I don't know what you're talking about," he said.

I searched his bald, alopecian eyes. "Out behind the copper beech?" I said.

Nothing for a moment. It felt like the big wintry wheel in the sky had stopped clicking on its sprocket. I think I even heard the clouds above us skid to a halt.

Then Todd Bunch extended his fist toward me. Not in a threatening way, although it did make me swallow again and quickly find my feet. His fist was very tight and trembling. It was as if he were doing his best to hold a freshly boiled stone.

His knuckles were white, his wedding band reflecting the harsh overhead fluorescent light I had installed after Christmas so the tenants wouldn't feel like they were entering a dark place when knocking on the door of their trusted, down-to-earth landlord.

Todd Bunch opened his fist to reveal a rent check, crumpled to the size of a piece of popcorn. He grabbed it with his other hand and attempted to unkink it. His hands were shaking, and he continued to breathe very slowly through his nose, working at the check, eventually smoothing it between his palms. He handed it to me and said, "The late fee's included." Then he turned and descended the back steps.

After I heard him key into his unit—perhaps thirty seconds later—I quietly went downstairs to the back porch and looked for the snowman. Although it was only just past noon, the thick cloud cover weirdly made it almost dark out. I flipped a switch to turn on the spotlight mounted over the front of the garage.

The copper beech lit up monstrously. Like a figure that could chase you down and ruin your life.

And the snowman was gone.

I ran back upstairs, taking two at a time, and called Mansard.

"Hey, Detective," he said, jokingly, but I had no time for that.

"It's gone," I said.

"Slow down," he said, "take a breath."

"It's gone," I repeated, not taking a breath, not sitting, completely winded from the sprint up the stairs.

"What's gone?" Mansard said. He was watching a rerun of The Honeymooners. I could hear Jackie Gleason railing on his wife. It irked me that Mansard was watching TV on the job.

"The snowman," I said. "The snowman's gone."

"Where did it go?" Mansard asked.

"I don't know."

He offered that perhaps it had returned to the North Pole with Rudolph and Santa Claus.

"Very funny," I replied.

"Well, it couldn't have melted."

"Not in this weather, no way."

"Huh," he said.

I couldn't tell if he was being sarcastic or sincere. "Yeah," I said. "Huh is right." The live studio audience was howling with laughter. Even through the phone it felt like they were somehow mocking me.

"Are you watching The Honeymooners?" I said.

He said that he was on his lunch break.

After a silence I said, "Are you still coming by?"

"Do I really need to?" he asked.

I didn't know what to say.

"Snowmen tend to crop up during snowstorms, kid."

"But with pink scarves?" I asked.

"I saw one wearing a sombrero once. It was wearing a sombrero and it had tortilla chips for eyes. Didn't warrant grounds for an arrest."

"But the pink scarf matches the mittens. The ones the Bunches threw out."

He asked me if I was in possession of the scarf.

I told him that I wasn't.

"What about the mittens?" he said.

I told him that I didn't have those either. I'd stupidly left them in the garbage. I was too panicked to get back to the house.

"Then there's not much I can do," Mansard said. "No scarf, no mittens, nothing to go on."

Suddenly someone in Mansard's office was talking to him. He

covered the phone. I could hear the muffled sounds of Art Carney making some indecipherable noise. Jackie Gleason was still screaming at his wife.

Mansard uncovered the phone and said, "I gotta go, Francis. If another snowman pops up, give me a call."

The dark skies persisted for a few hours and then brightened a bit, just in time for dusk. Consequently, it felt like the shortest day of the year.

At around four thirty p.m. my prospective tenant, Baylor Phebe, came by the house. To say that he possesses the largest stomach I've ever seen might be an understatement. It is exceptional, perfectly oval-shaped, and protrudes perhaps a full two feet from his waistline. It's strange because the rest of his body isn't in any way obese. He's certainly husky, but his midsection is completely and ludicrously incongruous with his legs, arms, head, and neck. It's a stomach out of a comic book. It looks almost like a prosthetic, as if it's been screwed on somehow, a Halloween gimmick.

His voice was deeper than it had been on the phone. "I shoulda worn snowshoes," he bellowed, stomping his boots on the porch, shaking my hand.

His paw is enormous. I noticed that he still wears his wedding band. After Sheila Anne divorced me, I continued to wear mine for almost a year. Now it lives in a matchbox on my writing desk. I like to think it's sleeping. Baylor Phebe has a vigorous, warm handshake and huge mountain-peak knuckles. This man could clear a bar, I thought. A bar and a smorgasbord. He stands a hulking six-three. His head is the size of a cinder block.

His broad Nordic face is marked with little broken blood vessels; purple and blue and pink spider legs drift across his nose and are faintly embedded in the yellow oysters under his eyes. Speaking of his eyes, there is an unmistakable kindness living there. Grief softens some people, distorts others.

After my mother died Lyman got weird and mechanical and emotionally distant. Cornelia's death turned him into the used-car-salesman version of himself. He got his teeth whitened and told more jokes and hung out at restaurant bars and started wearing Paco Rabanne. He brilliantined his hair and compulsively fiddled with the change in his pocket. And he bought a bunch of shit. Like a Rolex watch. And a nine-hundred-dollar Montblanc pen.

But back to Baylor Phebe's stomach, which has the same effect as a great Frenchman's nose—it somehow makes him more epic. I wondered what his students called him behind his back, whether the protuberance was the stuff of preteen mockery or legend. Songs could be written about Baylor Phebe's stomach. It could be the subject of a Roald Dahl story. And it also makes you think about diabetes.

He wore an augmented one-piece snowmobile suit. Augmented meaning an entirely different winter garment had been fashioned for the area covering his belly. A kind of torso shell of down-filled tufted nylon. It was sophisticated, festooned with snaps and a little marsupial-looking pouch, which had its own snap. There had even been an attempt, though unsuccessful, to match the color to the original one-piece. The patched stomach panel was a sort of hickory brown, whereas the one-piece was more straight-up chocolate. I wondered whether his dead wife had made the piece for him. Under a red-and-black-plaid wool hunting hat complete with earflaps, his hair was a thick yellowy silver, sprouting in all directions. His eyes were bright blue, the whites a bit dull but still white nevertheless.

I showed him the available basement unit—the small kitchen with its marble-top eatery nook, the bedroom, the living room/dining area, the bathroom where I had imperfectly set the base of the toilet, so that it's a hair cockeyed—and he immediately said he'd take it. He didn't ask questions, didn't even give me a chance to talk up the heating system or the amazing lack of sub-story mold or the necessity for the dropped gypsum ceiling or the pleasures of the house's lone true eco-friendly refrigerator.

"Is the size okay?" I asked. "I realize it's a little small."

"I don't need much space. Only enough for the couch to pull out."

I told him he could easily have a bed in the bedroom. "You can fit a king in there."

"The pullout's for when my daughter comes to visit," he explained.

I nodded. He seemed larger in the apartment than he did upstairs, as if he were slowly expanding.

"You don't mind the lack of sunlight?" I said.

"That won't make a difference. I'm mostly an outside guy."

Outside.

The word itself caused me to briefly relive my anxiety at the Dumpsters. The mad dash to the back porch, slogging through the depths of snow, everything speeding up on the inside but eerily slowing down on the outside, my limbs turning to lead. I could feel the cottonmouth coming on. I swallowed hard.

"I get plenty of sunlight," Baylor said.

I told him the apartment was his and he asked when he could move in.

"As soon as you'd like," I said. I added that we could even pro-rate the days for January.

"Great!" Baylor beamed.

I told him that per standard procedure, I'd need a final month's rent as a deposit, to which he replied, "No problemo."

His sudden Spanish made me smile.

It's worth noting that upon exiting the basement, while ascending the stairs, I observed Baylor Phebe to be much lighter on his feet than one might expect for a man of his size.

There was a young woman sitting on the floor in front of Bradley's apartment. She was very pretty, of mixed race, skin like caramel. Her corduroy jacket was too thin for the weather. Beside her lay a book bag and a large blond canvas sack, the size of a laundry bag, snapped shut at the top, and somehow bloated. The sack dwarfed the girl, who was text messaging on her cell phone.

"Can I help you?" I said.

"I don't know," she said. "Can you?"

She was tough, a little feral, maybe from East St. Louis.

"Who are you?" I said.

"Who the fuck are <u>you</u>?" she retorted.

I told her I owned the house.

"Good for you," she replied. She completed her text and sent it off.

I asked her if she was waiting for Bradley.

"Maybe," she said, not looking up from her cell phone.

She smelled of patchouli oil and clove cigarettes. I thought maybe she was his pot dealer, that her book bag was full of those little tetrahedral terrariums containing helices of high-quality crystal-budded hydroponic. But it was the larger sack that was really getting the better of my curiosity.

I asked her if she was Bradley's girlfriend.

"Naw," she answered. "We just friends."

"Video game buddies?"

"He don't play video games no more," she said.

I was shocked.

She said that he didn't even have a TV. "Gave all his shit away," she added.

I asked her whom he gave the TV to and she said she didn't know, but that he'd given his PlayStation away as well. "He's been simplifying," she said.

I asked her what was in the sack.

She told me to mind my business and she said it like a man.

She was prettier when she didn't speak, with sharp hazel eyes. They were almost silver, these eyes.

"You mind me asking your name?" I said.

She asked me if I was conducting a census.

I told her that Bradley was sort of like my brother. "I used to be married to his sister," I explained.

"Oh," she said. "You <u>that</u> dude."

"Francis," I said.

"Yeah, Francis the Fuckup."

"The report's that bleak, huh?"

"Pretty bleak," she replied, "yep."

The central heating system kicked on. A deep whirring sound, almost subliminal, soothing.

"Why you so worried about Bradley?" the girl said. "He's just doin' his thing."

"Which is what exactly?" I asked.

Her phone chirped again. She read something off its screen, then wrote and sent a text. Her thumbs moved with exceptional velocity.

"So you're just gonna wait for him?" I said.

"That okay with you?"

Her phone chirped yet again and she checked it and shook her head.

I asked her her name.

"La-Trez," she said, the emphasis on the second syllable.

"Pretty name," I said.

"Thanks," she replied. "It's got a hyphen."

She stood and we shook hands. She was taller than I expected. Her legs were much longer than her torso. She hoisted her backpack. I didn't hear anything clinking around. For all I know there could have been actual books in there.

Again, her phone made a noise. Checking it, she said, "Fiendin-ass nigga." She asked me if it was cool to leave the large canvas sack in front of Bradley's door.

I told her I'd make sure he got it.

"Thanks," she said. "Tell him I said keep makin' your way."

"Keep makin' your way," I echoed.

She thanked me and descended the front staircase. She moved quickly, like an athlete, her feet a fast patter down the steps.

After I heard the front porch screen door open and close I unsnapped the huge sack. Inside was an enormous blob of string, the kind you might use to bundle packages. I dug my hands into its depths to see if there was anything else hidden—drugs, chemicals, bomb-making materials, what have you—but there was nothing but string.

I miss my wife.

It's late and I'm drunk as I write this. It's four in the morning—4:07 to be exact—and I can't sleep and there is a kind of postoperative ache deep in my side that feels like a rib has been removed, and for no good reason.

I spent the evening doing dishes, organizing bills, shelving paperbacks, anything to keep my mind off of Sheila Anne. I even went down to the basement and cleaned Baylor Phebe's bathroom again, though it was unnecessary.

I keep going over the bad nights, the irreconcilable moments, and when I really examine the peptic marital viscera in a hard forensic way there really isn't any one thing that I can point to. The end of our marriage lacks an event. Sure, we fought about little things. She hated that I often didn't get out of bed before noon. She thought I was wasting half the day sleeping and dreaming and drooling on my pillow. She never bought the argument that the artist needs to be afforded the time to let his unconscious flower. She liked to rise early and go running and eat organic granola and update our streamable Netflix cue and knock out at least two-thirds of the <u>New York Times</u> crossword puzzle. She got more things done before eight a.m. than most people accomplish in an entire day.

After the band split up, my attack on pursuing a career in rock 'n' roll waned. Contending with the inchoate narrative of the Third Policeman—really taking a long, mature look at it—would have been like being forced to eat potting soil. The very idea of touching my guitar made my stomach churn poisonously. I got a few offers to tour with another band, to replace a rhythm guitarist who had fractured the ulnar styloid process in his wrist. It would have paid pretty well and most certainly would have led to other opportunities, but I wasn't crazy about their music and I was just too damn sad about the Third Policeman's demise. That band, Natural Appliances, sounded like four other alt-country outfits from Southern Illinois shamelessly trying to ape Son Volt and early Wilco. I turned down two overtures from them and instead stayed in bed, a king-sized Swedish affair made with brass springs and authentic horsehair (a wedding gift from Sheila Anne's wealthy parents).

Then my mother died, and Morris left for North Carolina and my column in the <u>Pigeon</u> was no more, so I stopped going down to the at-home studio and a film of post-nuclear-holocaust-looking dust settled on all the recording equipment and I started getting flabby in the middle and some random hairs sprouted simian-like around my shoulder blades and I developed a sty on the lower lid of my left eye that looked unfortunately cystic and maybe even a little venereal and that same eye started twitching uncontrollably and then I tried to pop the sty with the tip of a safety pin that I'd sterilized with a Bic lighter but it made it worse and it took months to go away and even when the twitching stopped I developed a paranoia that the sty would return from a sneeze or from a brisk wind or from telling a little white lie about whether or not I'd called the cable guy to upgrade our package and Sheila Anne NEVER SAID ANYTHING ABOUT THE STY IN THE FIRST PLACE, the omission of which was a point of contention constantly dangling between us, and there were more than a handful of occasions when I couldn't get fully erect despite being thrillingly turned on by Sheila Anne's face and mind and body and something really intense was happening to my stomach, meaning I could often feel it digesting itself, and in the bathroom mirror I could see psoriatic wens forming on my scalp and sometimes I could smell a faint metallic rot escaping from my own mouth, which meant other people could smell it too, especially Sheila Anne, and when I would drop my towel post-shower to leg into boxer shorts or briefs or what have you, Sheila Anne started looking away, as in literally doing a disgusted one-eighty, and then I turned down another offer, this time to go to Madison and help the guy who ran Slow-neck Records start a new label, because I didn't want to live in Madison because it reminded me too much of the band failing and then I noticed Sheila Anne coming home later and later into the evening, like sometimes as late as tenish despite De-catur being ninety minutes away and she never got off work later than seven, and I'm sure she was doing some emotional screwing around with Dennis Church like Skyping with him from her office and maybe even engaging in cybersex, which still makes me brux because I start imagining Sheila Anne bar-ing her breasts to him and him making obovoid shapes of awe with his mouth and then getting the right laptop camera an-gle trained on his cock so it looks larger than it actually is and the simultaneous mewling and sounds of mutual suspira-tion and actual utterances like YOU'RE SO HUGE, DENNIS CHURCH, and I CAN FEEL YOU INSIDE ME, DENNIS CHURCH, and YOU'RE GOING TO MAKE ME COME SO HARD, SHEILA ANNE, and I'M COMING INSIDE YOU, SHEILA ANNE, and their embarrassed but honest laughter during post-jism jism-policing, with Dennis Church's conveniently placed box of scented Kleenex within arm's reach, and Sheila Anne Purelling her hands so it almost looks as if she's wringing his cyber sperm into her very being, and the convivial silly guffaws at their desperation and elation and the scintillatingly unbearable fucking vernal attraction for each other practically setting fire to the Internet waves they shared and then the plans they made and the conspiratorial low-voiced conversations Sheila Anne had, or maybe as a rule she spoke to him only when she was alone in her car or maybe they texted each other in code or maybe there was a whole narrative of digital subterfuge, like when he came up on her smartphone it said PHYLLIS or KAREN or fucking BLYTHE or some shit, and when did all the trickery begin and when did that (the trickery) start to get old or even unbearable and when did they finally declare to each other the promise that they couldn't stand to be apart for another hotfooted minute and did he use his last available frequent-flier miles to tear-ass it through the heavens to Chicago and Amtrak it to Decatur and fuck her in his rental car because they just couldn't wait to get to the Marriott and did she wax her pussy for him because I DID NOTICE THAT TOWARD THE END and when I asked her about it she said she just wanted to try it and the last time I went down on her I thought it was the best thing I'd ever tasted in my life and I still do, even better than birthday cake and vanilla ice cream when you're stoned, and I was in a kind of erotic schoolboy utopia complete with a fully engaged erection, maybe the largest it's ever been, but Sheila Anne kept making a face like I was trying to put chilled serrated salad tongs inside her and when I consider the moment she decided to wax her pussy for him I want to die, I want to take an entire bottle of painkillers, preferably Percocet because of its warm, steady undertow and downright goofy slow-motion feeling, and enter the perfectly configured Francis Falbo–sized death canoe that will float rapturously down the loving River of Neveragain and evaporate into sun splash and low satiny cumuli and the gentle infinitesimal breath of fluttering hummingbirds...

I called Haggis.

"Francis," he said.

He'd been sleeping, as one is expected to in the predawn.

"Can you get me some Percocet?" I said.

"Of course." He asked if I needed it right away.

"Later's fine," I answered, dreading the long hours ahead. Feeling sickened by it, actually.

"Your back's that bad, huh?"

"Yeah, it's bad," I lied. "It's turning into full-blown sciatica." I explained that the sciatic nerve is the largest nerve in the body and once inflamed takes a long time to tame.

"I'll be by later," Haggis assured me. "And I'll shovel again."

I thanked him.

Below, despite the hour, an occasional car passed, muffled by the snow-impacted street. Otherwise, the neighborhood was hushed. The only sounds were of the house settling, the cycle of the central heating system whirring on and off every twenty minutes or so. I wondered how many other Pollardians were awake at this hour, limping around inside themselves, doubled over in the marshlands of the dispossessed, their hearts like a cold damp toad in their hands.

This morning I woke around eleven thirty. I was hungover and dehydrated, with bloated bowels and a kidney ache. I had pissed the bed, which raises all sorts of concerns when one is thirty-six years old. Fortunately, the mattress was mostly spared because of the wicking action of my double-layer waffle-patterned thermals and the terry-cloth thickness of my bathrobe. My urine smelled sweetly of bourbon. I peeled off the soiled long johns and took a shower and made some instant Folgers.

I looked up the word agoraphobia. Agoraphobia: an abnormal fear of being in crowds, public places, or open areas, sometimes accompanied by anxiety attacks. Well, a standard definition just about sums it up.

I turned on the radio, which reported various school closings and highway maintenance in the southern area of the state. Somehow, between dawn and now it has snowed another eight inches.

According to the radio, things in Afghanistan are bad. An American soldier lost his mind and barbecued an entire Afghani family. Another head coach for the New York Knicks has resigned. And in local news, Bethany Bunch is still missing.

After I stripped and sprinkled baking soda on my mattress, I took my coffee to the window and peered out. Indeed there was a fresh hide of snow, with a bluish, lunar crust. An old four-door Buick was moving slowly down the street, spinning its tires. The two bald sycamores in front of the house were so heaped with virgin snow they looked put-upon, humiliated.

Across the street, in plain perfect sight from my attic window, the astomatous snowman was in Hazard Groom's front yard. Charcoal eyes. The carrot nose. The pink scarf.

I called Mansard and told him as much, not taking my eyes off it.

"So you're coming over?" I asked.

"Sure," he said, "I'll swing by."

At around two thirty p.m. Haggis shoveled the walkway and steps to both the front and back porches. He salted everything down too. This time he actually used a new snow shovel made of bright aluminum, which he said he'd purchased from Target.

When I came downstairs to meet him at the front porch I feigned stiffness in my back and lurched dramatically for the handrail.

"You might want to see someone about that back," he said.

"If it doesn't get better in a few days...," I said.

Haggis had also brought me a small blob of foil, about the size of a baseball, inside of which were two dozen Percocets. He could have charged me five bucks for each little white pill, which could double as Tylenol, but he charged me only sixty dollars.

"Enjoy the flotilla," he said. Then he told me about some new shipment of pills he'd just gotten in that were supposed to guarantee a fifty percent growth of your penis.

I considered the thrill of my penis doubling its size. The confidence it would inspire. The hefty bulge in my thermals. "I'll take some of those too," I said.

"Next trip," Haggis said.

Just as he was leaving, Baylor Phebe pulled up with a small U-Haul trailer attached to the back of his black Dodge Ram 1500. He parked in front of the Grooms' house and met me at the front porch. He walked like an escaped circus bear, making his own time in the world. We shook hands and I told him it'd be easier to pull into the back lot, behind the house, and unload from there.

"The aft staircase has a little more width," I explained.

"I don't have much," he said. "The whole kit and caboodle's in there." He pointed to the U-Haul. "Everything else is in storage in Cairo."

When he got back in his truck and pulled around behind the house, the snowman was gone from the Grooms' yard.

I stood beside Mansard on the front porch, staring across the street at the Grooms' yard. "It was right there," I said. "Next to the ceramic deer."

Squinting and visoring his eyes with his yellowed hand, he said, "The deer on our side of the tree or the deer on the other side of the tree?"

"On our side. That other thing's an elk."

"An elk," Mansard said, "right."

Certain men have smoked for so many years that you can actually smell the nicotine coming through their pores. In the summer mosquitoes avoid these men. You could probably put Mansard in a Speedo, stand him on a pontoon boat in a thriving Southern swamp in the middle of August, and do a field study on high levels of epidermal nicotine in congruence with mosquito avoidance.

He lit a Lucky Strike, pulled on it so that his mustache pulsed, and said, "Pink scarf again?"

"Pink scarf, yep."

"You're sure?"

"I'm positive, Detective."

He exhaled an incredible amount of smoke and said, "You realize you have cereal in your beard?"

I raked my hands through my beard. Two pieces of Cap'n Crunch tumbled onto the front porch. And another smaller item that might have been a crescent of fingernail.

"Why don't we cross the street," Mansard said, "and you can stand exactly where it was."

"I'm not going to do that." I said this resolutely, like a man refusing to eat a worm. I cited my back yet again. "If I slip and fall it could be disastrous."

He looked at me for a second, pulling on his cigarette. With smoke in his lungs, in that cool, small-voiced way, he said, "I feel like every time I see you you're in your pajamas."

To which I replied, "You've only seen me twice and these aren't pajamas. They're long johns."

"Are they?"

I looked down and I was wearing plaid flannel pajama bottoms.

He exhaled and said, "Look like pajamas to me." He produced a face that somehow made it seem like he was thinking with his mustache, as if whatever powers of sleuthing he possessed were sourced in those yellowing brown bristles. "You gettin' enough sleep there, Francis?" he asked.

I told him that I sleep just fine.

Then he touched his hearing aid and asked me if anyone else had ever mentioned these snowmen.

I didn't answer.

"Might it be possible that you're seeing things?" he said.

I couldn't even scratch the surface of this proposition. He smoked some more and ashed in one of the front porch's standing ashtrays, crushing the butt. I think he finished his cigarette in under six pulls.

"Have there been any leads on Bethany Bunch?" I asked.

He replied that there hadn't been a single one. "Best theory we've come up with so far is that she was kidnapped by someone passing through town. That it wasn't even premeditated."

"What, like someone saw her and just said, 'Come with me, little girl,' and walked her out of the Target?"

"Could be."

"Which means Bethany might have gone willingly?"

He said it could have been love at first sight.

"Which means it's possible Bethany wasn't exactly too keen on Mommy and Daddy."

"The mind of a three-year-old's not an easy thing to decipher," Mansard said.

"So, but what are we talking about, like a trucker or something?"

"More likely'd be a woman," he explained. "A little kid isn't gonna just start walking toward a big scary-looking trucker. We'd like to bring some dogs by. Get Bethany's scent."

I reminded him that the Bunches had thrown their daughter's clothes out.

"They've likely kept other things," he said. "Toys. A pillow. Her mattress."

"What if Todd and Mary don't cooperate?"

"It'd be in their best interests, don't you think?"

"Maybe they're freaked out by all the attention."

He knocked on their door. Out of the side of his mouth, negotiating his lips through his calico mustache, he said, "Freaks getting freaked out? They were trapeze artists, Francis. Why would a little attention bother them? They're used to performing in front of hundreds of people."

I told him that they just seem a little anxious.

"If they're anxious about people trying to help them find their daughter," he said, "then that says something right there."

Mansard knocked again.

"By the way," he said, "always knock, even if there's a doorbell." He was suddenly instructing me on the subtleties of detective work. He said that people were generally more likely to open the door if you knocked. "It's less heraldic," he added.

I told him I'd keep that in mind.

He stroked his mustache with one hand, pinching the midpoint, just under his nostrils, and spreading his thumb and index finger wide. An unself-conscious gesture shaped by years. He glanced at his watch and then produced a piece of chewing gum, a lone, old-fashioned stick of Wrigley's, still in its foil. He unwrapped it and folded it into his mouth a little obscenely. The piebald mustache began undulating as he chewed.

He pressed the doorbell now. "Doorbell is phase two," he instructed.

"What's phase three?" I asked.

"Occasionally I'll go to the side of the house and tap on a window. Columbo would do shit like that. Or he would pretend to be the plumber. Or he would just break the hell in somehow. Columbo was a fucking god."

Still no answer, so he pressed the doorbell again. It was the same doorbell we'd had since I was a kid. I'd kept it as one of the original items. It was strange to be so familiar with its two-part tone yet feel so far away from the rooms that used to be on the other side of the door.

I asked him if he was going to go tap on a window.

"Not just yet," he replied. He explained that phase three was a big jump. "Once you start tapping on windows you have to see yourself actually breaking into the house. I'm not seeing that yet."

I nodded, a little baffled by the detective logic.

"And the next time our snowman makes an appearance, do yourself a favor and take a picture of it with your cell phone."

I couldn't believe I hadn't thought of that. "Good thinking," I said. I swear I could hear Mary Bunch quietly padding around inside her apartment. Mansard pressed her doorbell three more times, but there was no answer.

Down in the laundry room I was putting my sheets, thermals, and bathrobe in the dryer when Bob Blubaugh poked his head in.

"Bob," I said. "Hey."

He asked if he could show me something. There was a slight look of dread on his mostly neutral face. Or maybe I was projecting dread. I thought he was going to lead me to a dead rodent or some sort of unfortunate water leak caused by the extra eight inches of snow, but that's not what it was at all.

He led me to the storage room. He bent down and lifted the old rope rug that used to live on the Falbo living room floor. Again, the efficiency of movement. Nothing wasted. Total balance and coordination. He pulled at the rope rug, clearing away some floor space.

Underneath the rug was a door. An old iron door perfectly housed and hinged, rusted and ancient. I'd never seen this door before.

"How'd you find this, Bob?"

"I thought I heard something in here in the middle of the night."

"Like a person?"

"I don't know what it was. But something was moving around. It could have been anything. I wanted to make sure it wasn't an animal." He explained that back in Minnesota his family had similar rugs, and mice would get trapped under them. "When I pulled the rug aside," he said, "there was this door."

I yanked on its handle but it wouldn't budge. It was outfitted with a mortise lock, the same kind of system used to secure government explosives. The lock was much newer than the actual door. I pressed my ear to the single keyhole and listened but could hear nothing except my own blood pulsing through my head.

I called Lyman down in Jupiter.

"Son," he said.

In the background I could hear voices, laughter, clinking glasses, Frank Sinatra. He wasn't thrilled to be talking to me. Lately I've felt like some past-life irritant.

"We're sorta in the middle of somethin' here," he said. "Sissy's throwin' a cocktail thingy to try and raise money for African babies with cleft palates or some such."

"What's up with the door in the floor?"

"The door in what floor?" Lyman said.

"In the basement. Under Grandma Jelly's old rope rug."

"Oh, that."

"_That?_"

"It's a shelter."

"A _shelter?_" I said.

"Yeah, a fallout shelter, a bomb shelter."

"Since when did we have a bomb shelter?"

"We had it made before you were born."

"What? Why?"

"Why do you think? In case we got nuked by the friggin' Russians."

I asked him what year it was built and he said, "Seventy-one, I think. Your uncle Corbit was puttin' 'em in all over the Midwest."

I asked him how big it was and he said it was only a few rooms, maybe a few hundred square feet.

I asked him if it was furnished and he said that indeed it was. "With actual furniture?"

"With actual furniture, yes. Kitchenette, sofa, functional bathroom. Entertainment stuff."

"And supplies?"

"It's stockpiled."

"With what?"

"Canned goods, candles, a generator, cans of Sterno, flashlights, blankets, pillows, board games—"

"Board games?"

"Monopoly, Yahtzee, Scrabble, that sorta thing."

"Family night in the bomb shelter," I said.

"Gas masks too. And your mother loved pears, so there's a few cases of canned pears. Del Monte, I think."

"There's a mortise lock on it."

He asked what the hell a mortise lock was.

I told him it's the kind of lock the government uses for securing explosives. "In like pressurized bunkers," I explained. "The lock is way newer-looking than the door."

He said he had no idea why it would be necessary to have such a lock.

"Like I said," he continued, "your uncle Corbit built the damn thing."

I asked him why he and my mother never told me about it.

To which he answered: "I guess we forgot."

I asked him how I would get down there.

"Well, you need the key," he said. I asked him where it was and he answered, "It's definitely somewhere."

In the background an old lady made a whooping sound like she was getting goosed, followed by a chorus of elderly, wheezy laughter. I imagined oversized earlobes and insanely white dentures radiating through tan, leathery skulls. Rolexes and ship captain hats. Absurd alien-being face-lifts. Gauzy hair augmented with high-end toupees. Lifted, laser-corrected, macular-looking eyes.

I said, "I can call a locksmith."

"No," he replied. "I'll dig up the key. I think it's in a safety deposit box somewhere."

"And you'll send it to me?"

"Why are you so hell-bent on going down there?" Lyman said.

I told him that I'd like to know the house I've been living in for basically my entire life. "Which I'm now leasing to people who are depending on me," I added. I explained that as of tomorrow every unit would be filled.

"Good for you, Francis."

I told him that I didn't like keeping architectural secrets from my leaseholders.

"Fair enough," he replied.

"By the way," I said, "you still haven't seen the renovation."

"I'll be coming back north soon enough."

I told him that he'd like it.

"It's just not so easy being in the house. Your mother...," he said.

His voice went faint.

He hadn't cried at her memorial service. He'd mostly smiled and looked stunned. For some reason he handed out individually wrapped butterscotch candies to everyone, a random, out-of-nowhere gesture that had nothing to do with my mother, either side of the family, or anyone's purported love of butter-scotch.

Cornelia's service was held at an Elks lodge banquet hall in Skokie, just north of Chicago. There was a polka band and plum brandy, and the Wyrwas contingent was in full effect. Lyman pulled his hamstring dancing with Cornelia's beautiful young cousin, Aldona. I had to help him to the car.

Sheila Anne drove the whole way back to Pollard, where we had moved into my boyhood room during my mother's last weeks. Prior to that we'd been living in a two-bedroom apart-ment on the other side of town. Morris had been staying in our spare room, and we were still writing music in the base-ment studio space at the house, below Cornelia's hospice room. Although the studio was well soundproofed, we kept things quiet, on the acoustic side, using mostly guitars and a weighted digital keyboard that sounded like an authentic upright piano. The music we wrote was dirgelike—dreamy figments of sad-ness. This collection of songs—perhaps a dozen—was haunted, chorusless, and bridgeless. Drifty junk ballads that were as close to the concept of slowcore as anything we'd ever done. We felt this music deeply but I think it was ultimately too sad to share with anyone. We started to drown in it and I think this is one of the reasons why Morris ultimately left our apartment and Pol-lard altogether. The music started to digest us. There was no release in it, only a heavy, arterial thickening.

On the way home from Skokie, Sheila Anne and I were quiet as Lyman snored drunkenly into the passenger's side window, clutching his bad leg. Though I'd been too sad to dance, there was something incredibly life-affirming about the way the Polish side of the family celebrated, even in death. It was bitter cold that night, the middle of January, and the Lake Michigan wind we experienced walking the short distance from the banquet hall to the car is hard to describe, even in retrospect. The brutal indifference of novocaine thaw. Or an orchestrated attack of the nervous system that is both inside and outside you.

Into the phone I said, "Dad?"

"I miss her," he said, his voice cut in half.

"Me too," I said.

Only the sounds from the cocktail party. Hearing-aid chatter. Emphysemic laughter. Frank Sinatra and his big swinging band.

I was shocked. Hovering in that dead digital airspace was the closest I'd felt to my father in years.

Lyman cleared his throat and said, "I gotta go, son." His voice was a little ragged. He cleared his throat again. "Some former PGA golfer with ridiculous slacks and a bad dye job is makin' the moves on Sissy. I'll track down that key for you."

A few days passed. I couldn't wait for Mansard to politely ask the Bunches for some item of Bethany's for his dogs to sniff. I waited for Mary Bunch to leave the house, and when the coast was clear, in my bathrobe and wool slippers, I padded down to the first floor and tried to key into their apartment.

But they'd changed the locks!

They'd changed the fucking locks, which is an egregious infraction of their lease!

I went upstairs and retrieved a hammer from under my sink and broke a window and let myself in. It was one of the two small rectangular frosted windows inset in the mullions of their back door. The window broke cleanly in half and made surprisingly little noise. After I reached through the opening and turned their new deadbolt, I eased into their apartment, closing the door behind me.

I just sort of stood there for a moment. There was a sad, still-life quality to their furnishings. A weak, doleful light leaked through the slit in the living room curtains, grazing a lamp-shade, the top of an armchair, and their dull, pilling carpeting.

Their phone rang.

Which was so alarming that I almost released all matter that had been brewing in my rectum. I squeezed my ass cheeks to-gether as hard as I could, thrusting my pelvis forward absurdly.

Their message machine beeped and an elderly woman began speaking. "Mary," she said, "it's Mom. Just callin' to see how you guys are doin'." Her voice was faint, dry as tissue paper. "I sent you some of those ginger cookies you like so much. Did you get 'em? Just wanted to let you know that everyone here is prayin' for you and Todd and little Bethany. We love you very much. Call us back when you can. Your father says hi."

The machine beeped.

Mary's mom had a Southwestern lilt to her voice. I imagined her to be much older than she probably was, arthritic and shuf-fling, blind, losing her memory, swiping at invisible flies.

The answering machine somehow rattled my nervous system, and rather than begin my search for a "Bethany" item, I became obsessed with how to cover up my forced entry. I was suddenly sprinting upstairs to the attic. I put on a pair of old work gloves, pulled a brick from my bookcase, returned to the Bunches' unit, and threw the brick through the already broken window— chucked it with real reenactment accuracy—so it would look like a breaking and entering.

Then I absconded with their DVD player. Detaching it made my hands feel huge and blocky and it took way too long. I ran it upstairs and wrapped it in an old towel and pushed it under my bed. And then I sprinted back down to the Bunches' apartment because I had forgotten the hammer!

At this point my lungs were burning, as were my thighs. Somehow the hammer was on their kitchen counter practically with a spotlight trained on it. I couldn't place when or how I'd managed to put it there. What else had I done without realizing it? I seized the hammer with both gloved hands and started for the back door, but stopped yet again because out of the corner of my eye I could see that ONE OF MY SLIPPERS WAS JUST SITTING THERE, right in the little parabolic path between the kitchen and the living room, resting there like a felled bird of extraordinary evidence, so I spun, grabbed that as well, and hightailed it out of there.

Back in the attic I removed my work gloves and lay on the floor, my knees tented, my lungs chapped, my nostrils dilating like some oxygen-starved water buffalo. The whole event had probably taken less than five minutes but it felt like the heavy slow-mo physiological thickening of nightmares. I had officially committed my first felony. I burgled my family home.

Sure, Francis Carl Falbo had done his fair share of petty adolescent shoplifting. As a preteen Donkey Kong junkie he'd stolen money out of his mother's purse and even dined-and-ditched a few times in college, but that was lightweight stuff compared to what he'd just done in the Bunches' unit. I was enlivened and embarrassed and exhausted and I think I had a fever.

After I caught my breath I called Mansard, and instead of reporting the brick toss, I asked him if he thought I was a good person.

"I'm a detective, Francis, not a friggin' guidance counselor."

I had no reply.

"Do you think you're a good person?" he said.

"Yes," I heard myself reply.

"Then you're a goddamn good person!"

I apologized. Undoubtedly Mansard was starting to tire of me.

He accepted my apology and told me to take it easy.

I waited on the front porch for Mary Bunch to get home and told her the news there. "Someone broke into your place," I said. "Through the back door."

She had just gone for a jog. Her cheeks were red, her eyes tearing from the cold. She marched past me. I followed her around the porch to her back door, which she touched as if it were boiling hot.

"I was going to call the police," I said, "but I figured I'd wait for you or Todd to come back."

But Mary refused to call the police.

I followed her inside, where she immediately clocked the missing DVD player.

I told her my best guess was that it was someone looking to make a quick buck. "Pawning electronics is always a safe bet," I added. "Probably some random drug addict. Otherwise he would've taken more stuff."

She ran her hand across the surface of the shelf where the DVD player used to be. There was a small potted cactus I hadn't noticed before. Miraculously, in my panic to unhook and steal the DVD player, I had avoided getting punctured.

"When we moved in," Mary said, "you assured us this neighborhood was safe."

I told her this was the first incident in as long as I could remember, adding, "Pollard's not exactly the burglary capital of the Midwest." As much as I wanted to bring up the lease infraction of the Bunches changing their locks, I decided against it.

She asked me if I would accompany her as she looked in on the other rooms. "I'd feel safer," she added.

I followed her into their bedroom. The queen-sized bed was unmade, the sheets rumpled and twisted, the mattress ticking visible in places. The room had a smell of liniment and something sweet and gamy. The odor was oddly mannish, what I imagine a penitentiary to smell like. Clothes were scattered about. Athletic socks and T-shirts and sweaters. Boxer shorts. A black sports bra hung off the headboard. The source of the gamy smell was part of a Quarter Pounder with Cheese, still in its opened container. There was a sense that this was the room's constant state, that things were half-eaten and forgotten, that the Bunches never even thought to crack a window. There were no books or magazines, no TV. Only these strewn clothes, a dresser with two drawers half-opened, and a messy bed.

Mary asked me if I would open the closet.

I feigned vigilance, sneaking up on it and opening it quickly, in a move that probably resembled a suburban white man's version of kung fu. Inside the closet was a sad wardrobe that seemed to include mostly hand-me-downs from the early eighties. Cowl-neck sweaters and thick corduroy pants balding at the knees. Polyester dresses with explosive floral patterns. Paisley blouses. A few cheap men's suits in dry-cleaning plastic.

"No one's in here," I said, making a quick scan of anything that might have been Bethany's. But there didn't appear to be anything.

I checked under the bed and sneaked up on the curtains in the same way I had the closet. I think Mary found me to be brave and noble, really sticking my chin into possible danger, ready to go toe-to-toe with a drug-addicted, nunchuck-wielding intruder.

Next we went into the bathroom, where I crept up on the shower curtain, pulled it aside, and, literally, put my dukes up.

They used generic dandruff shampoo, Dove soap. A contorted washcloth, dry, clung to the spout of the bathtub like a palsied hand.

"It creeps me out to think that anyone was in here," Mary said.

Next was Bethany's room. Just as we were about to enter, Mary said, "I'd rather you not come in here."

I asked her if she was sure, if she felt safe enough.

"It's our daughter's room," she said.

I nodded, hugely disappointed.

She opened and closed the door so quickly I couldn't steal even the slightest glimpse.

The short hallway was dark. I kept expecting to be reminded of something, of the old version of the house. A smell like my father's aftershave or some abstract water stain that in my youth I mythologized as an extraterrestrial presence, but I had done such a thorough job with the renovation that all imperfections had been wiped, spackled, and painted clean. I'd inadvertently denied myself the sentimental pleasure of archaeology in my boyhood home.

At the end of the hall there was a phone book splayed in the corner, as if it had been thrown. I tried to turn the hallway overhead on, but the bulb had burned out.

The Bunches didn't have much, and their few possessions were uncared-for. Things seemed to have lost their purpose—for example, the phone book flung and left for naught, the dead lightbulb unchanged. I wondered if this translated to their daughter, if the reason they'd lost track of Bethany in the Target was that she had become just another faulty object to them, like a cracked dinner plate or a chair with a wobbly leg that gets relegated to the garage.

Mary came out holding a ceiling mobile of Muppet characters: Kermit the Frog, Miss Piggy, Fozzie Bear, Gonzo, etc. "This fell onto her bed," she said. "It keeps falling."

"I can fix it if you want," I offered.

"No," she said, pulling it close. "Thank you, though."

"Was anything missing?" I asked, not aware until I said it of how insensitive the question must have sounded.

Mary shook her head, opened the door, dropped the mobile on the other side, then closed it.

I really wanted to go into Bethany's room, but I knew I shouldn't push my luck. I was already improbably beating the odds. "You really should report this to the police, Mary."

"No police," she said again. "We're through with them. Please just fix the door."

"Of course."

"Maybe get us a solid one. Without glass in it."

I told her that this made perfect sense.

Then she asked me if I wouldn't mind sticking around until Todd got home.

I told her I'd be happy to.

She turned away, produced a cell phone, and went into the kitchen, leaving me at the threshold of their living room, staring at the vacant shelf where their DVD player used to be. The small cactus suddenly seemed like it possessed a human intelligence. After I left, it would tell Mary everything. I wanted to seize it and throw it out the window.

In the kitchen Mary was bringing Todd up to speed on the situation and insisted that they not report the burglary. She told him that I was there with her and that I'd promised to stay until he got home. Then she started whispering.

I found myself inching backward, toward Bethany's room. My hand found the doorknob. I turned it slowly and opened the door. The Muppet mobile was blocking the entrance, and I didn't want to step over it, out of fear that Mary had somehow strategically placed it. I didn't even cross the threshold.

There was a child-sized twin bed, immaculately made, a small white pillow, no headboard, a baby-blue cotton comforter crisply tucked into the mattress. There was also a canary-yellow ruffle around the box spring. Beside the bed, a stand with a Big Bird lamp on it, also yellow. The stand looked weirdly "country" and out of place, like it was something used for showcasing knickknacks at a Cracker Barrel gift shop. Opposite the bed was a short chest of drawers, mahogany. Everything that used to be contained inside them had obviously been sent to the Dumpster in that Hefty bag and was now long gone. The curtains, neatly drawn, were also yellow, but a sadder, flatter yellow than the box spring ruffle and Big Bird lamp. It seemed as if the winter sun were somehow avoiding them. This was my mother's hospice room, where she often groaned out in the night. Where there were screams for morphine and Dilaudid. Where she would often speak Polish, drifting in and out of narcosis.

The closet was closed. Next to the closet, on the floor, a small stuffed bear, brown, faced the corner, as if put there to be shamed. With every angstrom of will that has been genetically assigned to me I had to fight the urge to enter the room and take the bear. I quietly closed the door and returned to the living room.

Mary was still on the phone. After a long silence punctuated by some sniffling, she said good-bye and came back out into the living room, wiping her face.

I asked her if Todd was on his way and she nodded. I told her that as soon as he arrived I'd get to work on replacing their door.

Mary seemed to contract within herself like a sick child. For the first time I wondered how seldom she slept. How she got through each day. How little peace she felt.

She must have smelled the empathy steaming out of my pores because she said perhaps the most improbable five words to me since I've known her, which were: "Can I have a hug?"

"Sure," I heard myself say.

We took a half step toward each other and hugged. She forced her hands under my armpits and inside my bathrobe, where they interlaced between my shoulder blades. For a half second I thought she was going to perform some inverted version of the Heimlich maneuver. But it was an authentic hug and she pulled me tight, burying her head in my midchest region. Mary is a good deal shorter than I am so I rested my chin— or beard, rather—on the crown of her head, which didn't smell anything like the dandruff shampoo from her shower cubby. It smelled more like gloom. Like the funk of pure sebaceous gloom leaking through the pores of her scalp. A peppery, oily musk.

We clung to each other desperately. The heat from her face radiated through my many layers. I realized I was sort of pulling her into me. Her breasts, which felt surprisingly fuller than they appeared in her clothes, were pressing into my rib cage.

"Thank you," she said, still buried in my chest.

"You're welcome," I almost sighed.

"I'm sorry if I've been a bitch."

"You're not a bitch," I said. "You and Todd have obviously been through a lot."

The hug started to develop chapters. There was some shifting of weight and subtle movements of her hands, which were still interlaced between my shoulder blades. She sighed a little as well. I think our sighs occurred in roughly the same register, which means that mine were likely pretty womanish. She switched cheek positions, offered shallow breaths. A kind of laryngeal bellowing. I bellowed as well.

The hug was verging on novella length. Just when things couldn't get more bizarre I felt an erection coming on. And I was wearing loose boxer shorts under the plaid flannel pajama bottoms—which were also loose in that semi-pleated MC Hammer genie pants sort of way—so there was no way to prevent detection. We thawed out of our hug as it was about to get visibly embarrassing, and I turned and took a few steps, walking like some wayward, bowlegged Christmas soldier.

Todd Bunch entered through the front door, his face worried and ghostly white. He was wearing full firefighter regalia: the boots, the rubber coat with neon-yellow bands, the helmet, the vulcanized gloves.

"Was there a fire?" I asked, my hands forming a severe steeple in front of my pajama bottoms.

"Simulations," he said, and embraced Mary, who buried her head in his fireproof shoulder. She was like a dope fiend for hugs.

I stood there and awaited instruction.

Todd made severe eyes at me, but I think he was just generally freaked out. His face was incandescently alive. "I can take it from here," he said.

"Just knock on my door if you need anything," I said.

Todd somehow looked like a Fisher-Price fireman. A human-sized figurine with child-safety features.

As I was leaving, guarding my crotch with one hand, I reached down with the other and picked up the brick. "I'm assuming you don't want to keep this."

Todd shook his head.

I told them that I'd get to work finding them a new door.

When I got back upstairs, still erect, I slid the brick back into its position on the bookcase, which had been dangerously teetering.

Although at the embarrassingly young age of thirty-six, I am only infrequently visited by the Galloping Magic Cowboy of Natural Erection, once it's fully achieved, the only way to make it go away is by ejaculating. I thought of Mary Bunch, naked on the trapeze, high in the air, her nipples erect, her body glistening under the circus lights...I thought about taking her from behind, in her circus dressing room, the roar of the crowd and the smell of elephants and clown makeup...

Then I whacked off to great relief.

Before it got too late, I used my Makita drill to screw a piece of spare plywood into the mullions framing the Bunches' broken window panel. I said good night and repledged my promise of replacing their door.

They were grateful and exhausted.

Just as I was about to ascend the aft staircase, out of the corner of my eye, I saw another snowman. As soon as I spotted it I felt a chill pass through me. The snowman was at the base of the copper beech. The charcoal eyes. The carrot nose. The pink scarf.

My mouth went dry, and there was a strange pulsing in my head. I took a few steps toward it, my nose nearly pressing against the back porch's cold screen.

"Everything okay, Francis?"

I turned.

Baylor Phebe was standing behind me.

"You look like you just saw a ghost," he said.

I said hello to him.

He told me he was just going to go get a few things out of

his truck. "My phone charger. My Bonnie Raitt CD. Can't fall asleep without my Bonnie Raitt."

I said, "Baylor, can you do me a favor?"

"Sure," he said. "What?"

"Tell me what you see when you look at the tree in the backyard." I moved aside and he stepped toward the screen and squinted.

"I see a tree," he said.

"Anything else?"

"Nope, just a big old tree. And a heckuva lotta snow. Why, you got coons or somethin'?"

"No," I replied, "no coons."

"Cause I can certainly help you on that front. I've never been known to hesitate when it comes to dispatching a meddling coon."

I thanked him and he headed out toward his truck. I turned on the floodlight over the garage. From his driver's side door, Baylor waved appreciatively, but I wasn't thinking of him.

He was right. At the base of the copper beech there was nothing but snow.

PART THREE

LIFE
DRAWING

February 25.

It's been a month since I picked up these pages.

Pollard is still locked in snow, though it's lost its immaculate gloss and shimmer. The cross-country skiers have gone away and the three neighborhood yards within view of my finial window are now maligned with little carbonized monuments of dogshit. The dogs themselves bark through the night and I'm starting to think they're trying to tell me something. Perhaps there is some encoded pattern in their leavings, a secret escape map that will lead me out of the upside-down Arctic forest that has taken over my mind.

My bad molar isn't so much painful as it is just strange getting used to. I'm sure the tooth's nerve has long lost its purpose and I worry about winding up with a postapocalyptic face once the decay has rotted through my jaw. I've called Dr. Hubie three times now to request a home visit but I can't get past Julie Pepper, who diplomatically deflects the idea with the skill of a world-class badminton champion.

Nearly two months have passed since Bethany Bunch's disappearance. Recently someone staked a realty sign in the front lawn, only the culprit had painted over the actual firm's name and in large red horror-movie letters had scrawled the words BABY KILLERS LIVE HERE. Baylor Phebe extracted the sign and brought it up to the attic before anyone else in the house could see it.

"Those poor people," he said of the Bunches.

His kindness verges on the ecclesiastical. I'm starting to believe he might be the Kindest Man on Earth.

Now the sign is living under my bed, ironically on top of the Bunches' DVD player, which is still wrapped in a towel.

Three days ago Baylor invited me to go ice fishing with him. I ran into him while re-stapling insulating cellophane to the screened-in panels of the front porch.

"Up at Lake Camelot," he said. "They got bass the size of Toyotas. Ever been ice fishing?"

"No," I said.

"The best way to take your mind off stuff," he said. "They got a great waffle house right near the lake."

I told him I would think about it. The idea of being in that much open space makes me start to sweat and claw at my face.

Bradley Farnham is a UFO personified. There are occasional sightings, but these are mysterious and often from a distance. I knock on his door every few days but there is no answer.

It's past time to start harassing Harriet Gumm for February's rent. It's her first delinquency. The lease gives each tenant a six-day grace period before I charge a $25 late fee. Lyman's lawyer, Marty Moynahan, felt this was more than generous. I've only had to tack on a late fee once, which was to the Bunches after their fourth month in the building. (I waived it in January, the month Bethany went missing, but the Bunches insisted on paying it anyway.)

My first nude modeling session with Harriet Gumm is scheduled for four p.m., five hours from now. For the past few days

I've completed fifty sit-ups and fifty push-ups; the sit-ups in two sets of twenty-five, the push-ups in five sets of ten. These numbers are staggeringly low for a grown man who doesn't suffer from muscular dystrophy or some other related disorder. My chest is sore, almost depressingly so. It feels like what little pectoral muscle tissue I possess is full of crushed glass.

And then there's this: Three nights ago I think I tried to kill myself. I took one of Haggis's Percocets and then another. I drank a few fingers of bourbon and looked at the blob of aluminum foil containing the rest of the deal. The rest of my life represented by a blob of aluminum foil seemed somehow appropriate.

I thought about Sheila Anne. I imagined the children we would never have. Freckle-faced, with huge, wondrous eyes. The stray dogs we would never take in. The old farmhouse we would never fix up.

I lay on my stomach and stared at our wedding Polaroid magnetized to the bottom of my minifridge. I couldn't stop thinking about those first weeks when we fell in love. How we laughed together at our clumsy sex. How while following the band around on the road she'd run out of underwear and had to start wearing my boxers, which made her legs look thin and coltish and beautifully pubescent. How we couldn't stop listening to Silver Apples, of all things. That never-ending feeling— which, for her, had ended so resolutely. I contemplated my general ineptitude and sexual inconsistency.

I thought about being found dead in the attic of my family home. One of my tenants knocking, the smell of my decomposed body fouling the uppermost story, Todd Bunch, Pollard's newest fireman, breaking down my door with an official firehouse axe to discover the worms boring into my flesh. My body voided of all waste and humors. Ants feasting on the jellies of my eyes.

About twenty minutes into all of this gloom and doom I started to get really really really high and put on an early Flaming Lips record and wound up having one of the best times in recent memory, just sort of drifting around the attic like a helium balloon being batted about by a declawed kitten. I swayed and giggled. I pushed off the walls and swooned. I rolled onto my back and bicycled my legs. I fell asleep on Haggis's promised flotilla. It was a flotilla of Venetian gondolas drifting down a warm, loving Italian river. Thanks to the beauty of Percocet and the Flaming Lips, I made it through my darkest hour.

But back to that delinquent rent. Onwards!

I will first pose for Harriet Gumm and do the hard-core landlording afterward.

About posing nude:

I worry about my average penis. Will it relax and hang naturally? Or will it retreat, assuming the form of a young acorn facing its first brutal winter? Yes, I worry about size. I worry about length. I worry about girth and general penile attractiveness.

I also worry about farting, or somehow stamping the stool. Yes, potential stamping worries me too. I long for deliverance of that sanitary doily.

Despite these fears, which I accept as normal asinine frailties of the human condition, I have to admit that I'm looking forward to sitting for Harriet Gumm. It'll be like entering an unknown cornfield without an exit strategy. Or like the first day of Intro to Spanish.

Earlier, as I was retrieving the newspaper from the front porch mailboxes, I ran into La-Trez tear-assing it down the stairs from the second floor.

I said, "La-Trez with a hyphen."

She stopped halfway down the staircase. Per our previous encounter, she was wearing her corduroy coat and backpack.

"Hey, Francis," she said.

"Another delivery?" I said.

She didn't answer.

I asked if Bradley was home and she replied, "Naw."

Then I asked her how she kept getting into the house.

"Front door's mad open," she said.

I tested the door. It opened with ease. Someone had used silver duct tape to cover the latch plate so the latch wouldn't catch the strike. I removed the tape and placed it in the pocket of my bathrobe for future reference. I assumed Bradley was the culprit, since he was the only one with a mysterious visitor.

La-Trez descended the rest of the stairs, but I stood in her way, my arms folded before me. I said, "Whatever you're up to—"

"Excuse me," she said, squeezing by and scooting out of the house, the smell of sesame flowering briefly in her wake.

The door latched cleanly behind her.

I went up to the second floor, where another large canvas sack had been set beside Bradley's unit. I opened it. String again. As before, I dug my hands in deep. Nothing but string.

It's late again. Just after three a.m.

The house sleeps below me. Only the low-end hum of my minifridge and the gentle hiss of my humidifier. I'm beginning to believe the humidifier knows my thoughts. Perhaps household appliances attain a human intelligence after logging enough hours with you. My humidifier knows my thoughts and my microwave may be out to get me. But at least I know where they are. If this gets any worse I suppose I can just start unplugging things.

I am now writing longhand, using a cheap ballpoint pen and an old spiral notebook. That's how it's going to be for a while, for reasons I'll get to. I'll have to transcribe these pages with the Corona later, in fits and starts.

Disrobing for Harriet Gumm was easier than I'd thought. While engaged in this task, I realized I was actually disrobing a robe, which made for a clever syntactical distraction. Perhaps not dissimilar to undoing a hairdo. Or dismembering a member.

It was late afternoon but felt like early evening. When she opened the door, she actually said, "Welcome," as if she were the madam of some eighteenth-century brothel. She had taken down all the art.

She closed the door and I stood there. The overhead light was faint. Like really, really faint.

I pointed up to the fixture and asked if her lights were on a dimmer.

"I use low wattage for first-timers," she explained. "We'll raise the lights with increased comfort level."

The stool, which, in fact, did <u>not</u> have a protective doily on it, was perfectly centered in the room. There were four easels positioned around it.

Harriet wore blue jeans and a navy cardigan over a white blouse with a lacy collar. She was barefoot. Her toenails were polished red. Her eyes were made-up. She was less goth and more preppy and I wondered if she created a character for each new subject. She smelled like peppermint soap.

"So let's get started," Harriet said.

There was suddenly something overly calm and medical-assistanty about her.

I asked if I should disrobe right there, in the living room, or if there was some other, more appropriate place, perhaps a folded screen to change behind.

"I've turned the heat up," she replied.

When I asked her why the heat was relevant she said that the living room, which she actually called "the modeling room," should be a comfortable "nudity temperature." The word <u>nudity</u> hit me square between the eyes like a Ping-Pong ball.

"But by all means," she continued, "feel free to use the facilities."

I crossed to her bathroom like a man forced to walk toward a large sleeping bear. I closed and locked the door, turned the light on. Taped to the medicine chest, as if Harriet had known I'd opt for the john, was a note:

> Mr. Falbo,
> Don't be nervous. You're going to be a great subject.
> Sincerely,
> Harriet Gumm

I hung my bathrobe on the hook in the door. I peeled my double-layered thermals off, folded them neatly, and placed them on the toilet seat, after which I removed my slippers and merino Ingenius socks, inserting the socks into the slippers, and then gently placed the slippers on top of the thermals. I'd never undressed this carefully in my life. There was a geriatric, ritualistic quality to my movements. It felt like I was about to receive my first colonoscopy.

I was naked.

I took the note off the mirror and stepped back a ways to do a quick survey. The recent sit-ups and push-ups didn't seem to have made much of a difference, and the large brown mole in my navel looked like it always does: sort of sadly forced there, a cruel anatomical joke.

I will admit that, before the session, I performed some subtle pubic topiary. I used the edging feature on my now retired electric razor. In Harriet Gumm's medicine chest mirror my penis looked acceptably average. It was the genital equivalent of Hall and Oates's "Method of Modern Love." But I was grateful, if only for aesthetic purposes, that Cornelia and Lyman had chosen to have me circumcised. I tugged on it once or twice and headed out.

Harriet was standing beside one of the four easels, upon which a large sketch pad had been placed. She looked big-eyed and wise and a little savage. "Is it warm enough?" she said.

I nodded and mustered all my will to resist planting a fist in front of my dick. I kept waiting for her eyes to drop and check out the goods, but she calmly kept staring straight into my eyes.

"To the stool?" I asked. My voice had been cut in half, which used to happen a lot in the early days of fronting rock bands. The first thing to betray a front man's false poise is his voice.

"To the stool," Harriet replied.

I cupped my balls, sat on the stool, and then released them so they dangled comfortably. Were my balls too fuzzy? Should I have trimmed those as well?

The stool was much warmer than I'd anticipated, but the aforementioned lack of a sanitary doily was dismaying.

Harriet must have sensed my unease. "Don't worry," she said, "I always disinfect the stool."

She was witchy, this girl. A witchy little preppy goth.

I nodded and simply sat there, the arches of my feet forming tensely around the stool's little dowel support. My palms were on my knees, my head lifted high off my neck. My posture was probably too good. I think I might have been trying to elongate skeletally as well as genitally. For some reason I was aware that my nipples felt like they were more alive than usual. Like they both had individual brains. Or like they might form mouths and start meowing. And I decided to share this with Harriet.

I said, "I feel like my nipples might form little mouths and start meowing."

"Kitty titties," she said. It was the cleverest thing anyone had said in weeks.

Harriet continued to stand beside the easel, about five feet from me, taking me in. At this point she'd ceased committing her gaze to only my eyes and by now had surely assessed other parts, zones, limbs, joints, rogue hairs, skin tabs, and lumps.

Harriet proposed that we do a trust exercise. She told me to close my eyes. She would walk circles around me and while she did this would meditate on really seeing me, meaning beyond my physical being to my essence and my goodness and the primordial flickering of my soul, etc., etc. In a soft, pleasing voice not unlike a voice you hear on a commercial for feminine protection, she told me I should focus on relaxing, that I should simply surrender to the nonthreatening circumstances and "breathe into the experience," a phrase that immediately made me imagine I was kneeling over one of those CPR dummies with the bald brainwashed eyes that never close and whose bodies cease existing after the lower torso.

Harriet said that at some point, after x number of revolutions, we would switch positions; that at this important flash point of the exercise she would take her clothes off and sit on the stool herself, and this would be my cue to begin circling her. In terms of deep-sea imagery, there was a sharks-zeroing-in-on-prey kind of thing going on.

She started walking circles, sylphlike and confident. "The only rule," she said, "is no touching." She told me to close my eyes and I did so. "And while I'm circling you, just be sure to keep breathing and connect to your breath. And later, while you're circling me, only breathe through your nose. The person on the stool keeps their eyes closed until the other person is done circling."

An interesting, not entirely logical set of ground rules. Sort of a child's made-up game.

I asked her how many times she intended on circling me and she said she wasn't sure.

"Like hundreds?" I asked.

"Maybe," she answered. "Maybe twenty-seven. Maybe three. Keep your eyes closed now. Remember, trust."

I could hear her bare feet padding around me. Her refrigerator hummed. The low-wattage light buzzed overhead. We were quiet for what might have been thirty seconds, but it felt like an eternity.

Thoughts were suddenly skittering through my head. Thoughts about quantities of Percocet and the Bunches' new door, which was way more expensive than I thought it would be, like $478, and thank God Home Depot delivered and my dwindling supply of canned food and was I maybe starting to eat like a man stranded in an Arctic wasteland who'd happened upon a crashed propeller plane and the madness of astomatous snowmen that might be existing only in my mind and I was really pleased as punch that I hadn't needed to fart thus far and Detective Mansard's hearing aid and his bristly nicotine 'stache sort of floating independently through space like it had its own wandering intelligence and why all of the sudden is there this sort of constant intestinal gurgling going on in my lower depths and can Harriet actually hear that and was I going down low enough on my push-ups and was my bad molar releasing an odor and my mother in a white hospital gown walking through a field of blood-orange poppies sort of half doubled over because Lyman the abstraction of him at least had forgotten to reload her morphine plunger which she'd dropped somewhere in the sea of all those poppies and Sheila Anne sleeping on Dennis Church's tan, fit chest and less-than and greater-than signs coming out of nowhere and storming my thoughts guerilla-style and what the hell is Bob Blubaugh doing with his life anyway and the sound of a lone tennis shoe knocking around in the dryer unit and Baylor Phebe's almost grotesque kindness and will this winter ever cease or has the environment finally surrendered to the inevitable demise of the planet and Bethany Bunch flying upside down like a high-end chess piece flipped on its crown but traveling at some unbelievable speed through dark starlit skies and never stopping and why am I so overly concerned with my tenants' lives when I should be trying to hunt down the three members of my former band and maybe solve some problems of my own, mainly this thing of not being able to step away from the actual structural confines of the house without feeling like the world is tetrahedrally closing in on me—

"Your turn," Harriet's voice issued from the darkness.

I opened my eyes. She was standing before me, naked. She was so beautiful that I almost barked like a seal. I'm not talking about parts. I'm talking about the whole of her. Harriet Gumm is Beauty Incarnate in the way that Hershey's is Chocolate or a Mustang GT 5.0 is Horsepower. Her youth is astonishing, the quality of her skin crushingly, intensely perfect.

Again, it was all very touching, not sexual.

"May I?" she said, pointing toward the stool.

I dismounted and she took my place, crossing her legs. She closed her eyes and I started circling her.

She reminded me to breathe through my nose.

I asked her if it was okay to look at her.

"You can look wherever you'd like," she replied.

I walked exactly twenty-seven circles around her. I know this because I counted them, half under my breath, all the while breathing through my nose.

Harriet has a faint reef of acne across her upper shoulders, sharp bony points to her elbows. She also has a small brown mole perfectly assigned by some higher power to live at a point between her shoulder blades that almost seems like the actual center of her being. I imagined our moles sort of docking, which made for an interesting physiological composition, my stomach joined to her back, our congenital markings informing each other, causing something miraculous to happen, a volcano birthing a tornado of hummingbirds in some distant land.

I wanted to lie at her feet. I wanted to place my head in her bare lap and breathe in her scent and moan like a cow.

"Okay," I said, and stopped circling her.

"Okay," she said, opening her eyes.

I replaced her on the stool.

She picked up her clothes off the floor and put them on matter-of-factly, layer by layer, as if we were in the locker room of a same-sex gym class. Then she reached into the apple box of chalks and charcoal stubs, stood before the easel just to my left, took me in, biting her lower lip, presumably deep in thought, and started to draw. I never mentioned the rent.

*   *   *

When I returned to my apartment, the attic door was ajar.

I slowly pushed it open, half-expecting to see Todd and Mary Bunch holding their DVD player or one of my body hairs, forensically confirming my burglary. But that's not who I was greeted by—no, not even close.

Glose was asleep on the bearskin. Or appeared to be. Was it really him?

Had my session with Harriet Gumm unlocked some metaphysical slipstream and somehow conjured the Third Policeman's troubled, meta-destructive drummer?

He was asleep on his back, per normal, which I've always found to be incongruous with his insane unpredictability. You expect someone who thrives in chaos to sleep as if he's been thrown from a speeding car, but Glose always sleeps with perfect, sublime stillness, no matter how cramped the quarters or noisy the conditions. In waking life he is a human disaster. In sleeping life he's like some sort of Zen master of unconsciousness, transcending all circumstances. It used to really piss me off, especially when band funds were low and the four of us were forced to negotiate a thirty-dollar motel room—say, for instance, the Rodeway [sic] Inn, just off Route 26 in Ogallala, Nebraska, where the carpet smelled like a breakfast burrito. If I got the floor I would toss and turn all night, practically wrenching my shoulders out of their sockets. I'd often wind up sleeping in the van. If Glose got the floor he would lie on his back, tilt the bill of his Mao Communist cap over his eyes like some Dust Bowl hobo on a freight train, and sleep like the dead for ten hours. He wouldn't even bother taking off his shoes.

His hands were crossed under his chin now, like a vampire in a coffin, his disposed figure perfectly still, as if carefully arranged for a viewing. His black hair had grown long. It was dry and unhealthy-looking, graying in splitting, wayward strands. He had a few days' growth of a beard going, dark like his hair. His beard starts way high up, like almost under his eyes, and when he doesn't shave, it gives him the air of an irritated bandito. He was thinner, his big-boned build looser now, whereas normally it was overly fleshy, usually a little flabby. His fungal toenails were extraordinary to behold, with so many colors marbling their thick yellow carapaces that they seemed almost artistically manipulated.

He must have felt the air shift when I opened the door, as his eyelids separated in that strange, indifferent mechanical way of crocodiles. It was downright fucking spooky. I almost thought he was still unconscious, between planes of existence.

After a quiet moment he said, "Francis." His voice was soft, weaker than I remembered.

"Glose," I replied. "What a surprise."

"I would've called but I lost my phone."

I mentally scrolled back to the last time I'd seen him. I couldn't place it. Was it before or after Kent had moved to the Upper Peninsula of Michigan? For the life of me I couldn't locate his last day in Pollard. Glose was like that. He never said good-bye, would just disappear, abandoning IOUs, dirty laundry, drumsticks, percussion toys, half-eaten sandwiches, unresolved arguments, etc.

"I really like this bearskin," he said.

"Yeah, I'm pretty sure it's yours." I told him he'd left it in a box in the old rehearsal space. "You found it in that weird thrift store in Joplin," I added.

He said, "Joplin…" as if the town itself was a confusing half-memory.

"Joplin, Missouri. We were on tour. You bought the bearskin and Kent bought the little taxidermy bird. I think it was a finch."

This didn't seem to register. It hurt me deeply that Glose was forgetting things band-related. This was real history, spent in rented vans and cheap diners and venereal-smelling roadside motels. We crashed on friends' living room floors when we were way too old to be crashing on friends' living room floors.

The anecdotal stuff is the beautiful part of rock 'n' roll. Like when Kent, because of his cat allergy, slept on a pontoon boat, where he was attacked by the same dander-rich cat that had driven him sneezing and teary-eyed from the lake house in the first place. All these weird experiences on the road. The strange conversations at three a.m. The incessant two-lane highways. The water towers and farmland architecture. The bizarre small-town mom-'n'-pop thrift stores. The flea markets and pancake houses. The post-hangover conversations with teenage cashiers at gas station snack bars.

About the bearskin I said, "I had it flattened and cleaned. Figured you were through with it."

He neither thanked me nor confirmed his ownership of the bearskin. He simply watched me with his crocodile eyes.

I asked him how he'd gotten into my apartment and he said that the door was unlocked. "I knocked," he said, "and it just sort of opened on its own."

I never leave the attic apartment unlocked. It's one of my more responsible adult habits. But I had to believe Glose. My lock is a Sunnect Advanced Protection digital deadbolt. And my attic door is made of steel. There's no way he could've picked the lock.

I asked him how he knew to look for me in the attic and he said he studied the mailboxes. I asked him how he got into the house and he said that the front door was ajar.

He said, "I've come a long way, Francis."

I wasn't able to engage with him about his personal journey just yet. I was still dealing with the possibility that he might be a figment of my imagination. Or here simply to ruin my life.

He told me I had a righteous beard and I thanked him. He told me I've always been so clean-cut.

"Not so much anymore," I offered.

Then he slapped at something on his neck and said that he keeps having this recurring dream that he's grown a full beard. "But it's a beard made of almonds," he added. "And I'm on the run from the Almond Pickers."

I asked him who the Almond Pickers were and he said he wasn't entirely sure but that they wear these safari hats with the words Almond Pickers on them. "And they're chasing after me with sacks to put the almonds in and they're fucking fast as cats."

I told him that it would be really weird if he was on the run from the Almond Brothers. "Like if they were really the Allman Brothers but changed their name just slightly for the purpose of hijacking your dream."

We laughed and that made it official: I wasn't hallucinating. In our finest hours, this was the way the band came up with song ideas. We were at our best when we were goofing off. And we were at our very best when Glose was at the center of it.

His teeth were dim, his tongue chalky white.

"Homonyms," I said.

"Homonyms," he echoed.

He propped himself up on an elbow. He wore a gray hoodie

over his signature kelly-green Girl Scouts of America T-shirt and old split-pea-colored Levi's cords with holes in the knees. Black hair was tufting through the holes. No winter coat. No socks on his feet, not a pair of shoes in sight.

"Can I get a hug?" he said.

I approached him and he stood. Getting to his feet was maybe a seven-part move. I suspect his body carries so much survival inflammation that he probably suffers like an old person with rheumatoid arthritis. His breath smelled like the back of a garbage truck and his clothes stank of body odor and stale feces and mold. I worried about acquiring bacteria, but we hugged nonetheless. At the height of our embrace he sort of sighed. Something felt irretrievably lost about him. Like parts of his soul had gone missing. When the hug was over there were tears in his eyes.

I asked him where his shoes were.

Clearly embarrassed, he said, "I don't seem to have any at the moment."

"You've been walking around barefoot? In this crazy weather?"

"Just for the past few days." He said that he'd been wrapping his feet in newspaper and plastic bags.

In addition to the psychedelic toenails, he appeared to have trench foot. Both feet were cadaver white, wrinkled, maligned with crust and abscesses.

I went into my minicloset and pulled out a pair of old Doc Martens that I hadn't worn in over a year. They were still in pretty good shape, a bit scuffed up, but with solid soles. I also grabbed a pair of winter socks for him. I handed him the shoes and socks.

He said, "Thanks, Francis."

I think it was the first time he'd actually thanked me. As in ever. And when you've been deprived of that from someone, no matter how much bitterness and vitriol you've stored up, it can still be touching and it was.

But then he followed it by asking, "Would it be too much trouble if I crashed here for a coupla days?"

I noticed that I was crossing my arms in front of my sore chest, sort of defensively. I asked him if he'd called his mom.

"I don't think I can do that," he said.

At nineteen, after one semester, Rodney Daniel Glose dropped out of Waubonsee Community College to join an eight-piece Chicago-based stunt-band called the Spirit Dicks, whose shows would often devolve into paintball wars with their fans. They had two drummers, one who'd bite a beat and one who'd enact a kind of mathematic score of war. Glose was the latter drummer. The Spirit Dicks died after the band's lead vocalist was sent to Cook County Jail for stealing high-end Winnfield executive chairs from the Libertyville office-furniture warehouse where he was a part-time loading dock worker.

When Glose dropped out of Waubonsee Community College and moved to Chicago, he broke his mother's heart. Lorna Glose still lives in the small tar-paper house where her only son was born, on the east side of Aurora, Illinois.

Glose's father is an unknown entity. Kent, for reasons that were never entirely clear to me, believed him to be living on a pot farm in Jamaica. I'm still not sure how Glose wound up in Pollard. Morris and I met him at the Crooked Dog, a now defunct bar where he briefly worked busing tables. One night he overheard us talking about forming a band and he started talking about drums in a cool way, particularly about the idea of melodic drumming, so we invited him to jam with us. He blew our minds on a makeshift kit and the rest is history.

"Don't worry," Glose said, "you won't even know I'm here."

With a dirty index finger he probed inside his ear, employing a slow, churning technique that issued audible squishing noises. Critters were inside him. Did he have lice? Crabs? Or worse yet, scabies?

I wanted to scream at him for killing our band, something I'd never done. I wanted to scream so fucking loud that his face would cave in from the megahertz, but instead I said, "I'll track down an air mattress for you."

"No need for that," Glose said, ceasing his ear probe. "I'm happy on the bearskin."

Though I knew I was in for trouble, I nodded.

And thus the mooching began. And thus was I forced to abandon my typewriter, at least for the time being.

I called Haggis and traded the Bunches' DVD player for a month's supply of his new penis-enlargement pills. When he came to drop them off, I met him at the front porch.

"So they really work, huh?"

"They've put an inch on me," he volunteered.

I handed him an old Pollard Memorial High School gym bag containing the DVD player. He held his fist out and I bumped it idiotically.

"You could probably get a hundred bucks for that," I said of the DVD player.

"Oh, I'm not sellin' it," Haggis said. "It's gonna be the main cog in my new backseat entertainment system."

"In the Nissan?"

"Hells yes in the Nissan. I got me a twenty-seven-inch, high-def LED monitor, Bose speakers."

He was in good spirits. I wondered if the penis pills were helping his mood.

"I might get a hibachi," he said, "start hosting client barbecues."

I told him I was impressed. And I was. Here was someone finding great joy and purpose in the confines of a compact car.

Afterward, he shoveled the front and back porch steps, and the walkway from the street.

For the first time in years Hazard Groom's wife, Eugenia, crossed the street and buzzed the attic apartment. The last time she had paid a visit to the house was after my mother died. On that occasion she had dressed in all black, complete with a mourner's snood. She brought with her a huge bouquet of red carnations and was so made-up she looked waxen. You would've thought it was <u>her</u> mother who'd died and that she was coming over to borrow an egg for some memorial cake she was baking.

When I met her on the front porch, she seemed deeply troubled. I thought maybe Hazard had suffered a stroke, or worse yet, died. Somehow I always expect senior citizens to go in the winter. Their fragile, brittle bones turning to glass, their hearts winding down like shrinking, faulty clocks. Their lungs thinning to faint sacs of frost. Hundreds of Pollard seniors slowly teetering while filling the teakettle or reaching for the refrigerator door, landing face-first on their cold kitchen floors.

I brought Eugenia Groom around to the side porch and we sat on the wicker furniture, which was actually colder than the air.

I said, "What can I do for you, Mrs. Groom?"

Eugenia Groom has been wearing the same brown wig and identical shade of tuxedo-red lipstick since the midseventies. She is pretty the way an official Susan B. Anthony one-dollar coin is pretty. Her voice is a faint warble of desperation, perhaps more suited to a pigeon than a woman. You always feel like you're going to have to console her when she approaches you. She trembles and moves at the same steady pace as, say, a canoe. How she's survived all these years with a bombastic legendary football coach for a husband is anyone's guess. Kent used to joke that she might have some kind of unexpected jack-in-the-box energy in bed.

For this particular visit she wore an orange silk headscarf over her wig, black suede gloves, and black heels over sheer nylon stockings. Her navy mackintosh had specks of powder on the shoulders, which I assumed to be some sort of scented talcum that had escaped from her wig. She obviously hadn't yet beheld the beard I've been farming and I could tell she was trying to make sense of my new look. Was the nice boy from across the street, the one who used to deliver her <u>Chicago Tribune</u> and play in those silly rock bands, still in there somewhere?

She removed her gloves, placed them in her lap, and took my hands in hers, which I was sure meant Hazard Groom had indeed died. For a moment, she ceased breathing, enlarged her funereal eyes, and, with an expression that was distinctly corvine, said, "Francis, you have circus killers living in your house."

I took my hands back. "Mrs. Groom," I said, "if you're referring to the Bunches, I'll have you know that they are very nice people."

"They're cold-blooded killers. Circus killers."

I told her that there was absolutely no evidence that they'd done anything to their daughter. "They're actually going through a lot right now," I added.

"They're killers from the circus," she said.

She was starting to seem downright robotic with the variations on the "circus killers" refrain. It was as if she'd been somehow digitally downloaded with a well-mastered MP3 track and some fellow neighborhood witch huntress was zapping her with a remote from behind a nearby snowy hedge.

"It's unfair to say that, Mrs. Groom, it really is."

She cleared her voice and continued: "Gene and Cathy were wanting to bring the grandkids over this weekend, and I have to say it makes Hazard and me very uncomfortable knowing that these people are right across the street."

The thing that drove me craziest was her gentle, warbly voice. She really was scared to death.

I assured her that she had nothing to fear. "They're good, normal people," I added. "Todd is a fireman and Mary watches George Clooney movies."

"That's all a front," she replied. "Can't you see that?" She went on to say that she could see it—meaning their obvious murderous guilt—from all the way across the street, plain as day. "It's all a performance," she said.

For a moment I doubted myself. Was it all a performance? Were my initial suspicions about the Bunches correct? Was I being fooled?

Eugenia added that Hazard had wanted to join her on this visit but that he was too upset.

I imagined Coach Groom standing behind the drapes, even-faced, smoking a pipe, his arteries thickening with a slow dull rage, poised to call out to the neighborhood with a bullhorn and unleash the ignominy, leading end-zone-style chants against the Bunches until they came out to face the throng.

I suggested that she meet the Bunches for herself. "They're probably home right now," I said. "Let's go knock on their door."

She stood and put her gloves back on. "I don't think so," she said, her voice quavering ludicrously.

"You're wrong about them," I said to the back of her mackintosh.

She clicked across the porch, faster than I've ever seen her move.

"At least meet Mary," I called after her.

But she exited without a response, scooting across the icy street in her heels, as if chased by winter bees. Hazard Groom was already at their front door, just as I'd imagined him, stalwart as a can of nails, ready to let her in.

It's March at last.

Glose has now stayed for three days and into a fourth.

From the Internet, for thirty dollars, I bought him Calming Cleanse Delousing Shampoo and Conditioner. I paid for overnight shipping. The kit came with a comb and an instructional booklet. We didn't discuss the critters that were living on him. I just handed him the little clear plastic zipper pack and he read the label and nodded.

"Three showers should do the trick," I said.

"Like three in a row?" he asked.

I've heard about how homeless people resist showers because the high-pressure directional water feels like pins and needles. Had it been this long since Glose had actually bathed? "Maybe take one now," I offered gently, "and then again tomorrow morning and the following morning too."

Equally gently he replied, "But I could use it more than three times, Francis. Just to be safe."

"Sure," I said, noting how he'd affably feathered my name in there, practically childlike in its benevolence. "Just to be safe," I echoed.

Even more gently he said, "Like I'd be willing to do six or seven showers with this stuff."

"Probably a good plan," I said.

In this precise moment there seemed to be some tacit agreement cemented between us that Glose would be living with me indefinitely.

Just to be safe, I took these pages, along with my Corona, down to the laundry room, where I hid them in a wooden box on top of the cupboard over the washer and dryer. I loathed the idea of Glose snooping around in this manuscript. I figured the last place he would go looking for anything would be a room where things were cleaned. I am tired already of writing longhand and will hope for some typing sessions, or at least transcription, in the basement.

I was back on the stool once more, post–encircling exercise, as naked as a man on a stool can possibly be. Harriet Gumm was at the other end of the room this time, manning a different easel, focusing on my posterior side. At first it was strange being drawn from behind, Harriet as an unseen omnipotent presence, a disembodied voice, no doubt cringing at my bits of back hair, acne scars, and other imperfections.

I've been on the penis-enlargement pills for four days. They don't seem to be making a difference. I keep checking myself in the bathroom mirror after I urinate, which means I have to stand on the toilet, an act that makes the dick check oddly surgical, as it's only my crotch framed in the medicine chest. Without the rest of my body as a proportional context, it's not easy to assess progress. If anything, I think the pills are making my penis sort of, well, more brownish. Meaning the color brown. Like cooked-hot-dog brown. Or Buster-Brown-shoes brown. Maybe that's the first step: a slight penile darkening, to be followed by incredible, rapid growth.

Let's hope so.

For the first few minutes of the session I felt like prey to the huntress, but the trust exercise took the edge off and I was able to surrender to the new subject-artist relationship and connect to my breath, which smelled like way too much Dentyne Ice, a gum I've been chewing inordinate amounts of to ward off any bad odor my troubled molar might be releasing. And to ward off any possible Glose funk I might be absorbing, I'd showered so thoroughly that the soles of my feet were pruning.

I could feel her gaze crawling on my spine like a slow, deliberate beetle. I was surprisingly unaware of my brown penis. Or my brown mole, for that matter.

I think she went from chalk to charcoal or charcoal to chalk because the sound on the paper changed. Or maybe it was simply her technique that changed.

I asked if she would show me what she was working on but she said no, which I found to be a double standard, seeing as Keith's study was on the wall when he walked in, and I told her as much.

"You can come to my thesis showing and see it all then."

"When's that?" I asked.

"Beginning of May. By that time maybe your back will be healed." She told me it seemed like it was getting better.

I replied that sitting on the stool didn't seem to bother it so much.

"Posing has medicinal effects," she said.

At this point, the beginning of May seemed like a year away. Would I still be faking a bad back? Or would I have to come up with a more elaborate physical affliction, like bursitis or some unexplained adult version of rickets? Worried about what I would look like as a purchased, bonded, freed, and educated slave, I asked if she was crafting me the same visual narrative as her other subjects.

"No," she said decisively. "Not at all."

"Will my story relate to theirs?"

"Almost completely," she answered obliquely.

I was suddenly all too aware of my penis and my mole.

The moon is full tonight. I have been watching it through my finial window. So bright you can actually see its shadowy depressions and fault lines. Its ghostly seabeds and phantom continents. The cloudless icy sky. Frozen winter stars. Astral penumbra. Endless glittering space.

All is quiet in the house. Only the heat turning itself on and off. The occasional toilet flushing, sending a rush of water through pipes; that distant, mysterious sluicing sound.

I am writing longhand again tonight, unable to leave the attic.

Glose is asleep on the bearskin. He sleeps so much and so unfathomably deeply it makes me jealous. Since the three consecutive showers, I've rarely seen him get up, even to use the bathroom, eat, or drink a glass of water. I get the sense that he's in the throes of some essential restorative process. A kind of half-conscious hibernation. In recent days, the few times he's been conscious, he's been pretty quiet, if not a little dazed, occasionally emitting a faint sigh that sounds like a release of air from some unseen anatomical valve. At some point I will enter the attic apartment and he will have transformed into a jungle cat.

Or just a big plate of ham.

There is still an odor, an almost blinding halitosis, which I worried at first was from my molar, but realized, almost with relief, was emanating from Glose, even after the third shower. While working at my desk I've taken to blowing a small fan in his direction. A fan in the winter (it's early March, but still winter in this part of Illinois) is absurd, I know, but it seems to organize his breath into a kind of rectangular mass that lives with him on his side of the room.

Yes, I now find myself in a my-side/your-side situation. I offer him Dentyne Ice, which he refuses. I even left a new tooth-brush, still in its plastic, propped on the second shelf of my bookcase, within his direct line of sight, but he either hasn't seen it or doesn't care.

It's like we're at summer camp. Or in prison.

The Bunches purchased a new DVD player, and earlier, when I went down to check on them, they were watching one of the many George Clooney movies in which he is hapless and no-ble and charming and a lothario and sort of athletic and sort of unathletic and brilliant and self-effacing and chiseled of jaw and emotionally moving and larky and alpha <u>and</u> beta male and a good maker-of-pasta-sauce and coordinated and uncoordinated and doggedly moral yet in spurts totally Machiavellian and cut-throat and a good listener and a naturally talented masseur of the shoulder and neck areas belonging to women half his age (who would've thought!) and not bad with a hammer and good <u>and</u> funny in bed and not half-bad in a batting cage and maybe a secret genius with shy, reluctant borderline-autistic children—he is miraculously all of these things! The characters he portrays always seem to be fated (or is it blessed?) to float through a comic, prelapsarian world of mild conflict and even milder resolution, and one populated mostly by girls with great legs.

I guess I'm just jealous.

I will never have a life that resembles a George Clooney movie and I will never look like George Clooney. I will forever be an averagely handsome guy who looks slightly better while playing the electric guitar. That only gets you so far. And when you stop playing your guitar in front of people that doesn't really get you anywhere.

Anyway, Todd answered the door. He was wearing a gray hooded sweatshirt with matching bottoms, and hiking boots, the laces undone. His horrent red hair looked like a mass to be sanded, not barbered. He resembled a Sears catalog model clutching a garage-door opener. An odor of Mexican takeout wafted warmly toward me. Todd was holding an open two-liter bottle of Citrus Drop, whose off-brand label seems somehow more suited to dishwashing detergent than lemon-lime refreshment. The only light in their apartment—the spill from the living room TV—played over Mary's legs, bare and silvery, extended from the calico sofa. George Clooney's unmistakable voice—that finely tuned Instrument of a Nation—soothed and sedated their home with its sterling, mellifluous baritone.

Todd said, "Hello, Francis."

"Todd," I replied.

He was squinting at the glow from the back porch light behind me, which they've been leaving on lately. Half of me believes they keep it on in case Bethany miraculously appears in the backyard, as if deposited there by a flying saucer, and so I allow them to leave it on.

"Clooney," I said, referring to the movie.

"He's the real deal," Todd replied.

I have recently gotten into the habit of combing my beard and I was suddenly paranoid that Todd knew, and that in his mind it made me sort of gay.

Todd said, "Did you want to talk to Mary?"

"No," I replied, "I just wanted to make sure everything was okay down here."

"We're fine," he said.

"The new door giving you any problems?"

"No problems, no."

I told him that the Home Depot guy could come back if it needed adjusting.

"Door's perfect," Todd said, neutral as the door itself.

My real purpose for the visit was to delicately broach the subject of their having changed the locks. I figured enough time had passed since the staged burglary and for the life of me I just couldn't let it slide. The landlord-tenant collusion was making me feel cowardly and small-balled. I was about to ease into the issue when I noticed that a black video camera had been installed in their ceiling, just beyond the threshold of the rear entrance, maybe six inches in length.

"Surveillance," I said, pointing to the camera. Again, the first thing that came to mind was lease infraction. Were they allowed to drill into the ceiling? Was unapproved surveillance permitted?

Todd simply nodded and said, "There's one above the front entrance too."

"Wow," I said. "Was that expensive?"

"More than we can afford right now, but it makes Mary feel a lot safer."

"Good investment" is all I could come up with. So in a matter of days, they'd replaced their DVD player and installed a hi-tech surveillance apparatus. What had happened to their so-called low-income pressures?

"Yesterday at the bank," Todd said, "a woman walked up to Mary and told her we were going to rot in hell for murdering our daughter."

That was stunning to hear and I told him as much.

He said, "People, you know?"

"Fucking. People," I echoed.

He asked me please not to swear and I apologized.

"This detective keeps calling too. Wants something of Bethany's for some dog to sniff."

"Do you have anything you can give him?" I said, picturing the teddy bear.

Todd replied, "We don't want dogs sniffin' on her stuff."

At this point I had forgotten why I'd knocked on their door.

"I better get back to the movie," Todd said.

"Of course," I said. "Have a good night."

So yes, the full moon in all of its ancient glory…

After my visit with Todd Bunch I received an incoming call on my cell phone from an unfamiliar number. For a moment I thought my grandma Ania, Cornelia's mother, had finally died. I had always thought it to be a turn of ugly poetry that she was forced to outlive her daughter, to bide her time in a North Shore rest home that Lyman generously pays for. Grandma Ania's husband, Grandpa Radek, died in his sleep only a year before his daughter. So Grandma Ania is no stranger to the indifferent machinations of her Catholic God. Her grief has become a kind of unrelenting season of cold wind. The few times I've visited her at the nursing home she was withdrawn, virtually wordless. We ate microwaved tomato soup and Ritz crackers while she sat before a book of crosswords, a rosary wrapped around her left hand, not being used for any prayer ritual but seeming to function as a kind of apotropaic talisman, to fend off whatever badness is left for her in the world. The rosary might as well have been a fork or a steak knife.

I let the call go to voice mail, but it wasn't from Grandma Ania's nursing home—it was from Sheila Anne.

At the sound of her voice my kidneys lightened, my lungs tingled, my heart wobbled. A sudden and serious hyperawake feeling took hold of me. A feeling so potent it made me think I've been living as the revenant version of Francis Carl Falbo, a mere shade of who he was. Hearing her recorded voice made me whole again, albeit briefly, and my organs were inspired to manufacture something other than insulin and bile. Nerve endings fluttered. I think I felt the thrill of positive adrenaline for the first time in untold months.

On the message Sheila Anne said she'd been trying to reach Bradley to no avail. She wondered if I might be so kind as to go knock on his door, just to make sure he was okay. She also said she hoped I was doing well and that if it wasn't too much trouble would I mind calling her back.

I played the message maybe sixteen times, not even really dealing with its content but letting the music of her voice wash over me while I desperately searched for signs that I was still taking up space in her head, little clues scattered in between the vowels and consonants. She sounded healthy, present. Dare I say amazing?

I almost vomited.

But I didn't puke. Because I still have pride. Which gives me hope.

I swallowed hard several times and forced myself to stop replaying her message by putting my cell phone in my minifridge and closing the door.

Glose.

Day 6.

We were listening to the Alan Parsons Project's <u>Eye in the Sky</u>, whose first two songs, "Sirius" and the title track, are prog-rock masterpieces. The rest of the album has a hard time measuring up.

Glose was still sporting his kelly-green Girl Scouts of America T-shirt but had degenerated to wearing nothing from the waist down. Meaning he was half-naked and it was the wrong half. And the bottom of his T-shirt was rolling up, so his fleshy, simian stomach was sort of spilling out indiscriminately, his navel an unseen, unsolved mystery. I have no idea what became of his corduroys. Perhaps they were so threadbare they simply dissolved.

Unbeknownst to me, Glose and I were about to embark on our first full-fledged conversation since his arrival.

From out of nowhere, with Alan Parsons's rueful voice singing in the background, Glose said, "I do think about doing stuff."

Out of respect for the rarity of the Third Policeman's drummer actually sharing a thought approaching the complexity of self-examination, I let a few measures play. "Like what?" I eventually asked.

But he drifted off like he was on Vicodin and Blue Nun wine, which used to be his favorite little post-gig cocktail.

"Like getting a job?" I tried again.

"Maybe," he replied, drifting back.

I told him that gainful employment is never a bad thing.

He said that his skill set was sort of limited.

Beyond the drums, I tried to make a mental list of Glose's

various abilities. One thing he can do is foretell the future, mostly bad stuff that's between people. Like who will stop loving whom and who will cheat on whom first, that sort of thing. Or on a less dramatic, smaller scale, who will forget their cell phone during the load out or who has enough money to buy him breakfast at the nearest Denny's. It goes without saying that he's an incredibly talented parasite, but in terms of one's skill set that would be useful only on like some new reality TV series about competitive mooching.

"I like plants," he said, somewhat proactively. "I could work with plants."

"Like at a nursery," I offered.

"Or at a floral shop."

He seemed to follow the thought around the few feet of airspace between him and my bookcase as if it were a pulsating firefly...but then something short-circuited and his head returned to rest.

I asked him if he'd consider asking for his job back at the stand-up MRI clinic.

He said he couldn't go back there.

"Why not?" I asked.

"Because they caught me peeing on the ficus tree," he answered.

Clearly, nontoilet urination is a thing with Glose. Is this why he liked plants? So he could have a place to go to the bathroom?

I said, "You could teach drums."

But he said he'd sold his kit in Morgantown, West Virginia, for five hundred dollars, which meant he'd no doubt sold it for two-fifty.

"That kit was worth a grand, Rodney. You sold your cymbals too?"

"I sold everything."

"Those cymbals were artifacts," I said. He could've gotten five hundred for the cymbals alone. They were incredible—warped and cracked, producing sounds that any drummer would give an eye for. Whenever we played a gig, the drummer of the band following us was inevitably in awe of those cymbals. They were legendary. Turned out he'd sold his drums to some college kid who'd let him crash on his sofa for a few weeks.

I asked Glose where else he'd been.

"Pittsburgh," he said. "Portland, Maine, New York."

I asked him what he was doing in New York City.

"Not a lot," he replied.

Which meant he'd probably been mostly drinking other people's beer and getting into fights. He said he was there for around a month. He'd answered an ad to do some session work with a band, taken the train out, auditioned, and landed the job in a matter of two or three days. The band was called Scherzando, "a sporty gay jam band," according to Glose. "Sporty" because they dressed in tennis whites, and "gay" because he didn't like their gimmicky music, which he said sounded a lot like the Three's Company theme song from the famed American TV show of our youth. Although they did pay Glose several hundred dollars for his session work, he didn't last with Scherzando beyond a gig.

He said he'd stayed in the East Village with a woman named Fat Judy, Scherzando's main weed provider, whom he'd met during his few days of session work when she stopped by the studio to make a transaction, but that it hadn't worked out.

I asked him what happened between them.

"She caught me trying to step to this friend of hers."

Though I had a pretty good idea, I asked Glose to clarify what it meant to "step to" one's friend.

"Well, I was sort of boning her," he explained. "In Fat Judy's bed. And then Fat Judy walked in."

I said, "Oh, Glose..." I said it like his mother might have said it because that's what Glose does to you; he makes you feel like a worrying, bone-tired mother.

He explained that while he was having sex with this other woman, missionary style, Fat Judy rushed him like a hotfooted outside linebacker and slugged him real hard between his shoulder blades, which knocked the wind out of him. And then she grabbed this little aluminum baseball bat she kept under her bed and started swinging for the fences. It turned out that while Glose was staggering around from the blow between his shoulder blades, Judy took a serious home-run cut at him, like one that completely spun her around, but lucky for Glose she missed him completely but accidentally connected with her so-called friend, whose name was either Nono or Norca, cracking her skull open like a soft, ripe melon. Understandably, everything ended right then and there.

I said, "Jesus, Rodney."

Glose went on to say that Fat Judy called 911, and then went into first-aid mode, trying to keep Nono/Norca's brains from spilling everywhere. While running for his already ramshackle woebegone life, Glose grabbed as much of his stuff as he could, but wound up leaving a lot behind.

The point being, this was how he had lost his first batch of belongings, before Morgantown.

"So that was New York," I said.

"That was pretty much it for New York, yep."

Then, almost as a minor post–punch bowl afterthought, he told me he'd seen Sheila Anne. Apparently she'd walked right past him on the street. Glose was sitting on First Avenue, wedged between storefront doorways in a kind of homeless person's municipal alcove, begging for change with a sincere, straightforward cardboard sign that said TRYING TO GET HOME, his main strategy for acquiring Greyhound bus fare.

He'd seen Sheila Anne.

I was stunned.

My throat made a strange dry clucking noise. I clucked three or four times. I could feel my tongue contorting into a garden slug.

I asked him if he made contact and he said he called out to her but that she was wearing headphones, that she didn't even see him, that she was walking really, really, really, really, really fast like they do in New York. I imagined Sheila Anne's hip flexors getting really, really, really, really, really supple and defined.

Then Glose said, "But you know what was weird?"

Of course I bit and said, "What?" and he went on to say that, despite all the East Village noise—that purported grinding cacophony of First Avenue—he could've sworn she was listening to the Third Policeman's <u>Argon Lights</u>. Not at all far-fetched if you've spent countless hours recording, mixing, and listening to your own music. The melodies and moments float in your unconscious like the pains and joys of adolescence.

"Track two," he said, "'Know Your Beholder.'"

"Wow," is all I could muster. A beautiful warmth passed through my body. It started in my stomach and radiated outward.

"Know Your fucking Beholder," Glose repeated. "How 'bout that?"

The highest note I've ever made escaped my mouth, a sound birthed from some tender abscess in my heart. I asked Glose how she looked and he said "fucking amazing," that it was July, that it was hot as lion's breath, that the streets were baking and smelled like an odor he couldn't even describe, that she was dressed for work, that she was wearing a skirt and a blouse, with nice shoes.

"Heels?" I said.

"I think so," Glose replied.

I imagined her calves, their faint, lovely clefts.

"I guess I shoulda ran after her," he said, "but my sign was pretty big."

Sheila Anne probably would've taken him in. She always liked Glose, despite his antics. Whenever I would express my frustrations about him, she would say, "How can you be mad at Glose? That's like being mad at a big dumb dog."

When the instrumental track "Mammagamma" began we were quiet. I've always thought it to be the most underrated song in the Alan Parsons Project catalog. The layered synth is incredible. I let it mingle with the unexpected warmth I was feeling.

Hearing that Sheila Anne was still listening to our music as recently as last July, more than a year after she'd left, gave me hope. I sang the lead vocal on "Know Your Beholder." In spite of everything, she was still spending time with my voice in her headphones.

About halfway through "Mammagamma" I said, "What if I helped you buy another drum kit?"

"You would do that?" Glose said.

I told him I wouldn't even ask him to pay me back.

"Hardware and everything?"

"Cymbals, hardware, everything," I said.

Glose rubbed at the halo of eczema around his mouth and said, "Maybe like a little jazz kit."

"A jazz kit, sure."

"Where would I set up? In the basement?"

I told him I couldn't do that to my tenants.

"The garage?"

"It's too full. Besides, it's not soundproofed. You'd have to rent studio space. But you could afford that if you got a job. And you could give lessons on the side, which would easily cover your overhead."

Glose thought for a moment and said, "That seems pretty complicated."

I told him that it might take some getting used to. "But look at me," I said. "I never thought I'd wind up being a landlord. And I'm pretty good at it."

The Eye in the Sky ended. I didn't bother taking the record off the turntable. I just let the needle float in the gutter and the tonearm eventually returned to its first position.

You could suddenly hear music drifting up through the acoustic vinyl of Harriet Gumm's unit on the second floor, just below us. She was playing Angela Bofill's R&B dance-pop classic Too Tough.

Glose said, "I could help you too, Francis."

"In what way?"

"With your issues."

"My issues?" I sort of barked and snickered—an extended snicker, actually, demonic-sounding. I was snickering so hard I almost banged my head against the granite inlay top of my kitchen island.

Glose asked me why I was laughing.

"Because it's funny," I cried.

"What's funny?"

"You telling me I have issues. I mean, you're the one who's

been lying on my bearskin, like not leaving it in some sort of John and Yoko protest way." I had to take a breath. The words were tumbling out too fast. "And I'd greatly appreciate it if you started wearing clothes," I continued. "This isn't some old-world bathhouse." I laughed yet again. "And when was the last time you showered?" I added. "You're enacting some bizarre first-person ethnology study on my living room floor and you're trying to tell me I have issues?"

"You do, Francis."

"Don't call me Francis, Rodney."

He said, "I've always called you Francis, Francis. You have issues."

I told him to name exactly one.

"You like to use big words," he replied. "You just did in fact."

"What big word did I just use?"

"Ethanol."

"Ethnology?"

"I mean ethnology."

"That's not a big word!" I said. "It's not big at all!"

"It's like a word out of a crossword puzzle, Francis. Don't get mad."

"Don't call me Francis!"

"You're shouting."

"I am not!"

In some childish act of defiance Glose removed his Girl Scouts of America T-shirt and tossed it over his shoulder, revealing his hairy pectorals, which drooped in the manner of listless, flea-bitten spaniel ears. He was sitting Indian-style now.

"Great," I said. "That's just great. Now you're actually fully nude. Did you go away and become a fucking nudist?"

Glose said, "Did you not go anywhere and become a <u>thermal-ist</u>?"

It was the first cruel thing he'd said since his arrival. It was cruel and surprisingly witty and it stung. That was the thing about Glose. He was never cruel to anyone, except for Kent, of course. And to other bands' bassists, when he'd head-butt them for no reason. But that was somehow sort of fun-spirited, or at least he thought it was. He was inexplicably, carelessly, boyishly sweet, even during his most idiotic moments.

I took a breath. "Did you lose your clothes, Glose?"

He didn't answer.

"Rodney?"

He scratched petulantly at his chest, refusing to make eye contact with me. A big sad half-man, a kind of forlorn, imperfect, nutritionally challenged Sasquatch.

I gave him a moment and said, "Do you have any belongings at all?"

Finally the story began to emerge. Glose said that after he managed to get out of New York he'd been hitching rides west, with the hope of returning to Pollard. He'd fallen asleep at a rest stop in western Pennsylvania—one of the huge ones where you can take showers and have indoor picnics and traipse around in video game arcades and whatnot—and someone took his duffel bag, which had everything in it: his wallet, his ID, his clothes, his phone, the last few bucks he'd scrounged together on the streets of the East Village, everything. And then, farther west, he got caught stealing a taco, one measly taco from a truck-stop Taco Bell. An undercover cop caught him wolfing it down and displayed zero sympathy for the no-doubt itinerant, slightly suspicious-looking creature we know as Glose, who then had to spend the night in a highly impersonal little mint-colored cinder-block jail cell outside Terre Haute, Indiana, that smelled like balls and stale sperm and chewing tobacco.

It was a terribly sad story and I believed it. Part of me subscribes to the notion of karmic whiplash, the folksy logic that Glose was being punished not for the taco theft, but for the havoc he'd wreaked on Fat Judy.

We fell quiet. The house made a sound. It wasn't the heat and it wasn't the plumbing. It was deeper, sadder. A brief, almost human measure of grief that had been trapped in the floorboards. A sorrowful groan released into the wintry night.

And then again, it might have been my intestines.

"What's with all the snowman drawings?" Glose said. "There's like a thousand snowman drawings all around your desk."

I told him that my desk was my private area. I said, "Why are you looking in my shit, Rodney?" I was suddenly paranoid that he was looking in my notebook too, which I'd been especially careful to hide after each use.

"As far as I can tell those snowman drawings are on public display," he said.

"Well they're not."

"Then don't Scotch tape them to the wall."

I looked over at my desk and he was right. There were snowman drawings everywhere. It looked insane.

"You've been crying in your sleep too," Glose added.

"I have?"

"Two nights in a row now. Full-blown crying."

I tried to imagine the sounds I was making in my sleep. Were they whimpers? Sobs? Were they similar to the noise I just heard the house make? Were these little fits of anguish getting recycled into the floorboards? I couldn't even remotely go there.

Instead I glanced away and said, "You got thrown in jail for stealing a taco?"

"Look at me, Francis."

I turned back to face Glose.

"You cry in your sleep like a battered woman on food stamps," he said. "So don't try to pretend that I'm the only one here with issues."

I removed my cell phone from the minifridge and went into the bathroom and called Sheila Anne. My teeth were chattering so intensely I could feel my beard oscillating. I tried to dial her number three times but I couldn't because the teeth-chattering problem started spreading throughout my whole body. I skeletally trembled for a solid minute. Then I started yawning. I sat on the toilet seat and yawned until my jaw was legitimately fatigued. After several deep breaths I managed to dial successfully.

Her phone rang four times and went to voice mail. Which probably meant that she watched it ring and actually watched my name come up on her cell phone screen and thought about it, but maybe Dennis Church walked into the room in banana-colored bikini underwear with like a foamy toothbrush in his mouth or maybe she was alone and she simply got nervous, which is okay because her getting nervous means that she still has something for me no matter how small, even if that something's as infinitesimal as a grasshopper's eye, there's still a piece of me lost in her, some microscopic particle floating around in her bloodstream.

Again, her voice all but cleansed my soul.

I didn't stammer. I told her that I hadn't yet checked on Bradley, but that I would, and that she shouldn't worry too much about him, that from our limited contact he seemed busy and well. I even lied and told her that lately he'd been surprisingly friendly, that once we even fist-bumped after I'd handed him some of his mail that had been accidentally mixed in with mine, and that he'd thanked me and said, "Good lookin' out, bro." And I told her that she should feel free to call me back if she wanted, that it would be nice to speak with her live. I told her that I hoped things were great with her and that New York, New York, Big City of Dreams, was giving her everything she needed (yes, New York, New York, Big City of Dreams, conspicuously the city itself and <u>not Dennis Church</u>). Idiotic and about as transparent as a wolf made of gossamer, I know, but there you have it.

And then, after swallowing hard and holding my breath and flexing my larger muscle groups, I lost all control and told her that I missed and loved her and that I thought about her all the time and that <u>FOREVER</u> is a word that keeps lighting my long sleepless nights like the HOLLYWOOD sign itself and I wished we could eat vegetarian lasagna and drink Maker's Mark out of kooky ceramic gift mugs and listen to questionable Fleetwood Mac records, even the ones that were made before Stevie New York Nicks and Lindsey Buckingham Palace joined the band, and laugh while making uncomplicated but prestigious missionary-style love like in the Olden Golden Days of Fran and Sheila Anne, and just as I was about to keep unraveling like so much yarn thrown from the window of a speeding train her voice mail beeped and the cruel God of Digital Limitations cut me off.

I thought of erasing the message and starting over, but I figured all I would do is skip all the stuff about Bradley and just say how much I missed and loved her and thought about her all the time in as many clever ways as I could fit into her three-minute incoming message allotment.

And then I would do it again.

And again.

And again and again and again and again and again until my cell phone would run out of battery power and I'd have to start scrambling around looking for the charger.

After I hung up, I flushed the toilet, emerged from the bathroom, sat at my kitchen island, and pretended to read the <u>New York Times</u>. Glose was still nude, but he'd been considerate enough to pull part of the bearskin up through his legs so that it covered his crotch, diaper-like.

I repeatedly glanced over at my phone—which was no less than six inches away from my right hand—waiting for the screen to light up. Sheila Anne never called back and I had an impulse to take a hammer to my cell phone, the kitchen island, and at least two walls' worth of attic Sheetrock, but I didn't. Instead I just sat there for a while, my fingers stained with unread newspaper ink, and watched Glose sleep.

I happened upon Baylor Phebe on the back porch. I'd been down in the laundry room, transcribing the work from my notebook. He was wearing a beige broadcloth suit and brown wing tips, along with a white shirt and navy tie. In one hand he held a classic leather briefcase and in the other a brown fedora, which was perched on the outermost concavity of his tremendous stomach. He was pacing back and forth, muttering to himself. He seemed emotionally distraught and overwhelmed, at once sad and enraged.

For a moment I thought I'd managed to rent an apartment to a lunatic. He didn't hear me behind him. When he turned, his face was flush and glistening.

"Hi, Baylor," I said.

"Francis." He said my name like he'd been punched in the face, breathing hard, really worked up.

I asked him if everything was okay.

"Everything's fine," he replied.

But his eyes were moist. A tear escaped and ran down his cheek, though he caught it with the back of the hand holding the fedora.

I told him he seemed upset. Frankly, he seemed out of his mind, and in my head I was going over what civic service to call—the police? the fire department? the mental ward? Was there even a mental ward in Pollard, some dank subterranean padded wing at the local hospital? Or would the white-coats have to come all the way from Decatur with their hypodermic needles?

Baylor set the briefcase down, reached into the interior breast pocket of his suit jacket, and produced a slim paperback volume of Arthur Miller's <u>Death of a Salesman</u>. "Would you mind drilling me on my lines?" he said. "I have a callback in about an hour. My apartment was starting to feel pretty claustrophobic, so I came up here."

"You're an actor?"

He explained that he'd been taking classes at Willis Clay, and that his teacher was directing <u>Salesman</u> at the local community theater. She'd managed to persuade him to audition for Willy Loman, the legendary lead role. "I'd really appreciate it," Baylor said. He proffered the Miller play, opening to a page in act two.

"Pollard has a community theater?" I said.

"Bicentennial Theater," he said. "Over there by the Lutheran church. Two hundred seats. Carpeted dressing rooms. Decent wing space. Real nice facility."

You think you're familiar with your hometown and suddenly there's a community theater that you've never known about.

"My lines are highlighted," Baylor said. "It's not quite four pages."

I took the play from him and set my notebook down. Sure enough, he'd highlighted all of Willy's lines throughout the four-page section.

Baylor set things up for me. He told me I would be Bernard, a neighbor boy whom Willy runs into at Bernard's father's office. Bernard, an adult now, like Willy's two sons—Biff and Happy—is on his way to visit a successful friend in Washington, DC. He's come by his father's office to pick up a nice bottle of bourbon he's going to give his friend in DC. Bernard has done better, financially, than Willy's two sons, and the kicker is that Willy is out of a job and he's at Bernard's father's office with his tail between his legs, about to ask his longtime neighbor for a hundred and ten dollars so he can pay his life insurance bill. He can't draw the money from his bank account because he doesn't want to alert his wife, Linda, who thinks he still has a job. The second kicker, the spiritual piranha nipping at the gelatinous, worried-thin membrane of Willy's soul, is this: Charley, Bernard's father, has already offered Willy an entry-level job that pays fifty dollars a week, but Willy is too proud to take it, feeling it is beneath him.

I asked Baylor if Willy and Bernard are happy to see each other.

"Frankly," Baylor said, "I don't think Willy's happy about much of anything."

As we began to read the lines, it became clear that half of the Willy-Bernard encounter is a study in denial, during which Willy is unable to acknowledge that his son, the once-heralded high school quarterback Biff Loman, is lost in the world, without a job, without a wife, without any discernible future. The scene turns on a tragic rusty dime when Willy finally stops with the collusive small talk and asks Bernard his opinion of why Biff never made it.

"What—what's the secret?" Willy asks the successful Bernard.

There was a soft, earnest plea in Baylor's voice when he said it. He dabbed at his brow with a period handkerchief, hemispheres of sweat metastasizing under the pits of his suit jacket.

As Bernard, I went on to tell him that after Biff had flunked math, he never took summer school to make up the subject.

"Oh, that son of a bitch ruined his life," Baylor bellowed, referring to Biff's math teacher. His teeth were dim and fulvous in the dying porch light. His spine slackened and his large leonine head fell forward as if coaxed by an elusive, distant warmth.

After some more back-and-forth, Baylor achieved a heartrending moment when I told him that Biff failed to sign up for the summer school class after returning from a trip he'd taken to New England to see his father. Biff was ready to enroll in summer school, I said, he wasn't beaten. But when he came back from visiting Willy, he simply didn't bother. There was an implication of guilt loaded in whatever had happened during that trip.

The stage direction read <u>Willy stares in silence</u>, and Baylor simply looked out at the copper beech, staring off as if he were glimpsing some haunted memory. The hair on the back of my neck stood on end. I don't even remember the rest of the scene. There was something about that unadorned moment of Baylor-as-Willy staring at my mother's favorite tree that just about took my housebound breath away. I almost had to go to a knee.

"That's it," Baylor said, sort of thawing out of character, rolling his shoulders as if working through arthritis.

"Wow," I said, handing him the play. I told him he'd been perfect with the lines and that I couldn't imagine him not getting the part.

"You weren't so bad yourself," Baylor said, deflecting the praise. He returned the play to the inside breast pocket of his suit jacket.

I considered my relationship with Lyman. At best he had mildly supported my artistic pursuits. He'd occasionally come to gigs and he would read my column in the Pigeon, but it seemed dutiful. Part of him wanted me to take over his accounting firm, and he's always been disappointed that I didn't follow in his footsteps. I did work in his office the summer between my sophomore and junior years of high school, but I found it to be the dullest environment I could possibly imagine. The truth is that, beyond the genetic material, there really isn't much connective tissue between Lyman and me, and there never has been. Since my mother died, he's been turning into a kind of distant uncle who is good at card tricks.

"Your daughter's your only child?" I said.

"She is," he offered. "She lives up in Milwaukee. Just left her husband. Found out he was running around on her. She's been going through a rough patch."

I didn't know how to respond about his daughter's sad life up in Milwaukee. I thought I might relate to her pain, but the mention of the infidelity only made me feel bitter.

Baylor shook his head and looked out at the copper beech again.

"Well," he said, "I better get over to this audition. I feel like lobsters are square-dancing in my stomach."

"Do what you just did," I said. "You'll get the part."

"You really think so?" he said, hopeful, boyish even.

I told him I did.

He put the fedora on and grabbed his briefcase and exited the porch.

"By the way," he said, holding the screen door open, "don't forget about that ice-fishing trip. I called up to Lake Camelot earlier today and they said the ice is still good for a few weeks. Think about it."

I told him I would.

Then he told me to tell him to break a leg. "It's good luck for thespians," he said.

"Break a leg," I said, grabbing my notebook, my voice maybe a shade wobbly.

The screen door banged shut behind him, and I made a mental note to fix the pneumatic closer.

Dusk had fallen into darkness. I checked my cell phone. It was nearly eight p.m. Baylor got into his truck and pulled out, the dashboard light glowing softly on his face. I thought it was somehow poignant that he hadn't bothered wearing a coat in the thirty-degree weather. Something about a man starting to forget all the little things felt uncomfortably true.

The following afternoon, after a short session with the Corona in the laundry room, I ran into Mary Bunch near the mailboxes. I hadn't seen her since the night I witnessed her bare legs in the light of the George Clooney movie. She was dressed in thick beige corduroys and what might have been one of Todd's plaid flannel shirts. She looked as if she'd been sleeping or, more specifically, that she'd fallen asleep in her clothes.

From behind her back she produced the small teddy bear from Bethany's room. "This was Bethany's," she said, offering it to me. "I can't have it around anymore. It's just too much."

One of the bear's eyes was missing.

"I'll cherish this," I said. And when I said it, I really believed it. I saw myself taking it up to the attic and gently laying it in a shoe box lined with tissue, making a little shrine.

Mary turned and went back into her unit.

Then, for more than an hour, I agonized over whether to call Mansard. I couldn't focus on anything else. Wanting to avoid Glose, I mostly paced the porch, clutching the teddy bear and probing my bad molar with my tongue, a terrible new habit that had me twisting my face into strange contortions. At last I called Mansard, deciding it was best, though at this point, if the Bunches had done something to their daughter, I'm not sure I wanted to know.

He came by not long before six o'clock, as a weak sun was sinking into the gable of the Grooms' roof. Mary had gone for a jog, nodding as she passed me on the porch, and Todd hadn't yet returned from work.

My neighbors to the left—the Coynes—had been having some sort of family gathering. Cars were parked four deep in their driveway, as well as along the curb in front of their tall, majestic Tudor. Neil Coyne, the son of a lumber baron, had inherited the family business and, like me, his family home. There were four or five kids in their front yard, taking advantage of the last of the daylight by hurling snowballs at blackbirds so large and thickly feathered they looked like ravens wearing mink stoles.

Per usual, Mansard and I met on the front porch, near the mailboxes. When I handed him the bear, he pulled a large Ziploc bag out of his overcoat pocket, put the bear in it, and sealed it. I asked him to please hide the bear on his way out, in case one of the Bunches suddenly appeared. He tucked it under his arm, inside his overcoat.

As he was heading to his car, I said, "After your dogs are done with it I'd like that back."

"You like teddy bears?" he said with a slight smile, mostly obscured by his mustache.

Avoiding the attic, I fell asleep on the wicker love seat on the front porch, right where it starts to turn the corner, and had a strange dream about Glose in which he was flying on a trapeze above a pit teeming with bears. He wore his kelly-green Girl Scouts of America T-shirt and nothing else. At first he seemed adept on the trapeze—accomplished even—but it became clear that he would never get a rest, and he started losing his grip. The bears groaned hungrily below Glose, showing their fangs, and there was the feeling that nothing could be done to save him. Somehow I recognized my own voice in the bears' groans. I woke to Bob Blubaugh's hand on my shoulder.

"Bob," I said, "hey."

"You were crying in your sleep," he said. He was wearing a down winter parka and kneeling beside me, his face so close I could smell the soap he uses and see my reflection in the tinted lenses of his glasses. The cleft in his chin was perfectly centered, anchoring the symmetry of his face.

There was a terrible ache in my chest and my face was wet and I was shivering. "What time is it?" I said.

"It's almost ten o'clock."

I'd been asleep for four hours, and despite the space heaters I'd installed on the porch, I was chilled to the bone.

"For a moment I thought you were dead," Bob said.

"Dead?" I replied. I sat up. My bathrobe, which had gotten a little crisp from the cold, made a crunching sound. My body ached all over.

"You were sleeping so soundly you didn't appear to be breathing. But then you started crying."

I thanked him for checking on me and headed for the aft staircase.

"Ever find out what that door in the storage room leads to?" he asked.

"No," I lied. "But I'm on the case."

When I got back to the attic, Glose was wearing my thermals. He had also arranged his hair into pigtails, gathered at his skull with silver duct tape. It was the exact same kind of duct tape I'd peeled off the front door's latch plate, after my encounter with La-Trez. He'd taken Kent's bass out of the gig bag and was holding it in his lap. I could see that he was also holding a fork, which he'd been using to carve several words into the front of the bass, above and below the strings:

KENT IS BENT
[strings]
AND FRAN PAYS MY RENT

"Take those off," I said, meaning my thermals.

Glose set Kent's bass on the bearksin, rose painfully in one of his now patented multipart moves, and removed my thermals, letting them fall beside him, revealing a hellacious shit stain in the bottoms.

Once again, he was naked. He stood before me, his body

hair a collection of black and brown cyclonic swirls. Like a gorilla going through chemo. His penis, which I tried hard but failed to not look at, was like a little pale turnip poking through a patch of rich, furry soil. And he does indeed have three testicles.

"I ate some sardines," he said.

"How many tins?" I asked.

"Just one."

"Just one?"

"I mean two."

I told him I could smell it on his breath.

He breathed on me, a calm act of defiance.

I was assaulted by sardines and intestinal rot and distant garbage trucks. "Classy," I said. "Thanks."

"Sheila Anne left you," Glose said, "because aside from your songwriting you never take any risks. You're too safe. It's like your balls are contained in little quilted protector pouches."

I punched him in the face.

Which was like punching a granite bust of Hippocrates.

I grabbed my hand and made a sound that a dog running into an electric fence might make. I fell to my knees. The pain traveled from my fist to the back of my brain and back to my fist. It was a white-light kind of pain. I started to pitch over sideways, but Glose inserted two fingers into my nostrils and lifted, which made me stand. When I was nearly in full relevé, he swabbed the inside of each nostril with his fingers.

Then he fed me my own mucus. Definitely one of the strangest moments of my life. My right hand was aflame with pain. My nostrils felt permanently stretched.

Glose pulled his fingers out of my mouth. "Good punch," he said, and spit blood. Some of it sprayed onto my bathrobe.

We faced each other on the bearskin in a stare-down, the gamy, adipose smell of his fingers thick in my nose.

I was hoping to have at least knocked a tooth out, or broken his nose, but I had mostly just hurt my hand. With great pain, I opened and closed it. "Your face is like a massive mineral," I said.

"I actually ate three tins of sardines," Glose said. "And two microwave raviolis."

We were breathing in an animalistic fashion, through mouths and nostrils. His breath was warm and fecal. "Have you even once reached out to Kent?" I asked.

Glose shook his head.

"You know you just about did his head in."

He replied that Kent had fallen in love with the wrong homophobe.

"Do you ever wonder about Morris?"

"Not really," he answered. "Morris was always in his own world. Good dude. Great musician. A little too <u>Lord of the Rings</u> for me."

"What about me?" I said. "Did you ever think about me?"

"In the same way you think about a cafeteria plate," he said. "Or like an envelope." He wiped blood from his mouth with the back of his hand and said, "I think we needed a chick in the band. She coulda played keys. Sang all the high parts. A chick is good for balance—pH balance."

"<u>Potential Hydrogen</u>," I said. "Good album name."

Using thumb and forefinger, Glose grabbed one of his two front teeth and made a wiggling motion.

I asked if it was loose.

"Just a little," he replied. "Don't worry, it's not going anywhere thspethial," he added, exaggerating a lisp.

I asked him to tell me what had happened to him out on the road, after New York.

He stopped wiggling his tooth and said, "I found my father."

"Oh," I said. "Shit."

"His name is Dale," he started in. It turned out he lived above a small-engine repair shop. His apartment was like a maintenance man's closet. TV Guides and horse-racing forms everywhere. A bare fifty-watt bulb hanging from the ceiling. Glose had shown up right before Christmas and there was a bluegrass-blue University of Kentucky Christmas tree in the corner with blinking lights that pulsed "Wildcats Are Number One." His father was watching the Home Shopping Network. He looked like a man who'd survived something horrible, Glose said. Like he'd been struck by lightning or attacked by killer bees and never really gotten over it. Glose didn't recognize himself in the man at all. He spent all day with him in his little room with the flashing blue Christmas tree, but his father didn't know who he was. He told him his name and that he was his son, but the guy just kept watching TV.

I started to feel really uncomfortable speaking at such close proximity to a naked man with three testicles and a bloody mouth. I told him that I was sorry and I called him Rodney and said that meeting his father like that had probably been terribly painful.

Glose simply nodded and we said nothing else to each other for the rest of the night. I lay down on my bed and he sat on the bearskin, my thermals still bunched beside him. At some point he gathered the bearskin around his shoulders, sort of enfolding himself in it, and fell asleep sitting up.

The following morning Glose wasn't simply enfolded in the bearskin—he was actually wearing it. He'd fitted the hollow of the snout over his head like a hat, the rest of the skin unfurling across his shoulders and down his back. He looked prehistoric and stunned.

I had to go downstairs to meet the meter man, a nice older-middle-aged guy named Randy who's been wearing the same St. Louis Cardinals cap for as long as I can remember.

It was snowing again. It was March 6, and, yes, snow was falling. A light, unthreatening snow, but snow nonetheless. I hadn't slept all night and couldn't put two sentences together. After Randy finished his meter reading at the side of the house, he returned to the front porch and told me to have a nice day and I told him to have a nice car.

"A nice what?" he said, clearly confused.

"Day," I said. "Have a nice day."

When I came back from speaking with the meter man, Glose was sitting Indian-style, staring out at nothing in particular, the snout of the bearskin still crowning his head.

I told him he had to leave and he looked off toward nothing in particular some more and nodded.

"I'm sorry, Rodney, but this isn't working."

He nodded again.

"I mean, if we were playing music or something..."

He nodded a third time.

I told him I was sorry about his dad and that whole situation but that things were just too cramped in the attic. I wrote him a check for a thousand dollars, and as I was writing it, Glose requested that I make it out to cash and I said I would. It occurred to me I was essentially paying someone to stay out of my life.

"Can I keep the bearskin?" Glose asked, a little sadly.

"Sure," I answered, "it's yours." I had spent all that money flattening and steam-cleaning it, and I knew I would miss it, but it was his after all. By now it no doubt smelled like him anyway.

After I handed him the check he continued to just sit there. I offered my cell phone.

"Maybe call your mother," I said.

He nodded and accepted the phone.

I told him to leave my cell phone on the table when he was done with it.

He nodded again.

I was too bitter and sleep-deprived to say good-bye, so I simply walked out. Before I shut the door, I said, "Please don't take Kent's bass."

"I won't," he promised.

I went down to the laundry room intending to transcribe more of these pages but wound up sitting on the floor beside the Corona. I cried a little. Before I did so my body convulsed like I was going to vomit. It was more a series of whimpers than an arrangement of actual consistent-sounding crying. Whatever slim chance there had been of getting the band back together was totally fucked now. And no matter what I had told myself, no matter how truly awful things had been at the end, I knew I was always secretly hoping for a reunion.

The truth is that we weren't complete without Glose. Without his drums, his voice, his Kaoss Pad skills, and his lunatic senselessness, we were just another highbrow art band, a little full of shit and full of ourselves, pretentious even. Glose brought chaos and weirdness and, dare I say, a spirit of joy to the music. It was hard to admit, but he might have been the most important piece of the puzzle and now that was all over.

The Third Policeman was truly over.

Someone had dropped onto the laundry room floor a piece of Snuggle fabric softener, which I used to dab at my eyes and upper cheeks. I think it was the first time I had actually released tears into the full volume of my beard, which absorbed whatever wetness I didn't catch with the fabric softener. My face smelled like bluebells and buttercups and black-eyed Susans.

I grabbed my typewriter, along with the box containing this manuscript, and headed back upstairs, vowing to never again allow myself to be displaced from my writing sanctuary, where I now sit once more.

When I got back to the attic, Glose and the bearskin were gone. He'd left my cell phone on the table and he hadn't taken Kent's bass.

Three days later, on March 9, the teddy bear arrived in a small cardboard box. Inside, Mansard had left a note, which simply said:

> your bear

Its other eye was now missing. I imagined Mansard's hounds playing tug of war with it, trying to eat its face. Bethany Bunch's bear was blind. I did put it in a shoe box lined with tissue— well, quilted toilet paper actually, but it gave the same effect. I was placing the shoe box beside my bookcase when there was a knock on my door.

A wide-eyed, smiling Baylor Phebe greeted me when I opened the door. He was wearing a big orange T-shirt that said I'M THE GUY IN THE BIG ORANGE T-SHIRT.

"I got the part!" Baylor boomed. "I got Willy Loman!"

I congratulated him vigorously and we high-fived. It was

maybe the third time in my life I had executed a sincere high five. Our right hands met squarely and made a fleshy thunderclap.

"And you helped me," he said. "I owe you."

I told him he owed me nothing but the monthly rent, and he said, "But I do, though. Rehearsals start next Monday, week from today, and then I'll be busy. Come ice fishing with me this weekend."

I told him that I'd love to but couldn't.

"Oh," he said. "Why not?"

"Because I'm agoraphobic," I replied. It was the first time I'd admitted this to anyone. It flew out of my mouth like some harmless biographical fact, as if I had said that I was a registered Democrat or a lover of Vermont cheddar cheese. I explained to Baylor that I hadn't been able to leave the house in over two months.

"Well, that's awful, Francis. Have you tried talking to anyone about this?"

I told him he was the first person. I told him that I had more problems than I cared to admit. "Not unlike Biff Loman," I added.

He said he was sorry to hear this and wanted to know if there was anything he could do.

I told him that I hoped to eventually get over the condition, and related some inane bromides about time and wounds healing and letting scabs be scabs.

"Scabs are scabs for a reason," Baylor offered, gentle as a priest.

I asked him not to tell anyone.

He promised he wouldn't, and then his face got stuck, meaning his upper lip got trapped on his upper gums so that his big blond horsey teeth looked skeletal and terrifyingly alien, but then his upper lip flipped back into place and he resumed being overjoyed. "You should see the woman playing Linda," he said, thrilled as a Cub Scout on his first canoe trip. "What gorgeous arms on that one. I think her name is Roberta. She's from Centralia."

I congratulated him again and we actually hugged, which was sort of hard to pull off physics-wise because of his enormous stomach. I had to stick my ass out and shift my weight onto the balls of my feet, which put a lot of stress on my lower back. For the briefest moment I thought how ironic it would be if a hug were to cause me to slip a disc in reality, to precipitate a nonfictitious back injury. What a funny story this would be for later in life, gathered around a hibachi, turning hot dogs with a barbecue fork while friends and family—whoever they might be—allowed me to regale them with the funny anecdotes of my pre-midlife life as a housebound landlord whose only friends were his tenants.

That Friday, March 13, Baylor left a note on my door:

> Francis,
> Come visit me when you get a chance. I have a surprise for you.
>
> > Your Friend,
> > Baylor

Saturday afternoon, following instant oatmeal and equally instant instant Folgers, I went down to Baylor Phebe's apartment.

He greeted me with his big yellow smile.

To my surprise, he owned taxidermy. Mounted on one wall was a bear's head, the fangs yellow. In the corner facing the door, a full coyote, stoic, with colorless glowing eyes, the pupils sickle-thin, rearing back on its hind legs, its front paws perched on a woodland stump. And the bust of some sort of big-game cat mounted over the entrance to the bathroom, with craven, amber eyes.

"What's that?" I asked, pointing to the cat.

He said he'd found it at a flea market in Mississippi, while on a fishing trip at the Tunica Cutoff.

"It's a cougar," he added. "Eighty-five years old."

There were also a pair of deer-hoof lamps on either side of his plaid love seat, a largemouth bass that looked like it might break into song mounted over the kitchen nook, and a little red fox on a shelf containing bowling trophies and framed fishing lures. Arranged on the wall opposite the love seat was a huge flat-screen high-def TV.

Baylor was holding a remote. He pressed a button. "Check this out, Kemo Sabe."

The TV pulsed to life in vibrant high-def Technicolor. On the screen, an ice-fishing video game.

Baylor handed me a controller. "Let's fish!" he said.

We Wii ice-fished for three hours.

Baylor was having the time of his life and I have to admit it was pretty fun. Not normally a fan of video games, I gave myself over to it and things got pretty competitive. Baylor wound up out-ice-fishing me four to three in a best-of-seven series. After ice fishing we ordered pizza and bread sticks with marinara dipping sauce, which Baylor insisted on paying for.

While eating the pizza I noticed an eight-by-ten photo of a woman, framed in gunmetal, set beside the bowling trophies. The woman was very pretty, with a high forehead and prominent cheekbones. "Is that your wife?" I asked.

"That's Ellen, yeah."

"Pretty," I said.

"She was a beauty," he agreed. "Hard to believe she's been gone three years," he went on. "She died on June fifteenth."

I told him about my mother.

"Was she ill?" he asked.

I told him about her cancer, her long battle with it.

"That's a real shame," Baylor said. "Ellen had a thrombotic stroke. Blockage in her carotid artery. Didn't even know it was there. A freak occurrence. She passed out while she was taking dishes out of the dishwasher. Fell to the floor like a coat off a coatrack. I rushed her to the emergency room. Her face turned this deep, strange blue in the truck. Three hours later she was dead. Nothing they could do. She was only fifty-four."

We ate pizza. Baylor made terrific masticating noises. There was something unconsciously savage about how he devoured each slice. This man was made to ingest large amounts of animal fat and survive in the Arctic.

After a silence, Baylor asked me about Lyman. "Is your dad still alive?" he said.

I said that he was and he asked me what he did for a living and I told him that he'd had his own accounting firm but that now he's retired and living down in Florida. "After he remarried he gave me the house," I added.

"You two close?" he asked.

"No," I said. "Not really. When I was a kid we might've been. He used to take me bowling. He was an excellent bowler. Probably could've gone pro. So we'd bowl. And there was a period we'd go metal-detecting up in Starved Rock State Park, but that didn't last for very long. When I got older, we didn't have many common interests and sort of drifted apart."

"Sorry to hear that," Baylor said. "Were you close with your mom?"

"Pretty close, yeah," I said. "Especially toward the end when she was in hospice."

Baylor nodded respectfully.

All the things we must survive. The list just keeps growing. The deaths of others and heartbreak and taxes and the slow, deliberate failure of the body. I realized that Baylor Phebe might be eating himself to death, pound by doleful pound. Perhaps he thought that soon he would be with Ellen, their ghost selves reunited in the spirit world. Or is the truth more plainly stated in Baylor's taxidermy? We are beings who simply expire. Creatures who are killed or die freakishly, without warning, and become blue-faced objects. Things. The only remains our skulls, our teeth, our bones. Calcium and marrow. Some two hundred interlocked artifacts. Left to clatter in a casket or to be anonymously fed to a conflagration, transformed into gray silt, and flung into a dull, disinterested wind.

Hopefully those left behind memorialize us by mounting our bust on a piece of thick, sturdy wood, by keeping an eight-by-ten photograph next to the bowling trophies, by visiting the hunk of chiseled marble marking our grave, by lightly grazing a brass urn with their fingertips.

*   *   *

The following afternoon, Bob Blubaugh knocked on my door.

"Bob," I said.

He told me that morning there had been a strange man sleeping on the floor of the laundry room, in front of the washing machines. He said that the man told him he knew me. "He seemed nice enough, but I thought I should tell you," Bob added.

"Was he sort of hairy?" I asked.

Bob said that he was wrapped in some kind of animal skin.

I went down to the laundry room. Glose wasn't there but I could smell that he had been. I checked the storage room, then the boiler room. No sign. I went up to the porch, half-expecting to find him sprawled on the wicker furniture. But he was nowhere to be found.

The next day, Monday, a piece of Baylor Phebe's mail was accidentally placed in my mailbox. The return address said it was from Emily Phebe, who I assumed was his daughter in Milwaukee.

I went down to the basement and knocked on Baylor's door, through which I could hear the ice-fishing video game music.

Glose answered the door. He was holding a Wii controller, and the game was on pause in the background.

"Glose," I said.

"Hey, Francis."

I asked him what he was doing in Baylor's apartment.

"Just hangin' out," he replied.

"Just hangin' out," I echoed.

"Yeah, just hangin' out," he echoed my echo.

I asked him if Baylor knew he was there.

"Uh-huh," Glose answered. His mouth was a wolflike rictus, his tongue a chalky gray lump. He spoke through soft, lazy consonants.

I asked Glose where Baylor was, and he said, "Rehearsal. First day. You want me to give him a message?"

"No," I said. "No message."

Finally, he closed his mouth.

"How did this happen?" I said.

"What?" Glose asked indignantly, almost naively.

"You cohabiting with Baylor."

"He likes me," Glose replied.

"Did you knock on his door?"

"He saw me under the tree."

"What tree?"

"The one in the backyard."

"The copper beech?" I said.

"Yeah, that big tree. He saw me sleeping under it and invited me in."

"And then one thing led to another," I said.

"One thing led to another," Glose confirmed, "yep."

I decided against leaving the letter from Baylor's daughter with Glose. I considered calling the police and pressing charges, but for what? He wasn't loitering. And Baylor clearly trusted him enough to leave him to his own devices. Technically there was no lease infraction.

"Do you want to do some ice fishing?" Glose asked.

"No," I said. "No thanks."

He told me that Baylor said I was pretty good at it.

Before I turned to leave, I noticed the bearskin perfectly centered on the floor, in front of Baylor's flat-screen.

Glose clocked me looking at it. "Blends in pretty well, don't it?" he said.

I was furious.

When I got up to the attic I reconsidered calling the police. I even dialed Mansard but hung up, figuring it was a lost cause. Glose was clearly taking advantage of the KINDEST MAN ON EARTH, but until I spoke with Baylor about it, there was really nothing to be done.

I poured two fingers of bourbon and downed it.

And then two more.

And then two more.

Once I was good and silly drunk, for some reason I became overwhelmed with the desire to read Emily Phebe's letter to her father. I had never opened another person's mail before and I was well aware of the consequences—mail theft is a federal crime, after all—but the bourbon had obviously gotten my courage up. Why a piece of Baylor Phebe's familial correspondence was so intriguing to me is anyone's guess. The man had just opened up to me about his wife, and I'd reciprocated, telling him about my relationship with Lyman and my mother. There was nothing sneaky or duplicitous about Baylor. As far as I could tell he was about as mysterious as a box of baking soda. Perhaps breaking into the Bunches' unit had unlocked some creepy need to collect more secrets about my tenants.

I steam-opened Emily Phebe's letter to her father. It was handwritten, maybe four pages, front and back. She had composed it in blue ink and her penmanship was a thing of cursive beauty. I typed it out, adding it to these pages.

Hi, Daddy...

Is Pollard as cold as Milwaukee? I thought global warming was supposed to heat the planet up, not extend these bitter winters. It still feels like the middle of January here, with not much hope in sight. I think we've cracked forty degrees only once so far. I wish the spring would come already; it might help me shake this awful mood.

School is good. My sophomores are reading <u>The Catcher in the Rye</u>, which always makes for stimulating conversation. It's the only book on the syllabus that rivals all the vampire and wizard literature. And I'm always surprised at how many kids <u>don't</u> like Holden Caulfield. The class debate about his attitude toward life is enough to warrant a documentary film. And you'd think Holden would have all the boys on his side, but it's completely unpredictable. This semester, his most staunch supporter is an African-American girl from West Allis named Chiney, who hardly ever talks in class. I think Salinger would be happy. Next up is <u>Of Mice and Men</u>, which you know I Love Love Love. It's a short one, so we're able to read it aloud in class. I keep trying to lobby the English chair, Dr. Lowry, to start allowing me to add some newer, fresher YA titles to the syllabus, but he always brings up parental concerns and permission slips and possible problems with the board, etc.

It really irks me that we can't be a little more risky with regard to materials selections. I mean, we're one of the top private progressive-minded schools in the state! We should be able to feel confident in offering cutting-edge literature to our first- and second-year high school students! It's not a parochial school! This isn't the 1950s!

Okay, I'll gracefully step down from my soapbox now.

So I have a week off for spring break. They scheduled it late this year, for the week of April 14, and I was hoping to come down to see you. I'm happy to sleep on your sofa, but if it's too cramped I can stay at a hotel. I looked into some of the local places in and around Pollard and they all seem affordable.

Speaking of Pollard, it seems like you're pretty fond of it, and your new place too. I'm glad you had the good sense to finally move out of that weird truck drivers' motel, which was costing you way too much money.

Were you able to get any of your taxidermy in there? I hope you at least decided to mount your cougar head—you know how much I love that piece.

I'm so glad you're enjoying being back in school. That acting class sounds really interesting. What's this "sense memory" stuff about? Sounds a little like psychotherapy. I'm anxious to hear more. I wonder what Mom would think of this newfound passion of yours? She'd probably get a kick out of it. She always had a flair for the dramatic.

So now the sad stuff:

I'm not going to lie—it's hard living alone. As much as I hate Cole for what he did—and I do hate the selfish goat—I miss his companionship. I think he's going to marry that girl he's with now, Jillian or Gillian or whatever her elfin name is. I found out that she's only twenty-three. Cole turns forty next month. He's old enough to be her father. I imagine him taking her to ice-skating lessons and then out for hot chocolate afterward. And then for a winter pony ride at the petting zoo. His little daughter-bride...

I should stop about Cole. It only makes me start to shut down.

I actually got asked out on a date the other day. This new science teacher approached me in the teachers' lounge. His name is Paul Prisby, which sounds like a character out of a Jules Feiffer comic. He seems nice enough, but I'm not ready. He asked me to dinner but I told him I already had plans. He's not bad-looking, either. A little balding on top, but that doesn't bother me so much. He might be eccentric, which could be interesting. What I mean by eccentric is that I saw him carrying a book by Flaubert. We'll see...

And, Daddy, I feel like I need to tell you this too...I stopped going to church. I'm not saying that I'm giving up on God entirely, just taking a break for a while. Please don't be too disappointed (I know Mom would kill me). It's just that I see all those other families in church and I get so angry, which makes me feel like a phony (now I sound like Holden). I'm not saying I'm done with religion forever, only for the time being.

And, Daddy, I want to encourage you to get the Lap-Band surgery. I know your cholesterol is by no means a disaster and your blood pressure has improved, but Dr. Noyes did say that it could add years to your life, potentially many years. Call me selfish, but I'd like to have you around for as long as possible. I know you've tried Weight Watchers and didn't like it, and you've cut way down on the calories in other ways (at least you tell me as much!), but unless you start seriously exercising, you're not going to lose that weight and that's what Dr. Noyes is most concerned with. Diabetes, heart disease, you know the drill. And I know I don't need to bring up what happened with

Mom. Anyway, can we at least talk about it when I come visit? I promise not to be too pushy.

I know you're not much for Facebook and the Internet, so I'm doing the old-fashioned thing and including a photo strip. You asked to see my hair back at its natural color, so here it is. I hope you like it. Brown as brown can be. Brown as a squirrel. I think it makes me look older, maybe even a little like Mom.

Anyway, I love and miss you tons. Hoping to see you in a few weeks.

Love,
Emily

She had included a strip of photos taken at one of those instant booths that produce a series of four vertically stacked color snapshots. She was more attractive than I expected, with a pretty, pixie-ish face, dark hair, and warm, round, deep-brown eyes. Doe-eyed, you could say. I guess I'd assumed that she would've inherited her father's considerable size, but unless she is pear-shaped or possesses some sort of unexpected, magnificently large ass, this didn't appear to be the case.

Somewhat sickened by violating Baylor's privacy, I carefully returned the pages of the letter and the photo strip to the envelope. I could feel the guilt settling heavily in my bowels. Shame loves the alimentary canal. I used a large blob of Scotch tape, dabbing it along the enclosure line to create some adhesive gum, and resealed the envelope. Then I went down to the front porch and used the master postal key to open the mailboxes and dropped the envelope into Baylor's slot.

* * *

That night I found a bug in my pubes.

I was pissing into the toilet and I screamed like a woman. It appeared to be a small black aphid. And then I found two more in my beard. I combed through it, looking into the bathroom mirror, and saw red bites, fine as pinpricks, then found bites on the backs of my arms too.

I noted my alarmingly dwindling food supply. (Glose.) And the leftover breath and body smell. (Glose.). I recalled all the unflushed contorted turds in the toilet bowl, the foul turbid water, the long black body hairs that had collected in drifts on the bathroom floor. (Glose again.) And Kent's vandalized bass.

I shampooed my beard and body with the Calming Cleanse delousing system. I lathered up three times, waiting until I was dry and then getting right back in the shower. I scrubbed myself raw. I clawed deep into the whorls of my beard.

Afterward I surfed the Internet for pictures of bedbugs and compared them to the small critters I'd pulled off me.

The following morning I called Orkin.

That afternoon an official Orkin inspector arrived from Decatur. He drove a charcoal-gray Hyundai and wore a crisp company uniform featuring a white shirt with red epaulettes, a black tie, and pressed khakis. He was also sporting a hard hat, which somehow added a science-fiction element to the proceedings. His name was Glen and he was clean-shaven and when he spoke he hit all of his consonants and stood in a military fashion.

I showed him my bug bites along with a few of the bugs that I had killed and put in a jar. I was terrified that they were bedbugs and that I'd have to burn my furniture and throw out all my records and dry-clean my thermals.

"They're not bedbugs," Glen said, "they're fleas. Do you have pets?"

I said that I didn't.

He asked me if I worked with animals and again I said no.

Then he asked me point-blank if I had intimate relations with dogs. If I cuddled or slept with one.

"I don't have intimate relations period," I answered, trying to be witty. Which was probably too much information and fell flat with the humorless Glen. Then I told him about Glose staying with me, referring to him as "an old friend." I said that he'd been sort of itinerant; that he'd been wandering around the country, down on his luck, not bathing, hitching rides, crashing on people's sofas; that I had let him stay at my place for a few weeks.

I have no doubt that Orkin Glen imagined me having rough anal sex with a homeless person, and that he considered fleas to be the least of my worries. Despite what Orkin Glen might've thought, I thanked the God of Home Infestation that these pests weren't bedbugs.

"The flea problem is serious," Orkin Glen continued, matter-of-factly. "And they're mature fleas." Meaning they'd apparently been living and feeding off Glose for some time. And now they were living and feeding off me. "I'm going to need a few hours," he said.

He went down to his car and returned with two large cylindrical containers of chemicals. He told me that after he was done fumigating I should be sure to wash any dishes that had been left in the open air and that it'd be wise to start using a new toothbrush.

While Glen did his thing I took my laptop down to the porch and read <u>Pitchfork</u> and felt jealous of the new crop of important emerging bands with cool names like the Department of Motor Vehicles and Excellent Day to Run Away. I did my reps of push-ups and sit-ups.

After that I sat really still, imagining Glose's body teeming with fleas. I fantasized about them boring into his ears, nesting in the sores on his feet, mating in his nostrils, eating him alive.

Glen bombed the attic with a powerful insecticide that cost me $375. Now there is a faint chemical smell, like the smell of burnt napkin crossed with new-car smell. When I wake up I feel like there's a coating on my teeth.

So where does this leave me? How am I feeling? I've gotten to the point where I want to make Glose disappear. And in a real way.

Haggis has an acquaintance whom he refers to as "the Concierge." I have heard many anecdotes about the Concierge. For the right amount of money the Concierge can make pretty much anything happen for you. According to Haggis, for three hundred bucks he'd recently set someone's car on fire so the person could collect the insurance. For seven hundred he drove a golf cart through a plate-glass window. The word on the small-town street is that in addition to these larger acts, if the price is right, he can also procure anything for you, from chemotherapy kits to certain kinds of high-end African snakes to untraceable fatal substances, meaning poison.

I called up Haggis. "What if I wanted him to kidnap someone," I said, "drive them a thousand miles away, and just drop them off? How much would that cost?"

Haggis's gut estimate was that the Concierge would do it for a grand, plus expenses. "But I couldn't tell you for sure," he added. "Want me to reach out to him?"

"Why not," I said.

"Any major conditions?"

"I would just ask that the Concierge guarantee me that this person never returns to Pollard."

"So you're saying you'd want him dead?"

"No," I said, "not dead, not that."

"Blinded."

"Not blinded."

"Maimed."

"Not harmed in any way. Just get him a thousand miles away and drop him off in like the middle of a field of red sorghum or something."

Haggis called me back fifteen minutes later. "The Concierge can make it happen for two grand," he said.

"Guaranteed?"

"Guaranteed. But he's going to have to kidnap him, which will be somewhat hostile."

I told Haggis that I didn't want him harmed, just displaced.

Haggis replied that he didn't think any excessive pain would be necessary. According to Haggis, the Concierge had also told him that he thought red sorghum grew only in Uruguay and to make that happen it would cost an additional grand.

I told him that sorghum was a chief part of the Illinois agricultural harvest. "It's like the third most harvested crop," I said.

Haggis simply stated that the Concierge had his own take on things.

"Never mind," I said. "He's taking this too literally. It doesn't have to be a field of red sorghum. It can be any field. It can be a forest. Or a pasture. Or a glade, whatever an actual glade is." I could hear Haggis writing all of this down. I asked him how the Concierge was planning to abduct the person. Haggis said that he didn't have the slightest idea, that the Concierge was a person of many, many means.

"The Concierge is going to want to speak with you on the phone," Haggis said. "He's going to need to know the subject's height, weight, exact address, the best time of day for the abduction to occur, and a list of any serious allergies or phobias. Can I give him your number?"

"That's cool," I said. "The cell."

I was in deep.

I went down to the basement and knocked on Baylor Phebe's door.

Glose answered. He was wearing new clothes: khakis and a plum-colored turtleneck sweater, along with my Doc Martens. He had tucked the turtleneck into the khakis and was also sporting a new leather belt. In these new clothes he had the air of someone who smokes a pipe and jots things down in a little leather-bound journal.

"You look like a homeroom teacher," I said, then pointed to the turtleneck. "Is that cashmere?"

"You're still mad at me," Glose replied.

I couldn't even fathom the depth of my anger. As much as I was attempting to stay even-keeled, my face was likely giving me away. For all I know my beard was glowing red.

"You have to let go of all this anger, Francis."

I asked him if he was allergic to anything.

"Not that I know of," he said. "Why?"

I told him that I was thinking about organizing a big meal for everybody in the house. "Like a post-winter feast," I explained.

"Word," Glose said. "Baylor's got all this frozen venison," he added. "I'm sure he'd love to contribute. We could make a stew."

Yes, we, as if they were lifelong companions, a couple even. The absurdity was bewildering. I was starting to understand the concept of one's blood boiling. I felt this most intensely in my mouth. I could have spit flames. "How are those shoes treating you?" I asked.

"They're great," he said, seemingly both sincere and appreciative.

At least acknowledge that you're a conniving prick, I thought. At least have the decency to leaven your responses with a bit of irony.

The Wii ice-fishing game was on Baylor Phebe's high-def flat-screen. Glose had paused it and the wheedling music played like a bunch of mad elves on helium.

"You still gonna buy me those drums?"

"Probably," I said as I imagined him waking up in some random field of dirt a thousand miles away, utterly lost, confused, terrified, thawing into consciousness. The image thrilled me to no end.

That night the call came in.

The last thing I expected was for the Concierge to be a woman. Or a digitized woman's voice, at least. The voice wasn't dissimilar to the one featured on a dashboard GPS. It was a little eerie, a touch soothing. When the call finally came in, the word BLOCKED flashed on the window of my cell phone.

"This is the Concierge," she said when I answered. The voice was too human to be a speech synthesizer, and yet too measured, too consistent in the music of its vowels, to be purely human. It was certainly anthropoid, but weirdly tweaked, and I was convinced the natural voice was being bused through some digital device.

"Oh," I said. "Hi."

"Mr. Haggis has informed me that you would like to partake of my services, Francis." She asked me to tell her my needs.

I told her that I needed someone to be relocated.

"One thousand miles away," she said.

"A thousand miles," I confirmed. I reiterated to the Concierge what I had told Haggis: that I wanted "the subject" to be taken this distance from Pollard and left in a field of some sort, and that while I didn't want the subject physically harmed, the subject should be left without either financial or communication resources, as far from civilization as possible. I said that I'd like the subject to be left with a few days' supplies of food and water to get him through.

And then she listed a number of rural areas that are at or slightly beyond the thousand-mile radius perimeter with Pollard as the center point. They included Laredo, Texas; Artesia, New Mexico; Cortez, Colorado; Gannett Peak, Wyoming; Malta, Idaho; Indian Head, Saskatchewan, Canada; Pikangikum, Ontario, Canada; Chicoutimi, Quebec, Canada; Raymond, New Hampshire; Salem, Massachusetts; Kathleen, Florida; and a defunct offshore oil rig somewhere in the Gulf of Mexico.

"Do any of these places interest you?" she said.

I told her that they all did, except perhaps the oil rig, but that I would leave that up to her, that I preferred not to know.

She gave me a post office box address and instructed me to send a photo of "the subject," as well as the details Haggis had already asked me to collect. After she received this she would send a letter confirming receipt, at which point I would be expected to send one thousand dollars cash—half the fee—to said post office box. Then she would text me with the date and time that the abduction would take place. Upon completion of the job, a series of photos would be mailed to me confirming the subject's displacement, at which point I would have seventy-two hours from the date of the postmark to pay the balance of the fee and the Concierge's expenses.

"No harm to the subject," I repeated.

"Although a little force might be required to detain the subject," she replied, "once in custody, no further harm will be necessary."

The following day I returned to the basement and knocked on Baylor's door once more. Again, Glose answered. He was wearing another new outfit: blue jeans and a baby-blue oxford, Top-Siders without socks. He was holding a large pizza box, open. It held three pieces of pepperoni pizza, one half-eaten. His mouth was impossibly full.

"Rrizza?" he said.

"Already ate," I replied. "You look great."

He thanked me as marinara slop pushed grotesquely through the tight hole of his mouth.

I told him that the homeowner's insurance guy had called and I needed to photograph everyone's apartment. "Just a rudimentary thing for their files," I added. "Do you mind?"

"Not at all," Glose said, stepping aside.

I stood in the center of the living room and used my cell phone to photograph each wall. I went into the bathroom, which was spectacularly clean. No signs of Glose Entropy. No awful smells. No sunken turds in the toilet. No drifts of simian hair under the sink or boogers on the medicine chest mirror. I photographed the shower and the sink. I came back out and photographed the kitchen.

And then I asked Glose if he wouldn't mind standing under the cougar head. "I should give them a sense of scale," I explained.

He stood under the cougar head, his arms spread in a kind of welcome-to-my-wonderful-life fashion, and waiting until he swallowed his pizza, I got three good shots of him.

On my way to the door I asked how Baylor was doing.

"He's great," Glose said. "Rehearsals couldn't be going better. I've been helping him learn his lines."

"Nice!" I said, perhaps a little cravenly.

"He has a day off on Monday. We might go ice fishing."

"Cool!" I said. "From the virtual to the natural world!"

"He's such a good dude," Glose said.

When I got back to the attic I uploaded the photos to my computer, hooked up my old color-printer-slash-fax-machine, printed the best picture of Glose posing under the cougar head, as well as the following information sheet:

Rodney Glose
5'11"
215 pounds
264 Oneida Street
Apartment 2B
Pollard, Illinois
Friday, 4 p.m.
No allergies.
No phobias.

The time of day would coincide with Baylor's rehearsal schedule, and thereby guarantee his absence. This seemed like a safe plan.

I continue to do my push-ups and sit-ups. I continue to take my penis-enlargement pills. Francis Carl Falbo is on a mission.

To what end, exactly, I cannot say, but this newfound devotion feels good. I haven't thought about Percocet or my desire to float away in a personalized canoe.

I am a man who does push-ups and sit-ups, and who takes penis-enlargement pills, this much I know for sure. I am this man.

Today Haggis stopped by to clean up the front steps and walkway. Though it hasn't snowed in days, they still need to be swept because the two-month-old snow—that old, gray molecular survivor crust—still blows around.

When he came upstairs I handed him an envelope containing the photo of Glose and the required information. He said he would express mail it to the Concierge for me and handed me a DVD.

"This was in that DVD player you gave me," he said. "I thought you might want it."

After he left I inserted the DVD into my laptop. It was a crude home movie of Bethany Bunch, shot in the Bunches' apartment. Bethany is wearing light-blue footy pajamas. She is simply standing, staring at the camera.

"There she is," Mary's voice says. "She can stand like a big girl."

Then Bethany teeters a bit, falls on her rump, and uncorks an infectious laugh.

"Can you stand back up?" This is Todd's voice now. "Can you stand for Daddy?"

And then Bethany pushes off the floor, her bottom high in the air, and manages to achieve verticality. She whirls her arms a bit, teeters again, and then comes to rest, standing successfully. Mary begins singing "Itsy Bitsy Spider." Upon hearing her mother sing, Bethany flails her arms again. She screeches with

joy. Mary and Todd laugh, and then Bethany face-plants, gig-
gling.

The home movie continues this way for eight minutes and
forty-two seconds.

After watching it I realized I might very well have taken from
the Bunches one of the last remnants of their daughter's existence.

March 24.

Though the sun is noticeably brighter, not much thawing has
taken place. No, not in Pollard. The snow that first arrived in
January and grew from there still covers the cold ground with a
dirty, willful crust. The pavement in front of the house is now
finally visible, though it's plagued with scores of salt rime that
resemble the archaeological markings of a vast school of prehistoric jellyfish.

I've been having a crisis of conscience, in turmoil about my
part in the displacement of Glose. I haven't been sleeping much.
I wake in the middle of the night, fearing someone's in the attic.
Glose or some shade of Glose. A silent figurant approaching my
bedside with a knife, ready to flay me, to delicately, surgically
remove one of my kidneys and force me to eat it.

I had planned to simply let the inevitable take its course.
After all, I reminded myself, I detested everything about Glose:
his smell, the maddening unconscious weeping he had brought
upon me, the possibility of petty and non-petty theft, the mali-
cious damage to my boyhood home. I only had to stay out of the
way, go on with my daily routine, to continue to enact my simple life in the attic, and his departure would be accomplished.
But I couldn't help myself. The guilt was too much. I began to
want to pull the plug on the whole operation. As his abduction

neared, I felt as if I'd been swallowing sand in little spoonfuls. I couldn't eat anything else. There was nowhere for the food to go. But I didn't contact the Concierge. The date was set, and despite my misgivings, I just let it come, like some slow, persistent green-eyed demon moving toward me through the fog.

Exactly four days ago this is what went down:

It was the day of reckoning, the advent of spring. Just before the appointed hour, I keyed into Baylor Phebe's apartment, having lost my nerve and come to save Glose before it was too late.

He was in the bathroom with the door closed, likely on the toilet, singing along to the Doobie Brothers' "What a Fool Believes," likely coming from some small radio Baylor kept atop the toilet tank. Glose was actually matching Michael McDonald's impossibly high, soulful falsetto. It occurred to me that I had always underestimated Glose's singing abilities. When we recorded Argon Lights he always nailed overdubs on his first take.

Baylor's apartment was neat, as usual, and smelled of shoe leather. The Concierge was scheduled to arrive in ten minutes. Per my last and final phone conversation with her ("We will never speak again," she said in her soothing GPS voice), I had sent to the designated Pollard post office box a copy of both the front door key and Baylor's apartment keys, along with half of the agreed fee, in cash, which I took from the secret stash that I keep in the attic to pay Haggis for the drugs and any contractors for the work they do on the house. The next wave of communication with the Concierge would also be via mail, when I would receive proof of the completed job with a photo essay and a short report, at which point, as agreed, I would have seventy-two hours to send the remainder of the fee, plus expenses, to the same Pollard post office box. It had been very simply set up, elegantly even. ("For both our safety," the Concierge had said.)

Rodney Daniel Glose, the former drummer of the late, once-promising south-central Illinois indie-rock band the Third Policeman, would soon be out of my house and out of my life, hopefully forever.

Except I hadn't been able to sleep the night before. I'd tossed and turned. I'd assumed the fetal position. I'd lain on my stomach. I'd tented my knees and done deep-breathing exercises. Nothing had worked. I kept imagining Glose being chased by bear, elk, wild boar, hunted by backwoods rednecks with slingshots and eighteenth-century muskets. I saw him being attacked by eagles or scorpions, envisioned him surrounded by crocodiles, or mauled by a shark after regaining consciousness and falling off a defunct oil rig in the Gulf of Mexico.

So now, after that sleepless night, here I was, in Baylor Phebe's apartment, prepared to come clean and call the whole thing off. I was standing just under Baylor's eighty-five-year-old cougar head, waiting for Glose to emerge, the Doobie Brothers' late-seventies hit a tinny, distorted transmission from the bathroom, when I heard someone behind me at the front door. At the insertion of the key, I quickly crossed to Baylor's coat closet and hid. Through a slat in the aluminum closet I was able to see into the living room.

A large man entered.

I assumed it was a man because of the size and the height, which I guessed to be around six-five. He possessed the broad shoulders of an NFL tight end. He was wearing all black—a sort of jumpsuit with a zipper down the front—and a black ski mask over his face, which I found to be wildly clichéd. When he saw the taxidermy coyote in the corner, his body snap-flexed into an impressive ready position, which he quickly released when he realized it wasn't real. His movements were silent and efficient.

Glose was still singing along to the final phrases of "What a Fool Believes," modulating a single line of Michael McDonald's harmonies, pitch-perfect.

The only thing giving the large man away was a tuft of blond hair sneaking out from under the back of his ski mask. Was this in fact the Concierge? Or did the Concierge have an entire roster of minions, different specialists depending on the job requirements?

The Man in Black now held a small dark handgun, complete with silencer extension. The toilet flushed, and Glose entered from the bathroom.

He was naked from the waist down, wearing the familiar Girl Scouts of America T-shirt.

I farted without sound, a horrifying two-measure whisper that was so hot it burned my left testicle and I had to bite my lower lip to keep from sighing painfully.

When Glose saw the Man in Black he ceased singing and made a noise that sounded like <u>whuff</u>.

He hadn't turned the radio off, and "What a Fool Believes" was now being followed by Whitney Houston's "I Wanna Dance with Somebody." This whole thing was going down to forgettable classic late-seventies and eighties pop rock—there was no way around it.

The Man in Black trained the gun on Glose.

Glose put his hands in the air like a bank teller.

"Turn around," the Man in Black commanded. He was trying to disguise his voice. It almost sounded like one of those overemphatic, looped American English deliveries so prevalent in seventies kung fu movies.

Before Glose turned around—during that slow, inevitable one-eighty—his penis appeared to shrink into the insanity of his dark pubic wasteland, his three testicles bouncing in their scrota, then coming to rest.

The Man in Black fired the pistol, which was quieted by the silencer. It made a little pim sound, and a tranquilizer dart with red plumage blooming from the aft end of its silver shaft landed in the center of Glose's sagging, dextral gluteal mass.

"Fung," he said, followed by the far more accessible, classic pain expletive "Ouch."

Literally "Ouch," as if he'd stubbed his toe or been bitten by a horsefly. And with surprisingly little volume. As if the dart had both been painful and hurt his feelings.

Glose took to one knee, then the other.

Whitney Houston was joyously singing for her life, mostly just wanting to dance with any loser with two feet and a haircut.

The Man in Black holstered his gun and from his back pocket produced a nylon duffel bag, also black, which had been tightly rolled. With great efficiency of movement he unfurled and unzipped the duffel bag.

Glose attempted to stand and made it halfway, but that wasn't going to work. He shuffled his feet, the world tilted on him, and he quickly returned to his knees. His arms swam out oddly, as if he were pushing through tall, snarly grass. Then he wheezed heavily and pitched onto his left side, no doubt unconscious as a sack of flour now, the silver tranquilizer dart's brilliant red fletching protruding from his hairy right ass lump.

The Man in Black then impressively negotiated flocculent, half-naked Glose into the duffel bag, zipped it closed, and hoisted the large heavy form onto his shoulder. With relative ease, I might add, as though hoisting a bushel of apples. He exited the apartment and locked the door behind him.

It happened that fast and that simply. All within the context of the Whitney Houston song, which was still playing.

After the door closed I realized I had been holding my breath for some time. I exhaled and urinated hotly down my leg.

At times I think I can hear the house speaking to me. The joists groan like some ancient suffering giant incapable of making words, able only to release these long, dolorous vowels. The exposed truss support beams creak under the eaves like drunken women shrieking. The wind skirls off the steeply pitched gable and through the cracks of my finial window, a spirit child beset by madness.

I have taken down all the snowman drawings and stacked them neatly in a box under my desk.

The mystery of Bethany Bunch lives on, though her presence still haunts my life. The Bunches seem to be drowning... drowning without water, how awful that must feel. To get to that place where even oxygen turns against you. I don't know how they keep going. I guess there is this will in us to continue clocking hours. This little bit of fight left.

Two days ago I was sanding Glose's fork-scrawled words off the front of Kent's bass when there was a knock on my door.

Every knock now stops my heart. If I'm going to be trafficking in criminal activities, however minor they may be, I need to grow thicker skin.

I set the bass down, counted to three, and opened the door.

It was Baylor Phebe. He looked troubled, with those sagging yellow oysters underneath his eyes and deep furrows marking his brow. Only he wasn't wearing a Willy Loman costume this time. He was dressed as himself.

"Baylor," I said, "everything okay?"

"Have you seen Rodney?" he asked.

"No," I said. "Why?"

Baylor said he'd been gone for two days, that he'd been pretty worried.

I told him that Glose and I were old friends and that he'd been known to occasionally up and vanish like that.

Baylor knew about our friendship and about the band, and said that "Rodney" had shared a great deal with him. He said Glose had even told him about his "condition," which was the main reason he was so surprised that he would just disappear without a word.

"What condition?" I said.

"His cancer," Baylor said. "You didn't know about it?"

I had to cover my mouth to keep from screeching like a monkey. Instead I closed my throat and feigned shock and awe.

"The poor guy has stage-four prostate cancer," Baylor continued. "He got it from working in that tire plant in Georgia."

I was gobsmacked. "I had no idea," I said.

"And they won't even honor his medical benefits."

Gobsmacked indeed. I offered that he might have gone to see his mother.

He said that Glose had never mentioned her and asked me where she lived.

"Up in Aurora," I said.

Baylor thought for a moment, his worried expression cauliflowering into one of downright terror. "I have to call her," he said. "Do you know her number?"

I told him that unfortunately I didn't and that she and Rodney had suffered a falling-out some years back. "But if he's stage four," I said, "I could totally see him going to spend some time with her."

"All he has," Baylor said, "is that little bit of money the tire plant gave him to try and keep him quiet."

"Did he say how much that was?" I asked.

"A thousand bucks," Baylor answered. "But you can't live on a measly thousand bucks when you have stage-four prostate cancer. You can't even <u>die</u> right with a thousand bucks."

A tire plant in Georgia? Glose was starting to get creative— downright imaginatively diabolical.

"But going to see his mother makes a lot of sense," Baylor conceded. "Hopefully she'll be able to help him. I pray to God I didn't do anything to drive him away."

I told him that I doubted that very much. Then, to change the subject, I asked how the play was going.

He said it had been going well and that they were scheduled to open in a few weeks. "Sometimes I feel like I have no idea what I'm doing," he said. "Like I'm onstage for no apparent reason. Just another piece of furniture floating around. Other times I feel like I'm getting closer to Willy's soul." He looked down at his hands, the fronts, the backs, as if he wasn't sure whom they belonged to. "Rodney helped me memorize my lines," he continued. "He's helped me so much."

I told him I had no idea they'd gotten so close.

"We've only been together a short time," Baylor said, "but his companionship has meant a lot to me. Poor guy didn't even have any clothes."

I told Baylor that I was sure he meant a lot to Glose too. "Maybe he'll come back to see you in the play," I offered.

Baylor said that that would make him very happy and added, "I really hope he's okay."

"Wherever he is," I said, "I'm sure he's there for a good reason."

*　　*　　*

Today a padded Jiffy mailer was delivered to my attention at the house with no return address. It turned out to be from the Concierge. Inside was a six-shot photo essay of Glose's thousand-mile journey.

Shot One:

The dashboard odometer of what appears to be a standard American-made car: 22,874 miles.

Shot Two:

Glose passed out in the backseat of presumably the same nondescript vehicle, his head resting on his right shoulder, his tongue lolling out of his mouth. He is wearing his Girl Scouts of America T-shirt. He looks pleasantly tranquilized. The shot is framed from the chest up.

Shot Three:

Nearly identical to the second, except that Glose is blindfolded with a ninja-black cloth, still in the backseat, still unconscious, in exactly the same position, his tongue still lolling.

Shot Four:

The dashboard odometer again, exactly one thousand miles greater than the figure in Shot One: 23,874 miles.

Shot Five:

This one is taken from the backseat, with Glose's head and upper torso in profile, his head still resting on his shoulder, his tongue still lolling, but with considerable salivary goop saturating the collar of his T-shirt. The back door is open, and in the background beyond Glose is a vast meadow covered in wildflowers. Definitely a warmer climate. Rolling verdant hills emerge from all sides of the meadow, hills so large they could be construed as mountainous. A lone, solitary bird, perhaps a hawk, is pinned to the pearly gray sky.

Shot Six:

Glose lying in the meadow, on his back, legs straight, arms at his sides. He is wearing a pair of navy Adidas sweatpants with yellow stripes down the sides and, on his feet, cross-trainers, as well as the kelly-green Girl Scouts of America T-shirt. Shot Six was taken directly over his unconscious body. He sleeps among bluebells, forsythia, common milkweed. The photograph is actually quite beautiful. It appears that it was taken at the magic hour. A radiant blueness haloes Glose—wildflowers bursting around the perimeter of his body, bees hoarding pollen, random weedy grasses in the midst of swaying. He is still blindfolded. A canvas backpack rests beside him.

Below the sixth photo, the following text:

> Nice doing business with you, sir.
> Sweatpants and cross-trainers are on the house.
> > Sincerely,
> > The Concierge

*   *   *

March 25.

Today I met the mail person—a stocky woman with thunderous calves and a face like a Gila monster—at the front porch and handed her an overly stamped padded Jiffy mailer containing one thousand dollars and addressed to the Concierge's Pollard post office box.

Weeds get pulled from gardens, dandelions from front lawns. Rotten teeth are extracted. Tumors plucked from among healthier viscera. The infected boil must be lanced.

So, yeah, Glose. That was that.

After the mail exchange I went up to the second floor and finally knocked on Bradley Farnham's unit. Now that the other business, which had been all-consuming, was done, I figured it was time to check on my former brother-in-law.

There was no answer, so I knocked again. I pressed my ear to the door and listened. Nothing. I pulled his key from my maintenance-man retractable key chain and let myself in.

The first thing that hit me was a sharp smell of glue.

The second thing was, well, string. The entire apartment was covered in string, everything neatly, meticulously upholstered in white string. Every square inch of wall and ceiling. The light switches, the electrical outlets. His sofa, his lamp, the floor. Neat, tight, parallel runnels of string.

I turned the light on. The overhead fixture in the living room, also covered in string, glowed softly.

I went into the bathroom. Same story. Every surface, every cubic inch of wall space, every corner, the shower curtain, the showerhead, the bathtub, the drain, the towel rack, the actual towel, the sink, the faucet, the hot and cold knobs, the medicine chest mirror, the doorknobs.

Incredible unending rows of carefully glued string. The

painstaking care was unbelievable. Each row appeared to be perfectly straight, creating an even, complete hide. Its raw commitment took my breath away. I started making that clucking noise again. I just stood there clucking, staring at all the string. I might have clucked for a solid minute.

And then I walked across a short hallway of perfectly upholstered string and went into the bedroom, where Bradley lay on his back, on his string-covered bed, under his string-covered ceiling, surrounded by string-covered walls.

There he was, lying very still, his hands at his sides, arms extended, his feet pointed up, completely mummified in string.

PART FOUR

THE
KEY

The Sun.

Oh the Sun, the Sun, the Magnificent Sun, that Holy Ball of Fire, that Great Gilded Orb of Hope.

It's finally April and only now, alas, has the center of our solar system decided to make a meaningful appearance. There is still snow, but it's melting, little by little, sending rivulets of dirty slush along the curbsides, an endless trickling score of meltwater. The minor music of neighborhood thaw.

In truth, the temperature has barely started to creep over forty degrees. It's not like sundials are lighting up south-central Illinois. The one thing I notice is the sound of cars starting with greater ease. The jumper cables have gone away, as has the cyclonic whine of spinning tires and the endless early-morning windshield chipping.

During the past few days I've effected one major change: I've reduced from two layers of thermals to one, which gives the false impression that I've lost weight.

After the bizarre double whammy of Glose's deportation and Bradley Farnham's string installation, things at the house have pretty much returned to normal. From behind my attic window I live out my days with classic rock (lots of Pink Floyd the past few days), good books (last week The Wind in the Willows, this week Bukowski's <u>Hot Water Music</u>), and enough hand lotion to make Internet porn feel just a tad friendlier.

The one thing I can say about the penis-enlargement pills is this:

Taking them makes you realize how often you look at your penis. I couldn't tell you with what frequency I used to examine the all-important reproductive organ, but I know that I now tug, measure, fiddle, coax, touch, chide, applaud, and just plain stare down at my Johnson at least twelve times a day. I've considered keeping a log of these activities, jotting down the minutiae like some obsessed horticulturalist studying a rare flower, but I opt not to out of fear of someone finding it. <u>Francis Falbo: An Almanac of His Penis and Other Scintillating Errata</u>.

I have not heard from or received any sign of Glose. I think of him as a vibrating killer bee that's been shooed from a stately room containing a comfortable chair. He's still somewhere in the chateau, buzzing down the hallway, plying his finely haired tarsi along a gallery table, or poised on a piece of crystal in a palatial chandelier, but here I rest in said comfortable chair, in profound, luxuriant denial that he might return, making a beeline (<u>literally</u>) for me and sinking his deadly barbed stinger into the side of my neck.

The thing with Bradley and the string was obviously pretty unsettling. I flash back to the moment I found him. I could still feel his warm, sour breath on my cheek coming through the openings at his nostrils, but he wasn't conscious. I poked and prodded him. I called out his name. I seized his shoulders and shook him, but he simply flopped around like a CPR dummy, so I phoned the paramedics and he was taken to Pollard Memorial Hospital to be examined. I gave the paramedics Sheila Anne's phone number, and through arrangements with her, Bradley was admitted to Decatur Manor, a mental-health facility where he's been for the past week or so.

I learned all of this from none other than Sheila Anne, who called to update me on her brother's situation and to tell me that she was flying in from New York.

She asked if she could see me.

Of course I said that that would be okay, but overplayed the cool—nonchalant as a jazz drummer wearing a Moroccan djellaba. I was so cool she thought I wasn't interested.

"Should I not have asked?" she said.

"No," I said. "Let's get together..." The only thing missing from my response was the word back, which would have fit nicely between get and together. Because still, two full years after her departure, that's all I've been able to think about:

Us.

And the far-fetched possibility of our reunion.

I told her that she would have to come to the house to see me, that I was nursing a strained lower back. (Yes, my fictitious ailment has become more specifically located in the sacral area. I've been boning up on my spinal vernacular. The disc between L5 and S1 is now bulging onto my sciatic node, though I didn't share these details with Sheila Anne.) Stairs were off-limits, I told her, strict doctor's orders.

She asked me how I had hurt my back.

"I sort of broke it getting over you," I joked.

Our digital cellular airspace all but went dead. I imagined her biting the inside of her cheek, which she always did when she was uncomfortable or disgusted with me.

I told her about what I'd done to the house, listing the various renovations, etc., how I was now living in the attic, and how, despite what might sound like a depressing garret life, I was a bona fide landlord.

"Lord Francis," she said.

We decided on seven p.m. for dinner. I said we could order sushi and drink Maker's neat, just like old times.

She said that she couldn't do sushi.

I asked her why and she said, "I'm sort of watching what I eat."

After the phone call I fended off a panic attack by punching myself in the thigh several times. Then I combed my beard and contemplated shaving it off, but ultimately came to the conclusion that fuck it, she should see me as I am now: messy-haired, thermalized, bathrobed, slippered, and wildly bearded.

I called Haggis and asked him if he wouldn't mind bringing me a new pair of slippers—they could be cheap. I didn't want Sheila Anne to have the satisfaction of knowing I was hanging on to vestiges of our marriage. The wool ergonomic Norwegian slippers were a gift from her after all. That night Haggis brought me a pair of fur-lined pleather slippers that looked like a pair of overstuffed carnival dogs.

When Sheila Anne was a few blocks away she texted me and I met her at the front porch. I had decided to put on actual clothes, which consisted of a pair of gray corduroys, a plaid flannel shirt with a navy-blue cardigan over it, and the slippers Haggis had brought me. I even wore a belt.

Sheila Anne arrived at dusk and parked her rental car out front. Her walk to the porch felt interminable. For a moment I thought I was dreaming. "Don't start sucking," I said aloud, and punched myself in the thigh.

Sheila Anne was wearing casual clothes, jeans and a sweater underneath a man's gray wool overcoat. On her feet, a pair of off-white Chuck Taylor low-tops. On her head, a wool hat, cornflower blue. She was dressed similarly to the days when I first met her when she was still living in Louisville. There was a careless, random logic to her style back then, as if she kept things in muddled piles and pulled her outfits out of them with little or no thought. I guess I'd been expecting the pharmaceutical sales rep. The corporate dealmaker. A pantsuit with heels. Bleached teeth and salon-fresh hair. An expensive scarf.

We hugged hello. She smelled citrusy, clean. She wore no makeup. There was still a faint blue vein on the wing of her left nostril. She appeared not to have aged a single day since she'd walked out, two years earlier.

She said, "You have a beard."

"I do," I said. "It's getting cowlicks." I showed her one and she tugged on it and I forced a smile.

"Just making sure it's real," she said.

I took her down to the basement, moving gingerly, feigning the bad back, and showed her all the renovations: the laundry room, the dropped gypsum ceiling, the storage space, the paneling along the hallway, the two apartments. She seemed impressed. Then we went upstairs to look at the pair of apartments on the second floor. When we reached Bradley's unit she placed her hand on the door.

"I want to see it," she said.

I keyed in and turned on the light. I hadn't touched the string. Everything was exactly as it had been. You could see the indentations of the gurney wheels and the shoe prints from the paramedics.

I took her into the bathroom. She opened the medicine chest. Even his toiletries were covered in string. A tube of toothpaste. A cylinder of shaving gel. A rectangle of deodorant stick.

Next was the bedroom. Sheila Anne was stunned, to say the least. At one point she lost her balance and had to use the wall to steady herself, obviously creeped out by the strange world her brother had created, the relentlessness of it, the actual texture of the string, the meticulous care.

She said that Bradley had told the psychiatrist at Decatur Manor that he was trying to become Nothing. That if he became string in a box of string he would become Nothing.

I asked her where he would even come across a concept like that and she simply shook her head. I told her about my few encounters with La-Trez, who seemed to have some vague romantic connection to Bradley, but that beyond this, he'd been mostly an enigma, hard to reach, remote even when talking face-to-face.

"He looks really thin," she said. "He was undernourished and dehydrated. They're feeding him intravenously."

Up in the attic we ordered burritos and chips and guacamole from Uribe's, a local Mexican restaurant owned by a former Chicago White Sox infielder. While waiting for the food, I offered a mug of Maker's neat but she declined.

"Water's fine," she said.

We sat together at my kitchen island. I asked her about New York. She spoke of the energy on the street, the sheer volume of pedestrians, the subway cars, the old Ukrainian Hall just outside her apartment on Second Avenue.

"So you don't live in a high-rise?"

"We live in a third-floor walk-up," she said. "Our living room floor tilts east to west. You should see how much speed a tennis ball can gain from one corner of the room to the other. But it has its charms."

Although her office was in Midtown, she said she was there only a few times a week and spent most of her time on the road or in an airplane, making sales calls. Her region was Pennsylvania, Ohio, and New York State. She didn't mind the travel but wasn't crazy about the hours. "There's lots of entertaining," she said. "Dinners, cocktails, schmoozing. It's a far cry from working at a south-central Illinois hospital."

"And Dennis?" I asked.

He covered New York City exclusively; he was the envy of all the other reps.

"But he's earned it," she added. She got up and looked out the window, gazing down at the street for a long time.

"What are you thinking about?" I asked.

"Your mother," she said. "Her last few days. I was thinking about how quiet things were. It was like the house was waiting too, like it had its own thoughts. It was so peaceful."

It was true—there had been a rare graceful silence during those last few days. Grandma Ania had come down from Chicago. My aunts and uncles and a few Polish cousins were there too. Some people read. Sheila Anne and I played gin. Nobody talked on their cell phones. If a call came in, the person took it to the back porch. It was strange having such a full house overcome with respectful quiet.

When my mother finally went, she did so serenely. I was in her hospice room with Sheila Anne, who sat next to me on an old love seat we'd moved in there. Lyman was asleep on the living room sofa. He'd been watching <u>The Money Pit</u>, Cornelia's favorite movie, with the sound turned down. My young cousin Bronia was asleep beside him, her head on his shoulder. Bronia's little sister, Halina, was next to her, also asleep.

The moment of death was barely discernible, like a patch of snow dissolving into a stream. The hospice nurse on duty, a fair, willowy man named Chad, had to tell us.

"That's it," he said. "She's gone."

I went out to the living room and put my hand on Lyman's shoulder. Somehow he knew from my touch. He simply looked up and nodded.

"You were so good with her," I told Sheila Anne, who was still looking out the window. "Lyman could barely go in her room. He was such a coward."

"I was just more comfortable around someone in decline. Don't be so hard on your father," she added. "He does the best he can."

I told Sheila Anne that I dream about my mother. That I often wake up with an ache. I didn't tell her that she, Sheila Anne, was involved in that ache too. I didn't need to. I'm convinced that part of leaving someone is carefully arranging the pain that will be left behind. Like gluing a broken dinner plate to the wall.

While we ate she said she liked what I'd done with the attic. "It's cozy," she offered.

I told her about all the stuff I'd had to clear away before the renovation. There had been boxes of clothes, an entire library of children's books, a baby crib full of cookbooks, endless stacks of telephone books, decades' worth of Lyman's <u>Sports Illustrated</u> and <u>Golf</u> magazines. Footlockers filled with old sheets— seemingly hundreds of perfectly folded sheets in nearly a dozen footlockers.

"I never would've thought your parents were hoarders."

I told her there'd been a family of raccoons, that I'd had to call the ASPCA and have them come down from Urbana so the raccoons could be removed "humanely." Which basically meant they were fed canned dog food laced with tranquilizers and then put in cages and flung in the back of a van so banged up it looked like it could have belonged to someone who'd acquired multiple DUIs.

"And now you have yourself a little bachelor pad," Sheila Anne said. She asked if I was seeing anyone.

"No," I said. "No one."

"Why not?" she said.

I offered something about the local slim pickings.

"Do you have to stay in Pollard? Couldn't you hire a super to be on-site here?"

"Where would I go?"

"Chicago, St. Louis, Cleveland. Anywhere. The women would line up."

A cold blade turned in my stomach. To change the subject and avoid the slide into self-pity, I asked her about Bradley, about what the mental hospital was planning for him.

They'd immediately started a round of psychoactive medication, she said. The diagnosis was mild schizophrenia with paranoid tendencies. He'd apparently tried to attack the nurses when they started removing the string he'd glued to his body. "He went at their eyes," she said. "He's in restraints."

I asked her what drug they had him on.

"Thorazine," she said, "the great affect eliminator. They theorize it'll be good for the paranoia and delusional stuff."

I imagined Bradley shuffling around in a hospital garment, blank-faced and drooling, with stunned koala-bear eyes, clutching an empty Dixie cup.

"I don't know where it comes from," she added. "Major mental illnesses don't exactly run in our family." She added that she'd always assumed Bradley's problems were far subtler than delusions of grandeur.

Then she asked me about my tenants and I went down the list. The Bunches and their missing daughter. Harriet Gumm, the artist college student. Bob Blubaugh, the Most Neutral

Man in the World. And Baylor Phebe, the sixty-two-year-old former-junior-high-school-teacher-turned-actor. I told her that he was a widower, that he'd been cast in the Arthur Miller play, that he had an amazingly large stomach and surprisingly light feet.

She asked about the band, where everybody was, if I'd been in contact with anyone.

"No," I said. "Everyone's doing other things."

I had no interest in bringing up the recent appearance of Glose and what I'd done.

Then she asked me if I was writing any music.

"I noodle around on the guitar, but that's about it."

"You're through with it?" she asked.

"I don't know," I said. "I'd like to think that I'll get hungry for it again at some point." I didn't dare tell her that the simple thought of being in public almost caused a panic attack.

After we ate I put on one of our favorite records, Steely Dan's Aja. Sheila Anne and I have always loved Donald Fagen's voice, but it's the band's arrangements, their studio work, and their overall songwriting that have consistently blown my mind.

As soon as I showed her the album cover, a certain sweetness passed over her face.

During the bass-line intro to "Black Cow," she laughed. Back in our marriage we'd endlessly talked about how the beginning of that track inspires an inexplicable silly feeling. It always made Sheila Anne imagine someone in a black turtleneck and handle-bar mustache, carrying a banana cream pie topped off with loads of Cool Whip, mischievously sneaking around to the beat in some totally choreographed tippy-toes way, looking for a face to victimize.

The sound of her laugh alone cured me of all my woes for at

least the next ten minutes. She had to know that by playing Aja I was pushing old sentimental buttons, but how could I not?

She said, "You know the guitar part in this is the background music on a commercial for a top-selling erectile dysfunction pill?"

"That's amazing," I said. "Good for Steely Dan."

"The important things you learn on the job." Then she told me she liked my beard, that it somehow brought out my eyes.

We were sitting on my couch now, our backs against the armrests, facing each other, the rich smell of Mexican food still lingering. I was drinking Maker's neat out of a coffee mug. I set the mug down and put my hands on hers. We took each other in for a moment. I was convinced that we were going to make out. But then she slid her hands out from under mine and returned them safely to her lap.

"How's the back?" she asked.

"Right now it's fine," I said. "This position is fairly painless."

It was more than painless, in fact, it was perfect. This was perfection. Just how things used to be. Mexican food and three fingers of Maker's and some classic vinyl.

"How did you hurt it?" she asked.

I told her it had locked up on me one day when I was bending down to pick up my laundry basket, that I had likely slipped a disc, but that "my spine guy" thought if I rested, the bulge would recede. I was so convinced by my own lie that I actually could see the moment clearly in my head: bending down to lift a laundry basket and then everything locking up, me crumpling to my knees, pitching onto my side, calling out for help from the laundry room floor. "All those years of lugging amps around," I added. "It was bound to catch up to me."

She'd slid off her sneakers and was flexing her toes to the music. She wore white athletic socks that had grayed on the bottoms.

During the title track, the epic "Aja," I asked her if she was happy.

"In what way?" she said.

"In the only way."

"You mean with Dennis?"

Hearing her say his name did something to my throat. It felt like my Adam's apple had been snagged with a fishhook.

"Do I not seem happy?" she said.

"Do you guys have this?" I said.

"It's different," she said. "We have our own 'this.'"

"The New This," I said.

"Yeah, the New This," she said.

"Good album name," I said. "The New This."

She just shook her head and smiled.

"What about 'stuff'?" I said.

"Stuff?" she said.

"Issues. Please tell me you have issues."

"Generally speaking, our 'stuff' is the good kind."

"Do you guys order Mexican food and put your feet on the sofa and listen to classic Steely Dan on well-preserved vinyl?"

She smiled again, impenetrably.

"Do you have equally argued, heated but spirited American film debates about Tootsie versus, say, Fast Times at Ridgemont High?"

"Or Blade Runner versus E.T.?" she said, playing along.

"I still can't believe how much you like E.T."

"I could never get how much you liked Cat People," she countered.

"Like," I said. "Let's keep it in the present tense. Cat People is a hidden classic. Twenty years from now Cat People will still be talked about. What would a nine-year-old boy in the middle of Illinois have done without Nastassja Kinski? You were only four then. You had no concept of how, say, A Flock of Seagulls was shaping the minds of a generation. You were busy watching Fraggle Rock."

"I was a pretty precocious four-year-old," she said. "And don't start dissing Fraggle Rock. Fraggle Rock was an allegorically complex weekly television masterpiece."

I drank from the coffee mug and said, "What would Dennis say if he saw us like this?"

She didn't answer.

"Would he be pissed? Would he want to fight me?"

She remained silent.

"I could still make you happy, Sheila Anne. I can change," I heard myself say.

She looked at me for a long moment. I had always thought she was most beautiful at the end of the night, when she was tired. Her lids would get heavy, her face would soften, the little cleft of worry between her pale peach brows would finally disappear.

She said, "I'm pregnant, Francis."

It felt like a low-flying jet had just decapitated me at the precise moment my heart crawled into my mouth.

I think an entire minute passed. I'm not sure I moved. I had the distinct feeling that I was turning to hay. Not a scarecrow, but an actual bale of useless lost hay.

Eventually Sheila Anne said, "It's one of the reasons I came here tonight. I wanted to tell you in person."

I asked her how far along she was and she said twenty-two weeks. I imagined the sonograms, the morning sickness, Dennis Church lovingly pulling her hair back for her while she vomits into the toilet.

"No sushi," I said. "I get it now."

"No sushi, no steak tartare, no raw cookie dough. No whiskey."

Another minute passed.

Some part of Dennis Church was inside her. A little blind fetus contorted into itself, translucently pale, palsied, parasitic, its alien head too large for its body.

To my mind came the word <u>defenestration</u>, the act of throwing a person out a window. I had an impulse to run at my lone attic window, to actually run <u>through</u> it headlong and defenestrate myself.

I drank some more bourbon and said, "So you're keeping it?"

"Yes," she replied.

I asked her if Dennis knew.

"Of course he knows."

I asked her if they'd been trying to get pregnant.

"Yes," she said again.

Her yeses were like little colored discs of poison I was being forced to swallow, and yet I kept talking. "So things must be really good," I said.

She nodded, sparing me the actual yes this time.

I told her she didn't look pregnant.

"Well, I certainly feel pregnant," she said.

I asked her if it was a girl or a boy.

"Boy," she said.

"When we talked about having kids you said you wouldn't want to know."

Then she offered the age-old platitude: "People change."

I'd always wanted to have a little girl, though it was something I never told Sheila Anne. We rarely talked about kids. We didn't have enough money, so it just wasn't practical. I wanted a little girl with Sheila Anne's strawberry blond hair and her freckles that emerged every summer, and with my mother's sad-sweet Polish eyes.

I told her not to take what I'd said about her not looking pregnant the wrong way. "You actually look pretty amazing," I said.

She thanked me, and I told her she always looked amazing and then I lost it bad. I started crying, and while at first I could swallow most of it, then there was too much, like an entire feast of sadness, and it just came out, raging up my throat like something I'd actually eaten. Part of me wanted her to be disgusted by it, to be driven away by such a lame, self-pitying response, but instead she took my head in her hands and lowered it to her lap.

She and Dennis Church were having a boy.

He would probably be beautiful. He would chase urban butterflies and frolic in concrete playgrounds. By the age of three he would learn to hail a taxi. They would take him to the opera at four. By five he would begin conjugating French verbs. He would be exceptional, perfectly appointed, a wunderkind. They would name him something like Hudson or Dane.

"Deacon Blues" started, the final track of side one, a seven-and-a-half-minute masterpiece that should be played while driving along some oceanside vista in a '65 Mustang convertible with the top down.

This is the day of the expanding man . . .

I imagined their little boy as a toddler with long Raphaelite hair (our little girl is trapped in this boy after all), then as a preschooler, then as a first grader with Popsicle-stained lips and mosquito-bitten arms (tough, urban mosquitoes), Sheila Anne walking hand in hand with him, dropping him off at some elite private school in New York City, wiping his face with a eucalyptus-scented Wet-Nap before kissing him good-bye.

After I stopped crying, when the song had finally ended and there had been a good minute of needle-in-the-gutter silence, without lifting my head from her lap, I looked up and told Sheila Anne that this small part of me keeps hoping against hope that she'll come to her senses and return to me, that eventually, inevitably, we'll find our way back to each other.

She nodded, clearly not in agreement, but to display a kind of dull, tragic acknowledgment.

"Do you ever think about that?" I asked.

Again, no answer. "You have every right to make me a monster," she said.

I told her that I wished there was a way I could hate her, that it would probably be easier that way, but that I couldn't succeed even at demonizing her. All the cheating and the secrecy at the end simply didn't have enough poison in them to blot out my deepest feelings. I admitted that I had drawn naked pictures of her in the margins of this manuscript, that the slippers I was wearing were in fact impostors that Haggis had brought by earlier, and that in truth I wore her ergonomic Norwegian wool ones every day, almost dutifully, and that I'd stowed them under my bed in an old pillowcase so she wouldn't have the satisfaction of seeing them.

We sat that way, with my head in her lap, for a long time. She even started to stroke my temples, in little counterclockwise circular motions, a tenderness that made me feel so vulnerable I had the sensation that I was turning to powder.

The bliss of that soft lap. Her delicate fingers. I felt like I had returned to some soporific velveteen womb world.

Eventually I fell asleep.

When I woke up she was in the bathroom, talking on her cell phone. She had powered down the turntable and re-sleeved the Steely Dan record, just as she would have when we were together. I wondered if she was enjoying revisiting these old simple rituals, or if they sickened her, if she was executing them only for my sake, as some gesture of forced kindness. By the time she came out of the bathroom, I was sitting up on the sofa.

"Dennis?" I said.

She simply looked at me.

I asked her if everything was okay.

"It's late," she said. "I should go." Another disc of poison, this one white. The colorless, tasteless killer.

"Stay," I pleaded. "Just this one night."

She said she couldn't. She had a hotel room in Decatur, and she needed to be up early for an important meeting about Bradley with the Decatur Manor head psychiatrist.

She came over and sat next to me on the sofa.

I wanted her to tell me that she still listened to my music. I wanted her to take my face in her hands and not put it in her lap but kiss my eyes instead. I would close them just before her lips met my lids, like a child getting tucked in. But neither of those things happened. What happened was she put her head on my shoulder and then I leaned my face on her head. I regretted the decision to not shave my beard, because if I had, then I would have felt her head with my actual face, which would have offered enough pleasure to last me another six months.

At her rental car we said good-bye and hugged and I held on a little too long. She indulged me and I'm sure it made her sick to be enveloped by all my neediness but she indulged me.

It was after three a.m. when Sheila Anne pulled off down Oneida Street. I found myself walking in the same direction, following her taillights, ambling mindlessly past the Schefflers' lesser Victorian; past Darrell and Carol Stroh's modern solar-paneled block-shaped monstrosity; past the Gordons' and the Neugabauers' and then the Lindholms' tall, thin Tudor; past a little powder-blue clapboard ranch house with pink shutters and barren flower boxes inhabited by an old widow with some imponderable number of cats.

I turned left on Geneseo Street and another left on Waverly Lane and I found myself heading toward an open field covered with snow. The field is long and contains a platoon of 500-kilovolt power lines that issue a drifty, somnambulant buzzing not unlike early-summer cicadas. This was where, as young boys, Kent and a few other neighborhood kids and I would play baseball and Smear the Queer and rough-touch football. In later years it became a favorite place to smoke cigarettes and roaches stolen from Kent's older brother, Harry, and where we'd drink twelvers of Old Style and pints of peach schnapps and Mad Dog 20/20 in addition to whatever we could smuggle out of our parents' liquor cabinets. The "Radio Trees," as we called them, seemed blessed with some miraculous Holy Hand of Youth, as the cops never made an appearance.

There is a stand of woods along one side, and I sat there in the snow and stared up at the blue-black sky, which was hung with a smattering of stars and a weak smudge of moon. I was still wearing only the cardigan and plaid flannel shirt. Haggis's gift slippers weren't suitable for this kind of adventure, but the cold felt good. The seat of my corduroys was getting soaked. The crisp, aqueous air was almost drinkable and I felt more at ease under the buzz of those power lines than I had in months.

For the briefest moment I thought I might be asleep, perhaps experiencing some sort of lucid dream. I leaned back on my elbows and let my shoulders meet the cold ground. The snow was bracing. My breath plumed above me.

Sheila Anne was well on her way to Decatur by now, and though it wasn't even a hundred miles away, I had the sense that she was traveling a much greater distance, some epic expanse you read about in frontier novels. I imagined her rental car as a hovering egg, slowly receding into the night until it was merely a speck, then nothing. A fleeting feeling of peace, unaided by drugs, descended upon me, perhaps helped along by the Maker's Mark, but there nonetheless.

I'm not sure how long I lay there. It might have been twenty minutes, but it also could have been hours. The power lines buzzed hypnotically. A distant dog barked. The breeze periodically rattled the naked trees. I ate a handful of snow. It tasted salty, dirty, earthen.

The first hints of dawn were washing out the moon and I took this as my cue to make my way home. When I got to my feet the back of my sweater was soaked, as was the seat of my corduroys and the back of my head. I walked away from the field, still feeling dreamy, half-expecting to encounter a talking animal, some Pollardian black bear, briefly emerging from hibernation to remark upon the shape of my soul or advise me about the direction of my life.

I turned right onto Waverly, and then another right onto Geneseo. I found myself walking down the middle of the street, passing trees and yards and cars and snow-heaped gables. Telephone poles and ceramic lawn creatures that seemed to follow me with their eyes as I passed them: a deer, a rabbit, a knowing red fox, a stone owl perched on a mailbox. The months-old remains of a Nativity scene, all the characters gone, but the manger, the firewood-quality lean-to, and the scattered hay still there.

There were lights left on in kitchens, garages with initials stenciled on their faces.

Moonlight glowed softly on the windows. My hometown asleep, breathing in unison. I had the sensation that they were dreaming me, that I was a mere figment of their collective slumber. My feet seemed to be moving on their own, slightly ahead of my thoughts.

As I turned onto Oneida Street, I could see my house wedged between the Schefflers' lesser Victorian and the Coynes' Tudor, my boyhood home small in the distance, fablelike, a place for dolls and miniature lamps and intricate toy furniture, too tiny to be any man's entire world, too insubstantial to be stuffed with misery and secrets and lost, rarefied air. I walked toward it, delicately drunk with the predawn air of this long, cold night, treading lightly through the rags of snow still plaguing the pavement, my feet surprisingly warm and dry in my new slippers. Eventually I made my way up to the attic, where I fell into a deep, dreamless sleep.

*   *   *

By the end of the first full week in April the snow had thawed and temperatures were consistently staying in the midforties. One day it reached fifty-two degrees and the Coyne children took their bikes out and zoomed up and down the street. The sound of birds broke with the dawn.

At night the stars were out, incredible in their arrangements, along with the soft blue pulsing of a distant planet.

With the warmth I've returned to wearing normal clothes. T-shirts and old sweats mostly. Jeans and cords. And Sheila Anne's slippers.

Two days ago, at long last, the key arrived via FedEx with a note from Lyman:

> Son,
> I found that key. Enjoy the shelter. Hopefully you'll never have to make use of it.
> > Love,
> > Dad

The lock was a little stiff, so I sprayed some WD-40 into the slot. The door wasn't as heavy as I'd anticipated. Beneath it, a cement stairwell led to a short cement hallway. With a flashlight I found a light switch and flipped it on. A fluorescent overhead flickered. The small gray hallway, smoothly paved, gave way to a four-hundred-square-foot room covered with gray industrial carpeting. There were three bunks housed in the wall—basically human-sized shelves with mattresses. They were neatly made with bottom and top sheets, generic wool blankets, and pillows. The whole shelter had the feel of a military barracks.

There was an old Sylvania SuperSet on a small stand and, underneath the TV stand, a series of board games from the midseventies: Monopoly, Yahtzee, Parcheesi, Operation. I thought it odd that a VCR was rigged up to the TV, since Lyman said the shelter had been built in the early seventies. In front of the TV stand a coffee table held magazines: <u>National Geographic</u>, <u>Sports Illustrated</u>, <u>Golf</u>, <u>Mademoiselle</u>. A small bookcase along one wall contained many of my mother's favorite paperbacks: John Irving's <u>The World According to Garp</u>, Styron's <u>Sophie's Choice</u>, Salinger's <u>Nine Stories</u>, Updike's <u>Rabbit, Run</u>, Anne Tyler's <u>The Accidental Tourist</u>, among others.

Also on the coffee table, which was set in front of a convertible oatmeal-colored sofa, was an electric daisy wheel typewriter, plugged into an outlet but powered off. There was no paper in it. Beside the sofa was a floor lamp, which contained an old fifty-watt bulb. I turned on the lamp and miraculously it worked.

The room smelled surprisingly fresh. I'd expected dust and mold. The ceiling joists were visible. The raw, unstained lumber looked freshly cut. The ceiling itself was perhaps seven feet high. It made you want to sit on the floor. The shelter had obviously been made well, airtight. Uncle Corbit and his crew didn't cut any corners.

Against another wall was a small refrigerator and a series of cabinets. In the cabinets, a huge assortment of canned goods, enough to last months. One cabinet contained four standard-issue military gas masks. Beside the gas masks, a sleeve of iodine tablets and a first-aid kit. There were a half-dozen office-cooler jugs of water lined up against the back wall, with a rectangular dispenser unit set beside them. A coffeemaker on a countertop, beside it an electric double-burner stovetop.

The bathroom, complete with a shower, sink, and toilet, was so small you had to draw your knees up to your chest just to be able to sit. I flushed the toilet, and it worked perfectly. On the top of the tank was a copy of Dostoyevsky's <u>Crime and Punishment</u>, half-opened, facing down. In the margins, my mother's tiny handwriting. Little notes in blue ink. Perfect as frost. She'd been underlining passages. It was a Penguin Classics edition, from 2003. It suddenly dawned on me that Cornelia had been using the bomb shelter as some sort of private sanctuary.

The shelter was powered by a dynamo generator that was outfitted with a car battery and a hand crank. There were three additional car batteries stacked beside it, still in their boxes. I cranked the generator several times. An orange light flickered and it whined to life. Beside it, on the cement floor, was a ham radio, which was plugged into the generator. It crackled to life. I felt like I was slipping into another time. I turned the dial on the ham radio, tuned in to what sounded like a traffic report. There was road construction on Interstate 55, thirty-minute delays on the outskirts of St. Louis. I turned off the ham radio, powered down the generator.

I was struck by the three bunks, each perfectly made in that hyperneat angular crispness of the Polish. My grandparents' home in Chicago had been as clean as a museum, everything in its place. My mother's folding of clothes fresh out of the dryer was a thing of military precision. She took pride in proper creases and sharp corners. There was careful consideration of the family unit. If something were to happen, she wanted our beds to be right.

One of the bunks had a slight depression in it. Perhaps this was where my mother took her naps, dozing off while reading? I inhaled deeply into the pillow, but it revealed nothing. It smelled mostly of camphor. Underneath this bunk was a cardboard stationery box. I opened it. Inside was a manuscript. The cover sheet read:

A Certain Kind of Melancholy Sadness
by Cornelia Wyrwas Falbo

I turned the cover page over to reveal a dedication:

<u>For Francis</u>

The long story, or novella, too long to reproduce verbatim here, concerns a young man, home from his first semester at an elite college in the Northeast. He sneaks into a neighbor's home and brutally murders a young couple with a hammer and then abducts their three-year-old daughter, all while she's sleeping.

He takes her in a car and they drive hundreds of miles away, through a blizzard, until they happen upon an abandoned farmhouse, which has suffered some terrible calamity. It still has furniture, pots and pans on the stove, canned goods in the cupboards, but everything is in disarray. The furniture has been toppled, flung every which way; things have been strewn from shelves. In one room, a grandfather clock has been driven through the wall.

The young man's name is Francis.

The little girl is simply referred to as "the Girl" or occasionally "the Young Girl."

Francis uses the hammer—the actual murder weapon—to fix up the house. He drives nails into the walls to hang fallen pictures. He repairs a broken section of the staircase so they can go up to the second floor, where things are in similar disarray. There he fixes up a bedroom, reuniting a mattress and box spring, lifting a bureau and pushing it against the wall, picking up the shards of a broken mirror. This is the room where they will sleep.

On one wall hangs a crucifix; opposite this wall, a framed painting of a clown with balloons in its cheeks. It used to be a child's room. The wallpaper—bear cubs on tricycles—suggests as much. The little girl opens a drawer to the bureau, removes a knit scarf, claims it as her own.

They go into the other rooms and take the blankets off the beds. They know they will have to endure the winter.

There is the sense that Francis is leaving the life that he knew; that he is leaving it forever. Francis never tells the little girl what he did to her parents and she never asks about them.

The little girl is happy.

It eventually becomes clear that the farmhouse has been damaged by a terrible storm. A part of the house, the back porch, had been ripped away. They find it hundreds of feet from the property, sitting in a frozen field like some kind of strange boat at the bottom of a dry riverbed. They find three bodies there as well, splayed a great distance from each other, a boy and two older people, perhaps the boy's parents, but it's impossible to tell because animals have eaten the flesh off their faces. Birds have pecked away the eyes. Their limbs are twisted in odd, inhuman ways. Were they the owners of the house?

Francis and the little girl decide not to venture outside until the spring.

There is a fireplace in the living room, a huge pile of wood beside the hearth. Francis opens the flue and builds a fire and warms them.

They discover canned goods in the cupboards. Jars of preserves. Cases of oatmeal and powdered milk. They will have food to last the winter.

Francis finds a rifle in the basement and a box of shells. They will be safe.

At night, despite his age, they sleep together in the same bed, but it's innocent. It's as if they are both young children.

Slowly, over a period of days, they clean up the house, right all the toppled furniture, put things back in the cupboards, restore each item to its proper place. Francis manages to pull the grandfather clock out of the wall. Once upright, it starts to work again. He sets the time to his liking, disinterested in it matching the world outside. He and the Young Girl are making their own time now, creating their own private history.

They start to wear the clothes of the dead family. Francis teaches the little girl to read and write.

One day a wolf gets in the house. Francis shoots it with the rifle. He skins and dresses it and they eat it. With its hide he makes the little girl a hat, and she wears it proudly.

After the snow stops, five cows suddenly appear in one of their fields. Three to milk and two to slaughter. Francis corrals them and keeps them in a shelter near the house.

One day the little girl asks Francis why they never leave. He promises her that someday they will. When the time is right they will go beyond the field where they found the bodies. But until then they must continue working on the house, repairing all that is lost and broken.

Toward the end of the story there is a strange jump in time— twenty-some years go by in a single paragraph. They are still living in the house, which has become a safe, reliable home. In a matter of sentences several seasons pass. The fields are flourishing, and Francis and the little girl have become successful farmers. They have many cows.

In the final paragraph Francis is middle-aged and the little girl is now his wife. It is winter again. It ends with them walking into one of their fields, trudging through the snow, holding hands, heading toward a dark forest. Francis places his hand on the now-adult little girl's stomach, suggesting a child.

It took me hours to read the story.

My mother hadn't bothered with numbering the pages, so I had no idea how large the manuscript actually was. Time seemed to stop. I was incredibly moved by it, though also disturbed, and I had a hard time fathoming why my mother had not only dedicated it to me, but also given the young man my name.

Was this abduction relationship somehow drawn from her experience with Lyman? Was the little girl her? Had Lyman kidnapped her from her Wicker Park bed-and-breakfast in Chicago? Had she seen him as having rescued her from some terrible life?

But if she was the little girl and I was Francis, what did that mean? Had my mother seen me as a killer? Her protector? Her lover?

The more I thought, the more confused I got. Perhaps there was no relationship to anything in her life. Perhaps she simply liked the sound of the name Francis—the music it makes in the reader's head—and the dedication had been a totally separate idea. The Francis in the story isn't physically described in any specific way. He is quieter than I was at that age, and certainly riskier.

I know this much:

I was surprised at how well my mother wrote. Not that I'm some expert. But her prose was clear and purposeful, with very few flourishes. I didn't catch a single spelling error. I wondered how long she had worked on it. How many drafts she'd pored over. There was a dark innocence at play, even in the simplicity of the language. The whole thing was deceptively complex.

I had no idea she'd had this secret life below the basement. This subbasement persona, if you will. I spent an hour scouring the place for more pages—I looked in cupboards, under sofa cushions, underneath the sink in the bathroom—but I found nothing.

Was this story her life's work? Perhaps, while Lyman was away at the office each day, she'd been shaping it for years, polishing each sentence like some hermit jeweler perfecting a diamond. Had Lyman even known that she wrote? You think you know your family—your own mother—and then this incredible secret emerges.

I fell asleep on the bunk and dreamed I was running through a field of heliotropes, running like a man whose legs were broken. I was barefoot and there were thorns hidden beneath the rich purple petals. The puncture wounds shot through my femurs. I had the horrible sensation that I was being chased by birds. They screeched above me, thousands of them, blackening the sky like pepper. I was running as fast as I could, stumbling across the thorny field, but it was no use.

When I woke, Bob Blubaugh was kneeling beside me. There I was again, reflected in the lenses of his tinted glasses.

I had no idea where I was. "Bob," I said.

"I heard noises," he said. "Someone was crying out. I thought something terrible was happening."

I asked him the time. He said it was nine thirty. I had been down in the bomb shelter for over seven hours.

"You were crying out," he said again.

I asked him what I was saying, and he replied that he couldn't tell; for a moment, he had thought it was an animal.

"This is some shelter," Bob marveled.

I took the stationery box with me. After I closed and locked the door, I added the key to my retractable maintenance-man leash and made my way upstairs.

When I emerged onto the front porch, a woman was sitting on the wicker furniture. She was reading a book, using her cell phone for light. She wore a winter coat and a Milwaukee Brewers baseball cap.

"Can I help you?" I asked.

"I'm just waiting for my dad," she said. "He told me to wait for him here."

"You're Baylor's daughter."

"Emily," she replied, nodding.

I crossed to her and offered my hand. "Francis," I said. "I own the house."

We shook. Her hand was small and delicate and cold.

"It's not exactly warm out here," I said.

"It's okay," she said. "I've been cooped up in the car all day."

I told her there was a pair of space heaters that I could easily get for her.

"I'm really okay," she insisted.

Though it was dark and she was wearing the baseball cap, I could make out her soft, open face, her round eyes. She was prettier than her photo strip. I invited her in for a cup of coffee but she politely declined.

"He said he would be here after his rehearsal. It shouldn't be too much longer."

She added that she'd driven down from Milwaukee and was planning on staying through the upcoming week.

"You came down for the opening?"

"Next Friday's the big night," she replied. "You going?"

I told her that I'd love to but I probably couldn't, citing my bad back.

She made a sweet face.

"Doctor's orders," I added. "Rest, rest, rest." I told her that I lived in the attic apartment and to feel free to buzz me if she needed anything and she said she would.

Up in the attic I reread my mother's story. Twice. I stayed up all night. I couldn't put it down.

Saturday morning I drafted a memo to my tenants, informing them of the shelter. I was careful to refer to it as a "shelter," not a "bomb shelter." I wrote that I felt it was my duty to share with them a part of the house that had until now not been known to me, that indeed didn't even exist in the blueprints. I wrote that the shelter had been built in 1971, described its humble furnishings, explained that it was equipped with plumbing and electricity, and offered an estimate of its square footage. I mentioned that though I hoped it would never come to pass, in the event of a storm or an actual bombing, all tenants would be welcome to use it. I also mentioned that I would be more than happy to give anyone a tour of the newfound sub-sub-story, and that its existence or necessary utilization wouldn't cause an increase in rent or any fees.

It was a dry, impersonal memo, and I found upon rereading it that I had taken on the style of my mother's unadorned, matter-of-fact prose.

I assumed that my night in the snowy field among the Radio Trees had cured me of my condition and I decided to take a walk. I wore normal clothes, along with old basketball sneakers and a pair of Terminator sunglasses that used to belong to Kent. It was a bright, sunny day. As I headed out, the neighborhood felt warm and welcoming. I chose the same path I had the night I followed Sheila Anne's car, walking past the Schefflers' house, heading toward the Lindholms' and the old widow's, turning left on Geneseo Street and another left on Waverly Lane.

But when I got to the threshold of the long field, now thawed, revealing long-dead grass, a thickening spread through my chest and an icy film coated the back of my neck. I tried to breathe through it and press on, but I simply couldn't. Before my legs locked, I was able to turn and head back. I felt my body willing itself to crawl into some random front lawn and assume the fetal position. It took everything in my power to not go down to my hands and knees.

The mailwoman passed me. She nodded hello, pushing her delivery cart. She had no idea of the terror I was experiencing, which made the few blocks back to the house all the more dreadful.

When I arrived at the front porch, I was relieved not to see anyone from the house.

I was cottonmouthed, my face felt heavy and hot. My hands were clammy and the back of my neck still freezing.

And now Easter Sunday has come and gone.

Earlier today the Coynes hosted an Easter egg hunt in their front yard. Neighborhood children attended in their Sunday best. Girls in peach and yellow dresses. Boys in short sleeves and clip-on ties. I kept scanning the little girls for Bethany Bunch, as if she might have been reassigned seamlessly to a cul-de-sac home three stop signs away.

There was an adult dressed up in a giant blue-and-white bunny suit, whiskers and buck teeth, big plastic saucers for eyes. He/she was hopping around the Coynes' front yard, terrifying all the children. There were maybe twelve kids, from three to perhaps nine years old. One was black. She seemed like the oldest, tall and thin with long coltish legs. She wore a white dress with little blue flowers.

The kids pinwheeled around the front yard, picking through the shrubbery and the little strip of ungrown garden along the side of the house, half-searching for colored eggs and half-avoiding the terrifying giant bunny that had stopped hopping and was now lurching around the yard, either fatigued or drunk or on the verge of a heart attack.

Eventually the giant bunny threw his/her arms in the air and left the children to their egg hunt.

I spent the afternoon in bed. I'd taken a Percocet for no good reason and wound up passing out with my mother's copy of Crime and Punishment on my chest. I'd fallen asleep just after Raskolnikov murders the pawnbroker and her half-sister. My mother had underlined several passages throughout this section, and I found myself dreaming that Mary and Todd Bunch had broken into my apartment and were coming at me with a hammer. Todd was brandishing it above his head like Thor. Whenever he swiped it at me and whiffed—vicious flailing attempts—the hammer detonated in the Sheetrock, riddling my walls with craters. The sound was deafening. Mary had yellow wolf fangs and stood by laughing maniacally.

I find that the Percocet triggers terrible nightmares. Then again, it could be the Percocet-penis-enlargement-pills cocktail.

An aside:

Charting the daily development of your penis is like trying to watch grass grow. Or some sleeping lizard stir at the zoo. The Komodo dragon will remain static for so long that it starts to become part of the rock it sleeps on. The smallest movement becomes a terrible, electrifying possibility. I hope my penis transforms into a Komodo dragon, a thing to behold, a creature to spellbind and inspire awe and shame. As for now, it's still an unexceptional gecko.

Today, the Monday following Easter, I called Lyman down in Jupiter. He was in the clubhouse of some fancy golf resort, playing gin.

"I'm killing this clown from Coral Springs," he said. "He keeps insisting on playing for a buck a point. I took three large off him yesterday. Sissy's at the bar with ancient Harley Dukes and his twenty-something child bride, Shoni, who looks like she walked out of a convention for airline stewardesses. Harley told me he just got his dick done in Boca. Apparently there's a little button he presses."

I gathered that "getting your dick done" meant getting some sort of surgically installed hydraulic implant. "Technology," I said.

"The things we pay for," Lyman added, always the accountant.

I told him that I'd gone down to the shelter.

"Please tell me the godforsaken toilet still flushes," he said. "You have no idea how much money I parted with just to have the plumbing rerouted."

"It works," I said. I told him I was impressed with the shelter.

"Your uncle Corbit did a nice job," he said.

In the dead air I could hear the murmuring of the clubhouse. I imagined wealthy seniors with cicatrix faces babbling on about the sexual conquests of the on-site golf pro and their Facebook grandchildren and the glories of pain relief. Blazingly white teeth and thousand-dollar podiatry sandals. Titanium hips and the cocktail-hour collusion of plastic-surgery converts. I imagined alligators hiding in all the water traps along the back nine. Puff adders coiled in the finely raked sand.

"Well," Lyman said, "is there anything else? I better get back to my game before my gin buddy comes to his senses."

"Did you know she wrote?"

"Did I know <u>who</u> wrote?"

"Mom."

"Your mother <u>wrote</u>?" he said.

I told him about the manuscript I'd found. "Sort of a novella," I explained. "It was in a box under one of the bunks."

"You sure it's hers?"

"Her name's on the title page," I said. I asked Lyman if he'd ever witnessed her in the act of writing.

He said that she liked to write letters, and that when they were first married she kept a journal. "But I never saw her do any <u>serious</u> writing," he added.

"She never mentioned that she was writing a story?"

"Your mother liked to <u>read</u>," he said. "Everyone knew that. She devoured all those books."

There was another pause. It was hard to believe that Cornelia could have been that furtive. I could almost hear my father's brain working. Had she had a lover too?

"So did you read it?" he finally asked.

I told him that I had and then he asked me if it was "any good," as if he were inquiring about a new brand of light beer. I said that I couldn't stop thinking about it.

When he asked what it was about I explained that it concerns a college student who commits a senseless violent crime and then abducts a little girl, after which they find an abandoned farmhouse and fix it up and spend the rest of their lives together.

Lyman said, "Wow, sounds intense."

I told him that she'd dedicated the story to me.

"Well, you two were always two peas in a pot."

"Pod," I corrected him.

There was another pause, during which I thought I heard an elderly person say, <u>I'll trade you my daughter for those car keys</u>. Or maybe it was, <u>I'll take your daughter to the South Keys</u>.

"What was the crime?" Lyman asked.

I told him that the college student murders the little girl's parents.

"Jesus crow," Lyman said. "As in cold-blooded murder? But why on earth?"

"I think to start his life over. You get the sense that his life is meaningless up to that point. That he's sort of blank."

"So he gets rewarded with a new life for murdering people?"

"It's more complex than that," I offered. "I highly doubt Mom was condoning murder."

"I knew she liked to spend time down in the shelter," Lyman said, "but I always thought she was just watching movies and reading those big Russian novels." He said she mostly went down there after I had gone to bed and that sometimes, with her insomnia, she would be there all night.

"Her prose is really beautiful," I said. "She wrote with a lean poetry."

"Look, kiddo, it seems like we're gettin' into a serious convo here and I'm in the middle of a card game. Maybe I should call you back."

I asked him if he wanted to read the story.

"How long is it?"

The question disgusted me. I was stunned that he would ask something so trivial. "She didn't number the pages," I said. "It's a quick read, though. I got through it in one sitting."

"Is there anyone like me in it?" he asked.

The self-involvement was mind-blowing. "Not really," I said. "But don't you want to know what she wrote?"

"Sure I do," he said, "sure. It's just that..."

He hesitated—and then, without warning, he was crying. Sniffling like a child, with a sound like little squeaks of air being released from a balloon. I imagined him turned into a corner of the clubhouse, covering his face with his trembling left hand.

Lyman becomes a complete stranger when he cries. I've seen it only twice. Once in 1986 when the Chicago Bears won the Super Bowl and the morning after my mother died. He was alone at the kitchen table, actually sitting on the table, as all the chairs had been taken into the living room. It was early, just before dawn, and everyone was asleep, scattered around the house, in sleeping bags on the floor, sharing the sofa, two to a bed, wherever there was one to be had. I'd been in the basement. I'd fallen asleep in a retired La-Z-Boy, in full recline, while looking at an old photo album. I'd come upstairs to use the bathroom. Lyman was in his pajama bottoms, bare-chested, crying his eyes out, driving his fists into his brow. He was at that age when all of his body hair was falling off, and his torso had lost definition, so he looked like a gargantuan toddler whom someone had deserted on the kitchen table. His face becomes completely different when he cries. His eyes disappear and his mouth sort of implodes, as though he's been forced to swallow some thick, bitter-tasting medicine.

"I'm sorry, Francis," he said from Florida, his voice clogged and small. "You know how much I love your mother..."

I told him that I did know.

"I guess there was this part of her that I never really knew," he said. "Go figure."

He apologized for losing it on the phone.

"It's okay, Dad," I said, and I told him how I'd recently learned that I cry in my sleep. "I don't even know I'm doing it," I added.

"Well at least you don't embarrass yourself in public like the giant asshead you're on the phone with." Lyman cleared his throat and said Sissy was waving at him to come rescue her from Harley Dukes and his child bride. "She's making the international choking sign," he said, laughing now. "It looks pretty serious over there."

Before we hung up I told him that I'd make a copy of the story and put it in the mail.

It's late.

I haven't slept. I'm convinced that from reading my mother's story I've somehow inherited her insomnia. Are sleeping disorders, like cancer, inherited, waiting for us as we slowly lean into our midlife? Waiting like a hawk hovering over prey, its shadow expanding as it draws near?

I've taken a Percocet but it's only relaxed me a bit. It tricks my heart and mind into a syrupy warmth, which makes me want to lie down on my back and float, but every time I close my eyes something jumps in my blood.

It's some untold predawn hour. I don't even want to look at my clock. Everyone, everything, is asleep but me. I can't even hear the neighborhood owl that's been hooting lately.

I've been tempted to go down to the shelter, to see if that would bring any relief, as it had for my mother, but something about the place feels haunted now. I'm afraid some new secret will reveal itself. Another manuscript in another stationery box.

Another story from Beyond.

Earlier tonight Baylor Phebe's daughter, Emily, buzzed the attic. It was her father's opening night and when they arrived back at the house Baylor was drunk.

"I need your help," Emily said into the intercom. "My dad's had a lot to drink."

When I met them downstairs, Baylor was yawing up and down the front porch, pushing off the screen panels, barking lines from the play, completely and classically shitfaced. He was wearing a charcoal-gray suit with a matching fedora and brown wing tips. His tie had been flipped over his shoulder and a big gravy stain spread across his dress shirt. He was so off balance I was convinced that if he didn't fall on his face and go crashing through the front porch floorboards, he would tear an ACL or break an ankle. He knocked over one of the Rubbermaid ashtrays. Emily followed in his wake, righting the ashtray, trying to guide him like some human dirigible that was losing gas.

"Spite, spite, is the word of your undoing!" Baylor cried to some phantom audience that seemed to be closing in on him with knives. "And when you're down and out," he bellowed, whirling on them, "remember what did it. When you're rotting somewhere beside the railroad tracks, remember, and don't you dare blame it on me!"

His eyes were wild, his head thrust moonward. He hissed sibilantly between sentences. The Kindest Man on Earth was suddenly a pathetically drunk and embittered runaway house beast.

"Daddy, come on now," Emily implored, coaxing him with her hand on his back.

He seemed to focus for a moment, grew very still, closing and then opening his inflamed eyes. He teetered, shuffled his feet, finding purchase. Finally he relented and she took him by the arm and guided him down to the wicker love seat, which I thought would surely cave in, but it didn't. She managed to get him to lean back on it. His enormous stomach rose and fell like some continent struggling to rise out of the sea. His breaths were long and deep and troubled. Emily undid the top button of his dress shirt and loosened his tie.

He passed out in about twelve seconds, his mouth wide open.

Emily explained that after the curtain call he wouldn't take his costume off. "He's still wearing it," she continued. "He hasn't come out of character the whole night." At first everyone was getting a kick out of it, she said, and he was the life of the cast party, but things started to turn dark and weird. "He kept quoting the play and telling the actor who played Biff that he'd better start thinking about his future in a real way and that he should give the pen he'd stolen back to Bill Oliver."

I asked if Baylor was maybe joking.

"He was dead serious," she said. "You could see it in his eyes. It was like he crossed over to the other side."

Apparently the director had to ask Emily to take Baylor home. She was worried that he wouldn't be well enough for the next evening's show.

I asked Emily how the actual performance had gone.

"He was magnificent," she said, stunned. "I had no idea he had this amazing talent. When he came out for the curtain call the entire audience leapt to their feet. I think it might have been one of the greatest nights of his life." Emily had the dazed, resolved air of someone who'd been forced to wrangle a tireless four-year-old all night.

I told her that I was glad to hear he'd turned in such a great opening night performance.

"You hear the spite!" Baylor suddenly growled, briefly coming to but quickly fading, his mouth again hanging wide open.

Emily said she'd never seen him like this.

I asked if we should maybe try to get him downstairs.

She suggested that we leave him be and let him sleep it off a bit.

I could smell the alcohol roiling out of his lungs. I asked Emily what her father had been drinking and she mentioned vodka. She said it was probably the first time he'd been drunk in years.

Her cell phone rang. She took the call on the other side of the porch, speaking softly.

In his sleep, Baylor said, "What—what's the secret?"

It was a line from the audition scene I'd read with him. I patted him on the shoulder and peered into his enormous hippopotamus mouth, which was plagued by what seemed to be hundreds of years of dental history. He had gold and silver fillings, bridgework, liver-colored receding gums, a blue incisor, yellow ancient molars, and an esophageal opening so large it looked like it might lead to some strange land of salivary Lilliputians.

When Emily returned she said she'd been on the phone with the assistant stage manager. "He's worried about the costume getting ruined. Wants to make sure it gets hung up and steamed in the shower."

I asked her if I could get her anything.

To my surprise she said, "You don't happen to have any pot, do you?"

I told her that I did but suggested we not smoke it on the porch.

"How about my car?" she said.

"Sure," I said.

Her car, a little Ford Focus, was maybe twenty feet away, parked in front of the house, but it might as well have been in the middle of the Sudan. By deploying some quick mental ju-jitsu, I convinced myself that it was actually part of the house, or at least a kind of friendly satellite. If I started to panic I could just open the door and run back to the front porch.

Emily went down to her dad's apartment and returned with a wool blanket. While she was arranging it over Baylor's titanic torso, I went up to the attic to roll a joint, after which I also reapplied my deodorant, brushed my teeth, and ran a comb through my beard. When I came back downstairs, I could see that Emily was waiting for me in her car, the silhouette of her profile poised in the driver's side window, her hands perched on the wheel as if she was about to pull away.

The walk to the car was interminable. I kept reaching out for an invisible handrail. My legs felt heavy and slow. My chest was seized with that awful thickening again.

When I arrived at the passenger's side, Emily leaned over and opened the door for me. I slid in, and out of some childhood habit, I put the seat belt on. It was the first time I'd been in a car in months. The smell was still that new-car smell, at once citrusy and sterile. It's the smell of loneliness.

"We going for a drive?" Emily said.

I undid the seat belt, embarrassed.

"You okay?" she asked. In the moonlight her eyes were big and round and cavernous. I noticed that she'd applied lipstick. "You look a little pale," she said.

My hands were shaking, and there was no hiding this fact. "I'm good," I said, producing the joint and a Bic lighter. Despite my trembling hands, I managed to light the joint, inhale, and pass it to her.

"This is so completely illegal," she said, and took a toke.

"Welcome to the dark side," I joked.

When she inhaled she squinted, like she was afraid of burning her eyelashes, then passed the joint back to me.

My head had started to race a bit and I closed my eyes and tried to imagine that I was back inside, up in the attic, on my corduroy chair, within arm's reach of my record collection, underneath the soft glow of my reading lamp.

"You sure you're okay?" Emily asked.

I opened my eyes and told her that in all honesty I was a little freaked out.

She asked if she'd done something wrong.

"No, I sort of have this problem," I said, and offered her a cursory definition of agoraphobia, citing the fear of crowds, public places, open areas. I told her how I'd ventured out only three times the whole winter; how the first time, in the back lot by the Dumpsters, I'd thought my heart was going to explode; how the second time, that dreamlike visit to the Radio Trees, had been much more pleasant; and how the most recent attempt had been a disaster. She asked me how long I'd had my "condition."

I told her that I wasn't exactly sure, that I stopped going outside sometime before Christmas.

"Did something happen?" she asked.

"Nothing out of the ordinary."

She said that being a landlord was probably the perfect profession for me. "You never have to leave for work," she said.

"It's done wonders for my weekly commute budget," I agreed.

She laughed and smoked. Then, like her father, she asked me if I was seeing anyone about it.

"The idea of having to go to some shrink's office just about does my head in," I said.

"Well, maybe you're improving on your own. At least you don't appear to be having a heart attack this time."

"It could hit me at any moment," I said. "I hope you know CPR."

She said she was certified, that it was a job requirement at the prep school where she taught.

"Do they drug test you?" I asked.

"I think they know they'd lose half the faculty if they did that."

Headlights emerged at the end of the block, ominously pointed at her car. As the lights moved toward us, we sank low in our seats.

Emily covered her face with her hand as the car slowly passed. "Is it a cop?" she whispered.

I mouthed the words I don't know.

After the car was gone she burst into laughter. She said she felt like she was fourteen.

We didn't rise back up in our seats. Framed in the windshield was our old sycamore, its naked branches silhouetted by starlight. It looked like a giant hag's hand.

"So what's your story?" Emily asked me.

"My story," I said. "I'm not sure it's all that interesting."

She said she wasn't easily bored.

I told her how I used to be in a band, charting a sad three-sentence survey of our brief flirtation with serious indie-rock success and our inevitable breakup just as the Lollapaloozas and Coachellas were in our grasp, how we'd had a record called Argon Lights that had gotten some attention.

"What's argon?" she said.

"Oh, a couple of things," I said. And I told her how as a young boy I used to spend a little time in the summer at an aunt's house, down in Carterville, a town that was the equivalent of a Norman Rockwell painting—not unlike Pollard, if you were to cut it in half and populate it with a lot of people carrying fishing poles and tackle boxes. My aunt lived on a road called Argon Drive, in a little blue clapboard house, and across the street loomed a pair of midcentury sodium vapor lights that looked like hovering UFOs. "I used to stare up at those lights and just get lost in thought," I said. "Thinking that there was this whole other world, this galaxy of possibility or something."

"So sentimental for rock 'n' roll," Emily teased.

"Well, there's the other thing," I continued, "which is that argon is a noble gas."

"Meaning?"

"Noble gases don't combine well with other elements but they're super stable, so they're often used in fluorescent lighting. I think Morris, our lead guitarist, liked that metaphor for the band. For both its stability and our individual weirdo factor."

"Do you combine well with others?" she asked, a hint of mischief in her eyes.

"I can combine," I answered.

"I'm sorry," Emily said, suddenly embarrassed. "I should have asked if you were married."

"I was," I said. "She left me for someone else." I did my best to say this without asking for pity, but I was starting to feel pretty stoned, so who knows how it came out.

I also told her that I had written for the local alternative newspaper until it folded, and how after my mother had died, I inherited the house from my father when he remarried and moved down to Florida with his new wife, a big-boned, kind-as-a-Christian-missionary woman named Sissy Bisno.

Neither of us acknowledged the fact that we shared the distinction of having dead mothers and widower fathers.

I said that I was happy learning the landlord trade, that I'd accepted my fate of growing old and hunchbacked, lugging around an above-average Black & Decker toolbox, becoming somewhat adept at operating various power tools, joining the ranks of that strange fraternity of ageless troll-like men with undiagnosed gout and hairy ears. "That's about it, I guess."

She asked me if she could see my ears. I showed her the left one.

"Doesn't look hairy to me," she said.

"You should see the other one," I replied. I told her that that's why I grew the beard, to pull focus.

I felt as calm as I had since my night underneath the Radio Trees. I didn't want to believe it, but maybe it was as simple as my out-of-house nervous system being somehow pacified by proximity to women.

"What about you?" I said. Based on the letter to her father (whose violation of privacy was lodged deep in my viscera like a small cold coin), I already knew some stuff of course, but I asked Emily her story.

She said she taught English at a prep school in Milwaukee and that she too had been married but that it hadn't worked out, that her ex-husband, who ran his family's construction company, left her for his secretary. She reported all of this very matter-of-factly, throwing away any hint of the pain or suffering it had caused.

Another shared distinction: the cheating spouse and failed marriage.

"A nymphomaniac with perfect skin and tiny little ankles," she added.

"Is that what men really want?" I asked. "Tiny ankles?"

"Tiny ankles and tiny minds."

"I always thought it was supposed to be big tits and slim hips."

Emily said that the secretary had that going for her too. "The girl's like some genetically perfect archetype," she said. "Put on the earth to make all other women feel terrible about themselves."

"And help keep the self-loathing genre of the self-help mass-market paperback firmly ensconced on the bestseller list," I offered, which I thought was a witty, if not downright erudite, thing to say.

Emily ignored the remark. She pinched her lower lip with thumb and forefinger and said, "I'd like to <u>break</u> that girl's ankles. Then she'd wind up bedridden and get fat and hormonally confused and grow a beard."

"Then your husband would leave her for another nymphomaniac," I said.

"With tiny ankles."

"And big boobs."

"And no waist."

"And then you'd have to break the new girl's ankles," I said.

"Anklettes," Emily said. "That's what she has—anklettes. Is that a word?"

"It is now."

We each took another hit from the joint.

"You don't have anything against beards, do you?" I said.

"Not at all," she replied. "I'm especially drawn to them when worn by fat nymphomaniacs with chronic ankle pain."

After a pause I said, "So we're both a couple of marital rejects." Though I was trying to make light of things, it was painful to say this and perhaps equally painful for Emily to hear.

Her only response was a nod. She seemed suddenly to contract within herself. Her eyes went somewhere else and her mouth shrunk.

I reached across the console and took her hand. I don't think I was trying to express any commiserative, sloppy, sentimental Woe Is Us plea, and it wasn't meant to be a sexual advance; I simply felt close to her.

In any case, Emily didn't resist.

We were facing each other now, and it was my right hand joined with her left, awkwardly arranged over the manual parking brake, which she'd engaged in its maximum erectile position, even though my street is as level as Nebraska, and for some reason, at that precise moment, the fact that she was the kind of woman who would do that seemed to me wildly sexy.

Her hand was warm and it felt smaller than it looked. She was a nail biter, it was clear, though that's something which has never bothered me. (Lyman always said that a woman with bad nails is likely a bad cook, just one of the many bits of folk wisdom he's come up with over the years.)

"I'm really stoned," Emily said after a silence.

I told her that I was too. And then I suggested that we go in and check on her father.

She nodded but we kept holding hands. For maybe thirty minutes. We didn't say much. We remained crouched low in our seats with my forearm and upper wrist draped over the parking brake. Some of that time we spent looking at each other, but mostly we just looked into ourselves or at the various surfaces and cubbies and dashboard circles and entertainment knobs of the car. Once, for a few minutes, we infinitesimally brushed our thumbs against each other, but that was so subtle—like an eyelash on a pillowcase—that I might even be imagining it. Finally we looked at each other and nodded and took our hands back and got out of the car and made our way to the front porch.

Emily woke her father up, and we manned either side of him and eased him down the stairs to the basement and into his bed, which was like moving some kind of undulating, soft-bodied refrigerator filled with an impossibly heavy liquid. Emily removed his suit jacket and shoes and his tie and put a pillow under his head, and I left to retrieve his blanket from the front porch. When I got back, the apartment door was closed.

I knocked.

Emily answered. She was brushing her teeth and wearing a long-sleeved Marquette University T-shirt. She looked beautiful with her scrubbed face and foamy mouth and tired eyes.

I handed her the blanket, and with her mouth full of toothpaste she said that maybe next time we could take an actual drive.

I offered my hand and we shook on it, but not in a businesslike way. It was as if we were holding the same warm stick that we'd stolen from a once-important but now extinguished fire.

I said good night and went upstairs, and here I sit at my desk, praying to the God of Idiots and Suckers for sleep, thinking of Baylor Phebe's daughter in ways I shouldn't, feeling swept up in something that will likely kill another part of me.

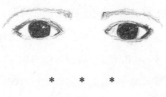

*   *   *

The next day, around lunchtime, I called Mansard.

"Francis Falbo," he said. "Newfangled detective. Seer of troubled snowmen. What can the City of Pollard do for one of its brightest, most creative sons?"

I asked him if his dogs had found anything.

To which he replied, "Not an eye-ota."

"Still no leads?"

"For all we know the little circus girl's turned to mist."

"My mother wrote a story," I told him. "I found it hidden in a box. It concerns a little girl who gets abducted."

"I'm still here," Mansard said. "You're talking and I'm eating a tuna salad sandwich on multigrain and I'm still holding the phone."

Just as I was about to launch into it, the Pollard tornado horn blared, a hellish note-bending siren that sounded as if it were being broadcast from some invisible south-central Illinois mountain. It was a common occurrence during the summer months, especially when mosquitoes were thick and the humidity insufferable, but this was too early for that.

"That's the twister horn," Mansard said. "Talk soon."

I sat at my desk, waiting for the siren to stop. It didn't. I opened my laptop and went to the local news site, which had a weather banner flashing on the home page. Apparently an entire family of tornadoes was heading directly for Pollard. They had started in Nebraska, cut through southeastern Iowa, and were now barreling into Illinois at some unfathomable speed. There was a terrifying photo. Four dark twisting tendrils, descending from the belly of the same beast, plowing through an empty field, the sky brown and bruised, a forest of lightning touching down. Apocalyptic to say the least. The website had a flashing band of text warning that the tornado family was twenty minutes away.

The horn continued.

I looked out my attic window. The sky was as blue as Easter. The whole thing seemed improbable.

I went down to the basement and into the storage room, where I pulled aside the rope rug and unlocked the shelter door. When I grasped the handle I felt a pain in my right hand, a reminder of the punch I'd thrown into Glose's face.

I turned the lights on and headed back up.

I knocked on everyone's door. Bob Blubaugh and Baylor Phebe and Emily were the only ones on the premises. Baylor was so hungover he looked like he'd been poured from cement and he moved as though he'd been struck by a car.

I went back up and left a note for Harriet Gumm, as well as one for the Bunches. It seemed odd that Todd and Mary were both gone. I figured Todd was at the firehouse and Mary out on one of her runs. Briefly I imagined her having to outrun one of the four tornadoes, tapping into some innate circus magic, bounding over parked cars, somersaulting through the air to beat the twisters.

The siren continued.

My fellow tenants and I were arranged around the bomb shelter like strangers forced to board a pontoon boat. There was a general feeling of dispersal, a drift toward the corners.

Hoping to bring everyone together, I offered the option of entertainment, showcasing the selection of VCR tapes. "Tootsie? Kramer vs. Kramer? Prizzi's Honor?" I said, but nobody bit.

Above us, the sound of low-end booms cut through the higher frequencies of the siren. I imagined entire houses flying through the air, compact cars lifting into the sky, garage doors slicing into the neighborhood tree line. I envisioned pedestrians running through the air with their arms windmilling, dogs and cats flung into chimneys, bicycles landing on rooftops, the Our Lady of Snows shrine spinning high above the city limits, Pollardians and bored motorists being spat into the stratosphere, Eugenia Groom's wig skittering across a barren cornfield on the outskirts of town.

Bob Blubaugh, who wore flip-flops, jeans, and a sweater, sat on the floor in one corner, Indian-style, reading a hardcover book, his eyes mysterious behind his amber-tinted lenses, his hair perfectly parted, not a single strand out of place. Abstruse as ever, he'd removed the book's dust jacket and was holding the book so that the title couldn't be seen on the spine.

Opposite him, clad in a black peasant frock, was Harriet Gumm, who'd run the entire way back to the house from the Willis Clay student gallery—some two miles—where she'd been working on the hang for her thesis showing. She claimed she'd sprinted through the streets of Pollard just as the tornadoes were hitting the city limits. The sky had turned a sickly dark green, she said, and there was a heavy taste in the air like iron, along with a terrifying quiet stillness in the trees underneath the sound of the tornado horn. Harriet had an aura of the possessed about her. She'd been forced to leave all of her hung pieces in the gallery, but had hoofed it back to the house to make sure the last of them wouldn't get swept away by the storm. Beside her was a large black cylinder, no doubt containing those remaining pieces, which I could only assume included the study of me. She guarded the cylinder as if it were filled with thousands of dollars of unmarked cash. After she spewed to us the things she'd seen and felt, she inserted earbuds and listened to legendary soul queen music on her smartphone, her large spooked eyes peering out from beneath a fringe of black bangs.

Baylor spent most of his time in the bathroom, shitting and puking and hocking loogies, by the sound of it. I have no idea how he'd managed to negotiate his mass into that cramped space. He would periodically emerge and apologize to the group, his voice hoarse and somehow deeper than its usual baritone. The hangover seemed to have shaken him in some existential way, as if he'd glimpsed his own mortality for the first time in years.

Emily sat on the sofa, a worried expression on her face. She managed to exchange a few texts with the assistant stage manager of the play, which had been canceled for that evening.

I sat on the bunk underneath which I'd discovered my mother's manuscript and spent the first hour or so rereading Cornelia's novella while the tornado siren continued.

Again, I was stunned by the storytelling, impressed with the prose, and convinced that my mother had spent a long time working on it. Nothing this good could be done quickly or impulsively. I imagined her hoarding her private thoughts, walking slowly around the house, working out the narrative complexities in her head, daydreaming about the two characters for years. Had she ever told anyone about it? Had she ever had hopes of publishing it or was the pure act of writing it enough?

Occasionally, in between paragraphs, I would glance over at Emily. I wondered if she remembered our time in the car or if getting high had erased it. I found myself searching her eyes, craving that flicker of recognition, but Emily was clearly preoccupied with her ailing father, a stitch of worry knitting her brows together.

The Bunches had yet to make an appearance and I was worried that they'd been swallowed by a funnel, their bodies divulsed, their skeletons cartwheeling through the apocalyptic skies.

Halfway through my mother's manuscript I was seized by the terrible thought that I could murder someone. Even with all the infuriating things I'd gone through with Glose, I'd never been visited by a homicidal impulse. I'm not sure if it was my mother's story working on me, the madness of close quarters, my erratic anxiety about the outside world, the sound of Baylor's intestinal suffering in the small bathroom, the chaos above us, the general downward spiral in which I had been engulfed, or the combination of all of it. But like the character whose name I shared in my mother's story, I could feel a murder in my hands, the thrill of it pulsing at my wrists.

The tornado siren seemed to be in cahoots with these thoughts. Like the Francis in the story, I imagined using a hammer. A classic iron carpenter's hammer, well balanced, with a long hardwood handle. But whom would I kill? And why—to what end?

Nevertheless, there I was, sitting with my mother's manuscript, actually seeing myself staving in some faceless person's head, the nauseating pleasure it would unlock. It made me sick to my stomach and I lurched toward the toilet, spilling my mother's pages to the floor.

Baylor was just emerging from the bathroom, having left a terrible smell in his wake, which I endured as I vomited into the toilet. Not much came out, mostly bile and air and a foul bitter taste. I flushed the toilet, vomited again, flushed once more, then just stood over the commode with my elbows on my knees.

I felt a hand on my back and turned.

It was Emily. "Are you okay?" she asked. Her warm, soft hand radiated between my shoulder blades. "You're shaking," she said.

The winding note of the siren keened above us, faint but certain. You could also hear the distant sounds of things cracking, like old ships tossed around in some epic sea storm. Perhaps houses on our street. Trees being ripped out by their roots. The pavement being halved.

I told Emily that I'd probably eaten something that didn't agree with me. I rinsed my mouth in the sink and wiped my beard.

"Here," she said, offering a cup of water from the cooler.

I drank the whole thing and thanked her. The space between us was charged with desperation. Our faces were so close that I could feel the heat of her sweet breath.

"Thank you for last night," she said. "I had a nice time talking to you."

Her throat looked so vulnerable, the skin above her collarbone soft and marked with a small dark mole. I raised my hand to touch it, placed my fingers beside her Adam's apple, where I felt her pulse. She placed her hand over my fingers. I felt intoxicated—both confused and enlivened by my dark thoughts of a few minutes before.

"Me too," I replied.

When we emerged from the bathroom, Baylor was sitting on the floor beside the water cooler.

Emily led me to the sofa and then got me some more water. When she handed me the cup, I asked her if she wouldn't mind bringing me my mother's scattered pages, which she was kind enough to do. Because they weren't numbered, I spent the next hour or so getting them back in order. Emily sat beside me on the sofa, trying to use her phone to field any news about the tornadoes. But the Wi-Fi had been down since the storm began and cellular networks were sketchy at best.

Though I'd never actually seen him cross to the other side of the room, Bob Blubaugh was now sitting near Baylor, fiddling with the ham radio. After a few minutes, he was able to tune in to a report that said the family of tornadoes—four in total—had moved some twenty miles south, toward Jefferson and Franklin Counties, but regardless, the siren continued.

"We should stay put," Bob suggested calmly, and we all agreed that it would be wisest to wait until the siren ceased. He was the most poised after all, and even though I was perhaps the only one who knew of his Olympic background, there was something about his vibe—the calm confidence—that suggested a quiet heroism.

Baylor's face had gone so gray it was practically green. We met eyes for the first time. It was strange that we were both throwing up, albeit for very different reasons.

"I think I damn near poisoned myself last night," he said, his back against the cinder-block wall, stomach spilling out in front of him. His sweatshirt now had several stains on it. "I hope I wasn't too much of an idiot," he added.

I congratulated him on opening the play and told him that his performance was already being called legendary.

"I probably killed so many brain cells I'll be lucky if I remember my lines."

His daughter told him to keep drinking water and he nodded and filled his cup and drank.

In the corner, Harriet Gumm continued to keep to herself. I found it curious that someone so self-possessed and provocative in a one-on-one setting was so withdrawn around the other tenants. At one point she opened her eyes, removed the earbuds, and said, "Where are the Bunches?"

We looked around at one another. Not a single word was uttered.

"I pray they're okay," Baylor finally offered.

This was the first time I had been in a forum with my tenants, but I wasn't about to broach the topic of little Bethany and start soliciting opinions. It was clear that, instead, it would turn out to be something we conspicuously <u>wouldn't</u> talk about. You could almost feel the subject braiding itself into some enormous knot of Unit 1 angst right there in the middle of the shelter.

Emily found a deck of cards among the board games and dealt herself a round of solitaire. I wanted to reach out and take her hand as I had the night before, but I was still stuck with those dark thoughts of violence and felt my stomach tightening once more.

After I finally got the manuscript arranged, I placed it in the stationery box and secured its cover. I decided that for the time being it was best to get a healthy distance from the sneaky, haunting prose of my mother's story.

At six thirty the siren finally ceased and we all rose and filed out of the bomb shelter. Harriet was first, with her large black cylinder, followed by Bob Blubaugh, with his hardcover book, and Baylor lurching behind him, Emily's hand on his back. I made sure all the lights were off and headed up to the basement. Then I lowered the shelter door and locked it.

I half expected to find the roof blown off. Or a tree driven through a wall. But there was no evidence that the tornadoes had even touched the house. Everything was in its right place. There wasn't even a cracked window.

We walked around the porch as a kind of forlorn, confused unit. The air coming in through the screened-in panels was thick, rich as earthworms.

Next door to us, the Coynes' Tudor had been all but completely demolished. The joints of the house were on full display now. The original beams and joists were exposed—ancient, discolored. The walls were torn here and there, revealing the skeletal lath-and-plaster. Conduit snaking every which way, like some giant android's circulatory system flung at the house in protest. Absurdly, a bedroom on the second floor appeared to be the only thing left intact, the bed still made. The living room sofa was abutting the space where the front door used to be. I imagined the door being sucked into a funnel, centrifuged, and spat into the Blackhawk River. There were parts of bikes and seemingly hundreds of books splayed, flayed, and heaped in an enormous pile. Broken glass glinted like gems. Their cat—an Abyssinian with yellow eyes—was slinking through the debris like a thief.

I would later learn that when the tornadoes touched down on our street, the Coynes were safely in the basement. Apparently, Neil Coyne pulled his shoulder out of its socket rushing his two children from their rooms.

We stood around the wicker furniture, staring at the wreckage in disbelief. It looked like a war zone.

PART FIVE

AFTERMATH

Two weeks have passed since the tornadoes.

The arrival of May has been a blur. Delayed no doubt by the local environmental confusion, the bees have finally appeared— the bees and the morning birds, chattering in the trees like church ladies gossiping in the parking lot of the cathedral I no longer attend.

There's a hornet's nest just outside my finial window. The deep slow buzz of their heavy wings is ominous and mechanical-sounding. They are industrious, a militant force. They have no faces, only soulless, malevolent, giant eyes. I fear they are geniuses and will somehow work their way through the screen and attack me in my sleep.

The governor of Illinois has declared Pollard an official disaster zone and the American Red Cross from all over the state has descended on us. Their Windbreakers, crimson with white letters, are a welcome sight. Relief workers have been picking through the remains of the neighborhood. The National Guard set up camp at the high school gymnasium, where they and the Red Cross and the Pollard Fire Department have been helping the displaced and the homeless. The gymnasium has been functioning as a kind of community checkpoint. If you can't find your home or your family, this is where you're urged to go. If you encounter a stray pet, bring it to the YMCA.

Current reports hold that fourteen people are dead, but several more are still missing. The death toll gets updated every day or so; it's gone from an initial three up to fourteen. One child, a four-year-old from Doheny Street, was crushed by a felled telephone pole. An elderly deaf woman, working in her garden over by the Blackhawk River and unable to hear the sirens, was sucked into the turbulent skies and has not been found.

The Red Cross is walking around, making calls on their cell phones, comforting the vanquished. There is something missionary-like about their presence in Pollard. It feels like they believe in God or some other mythical higher power. They are benevolent. They nod a lot and make concerned faces when they listen. They are huggers and shoulder squeezers. I suppose where devastation lurks God can't be far behind, the old cagey Trickster.

I keep thinking that this is what war must look like. This is what it must be like on a daily basis for people in Gaza, Syria, Cairo, Islamabad.

The images on the local news have been dizzying. One home was so annihilated that all that remains is the foundation, a pond of gray concrete. There are slain trees and far-flung telephone poles. A lone chimney, the house blown to smithereens around it. A granite public library lion sent through the storefront window of the H&R Block across the street. An automatic dishwasher planted two feet into a front yard, as if birthing itself from the soil. Two churches, St. Bart's and Annunciation, lost their steeples. The Pollard Little League fence, with all its hokey local business signage, wound up in a cornfield twelve miles away, hardly a buckle in its arrangement, hardly a placard out of place. A German shepherd was found on the roof of the Cineplex. A number of disparate birds—swallows, crows, doves, a pheasant—were discovered under a porch, huddled together as if from the same flock.

People are bivouacking on their front lawns, living in RVs and aluminum camper-trailers. Pup tents have been cropping up all over Pollard, Illinois, like dandelions. The Target, untouched, has been donating supplies to the Red Cross.

Surveyors and insurance representatives and city planning officials continue to mill in the middle of my street, drinking boxed coffee and eating donuts with sprinkles, matter-of-factly speaking into walkie-talkies as if they've done the drill a thousand times.

My neighbor Neil Coyne wears a sling, returning every so often to wade among the ruins of his home like someone encountering artifacts from another planet. At one point he bent down and picked up a toy train—obviously his young son's—only to drop it in exasperation onto the wasteland of debris.

The Coynes' unscathed second-floor bedroom is astonishing to look at. The king-size bed is, in fact, still made, two weeks into the cleanup, preserved perhaps as some defiant display of survival. At a closer look, one can see a framed family photo perfectly centered on the wall: the Coynes and their two children, no doubt done at the portrait studio in the mall. There is also a bureau with a small lamp on it, and a rectangular mirror, unscathed, over the bureau. Somehow this room was pardoned. Everything else was decimated. Their antique French snooker table, however—the late-nineteenth-century prize centerpiece of their family room— was discovered two blocks away with hardly a scratch on it, seemingly parked in the driveway of the Deardruffs', with the cue ball miraculously cradled in a side pocket.

Across the street, the roof of the Grooms' house was ripped off and sent to another neighborhood a half-mile away, where it landed on the roof of another house. A roof on a roof. Go figure.

The other day, as Hazard Groom stared up at his temporary tarpaulin roof riffling in the wind, I heard him telling his insurance rep that he wanted his old roof back. "I don't <u>want</u> a replacement," he bemoaned in his front yard, where his ancient oak had lost half its girth, as if reduced by chemotherapy. "I want the godforsaken <u>original</u>!" he shouted at the insurance rep—a black man in a white shirt and tie who wore an orange hard hat, as if he was one of Hazard's former football players.

Eugenia Groom, a pole of flesh with a hairdo and arms, stood a few feet away, the devoted acolyte to her husband's wrath.

A few hundred feet east of the Coynes' lies a car in the middle of the street, an overturned silver Hyundai, perfectly centered like some undergraduate practical joke.

A basketball goal hangs in the Schefflers' oak tree—the pole, the backboard, the breakaway rim intact, the whole thing looming high in the branches as if a giant plucked it from their driveway for his personal use.

In my backyard, there is a birdbath that no one has claimed. I have no idea where it's from. It simply appeared as if summoned by the copper beech. Harriet Gumm righted it and placed it in the shade of Cornelia's favorite tree. My mother would approve, I think.

Bob Blubaugh, who did a quick reconnaissance of the neighborhood, reported that two blocks away an aboveground swimming pool had somehow moved from backyard to front yard. There is a toilet beside it, the cistern cracked in half like a skull.

Since the catastrophe, the weather has been stunningly beautiful, with high blue skies and little wisps of clouds—watercolor skies, really—and temperatures in the low seventies. The trees are in bloom. The ivy in the Schefflers' gable is ripening, indifferent to the devastation. It's as if God is plying Beauty simply to stick Pollard's nose in the mess. <u>Don't you see what I'm capable of?</u> he cries out in a sinister, wiseass falsetto, mocking us.

Mine was one of three houses on our street that the tornado missed. As I watch the Coynes and the Grooms making sense of their annihilation, picking among the detritus, helping to direct upstate volunteers and Red Cross officials and men driving eighteen-wheelers who are strategically unloading land barges and positioning them in front of their homes, I can practically feel a spur of shame boring into one of my kidneys.

In the case of the Grooms, they've been paying off their mortgage for almost thirty years, only to have the roof of their home blown to kingdom come—or at least onto another roof—in a matter of seconds. The Coynes are decent people who keep to themselves. Their children are polite, if not creepily so, and they've lost just about everything. But in all honesty, lurking deeper, in some despicable hidden recess, I am joyful, almost maniacally proud of my luck.

Baylor Phebe has been going from house to house, transporting things in a wheelbarrow, befriending the neighbors as if he's running for a spot on the Pollard City Council. He returns to the house invigorated and in a full sweat.

The Miller play has been delayed, but there are plans to resume performances imminently. There was no damage to Bicentennial Theater, but the place next door, home to a local beloved hot-dog stand, the Willful Wiener, is now merely a gravel lot with a slab of concrete and several pipes jutting from the surface, as if there's some sort of surreal industrial snorkeling activity going on.

Emily went back to Milwaukee the day after the tornado. I was sleeping when she left, but she taped a note to my door.

It read:

> Dear Francis,
>
> I think you're sleeping. You must be exhausted. I had to head back to Milwaukee as my sophomores will be running amok without me.
>
> It was lovely getting to know you.
>
> Emily

Below her name she'd included her phone number and e-mail address.

The strangest news of the aftermath is that the Bunches are nowhere to be found. Their car, a white Dodge Neon, which they always parked in the back lot, is gone. I called the DMV, and their license plate number doesn't match any accident reports or unpaid tickets.

I also called over to the Pollard firehouse and spoke with Chief Hannity, who said that Todd Bunch hasn't reported for duty since the tornadoes. "It's really unlike him," he said. "The guy never missed a day. He was always on time, first guy here, last guy to leave. And he worked his tail off."

Next I called their bank, First Federal Savings, hoping to get the skinny on whether their accounts were still active, but the branch manager said she wasn't at liberty to disclose that information.

After knocking on the Bunches' door repeatedly with no answer, I decided to break in again. I had no choice, as I'd never resolved the issue of their changing the locks. Per the last time, I had brought the hammer with me, figuring I'd gently break a window—one of the two overlooking the front porch—but their door was actually unlocked.

They had left their furniture but taken everything else, including their surveillance system. I imagine that the two cameras and small monitor will be a part of their lives for a long time. I wonder how many hours Todd and Mary spend poring over footage, whether they sometimes see the pixelated ghost of their daughter flickering for a few moments.

In their bedroom, the bed was stripped, but the mattress and box spring remained, as did the headboard. The closet was cleared, save for hangers. The dresser drawers were bare. One drawer was actually missing, as if removing it whole had made for a more efficient exit.

In Bethany's room the bed was also stripped, the bedside stand slightly cockeyed. The diminutive bed made it feel huge in there, as if the room could swallow you up. The closet was empty. I closed the bedroom door and went into the kitchen.

There was a note taped to their refrigerator that read, "NO NEED TO RETURN THE DEPOSIT." The author of the note had really dug in with the pen. The ballpoint ink was practically etched into the surface, as if Todd had written it with a knife dipped in black ink.

I have no idea where they are, but clearly they'd had enough. I thought they'd at least stick around through the end of their lease. Pollard wasn't for them, though. Perhaps they've returned to the circus? Or maybe they're heading toward Mexico, where they will reinvent themselves yet again?

It saddens me that they didn't say good-bye, but it makes sense that they would use the catastrophe as an exit strategy. I imagine Todd gunning the Neon, his teeth clenched, his invisible braces glistening with saliva, Mary on the passenger's side, wiping tears from her puffy face, the backseat jammed with all the soft goods they could fit from their unit: clothes and bedding and pillows, the Navajo blanket, unwashed place settings, Bethany's Muppet mobile smashed up against the rear windshield.

Their unit will always be haunted, if not by Bethany or my mother or some monstrous combination of the two, then by something stranger, a thing sadder than death, a weaving of unresolved voices, a dissonant, lonesome keening reverberating quietly. A terrible blankness pervades the first floor now. Lives seem to stop in there. Or slowly get worse. I guess the word is <u>entropy</u>. I picture Mary Bunch shuffling around slowly, lost in her own house, approaching total inertia while the dishes in the sink pile higher. My mother losing consciousness, finally giving over to the warm river of morphine or Dilaudid or whatever powerful narcotic has taken over her bloodstream. Todd Bunch, wandering from room to room, moaning out in the middle of the night, opening cupboards, looking under beds, behind the sofa, searching for Bethany as if she were a misplaced beloved pocketknife.

Lyman called two days after the devastation. "I hear things are pretty bad there," he said. "They say it was the worst tornado in fifty years."

"Tornadoes," I corrected.

He asked if the house was okay.

"We got lucky. If anything, we subtly improved," I said, citing the birdbath. I told him about the Grooms' roof and the Coynes' Tudor, which was now part of the vast World of No More.

"You used the bomb shelter, I presume."

I told him it couldn't have been put to better use, and that I brought most of my tenants down there with me.

"Sissy and I sent a few g's to the Red Cross," he said.

I told him he was generous and he demurred, saying it was an easy write-off.

He and Sissy are planning a visit in August. I told him the first floor was available, now that the Bunches were gone.

"You lost your first tenants," he said.

"Yeah," I said, "they moved on."

Regret. It sits in you like a dead bird, swallowed whole, indigestible.

"The place is still furnished," I explained. "I'd be happy to make it nice for you and Sissy."

"I imagine we'll be staying at the Best Western," he replied. "It'll be better that way."

I dream of Emily Phebe.

Simple, reliable dreams. We're sitting on a porch swing, watching fireflies tumble through the air. Or we're in a canoe, the water underneath us placid, velveteen. The one I can't shake is where she takes my head, just like Sheila Anne did, and simply lowers it to her lap and I fall asleep there. I fall asleep even in my dream.

Eventually, in the dream, I wake up and she's not there. And then I wake up in reality and she's not here either.

On May 5 I attended Harriet Gumm's thesis show in a small, whitewashed student gallery in the Willis Clay Fine Arts Building. To put it mildly, it was a major step to venture this far from the house. As I prepared to leave, I was so nervous it felt like my sweat was sweating. My internal thermostat was going bananas. One minute I was freezing, the next I was having hot flashes like some menopausal housewife fanning herself in a supermarket checkout lane.

I decided against taking a Percocet. I wanted to do this straight.

It was the first time I'd taken my car out of the garage since December. For the past three years, since Lyman went to Florida, I've been driving his hand-me-down '84 Olds 98 Regency Brougham sedan. It's charcoal gray with whitewall tires. It has power steering and power windows. A fine leather interior. It smells exactly how a fine sedan with leather upholstery is supposed to smell: like success. Like an expensive set of golf clubs. It's the quintessential accountant's car. I wasn't sure if the thing would even start, but it fired up on the first turn of the key.

To help me relax I put on an old Sade cassette. Sade Adu, Queen of Smooth Jazz, the Quiet Storm, the R&B Soft Rock Chanteuse Extraordinaire. Face like an El Greco painting. As a sixth grader with maybe seven pubic hairs between my thin, rubbery legs, when I wasn't masturbating to Sade's debut album cover for Diamond Life I was imagining us (Sade and me) having a secret tryst in some faraway place like Mozambique, riding bareback on a horse, our golden palomino cantering through the streets of Maputo, me seated behind my mysterious songstress, reaching up through her blouse, cupping her soft Nigerian breasts.

As reported on the news and indicated by what went down on my street, there was a bizarre and seemingly selective randomness to the tornado damage. I drove past the Dairy Queen on Water Avenue, and there were easily a dozen people lined up at the counter. It seemed to be in perfect condition. The Hardee's, however, on the same side of the street, perhaps only five hundred feet away, was a pile of bricks and contorted conduit, with orange hazard tape and hurricane fencing enclosing the rubble.

The tornadoes wreaked very little havoc on the three-block-long Willis Clay campus. Apparently there was some water damage to a science building, which was caused by a ceiling sprinkler system getting triggered, but that was it.

At Harriet's showing, cups of red wine and cubes of cheese were served. The artist herself was in high spirits, greeting her classmates and faculty members primly, with an outstretched hand. She had painted her nails with black polish, which brought out the ghostly pallor of her fingers and arms. Her hair looked especially ink black and glossy and her eyes were made-up hauntingly. She wore a black gown and a black veil, as if she were attending her own funeral.

I was half-expecting to see her family there, but no such luck. There was nary a Gumm to be found. I guess she is more alone in the world than I'd assumed. I figured she was one of those privileged girls from the North Shore of Chicago with a proud extended family; a blue-blooded country-club dynasty clad in ice-cream-colored Ralph Lauren, the men in Top-Siders and Nantucket reds, the women in tennis whites.

The strangest part of the night was being there with my fellow subjects, whom I had never met. As requested by Harriet, our creator, her five subjects (Jershawn, Markeif, Keith, Cozelle, and I) were also wearing black. Markeif, the most stylish, wore a black suit with a black shirt and black tie, as well as black patent leather shoes. Jershawn wore black jeans with a black knit shirt, through which you could see the segments of his impressive six-pack. Cozelle wore a long-sleeved black T-shirt featuring Biggie Smalls and black jeans so sagging and baggy it looked as if he was carrying several servings of oatmeal on or around his haunches. Big Keith wore a black porkpie hat and a black Adidas sweat suit with white stripes down the sides of the legs, à la early Run–DMC. I wore a pair of faded black corduroys that were actually pretty gray and a black Third Policeman T-shirt that we used to sell at our gigs. Together my fellow models and I could have been mistaken for some traveling R&B wedding band. I no doubt looked like their weed-smoking white-boy bus driver.

Centered on the white ceiling of the gallery, in black type-writer face, Harriet had stenciled the following phrase:

THE SEVEN STATIONS OF O. J. SIMPSON'S AMERICA

ALL SUBJECTS

AS WELL AS THE ARTIST

ARE IN BLACK

SAY HELLO!

Harriet had given each subject his own narrative sequence. She hadn't framed the works, but had simply attached them to the white walls with some sort of adhesive.

Keith and Markeif shared a wall, as did Jershawn and Cozelle.

I had a wall all to myself and I was pretty shocked at my narrative.

First of all, unlike the others, my collection was in full color. I'm not sure if this was intended to be some sort of comment (the white man always gets a little extra!), or if it was simply an organic part of Harriet's process. I had been depicted, in succession, as a plantation owner who becomes an oil tycoon who becomes the owner of the Dallas Cowboys who becomes the president of the United States in blackface who becomes a clown who, later in life, in his geriatric twilight, becomes a gauzy-haired, sparsely bearded anorectic who's been outfitted with a bionic penis and is again wearing blackface.

In the first picture I am a vigorously bearded, licentious ante-bellum plantation owner, bare-chested, slightly more fit than I truly am, with abdominal quadrants that would rival Jershawn's, and am in the process of sexually exploiting a slave's wife, presumably Big Keith's, as he has been cast as the husband looking on from the shadows, barefoot and clad in a humiliating burlap pinafore, murder in his eyes. The sexual act is performed doggy-style, with my victim, a young, nubile slave woman, bent over a Louis XV fauteuil trimmed in gold leaf, facing the viewer, terror in her eyes, her hair lopsided as if it has just been violently snatched, while I, also facing the viewer, plow into her haunches with a wild-eyed look of depraved, insatiable glee.

As I was taking in the first of these fascinating horrors, Harriet sidled up and asked me if I approved of my narrative. She'd removed her veil, and her lips were so red and glossy they looked somehow fireproof.

I told her I was still absorbing it.

"It's okay if you hate it," she said.

I told her I didn't hate it at all, that it was simply a lot to take in.

"You were a great subject," she told me. "I enjoyed drawing you." And with that she returned to her mingling.

I looked around the gallery. At this point, in addition to those of us wearing black, there were maybe a dozen others. Most of them were young students, with strange hair and odd, makeshift clothes. None of them was wearing black. There were also a few others, older, in their forties and fifties, who I assumed were faculty members. They were not wearing black either. It was starting to feel like a conspiracy, as if my four brothers and I were about to be cooked in some ill-fated African-American bouillabaisse with a pinch of white boy thrown in for good measure.

I closed my eyes and imagined the path from the Fine Arts Building to the parking lot, calculating the amount of time it would take me to get to my car. From there the ride home was maybe twelve minutes. Three stoplights. A handful of stop signs, followed by the two-mile stretch along Calendar Road.

But the truth is, I was doing okay and I returned to examining my narrative.

In the second picture I had been cast as an oil tycoon, wearing a charcoal-gray power suit, my beard curly, seemingly bronzed, my hair slicked back like Michael Douglas's in the eighties, my skin healthy and aglow. I stand in the center of a dirt field, among a half-dozen or so oil derricks strangely reminiscent of the Eiffel Tower, my arms spread in a welcoming fashion, while Markeif and Cozelle—dressed in dingy coveralls, their faces dusty, their bodies racked with fatigue—tend to two of the derricks in the foreground. I sport a million-dollar smile, and behind me the sun is setting, casting violet and orange streaks across the horizon. The World of Oil is mine.

In the third picture I am the owner of the Dallas Cowboys. I am seated at a large ornate office desk with a Super Bowl trophy opulently displayed on a dais behind me. My hair, no longer slicked back, is slightly receding and has grayed in that distinguished, silvery way. Jershawn is also in my office, dressed in a Cowboys uniform, full pads and helmet, white cleats, striking a Heisman pose with a football tucked under his arm.

Next I am the president of the United States, standing in a desert landscape, shaking hands with a Middle Eastern diplomat in a large turban and gold sunglasses. I am wearing blackface and still have the beard. Behind us a McDonald's is being erected, and beyond the McDonald's, speckling the dunes, stretches a platoon of oil derricks, more spectacular than the previous ones, almost Seussian in their structural flourishes. To my right, arrayed in an impressive four-man formation, stand Secret Servicemen Jershawn, Cozelle, Big Keith, and Markeif, wearing dark suits, holstered sidearms, and sunglasses. My teeth look presidential, to say the least, in bright contrast with my blackface.

In the fifth picture I am removing my blackface and preparing to apply clown makeup. Seated at a vanity, I wear a big puffy red wig and a classic Bubbles the Clown costume, with long yellow goofball shoes. A small red tricycle is parked beside me. There are no other characters in the picture and I have no idea where it is supposed to be set. My beard is red like my wig. And I look like a fucking ass.

In the sixth and final picture I am a frail geriatric man, an octogenarian living on fumes, my hair gauzy, my beard wispy and intermittent. I stand at the sandy shore of some calm, cerulean body of water. My white cotton hospital garment has been pulled above my waist to reveal spindly bald legs and I am aiming a remote control at my erect penis, which is almost as large as one of my legs. Presumably, this is some sort of bionic, technologically enhanced penis, perhaps much like the one my father described Harley Dukes as having installed. To my left and slightly in the background, in the froth of the surf, Big Keith, cast as my driver, is poised in front of a white Ford Bronco, his arms crossed in front of his chest. In the backseat are a trio of buxom blond Dallas Cowboy cheerleaders, their garishly made-up faces and swollen breasts pressed against the glass. The Bronco is dressed with red-white-and-blue celebratory bunting. Girandoles of fireworks are exploding in the sky above and reflecting down onto the surface of the water.

While I was taking in this final picture, Cozelle approached me.

"You the landlord dude," he said.

"That's me," I said. "In the flesh."

"Cozelle," he said, offering his hand.

"Francis," I replied, and we shook in a brotherly manner.

Cozelle scanned the pictures. He must have sensed me contracting, wishing I could disappear. "You straight?" he asked.

I grasped, after a half-second misfire, that he was asking if I was okay, not inquiring about my sexual orientation. "I feel like if I turn around," I said, "the entire Willis Clay women's volleyball team will be pointing at my dick. Or tweeting about it on their smartphones."

"It ain't nothin' really," Cozelle said. "She's makin' fools of all of us in one way or another. Them volleyball bitches is all lesbians anyway."

I laughed so hard I almost snotted into my beard.

Cozelle then added that Harriet had defended her thesis with honors.

I told him I was glad to be part of such a great undergraduate success.

"You can't deny the girl can draw," Cozelle said, and then he joined Jershawn and Markeif on the other side of the room, where the two of them were speaking to a couple of young white female students. Markeif was holding the bottom of his tie, articulating with great charm and fervor the difference between the blacks featured on the tie and his dress shirt.

"This is midnight black," he said of the tie. "The shirt's straight-up ebony."

Jershawn added, "Shit is mad subtle, yo."

Big Keith was smiling incessantly and eating many cubes of cheese.

I found Harriet.

"You're sweating," she said. "You need a drink"—and she grabbed a clear plastic tumbler of red wine from a nearby skirted table.

I thanked her and asked what was next for her. I figured she had plans to move to the Chicago area or maybe even New York, a city with a thriving art scene. But she told me that she was graduating next week and planned on staying in Pollard.

"I have a good thing going here," she added. "I'd like to renew my lease."

I told her that this wouldn't be a problem. Her eyes wandered around the gallery. She was feeling a bit trapped, I could tell, but before I let her return to her schmoozing I had to ask her something. "So tell me what happens to the little girl in the forest," I said.

She replied that she hadn't finished that project yet.

I asked if the little girl was still lost.

"She's still definitely lost," Harriet said.

"By the way, you only gave me six pictures," I said. "The others got seven."

"You jealous?" she teased.

I asked her if that was intended.

"There's a reason for everything," she said, elliptically.

The room was filling up. Five or six people were gathered around the picture in which I was portrayed as a Yodafied octogenarian with a bionic erection. One of them—a young woman with pink hair—pointed at me, then turned back to the wall.

"You're a regular campus celebrity," Harriet said, before drifting away.

I remained at her showing for maybe another hour. I ate cheese and drank wine and managed to stay loose. I probed my bad molar with my tongue and wiggled my jaw. Eventually I settled into my role of Art Model in Black with a kind of forced insouciance.

Toward the end, a female student approached me—the one with pink hair who'd pointed at me. She had a nose ring so small I initially thought it was a piece of glitter stuck to her nostril. She could've passed for a young Ian Curtis from Joy Division.

"You were in the Third Policeman," she said.

"Truth is truth," I replied.

"I have that shirt," she added, referring to my black T-shirt with white lettering.

It wasn't the shirt, incidentally, that would have tipped her off about the band, since it doesn't say "The Third Policeman" anywhere. It simply says "Daddy's in the Old Hotel," which is the third track on <u>Argon Lights</u>. On the back of the shirt is a picture of Kent's father, Julius Orzolek, who has a face like a fat sick baby.

"You must be Harriet's friend," I said.

"I know her, but I wouldn't say we're friends."

"Mortal enemies?" I joked.

"Classmates," she retorted. "Same difference. I'm not much of a fan of her personality—she's a little self-absorbed for my taste—but she's a real artist." Then she offered that she'd seen the Third Policeman play at the Grog Shop, in Cleveland.

"You're from Cleveland?"

"Rocky River," she replied. "Cuyahoga County. It's like being from an Olive Garden."

"Because of the affordable family-style menu?"

"Because it's like the whitest place in America."

"That gig was a long time ago," I said. "How old were you, like twelve?"

She laughed and said, "I was fifteen."

She had a pretty smile. Her teeth were a little gray but in that perfect pearly way. She had sharp incisors and I thought how it would be a shame if she turned out to be a vegetarian. Her thin smooth face was more attractive than what she was comfortable with. She had little round soft fists for breasts, mostly obscured by a boyish Sonic Youth T-shirt. She was trying hard to hide her beauty, to broadcast to the world that she was authentically "alternative."

The Cleveland gig had been a memorable one. We'd played one of our best sets that night. We were incredibly connected, in part because of the rudeness of the sound guy—a strange middle-aged man with a classic mullet who'd treated us like some disgruntled villain in a Dickens novel might treat a band of chimney sweeps, ushering us offstage during the sound check without letting us work through a single song. As a result, we'd been turned up a little too loud, which caused us to bark some very punklike vocals and to listen to each other more closely, leaning into the music in ways that we hadn't in Chicago, at the Empty Bottle, the night before. The following week we were written up in their local alternative weekly, the Cleveland Scene, as being one of the most promising new indie bands to come along since Yo La Tengo.

"So what brought you to Pollard?" I asked, and she mentioned Willis Clay's fine arts program. "Ah, an aspiring fine artist," I said. "That's almost as dreadfully promising as being an aspiring musician. It might even be worse."

"Wow, you're not cynical," she said, then admitted that she and a couple of girlfriends also played in a band. She told me they gigged at some new bar on Calendar Road called the Flattened Fish and that I should come see them sometime.

I asked what her band was called.

"Temper Temper," she replied playfully, as if I'd just gotten angry and she was teasing me.

"I like it," I said. "What's your name?"

"Staley."

"Just Staley? Like Cher, or Sinbad?"

"Yep, just Staley," she said. "Argon Lights is a great album, by the way."

I thanked her with a sincere, humble voice.

"What are you doing these days?" she asked. "Besides modeling for slightly pretentious, horrifically self-indulgent, pseudo-feminist aspiring artists?"

I told her that as of late I'd been renovating houses.

"Do you enjoy that?" she asked.

"It gives me great satisfaction," I said.

"You guys should get the band back together."

I told her that we likely wouldn't, that as much as we loved writing the music, recording, and touring, there was just too much interpersonal turmoil.

"People pass your stuff around," she said. "I've burned Argon Lights for tons of my friends."

I said that although the band would appreciate people actually buying the record, I was glad nonetheless to hear that it was still making the rounds.

Despite the pleasant, seventy-degree weather, a dread of the outdoors had begun to build in me again. I pondered the walk to the visitors' parking lot, maybe only five hundred feet, but in my mind it stretched before me like an infinity. If I didn't leave right then, I might start freaking out. But there was something else. There was something about this pretty girl with the pink hair from Rocky River, Ohio, that was hiding behind the indie-rock tomboy persona. I wanted to get away from it, but I couldn't.

I told Staley I had to go and asked her if she would walk me to my car.

"I'll walk you to your car," she said. "Why not?"

I made sure to say good-bye to Harriet and congratulate her on defending her thesis with honors.

She was again wearing her veil. With rehearsed sincerity she said, "I couldn't have done it without you."

Outside, Staley ambled along exhaustedly, as if her thin pale frame were fighting off a virus. When she spoke, I recognized now that there was something of Sheila Anne in her voice. It was pitched at the same register; there was the same slow melody in her vowels. From somewhere on campus came the sound of turf sprinklers spritzing. We passed some fine small-college landscaping, a rampart of well-groomed hedges, and a manicured lawn featuring several abstract corroded iron sculptures that easily could have been mistaken for scrap metal tossed about by the tornadoes. Three baseball players in their uniforms walked by us, lazy as old Southern landowners.

When we reached the Olds we turned and faced each other.

Staley with the pink hair was suddenly flirty, almost coquettish. With an index finger, she pushed me, lightly, in the middle of my chest. "How old are you?" she asked.

"Thirty-six," I replied matter-of-factly. "Why?"

"You're fuckin' old," she joked.

For some reason I thought of Emily Phebe. Her round brown eyes, their warmth and depth. Only days before I had looked once more at her note and sent her a simple e-mail, writing, "Hey, thinking of you," leaving my cell phone number and wishing her well. She'd quickly written back, telling me that I'd been on her mind too and suggesting that we talk on the phone sometime soon. Outside of this e-mail exchange we hadn't been in touch, and yet here she was, on my mind again.

"I dig your beard, though," Staley said. "Can I touch it?"

I let her touch it and she dug her hands into it briefly. She tugged it the way Sheila Anne had only weeks before. Something went cold in me. It was as if she were tugging not at my beard but at some tired worn space in the center of my chest. Not quite my heart, but perhaps the hardened tissue around it.

I reached up and placed both hands around Staley's neck. My fingers were interlaced at the knobs of her cervical vertebrae. My thumbs met below the faint knot of her Adam's apple, at the soft recess there. I squeezed ever so gently. Her pulse throbbed against my thumbs. Her skin was so fragile, so pale, almost translucent. She simply looked at me. Our pupils seemed to be locked into the four inevitable points of a perfect universe. Just as I could feel the blood rushing to my hands I let go.

She didn't step back. She actually sort of smiled. "Kinky," pink-haired Staley said, her face a bit flushed.

I just continued staring at her.

She kissed me on the cheek, just above my beard, on the left side, and moved away. She walked backward for a few feet, still smiling, with a playful knowing in her eyes that sickened me, then pivoted and jogged back to the gallery.

During the drive home I was struck by the deep cobalt blue that dusk seems to thrive on, by the beauty of small-town streetlamps, by the sound of evening crickets—that hypnotic cresting throb—by the tucked-in quiet of the middle part of an evening in Pollard, Illinois.

When I turned onto my street there was a family barbecuing on a hibachi. I assumed they were new to the neighborhood, as I'd never seen them before. A man I guessed to be around my age with short black hair and a clean shave was turning hamburgers on a grill. His wife, a somewhat heavyset woman of mixed race, sat at a picnic table in their front yard, as their child, a little boy, maybe three, ran around a small mulberry tree.

Their modest ranch house used to belong to the Dabadudas, a family of staunch, bloodless, entitled Lutherans who rarely said hello to anybody. Their only child, Lawrence, was mostly known for getting punched in the face at the bus stop and mostly deserving it. (One time Kent put Lawrence Dabaduda in a headlock because he wouldn't give up his seat at the front of the bus to a boy who'd just broken his leg.) Mr. Dabaduda—I believe his first name was also Lawrence—often would mow his front lawn on a John Deere rider, which was totally unnecessary, as the lawn was about as large as a badminton court. Kent and I used to plant rocks in their yard and listen for the sound of the mower blades crunching them.

The house was now bandaged in blue plastic. Half the roof had been torn off and was temporarily patched over with long sections of tarpaulin. Despite the wreckage, they were making the best of things, enjoying their front yard.

I stopped the car and let my window down. I said hello to the husband and introduced myself. "Francis Falbo," I said, and told him I lived down the street in the old Victorian with the wraparound porch.

He reluctantly offered his name—Scott King—but didn't acknowledge his wife and son. He barely stepped out from behind his hibachi.

I told him I was sorry about his house.

He said, "Bad luck, I guess."

"Anyway, welcome to the neighborhood," I said.

He nodded and I powered the window back up. In the

rearview mirror I could see his wife still seated at the picnic table, pulling her son close.

Was Scott King distant because he knew I was one of the lucky few? Or had someone from the neighborhood tipped off him and his wife about my being the person who had harbored the child-killing Bunches? Or was he simply tired after a long day at the office, only to return home to a half-ruined house?

With regard to my "condition," it wasn't until I had parked the car in the garage and turned the headlights off that I had a problem. Sitting there in the driver's seat, I was suddenly aware that my feet were stuck. I grew short of breath. I groped the Olds's leather upholstery. My tongue contracted, my lips went numb, my lower back stiffened. Paralysis was rushing up my calves and soon would be at my femurs, my hip sockets, my spine.

I cried out for help but no one heard me. Where was Bob Blubaugh when you needed him? Or Baylor Phebe?

I started to hyperventilate. My lungs turned to paper, my jaw tightened, my hands became claws. Why now, when I was so close to being safely home? The agoraphobia gods were truly fucking with me, batting me around like a stunned mouse.

I managed to wrest my cell phone from my front pocket and selected the first number I recognized. It was Kent's. I waited for it to ring. But it went straight to voice mail:

This is Kent Orzolek, he said. I am not here. No, don't be fooled. This is merely my vocal instrument. Please leave a message. Don't be afraid.

Despite the many years in which we haven't spoken, something about hearing my best friend's voice helped.

Don't be afraid...

Almost immediately the panic faded, the paralysis lifted. My pulse slowed, my jaw released, my hands relaxed.

After the beep I simply said that it had been a while and that I hoped he was all right, that the winter hadn't been too rough in the Upper Peninsula of Michigan. I told him that I missed him and to please give me a call. I probably sounded a little desperate, but it felt good to leave him a message.

After that I was able to get out of the car and wade through the garage in the dark and make it across the backyard, onto the porch, and into the house.

The following morning I was determined to go back out into the world. I walked down the street, weaving through the various teams of volunteers, construction barges, and municipal vehicles, and knocked on the Kings' makeshift door, which was a piece of plywood bolted to a long two-by-four, enshrouded in blue plastic.

Moments later, Scott King's wife answered.

"Mrs. King?" I said.

"Yes?" she replied.

Up close I realized she was Indian, meaning South Asian, perhaps Sri Lankan or Bangladeshi. There's something about a South Asian woman trapped in the middle of Illinois that feels wrong. She should be wearing a sari and relaxing under a banyan tree, eating figs and breathing the silky air, not stuck in a tornado-beaten house wrapped in industrial plastic, waiting for her clean-cut husband to come home.

I offered my name and told her I lived in the neighborhood, that I had spoken with her husband the night before. "You guys were barbecuing," I added. "I was in my car. I rolled the window down."

She said nothing.

"What's your name?" I asked.

"Deepa," she said.

"Deepa King?"

"Yes," she replied, "Deepa King." She didn't speak with an accent of any kind. There wasn't a single note of exotic music in her voice and she was dressed like Oprah Winfrey.

Her little boy was suddenly standing beside her, hugging her leg, his dark head of curly hair vast and incredible.

I said hello to him and he just stared up at me with eyes so large and brown they might have been appropriated from a doe. "What's your name?" I asked the boy.

He didn't answer, just kept staring up at me.

"He's shy," his mother said.

I told Deepa King that I was sad to see her and her family so put out, and that my house, which was one of the lucky few in the neighborhood that hadn't been damaged by the tornadoes, was a converted apartment building and that my first-floor tenants had recently moved out without proper notice, and also I had an unexpected vacant unit that I would be more than happy to donate to her and her family until they got back on their feet. I wouldn't charge them anything, I said, not even for utilities.

Then, with an ultrastern expression, she said, "What's that?"

She was referring to Bethany Bunch's teddy bear, which I'd brought along with the intention of giving it to her son, who stared up at me. It felt like I'd known the boy for years.

"Here," I said, offering the teddy bear to him.

He didn't reach out to take it. He just kept staring. I felt myself falling into his brown, cervine irises.

"It doesn't have any eyes," Deepa King said.

The boy was frozen, clutching his mother's leg.

"Don't you want it?" I asked him.

"No thank you," Deepa King answered, adding, "I'll speak to my husband about your generous offer."

Before I could give her my phone number she closed the makeshift door in my face. Moments later the sound of a Master Lock clicking.

That evening it rained. A long, heavy, opiate rain. You could hear it detonating on the Grooms' tarpaulin roof, drumming on the eaves.

I went downstairs and walked around to the back porch. Beneath the copper beech the new birdbath had filled to the brim and was flooding over. I kept expecting to see dead birds spilling out of it. Little thrushes and blue jays and swallows.

The rain pattered melodically through the new leaves of the copper beech. It released the metal in the air. The back porch was cool and smelled like an ancient stone well that you happen upon in a field.

I went into the Bunches' unit and sat on their living room floor. They'd left behind their TV, their new DVD player, their TiVo. Their corduroy cat throw pillow was within arm's reach. I had an impulse to take it back up to the attic with me—I thought it would go well with the similar hide on my reading chair—but stopped myself. I had the crystalline thought that these items should be left alone. A kind of archaeological respect had to be paid.

I felt a terrible ache. An emptiness was expanding. An earwig skittered across the carpeting and crawled over the cable remote, then disappeared.

I could smell something sour, something decaying. I got off the living room floor and went into the kitchen, where I opened the Bunches' refrigerator, which they had turned off, perhaps a last-second bit of energy-saving generosity. Inside was a curdled half-gallon of milk with the top off, a cantaloupe turning bad, a bottle of Thousand Island salad dressing, and in the crisper a damp, putrefying head of romaine lettuce, floating in a film of brown water.

Was it in fact a gesture of energy-saving generosity or a final act of bitterness? I pondered whether they always left the cap off their milk, or whether perhaps, beyond their clothes and other soft goods, that little blue disc had been the one thing they'd taken with them, a souvenir to mark this terrible chapter in their lives. A thing for Todd Bunch to carry around in his pocket, to forever remind him of that fucked-up Illinois town where his daughter disappeared and the people called him and his wife murderers, where all he wanted was to live a normal life with a regular job and reside in a furnished home with no circus animals. An object whose dull plastic edge can be occasionally stroked with the pad of the thumb so he will never forget the awful inhuman capabilities of the neighbors and store clerks and coffee baristas and local news anchors of Pollard, Illinois.

I cleaned out their refrigerator, sprayed down the interior with a bleach-based disinfectant, and left the door open so it could air out.

When I got back upstairs I called Mansard's cell phone.

He said hello like he'd fallen asleep with his mouth full of Kleenex. He coughed and sputtered, cleared his throat. "Who is this?" he growled.

"Francis Falbo," I replied.

"They found her...," he said.

My legs gave out. I fell into my bookcase and sent a row of paperbacks tumbling to the floor.

Mansard told me that Bethany Bunch had been found at a high school track meet in Manteno, Illinois. A young father had come upon her stranded in the grandstand of the small high school football stadium. According to the local authorities, there was no evidence of abuse. She wasn't malnourished and she seemed perfectly fine. She was wearing a new cotton tank dress, robin's-egg blue, with little white daisies. The dress had been purchased from a Target in Merrillville, Indiana, and the tags were still on it.

"What about her parents?" I asked.

"I spoke with the sheriff's office up in Manteno about an hour ago," Mansard said. "The Bunches are with their daughter now."

I asked if he knew where they'd been.

"I figured they'd gone back to the circus," he said. "But apparently they'd just been driving around."

I got to my feet and adrenaline hurtled from my kidneys to my throat. My body was moving at breakneck speed. I was careening down the aft staircase, heedless of the unsuitability of wool slippers for sprinting on stairs. I found myself in the basement, pounding on Baylor Phebe's door. The thrill of Mansard's news tingled in my wrists, my fists, the tips of my fingers. There was no answer and I pounded more.

Moments later Bob Blubaugh opened his door and peered into the hall. "Everything okay?" he said.

"They found her!" I exclaimed.

"Who?" he said.

"Bethany Bunch!" I cried. "She's alive!"

He said that was great news and before I knew it I was rushing toward him. I hugged him with all my might, lifting him off the floor. I don't even recall setting him down. All I know is I was running up the stairs to the second floor.

"They found her!" I shouted down the hall. "Bethany Bunch is alive!"

And then I was coursing headlong down the stairs. I burst through the front door and scampered across the street. The rain was coming down hard—cold and aggressive—and the air was thick with ozone. On my way across the Grooms' lawn I almost knocked over their ancient ceramic deer, the one that had miraculously survived the tornadoes, as well as its new companion, a wide-eyed stone rabbit. My shin connected squarely with the rabbit, but at this point, pain meant nothing. I pounded on their door and in a matter of seconds, Eugenia stood on the other side, staring at me through its rectangular glass mullions. Her wig was a tad lopsided and she wore a yellow velour jogging suit top. Her folded arms made it clear that she wasn't going to open the door.

"They found Bethany!" I shouted over the din of the rain. "Bethany Bunch!"

She just kept standing there, staring at me, unblinking.

"She's ALIVE," I exulted. "They found her up in Manteno!"

Eugenia Groom's eyes scanned me, top to bottom. In her reserved, even manner she said something, but I couldn't make it out.

"What?" I squawked.

"You're bleeding!" she called out, loud this time, and pointed toward my lower leg.

I looked down, and indeed, blood was blossoming through a long white tube sock. And I realized that, underneath my bathrobe, my only covering was a pair of old fraying briefs and

mismatched tube socks. I must have looked crazy with excite-
ment, my shin gushing blood, my hair and beard soaked from
the rain, bare-chested under my robe.

"Isn't that great about Bethany?" I shouted.

Eugenia made a face that was almost a smile. Her lips went
flat against her teeth.

I turned and ran back across their yard, careful to avoid the
deer and rabbit this time. When I got to the attic, I lowered my
sock and cleaned the gash in my shin with peroxide. It stung but
I didn't care.

It wasn't until after I applied the Band-Aid and put on a new
pair of socks that I began to cry. When they came the sobs were
unbearable groans, like great sopping wads of grief being pulled
out of my throat, one after the other. I sat on the floor, with my
back against the kitchen island, as these unfathomable sounds
escaped my body.

The rain continued long into the night. Thunder gently bellowed. An occasional car sluiced by on the wet street below.
I fought the urge to start wandering around my house again.
Sometime near dawn, when the rain finally ceased, I pulled myself off the floor, moved over to my bed, and fell asleep.

The following afternoon I received an e-mail from Morris. We
hadn't been in touch since September, when he said his teaching
load was starting to get hairy. The family of tornadoes now
known as "the Midwest Marauders" had made national news,
and he wrote that he was worried about me. He'd heard about
the devastation in Missouri and south-central Illinois, Pollard in
particular, had seen the footage on CNN, and kept looking for
my house. Naturally it held meaning for him as well, since we'd
spent so much time recording in the basement during the early

months of the Third Policeman, and then, later, had written all that dirgelike stuff during my mother's decline.

Morris is still teaching, composing stuff on his guitar at night. "I've been using an old Fostex multitracker," he wrote. "Recording on cassette tapes just like I did when I was in high school. I'm loving all the care this requires. The Ping-Ponging. The weird, imperfect limitations of quarter-inch tape. The manual mixing down. Getting back to the analog ways."

He also mentioned that he'd met a woman. Her name is Mina Feer and she has two kids, six and four, both boys. Her husband left them three years ago and hasn't been heard from since. "She teaches reading to illiterate adults," Morris wrote. "They're mostly immigrants and middle-aged floaters who've somehow slipped through the cracks. Lost souls who were in jail or who've been fighting addiction or just plain homeless people trying to get off the streets for the first time, making a second or third go of it, attempting to get their GEDs." He added, "I think I'm in love, Francis. Mina is teaching me how to really share myself, to get out of my own head, to appreciate nature, children, the North Carolina sunsets, the goodness in the world. I never thought that would happen, Lord Francis. Like ever."

The shocking part of the e-mail, though, was that Glose had shown up on his doorstep. No possessions, no money, only a backpack. Morris opened the door to get the morning paper and there he was, curled up in the fetal position, under the mailbox. "He's sleeping on my floor as I type this e-mail," Morris wrote. "It's like he's been drugged and kept in a basement."

Something sank through the depths of my viscera, some irretrievable bitter silt that will never be metabolized, a permanent sediment that I will carry in my bowels well into my dying days.

Morris wrote that his heart broke when he saw Glose, that

our "beloved drummer" was severely dehydrated, crazed, mal-nourished, with blisters all over his feet and sores on his face. "Not sure what he's been through," he continued, "but it certainly seems life-changing."

The possibility that I have inadvertently done Glose a favor pisses me off to no end, and I am forced to admit, as I write this, that I have no love left in reserve for him, only resentment.

Morris went on to convey that recently he'd been thinking about the songs we were writing during my mother's illness. "They're good, Francis," he wrote. "They're simple, heartfelt, and you never sounded better. I still listen to them. It was a pleasure to work on those eleven songs with you. I know you were dealing with so much. I am proud when I hear them, as proud of them as anything else we did with the band. We allowed space. There's nothing tricky or ironic going on. Very few guitar flourishes. Only when necessary. Nice moody collage stuff. And just your voice and occasionally mine. They stay with you." He asked if I'd thought about doing anything with them, and urged me to either release the collection as an album or just create a SoundCloud account so that people could hear them. "I play them for my eighth graders—we do automatic writing exercises to them—I play tracks one through eleven. Forty-seven-plus minutes. I wouldn't cut a single song. Several students have asked how they can get them. I told them I'd have to consult with you before passing them around or making them sharable in any way."

Morris said that teaching, despite the heavy load, had recently been incredibly satisfying, that reaching kids was a far less cynical pursuit than playing rock 'n' roll to a bunch of people satisfied simply to be indie-rock sheep, interested only in participating in "the Currency of Hipsterdom...a bunch of bored, overeducated, privileged thrift-store drones who've already lost hope, whether they realize it or not." There's still an openness to twelve- and thirteen-year-olds, Morris continued. "They haven't been sucked down the drain of expectancy yet. There's still a fire in them. A genuine raw curiosity."

I haven't written back yet. I'm not sure what to say.

I miss Morris and I'm glad to hear he's in love with magnanimous, nature-loving Mina Feer and her two boys and that he's still so interested in those eleven songs we wrote.

After reading through his e-mail several times I attached a pair of speakers to my laptop, pulled up the mixes, and listened to them. Morris is right. They're simple. Some don't even have choruses. Most don't have bridges. One is a dirge in which we play very few notes and I sing, simply and plaintively, the two lines "A sparrow in her eye / Aflight on blackened skies" over and over, with "Behold the rain / Behold the water" serving as a kind of terminal couplet. This is the eleventh and final track completing what I only now realize is actually a song cycle.

There are images of ghosts, women walking barefoot through neighborhoods at night, entering homes they used to live in. There are iron objects being searched for at the bottom of a river. There are dark, solitary birds, the depths of sleep. Things underneath things underneath things. I was encouraged by the honesty of the songs, by the one-or-two-takes recording style that we stuck to despite patches of imperfect playing and singing, the weird background noises that the mics were picking up in the basement.

Sometimes you can hear the dryer churning. Sometimes you can hear the heat turning on. There are textures within textures.

At one point, Morris gently clears his throat after a take and immediately following this moment there is a faint, distant wail, my mother suffering in her hospice room. It's an excruciating animal noise, so pure it cuts through you. We left it in the mix. It all feels essential to the musical image. The impulse is true. There are no actual drums, only makeshift percussion: Morris lightly shaking a handful of change, me drumming on the face of my acoustic guitar with my fingers, Morris tapping on a hardcover book with the back of a spoon.

I called Julie Pepper and set up an appointment to come in and see Dr. Hubie.

"The back's finally better?" she said over the phone.

"Finally better, yeah," I replied.

The appointment was in the midafternoon and I was determined to have a positive experience. I'd spent a long night awake, convincing myself that fixing my bad molar was the first step toward a new beginning, both dentally and mentally. A successful visit would put me on a new path away from my dark thoughts.

I explained to Julie Pepper that I needed the whole thing done in one visit, that my time was limited, that in the coming weeks my calendar was full.

"Dr. Hubie is prepared to do it in one shebang," Julie Pepper told me.

And that's exactly what Dr. Hubie did. He stuck my jaw full of novocaine, drilled the bejesus out of the molar, extracted the dead nerve, inserted a titanium post, bonded and crowned it to rebuild the structure of the tooth, and completed the root canal—all in less than three hours.

Dr. Hubert Dembrow, lovingly known as Dr. Hubie, has tan, hairy hands and likes to talk about his golf game even though he clearly knows you have no interest in golf. You could be a side

of grade B beef with no ears or other human sensory character-
istics and he'd still regale you with his various tee drives, fairway
shots, and long putts from the fringe.

After the golf disquisition, he poked and prodded me with dental instruments. He told me he liked my beard. He told me he
thought I'd been doing a fair job of flossing. He told me my breath
had a nonoffensive peaty scent and asked if I was taking vitamins.

"Vitamin V," I told him.

"V?" he said. "What's that one?"

"Vinyl," I answered.

He laughed like an old family friend who knows too much
about your parents' marriage.

I cited the favorites from my record collection: the 13th Floor
Elevators' The Psychedelic Sounds of the 13th Floor Elevators;
Stevie Wonder's Innervisions; Prince's Sign o' the Times; Steely
Dan's Aja. The best part of the day was the laughing gas. I asked
for the "extra help," as Julie Pepper calls it. I had explained to
the ageless beauty with the dyed strawberry blond hair and spectacular legs that I was incredibly anxious about this particular
tooth, that I couldn't really articulate why, but that I was feeling
a terrible sense of panic.

"Don't worry about that," she'd said. "We'll be sure to give you
some extra help."

Nitrous oxide. God bless nitrous oxide.

I became warm all over. My brain turned into a loaf of angel
food cake. My eyes into daisies. I generally felt like I was being cradled in the arms of an enormous mother panda bear. The
word fluffy comes to mind.

While Dr. Hubie ground out the broken, decayed material, I
could see smoke rising out of my mouth, I could smell calcium
burning, but I was in those mother panda bear arms and every-

thing was right in the world of Francis Carl Falbo of Pollard, Illinois.

Before I left his office, in a voice that didn't sound like my own, I asked him how much laughing gas it would take to render someone unconscious.

"Not a lot," he said. "Too much—more than a fifty-fifty mixture of gas and oxygen—and you risk asphyxiation, even death."

I imagined pilfering a tank or two of laughing gas from his office. I'd sweet-talk Julie Pepper, tell her she has legs like one of the Rockettes. She'd show me some calf and twirl and curtsy and I'd swiftly grab a tank and fox-trot my way out of the office and into the Olds.

"Who are you trying to pull a prank on?" Dr. Hubie asked.

"Oh, just random friends and neighbors," I told him.

I must have been smiling through the whorls of my beard because he took my comment as a joke and laughed like a jolly small-town mayor.

When I got home early that evening I called Haggis and asked him if he could get me some nitrous oxide.

He said he could procure a tank for me. "There's a dependable dental assistant over in Decatur," he said. He told me it would run me a few hundred bucks. "But I'll throw in some ventilator tubing for good measure."

Several hours later he stopped by with a heavy cardboard box, and I met him at the front porch.

He wore flip-flops and a blue T-shirt with Woody Woodpecker on it. "You're wearing clothes," he said.

"Everything's been different since the tornadoes," I said, taking the large box into my arms and handing him three hundred dollars cash.

"The back is better?" he asked.

"So much better," I said, and twisted my trunk a few times, à la Chubby Checker. "Starting to feel like new."

"There's a small tank of oxygen in there, too," he said. "Use both tubes. Make sure to mix. And enjoy this lovely May weather."

I thanked him and headed upstairs.

With duct tape I was able to effectively rig the two ventilator tubes from Haggis's box to the snout of a gas mask I'd procured from the bomb shelter. From the box I also removed the two tanks—gas and oxygen—and joined the ventilator tubes at the other end to the nitrous oxide and oxygen tanks. I placed the gas mask over my head and turned the nitrous oxide valve maybe twenty degrees to the right. I matched it with the oxygen. I inhaled deeply three or four times and removed the mask.

I started laughing hysterically.

It might have been the best feeling I've ever had. Better than sex or theft or apple pie. Pure love. Pure hilarity. The absence of sadness, ache, confusion. And then the floating. That silly, expansive, slow elevation of my head and lungs and limbs. A feeling like your soul is just centimeters ahead of your body, directionless, undulating.

Just as I went for another round, when I was prepared to really open up the valve of the nitrous oxide and reach for the clouds, my cell phone rang. I pulled it out of my pocket.

It was Emily Phebe, the screen showed.

I closed the nitrous oxide valve and answered the phone. "Emily!" I said, practically singing her name like a summer-camp song. I felt like the giant balloon version of whomever I was becoming, about to float endlessly over the Francis Falbo Parade of Immanent Darkness.

"Hi, Francis," she said, but she was far less enthused and entertained than I. In fact, she sounded downright glum.

Hearing her say my name pulled me back to myself a bit. I asked her how she was and she said she'd had better days.

I told her I was sorry to hear that. It wasn't easy to work against the gas, to act mature and even-keeled. I was mostly in the mood to see how much gas it would take to render myself deeply unconscious, but I said, "Anything you want to talk about?"

And then she launched in:

Only a few hours earlier, her father, my favorite tenant, whom I hadn't spoken to in days, had suffered a massive heart attack and died on the stage of Bicentennial Theater. It purportedly happened during one of the final scenes of the play, when Willy Loman, beset by some form of high-stakes dementia, is speaking to Biff, who is not even present. Willy is counseling him as if in the past, egregiously out of time and place, encouraging his oldest, most painfully failed son to execute a flawless kickoff and run downfield and make the perfect tackle. Soon after Willy's exit we learn that he tragically takes his own life by crashing his car, in his mind securing a life insurance windfall for his family. This action happens offstage, and as a bitter turn of poetry, Baylor Phebe had, in fact, been seized by his heart attack just as he was stepping offstage. A strange confluence of art and life, and one real man's dream coming true as his character's dream is tragically ending.

Apparently the company of <u>Death of a Salesman</u> finished the final scene of the play, the requiem, not even remotely aware of what Baylor was going through. He was in the dark, in the wings, probably swimming his arms out, clutching at his shoulder and neck as angina gripped his giant chest. I imagine him going to one knee, perhaps shattering it, then the other, pitching forward and floating on the ocean of his belly while his soul wrests itself from his flesh, passes between the wings of his shoulder blades, and rises through the walls of the theater and into the calm, starlit night.

He never made it to the curtain call.

As reported to her by the assistant stage manager, Emily said that the audience—a full house—was collectively on its feet, calling for her father to take his bow.

"Apparently it was very sudden," Emily said. "The paramedics believe it was relatively painless. He was likely unconscious before the worst of it took hold." She was surprisingly calm and spoke through restrained sniffles. Her voice was deep and dry and tired.

I told her I was so sorry.

"I'm on my way down now," she said. "I'm actually at a diner in Joliet, just off of I-Fifty-five. Can I see you?"

"Yes," I said.

"You'll be at the house?"

I promised her I would be here.

"Good," she said. "I've missed you."

"Me too," I replied. The laughing gas was wearing off and a headache was forming in an orbit around my left eye. After we ended the call I took the gas mask in my hands and simply held it. I'm convinced that there are two lives that we get to live: an A Life and a B Life. They are presented to us by a whimsical universe at critical junctures when we least suspect this arrangement. This is not Fate I'm referring to. The concept of the A Life and the B Life is far trickier than that. What I mean is the life you're living and the life underneath the life you're living. One is polite, expectant, moral. The other is depraved, carnivorous, lustful, perhaps even homicidal. I'm not sure how often they intersect, or if one eventually takes over, but this is what I think I was experiencing as I sat there with the nitrous oxide—a strange, spiritual cloverleaf of my A Life and B Life—until I received that call from Emily Phebe.

Later I woke with a start.

I checked my phone. Emily had texted three times. She was waiting outside, parked in the front of the house.

We embraced on the front porch for several minutes. She smelled warm and sad, like fast food when it's left in a car, and I could feel my heart filling up.

We spent the next two hours in Baylor's basement apartment, sitting among his things, arranging them in prefabricated boxes that Emily had brought with her from Milwaukee. I built the boxes and secured the bottoms with a tape gun while Emily rummaged through her father's possessions.

Glose's bearskin was still on the floor, in front of the flat-screen television. After scanning it for bugs, I rolled it up and left it alone. It makes me sick to think that Glose could have taken advantage of Baylor. I guess bitterness can persist even during elegiac moments. It's a tenacious, angry dog with sharp teeth that won't die no matter how many times you kick it.

Emily packed all of her father's clothes in three suitcases, as if she were helping him prepare for a voyage by ship. She wept quietly, almost invisibly.

At first I thought it odd that we were packing up Baylor's things in the middle of the night, but I got the sense that Emily simply needed to do something practical, anything to keep her busy.

I took down the taxidermy, covered each piece with a plastic bag. I was careful not to touch any items that looked too personal. I left family pictures or favorite fishing lures for Emily. I cleared out the shower and the medicine chest, surprisingly bare for a man in his sixties. There was a bottle of Bayer aspirin, a tube of Pepsodent toothpaste, individual foils of Alka-Seltzer Plus.

When I was finished I joined Emily in the kitchen, where she was clearing out Baylor's refrigerator. I asked her what was next, meaning next in her life. She said she needed to visit the morgue in the morning and then bury her father.

"Bury him in town here?" I asked.

"Down in Cairo," she replied, "next to my mother's grave. I'll have to arrange a funeral. There's not much family left, but there are plenty of people from the junior high. They'll want to pay their respects."

I asked her if I could come with.

She asked me how I was doing with my condition.

"I've been venturing out," I told her. "Some days are better than others. I'm willing to risk it."

"Are you sure?" she said.

"I'm positive," I said. And then I admitted I was afraid of being alone. "I've been feeling far away from myself lately. Being near you would be good for me."

"Me too," she said.

Three days later, after Emily had taken care of various arrangements related to her father's death, we attended a small memorial service in the garden of a nondescript cemetery in Cairo, Illinois, where a few dozen people had shown up. The service was held in the afternoon, and following a brief rain the blue of the sky was eerily bright and the cloudless firmament seemed endless.

I wore a white button-down shirt and black suicide tie and a pair of wing tips that Lyman had given to me some years back. Emily introduced me to her father's colleagues as her friend and we held hands the entire day.

Ernie Glass, Baylor's old dove-hunting partner, the sturdiest seventy-year-old I've ever seen, shook my hand and said, "You're good."

I thanked him, although I had no idea what he was referring to. I took it to heart nevertheless and I think somehow that I needed to hear it.

At the burial, once the pastor had finished offering his bless-ings and various platitudes about Everlasting Life and Being with God and Passing into Heaven, Emily spoke on her father's behalf, thanking everyone for coming. We were all encircling his modest gravestone. Emily wept a bit but held firm and clutched my hand throughout. When she got to the part about Baylor be-ing buried beside her mother, she lost it, but in a way that didn't ask for pity, and when she regained her composure, she recited a Yeats poem that her father loved, "He Wishes for the Cloths of Heaven." She told those assembled that he used to read this particular poem to his junior high school students at the end of the year as a kind of blessing to them:

> Had I the heavens' embroidered cloths,
> Enwrought with golden and silver light,
> The blue and the dim and the dark cloths
> Of night and light and the half-light,
> I would spread the cloths under your feet:
> But I, being poor, have only my dreams;
> I have spread my dreams under your feet;
> Tread softly because you tread on my dreams.

After the service there was a small gathering in the back of her father's favorite restaurant, the Gem, where Baylor had proposed to his wife some thirty-five years earlier. The Gem is a mom-'n'-pop seafood restaurant with an enormous salad bar and everyone from the burial site heaped a plate and ate quietly to Lite FM music. I wasn't hungry but I forced myself through a baked potato, which I'd loaded up with fixings and consumed to Lionel Richie's "Truly," an eighties weeper that would have made me lose it were it not immediately followed by the Carpenters' "Top of the World."

I was never farther than an arm's length from Emily, who sat beside me and picked at a bare salad with many black olives.

At one point she asked how I was doing.

I told her I was okay. I knew she was checking about my condition, but I felt like I was answering a larger question.

"How are you?" I said.

She looked at me and smiled, but her brown eyes seemed to be aching.

There was something about watching Baylor Phebe's simple, unadorned casket being lowered into the earth that had brought me back to myself. And Emily's genuine concern for me at that little seaford restaurant in Cairo—was I okay?—even as she was picking at her salad and collecting shoulder squeezes from her father's friends and colleagues and touching each of their hands in a sincere way, made me feel something I hadn't in a very long time: that I was actually taking up space in somebody else's head.

We stayed at the Gem until the bitter end, and Emily put the whole thing on her credit card. It hadn't even occurred to me that she was going to be the one footing the bill, and I was touched by her generosity.

We drove back to Pollard in relative silence.

It started to rain again and the windshield wipers made dry weeping noises, as though the car were mocking us. Amid the silence the only sounds were the simmering rain and the low hum of the engine and the Dopplering swoosh of an occasional southbound car.

Perhaps twenty minutes into the trip, Emily thanked me for joining her, and before I could respond, she said that up in Milwaukee she'd been thinking about me a lot.

I told her that she'd been on my mind too and confessed to drawing her eyes in the margins of this manuscript.

She asked me if I was a good artist and I told her every face I draw winds up looking a little like a rabbit and she laughed and looked over at me and her eyes were so big and brown and kind I had the distinct thought that one could warm one's hands by them.

I asked her what her immediate plans were and she said she was going to have to head back to Milwaukee in the morning.

"What about bereavement leave?" I asked.

She said that the academy had given her a week off, but that she just felt like she needed to be in Milwaukee.

Then I heard myself asking her if I could come with her.

"Like just for the road trip?"

"I don't know," I said. "Maybe I could stay with you for a while."

Emily pulled the car over onto the shoulder. It was raining harder now and the wipers were really slashing across the windshield. She removed her seat belt and leaned toward me and rested her forehead on mine. Her breath smelled sweetly of black olives.

"You can say no," I offered.

She smiled and her eyes at such close proximity made a strange parallax. Eventually she nodded, which forced me to nod along, and then she drew her head back and put her seat belt on and we drove the rest of the way to Pollard.

The following morning, after I had secured the travel case over the manual Corona and packed a small duffel bag, while Emily was loading her father's last few boxes into the hatchback of her Ford Focus, I went into the backyard and with a small gardening spade buried my mother's manuscript under the copper beech, which seemed to me an appropriate gesture. I figured that if compelled someday I could dig it up and read the story again. I had the strange thought that the story will continue to write itself, that it will call to me when I'm an old man and teach me something about my life.

Although I offered to drive, Emily insisted. We took back roads most of the way through central Illinois. The farmlands were ripening. Fields of soybeans and wheat and cabbage. Corn was starting to rise. We passed silos and old, dilapidated barns and grain elevators and surprising rolling prairies that led to vast forests. In the weak blue light, the tree line barely discernible in the distance now, we happened upon a farmhouse that had been damaged by the tornadoes. There was a small barn, a stable for horses, hitching posts. One corner of the house had been torn away and the place appeared to be abandoned.

It was a simple two-story clapboard house. It was so far from the road it felt like a fable. Like if you started running toward it, by the time you reached the front door you would be changed forever.

Emily sensed my fascination with the house and pulled over onto the shoulder of the empty two-lane road. For the briefest moment I thought I saw a shadow pass across an upstairs shaded window.

"What is it?" she asked.

I simply said, "That house."

"What about it?"

I couldn't answer. Finally I said I was just amazed that it was still standing. I imagined all the things inside that had been tossed about by the tornadoes. Cabinets and tables and a library of books. A grandfather clock. I imagined an upside-down kitchen. Dining room chairs embedded in the walls. Half the staircase in some faraway field, leading to nowhere.

"Do you want to take a look?" Emily asked.

"No," I said, "let's keep going."

ACKNOWLEDGMENTS

I would like to thank Hari Kunzru, Hallie Newton, and my agent, David Halpern, for their careful, early reads of the manuscript, as well as my editor, Ben George, for his meticulous, passionate, and artful care.

ABOUT THE AUTHOR

An acclaimed filmmaker and playwright, Adam Rapp was a Pulitzer Prize finalist for his play *Red Light Winter* and is the recipient of the Benjamin H. Danks Award from the American Academy of Arts and Letters, among other honors. In addition to his numerous plays, he is the author of the novel *The Year of Endless Sorrows* and several YA novels, including *Under the Wolf, Under the Dog,* a finalist for the *Los Angeles Times* Book Prize. He lives in New York City.